Praise for the works of Catherine Maiorisi

A Message in Blood

Her characters are well-developed. PTSD and her sexual orientation are integral to the person she is, not just a quick paint job to make her more relevant. The LGBTQ community seems to recognize her skills; she has been nominated for at least two Lambda awards. While NYC is an iconic place to set a mystery, especially a police procedural, it is also a place the author obviously is comfortable in and can write about with authenticity. It is obvious fairly early that the bad guys are well-connected; what is not obvious...is where all the strings are connected. That was a pleasant surprise...

-reviewingtheevidence.com

This is such an excellent mystery series! It's really well done and each book is better than the last. This is the third and possibly final book in the series and I could not stop reading it.

The mystery is all contained in this one book so you could start the series here if you really wanted to. I would recommend starting at book one, *A Matter of Blood* or at least I would suggest reading book two, *The Blood Runs Cold*, first. The main character Corelli has had some incredible growth in this series. I like my detectives flawed and a bit moody so I always enjoyed her character but it's still great seeing the new person she is becoming. Anyway, there is the growth in Corelli, the experience and backbone her partner grew, and just other relationships that you would miss out on if you didn't start reading this series at book one...If you could not guess by my glowing review, I would absolutely recommend this series to all mystery fans.

-Lex Kent's Reviews, *goodreads*

This is a dark and intense book that shows some of the worst sides of humanity—but it also shows good winning over evil. The characters feel real, and the mystery is filled with twists and turns—I never saw the end coming. If you enjoy a well-written dark mystery, I would recommend checking out *A Message in Blood*.

-KRL News & Reviews

I love a good lesbian detective novel and this one is an excellent example as to why, there is nothing more satisfying as reading about a network of strong women, mostly queer who work together to find justice for women and girls. Fantasy? Maybe but a good one. In this book the author wanted to shine a light on the horror of child sex trafficking and I think she did an excellent job...There is a lot in this book which really shows the power of a good crime novel especially with a network of kick-ass, mostly female, mostly queer people determined to do what they can in a corrupt society.

-Claire E., *NetGalley*

Matters of the Heart

Matters of the Heart is a lesbian medical romance where a doctor and patient find love together. I don't know how Catherine Maiorisi did it...I recommend *Matters of the Heart* to anyone who's looking for a solid, traditional romance.

-*The Lesbian Review*

I'm a sucker for a slow-burning romance, and this one nicely hit that spot. As is made clear in the introduction, it's Maiorisi's first attempt at a full-length romance—previously she has been known for murder mysteries. If she wants to continue in this genre, she's off to a great start.

-*Rainbow Book Reviews*

A Matter of Blood

This is an excellent mystery and whodunit with well-developed characters, an interesting backstory and great potential. The action is fast-paced but nicely interspersed with moments of stillness and humanity....Well written, enjoyable reading. I literally can't wait for the next one to see where Ms. Maiorisi takes us with both the crime-fighting team and the prospective romance.

-*Lesbian Reading Room*

This book was a long time in the pipeline for Catherine Maiorisi, and it shows. The pacing is perfect, and there has clearly been a lot of work done over a long period on making sure that everything is just right. As a result, this is a really easy read that will hold your interest until the final page.

-The Lesbian Review

The Blood Runs Cold

While I did not read the first book in Catherine Maiorisi's Chiara Corelli series, this did not prevent me from thoroughly enjoying *The Blood Runs Cold*. Maiorisi populates her story with some much-needed diversity, but never strays into exhortative territory: these characters feel like individuals rather than stereotypes intended to fill a role (or purpose). The mystery is suitably complex, sure to keep readers guessing until late in the game.

-The Bolo Books Review

In most cases, I will say readers can start with the current book and not miss anything. With Chiara ostracized by other members of the department, readers should start with *A Matter of Blood* to get the full effect and the background of Chiara and PJ working together. Both books are fast-paced thrillers, where every minute could be their last, with no one to trust and nowhere to hide... Love page-turner thrillers? Pick these books up—then try to keep up with Chiara. It'll be a breathtaking ride.

-Kings River Life Magazine

An excellent police procedural with twists, turns and surprises. Looking forward to other mysteries featuring Chiara Corelli.

-Map Your Mystery

The Disappearance of Lindy James

This is not your typical Catherine Maiorisi book. It is a deeply involved fictional look at mental illness and how it affects the life, family and friends of Quincy, Lindy and their two young daughters.

The story is told through two narrators, Quincy and Lindy. We are inside Lindy's head as she devolves and it is a scary place. As well we are privy to the emotional ride Quincy faces as her family slips away. This is by no means a light read. The writing is solid with exceptional moments when describing the inner workings of Lindy's mind as she loses touch with reality. The storyline is intensely interesting as Quincy and Lindy's lives diverge. The sense of community is illustrated as both supportive and loving on the one hand and manipulative and false faced on the other. The dichotomy is displayed convincingly as we follow both narrators. I could not put this book down. And although this may be a challenging read for some due to triggers, this is an engaging story.

-Della B., *NetGalley*

4.25 stars. I'm a fan of the Corelli mystery series, however this is such a completely different theme, so I was curious to see how it would work for me. It was a tough read, but surprisingly good! Like in the mystery series, Maiorisi is not afraid to show the ugliness of the world, but in the end this book is about unwavering love... This is not an easy read and contains many triggers concerning religion in combination with homosexuality, so this might not be for everybody. It is a book I will remember though, it's very well written and I thought the insights in postpartum psychosis were very interesting and well done (to my limited knowledge on the subject) and their love for each other is something you can really feel even during the darkest parts of their relationship, which is quite exceptional. Recommend!

-Meike V., *NetGalley*

LEGACY
IN THE
BLOOD

And to my readers. I love Corelli and Parker and I love you for loving them. Thank you for continuing to read the series. I'm grateful for your support. Hearing from you is wonderful and I encourage you to contact me through my website www.catherinemaiorisi.com, Facebook and @CathMaiorisi on Twitter. Please continue to recommend the series to friends and relatives, and on social media. And, if you can, reviews are always welcome.

Note: I've said this before but it's important enough to repeat. The Corelli series is set in New York City but the NYPD portrayed in the books is my New York police department and all police procedures, characters and events are the product of my imagination.

Dedication

To Lee and Judy,
Who dared to read an early draft of the first Corelli Mystery, *A Matter of Blood*, my first attempt to write fiction.

Who have continued to provide thoughtful criticism on each book in the series.

Who are the best friends ever. Always there to support and encourage.

And to Sherry, as always.

CHAPTER ONE

In the predawn dark of Rockefeller Park, NYPD Detective Chiara Corelli walked briskly toward death. Her footsteps echoed in the silence broken only by the sounds of her breathing and the soft slapping of the water along the familiar Hudson River path.

She loved this time of day. Loved the freshness of the air. Loved the feeling of being cocooned in its velvety darkness, the feeling of unlimited possibilities as the dawn's light splintered the sky. But she missed the warmth of the sun. She tugged the collar of her coat higher on her neck. In comparison to recent weather, this morning was balmy, forty degrees headed into the fifties, but still cold enough to seep deep into her bones, as it had ever since she was shot. She shivered remembering that less than six months ago she was lying near death just minutes from here and only the quick thinking of Parker, her partner, kept her from bleeding out.

Like most things in life, some good had come out of the trauma of nearly dying. She had stopped fighting her feelings for her girlfriend, Brett, and had begun to deal with Marnie's death. And she and Parker had become friends. Or maybe she should say friendlier. Corelli took a deep breath, noting the hint of spring in the air. She wasn't fooled, though. March was freaky. One minute it felt like spring and the next you were in the middle of a blizzard.

When she arrived at Penny Park, she looked around to get her bearings and then ducked under the yellow police tape. She'd been here with Brett so she knew to avoid the many cartoonish bronze statues and large bronze pennies strewn about.

"Detective Corelli?" She squinted at the officer who'd recognized her in the dim glow of the park lights. "I'm Officer Lydia Ortega."

Corelli tried to remember the names of police she worked with but she didn't think she'd ever run into Ortega. "What do we have?"

"My partner and I responded to the 911. Tim Ryder, the guy with the dog standing there"—she pointed toward the staircase on the other side of the small park—"called it in at 6:14 a.m. He was the only one around when we arrived. EMTs declared the male dead and reported he was already stiff when they got here."

"Thanks, Ortega. What would we do without dog walkers to find the bodies?" Corelli didn't wait for an answer to the rhetorical question. "We'll talk to Ryder when we're done here. And good job taping the scene." Corelli signed in, pulled on booties and gloves and then went to the victim. She knelt over the body of the slender, youngish man with long blond hair, sprawled on his stomach next to the bronze sculpture of a cat. It was still too dark to see him clearly, but the reek of excrement combined with the lack of a pulse in his carotids confirmed he was dead. She raised her head to breathe in the briny smell of the Hudson River wafting on the breeze and came face-to-face with her pissed-off partner, Detective P.J. Parker, kneeling on the opposite side of the dead man.

"Damn it, Corelli, why didn't you wait for me to pick you up?"

She'd expected the anger but last night had been one of the rare times she and Brett had slept at Brett's Battery Park City apartment and Penny Park was just a five-to-ten-minute walk from there. And since her leg still wasn't strong enough for her to run along the river, the walk here was the next best thing. Besides, she didn't agree with Parker's assessment that she was still a target for some of their brethren in blue. "Like my text said, walking got me here faster than waiting for you to pick me up."

Parker wasn't buying it. "We agreed I would continue to function as your bodyguard as long as I felt it was necessary. Remember?"

"I don't give a f—" Corelli caught herself. She took some yoga breaths and swallowed the anger that was quick to rise at the least provocation. Parker was right. She had agreed. And she'd gone back on her word. "Sorry. It just seemed easier since I was so close."

Would Parker drag it out or accept her apology? Parker met her eyes. "Damn right you won't. Brett would kill me if I let anything happen to you." She dropped her gaze to the victim. "What do we have here?"

Forgiven. Or at least apology accepted. "You tell me."

After eight months Parker was exceptional at reading a crime scene. She really didn't need the experience but training her was a part of the deal they'd made after Corelli exposed a group of dirty police and found herself on the wrong side of the blue wall. At the time, neither wanted to work with the other, but they'd come to a mutually beneficial agreement. Corelli would train Parker as a homicide detective while Parker functioned as her bodyguard. The partnership had worked out well, at least from Corelli's point of view. She thought Parker felt the same but because of her inexplicable habit of dumping her anger on Parker and because of Parker's reticence, she couldn't be sure.

The sky was brightening as Parker stood and paced the area marked off by the crime tape. She smiled at the whimsical sculptures but her gaze was all business, scrutinizing the scene for any clue as to what might have happened here. Finally, she knelt next to Corelli. "No blood that I can see." She touched the man's carotid artery then his arm. "Male in his thirties, blond hair, brown eyes, no pulse, near full rigor, no visible blood, though we may find some under him. He's dressed casually in boots, a down jacket and jeans so not a jogger and no sign of a dog. Maybe he lives nearby and was out for a walk." She picked up his hand and studied his palm, then moved around to check the other hand. "His clothing and his hands are clean. His lack of calluses indicates a desk job rather than hard labor."

"Recognize him?"

Parker shook her head. "You know all these white guys look alike to me."

Corelli knew the joke was Parker signaling she wasn't holding a grudge. But then she never did, no matter how shitty Corelli treated her.

They looked up at the sound of Medical Legal Investigator Gloria Ndep's voice. Corelli glanced at Parker. As usual, she appeared professional when faced with the woman she may have been in bed with when she got called to the scene a short time before.

Ndep signed in, pulled on protective gear and then approached them. "Good morning, detectives, what have we got on this lovely day?"

Although Ndep wasn't a detective, she had medical, forensics and investigative training, a keen eye and an analytic mind. Corelli respected her ability to analyze a crime scene and read the victim. Sometimes Ndep saw things she and Parker missed. "We'd appreciate your take on it."

"Okay. Let's see what we can see." She pursed her lips and surveyed the area. "I guess it's called Penny Park because of those bronze pennies everywhere. But what are these funny little creatures? Is it meaningful that he died in the middle of these strange sculptures in this unusual park?"

"Good question. This whole installation"—Corelli waved her hand—"is a commentary on capitalism. The bronze sculptures are cartoonish representations of capitalists, laborers, bohemians, and animals interacting. It's political. Once we identify our vic, the reason he died here might become clear. Or not."

Ndep began sketching the scene on her iPad. Parker did the same with pencil and paper while Corelli took pictures with her iPhone.

"Morning." Lopez, the crime scene unit photographer, greeted them and immediately got to work photographing the body.

When Lopez indicated she gotten the pictures she needed in this position, Ndep put her iPad down and began her examination of the victim. "No visible wounds on the back of his head, neck, torso or legs." She looked at his hands. "Rigor. No rings. No calluses, nails manicured." She bagged his hands, frowned, then felt along his right arm. "The rigor makes it hard to be sure but I'd guess this arm is broken. Help me turn him, Detective Parker."

Lopez continued to take pictures.

Because of the rigidity, it was difficult to move him but with Corelli's help they flipped him onto his back.

"His face is clear." Ndep unzipped his jacket and pulled his sweater up. "No wounds that I can see on his chest." She pulled the neck of the turtleneck down. "Extensive bruising on his neck." She checked his eyes. "Red spots, petechiae in the eyes. Looks like he was strangled." She unbuckled his belt and unzipped his jeans. Parker helped her pull the jeans down. "No visible signs of sexual activity. Let's turn him again."

Corelli put her hand out. "Wait, let me take a picture of his face so we can use it to get an identification." She took several photos from different angles, then they turned him onto his stomach again.

Ndep pulled his jacket and sweater up and examined his back. "There's extensive premortem bruising on his back and around his kidneys. It looks like he has a couple of broken ribs. Livor mortis, where the blood pooled, indicates he was lying on his back after death. It's likely he was killed elsewhere and dumped here." She ran her fingers through his hair, then pulled the turtleneck down exposing the back of his neck. "The bruising on the front of his neck and his back indicates the killer strangled him from behind, maybe put a knee in the kidney area to weaken him." She took his anal temperature and made notes on her iPad. Parker helped her pull his pants up. Ndep searched his rear pockets but came up empty. "Help me tilt him, please." Parker and Corelli tipped him onto one side than the other to give Ndep access to the other pockets in his pants and jacket. She handed Corelli some change, a Metro card, keys, a pack of Marlboros, and a wad of cash.

Corelli dropped everything but the keys and the cash into the evidence bag Parker held out for her. "Three hundred dollars in fifties and twenties." She dumped the money in the bag, placed the keys in a smaller bag and pocketed them.

"Just this in his jacket pockets." Ndep handed Parker a crumpled piece of paper. She smoothed the page. "Looks like an invoice." She passed it to Corelli. "Do you think it's even related?"

Account number: 03151752
Amount: $4,000/month
Remit to: Deep Dig Excavation Services
305 Van Brunt Street #201
Red Hook, NY 11231

that artists and galleries attracted by cheap rents in the few, small prewar apartment buildings, lofts, and single and multi-family houses, discovered the beauty of the area. And even more recently, that small businesses and tech companies followed.

"Red Hook's waterfront is similar to that of Brooklyn Heights but unlike its upscale neighbor, it's relatively free of development. The fact that the closest subway is a mile away and local bus connections are not great is a good part of the reason. The presence of Red Hook Houses, one of the largest public housing developments in the city, may also have something to do with it."

Parker side-eyed Corelli. "Are you saying that the presence of poor and minority neighbors has kept developers from exploiting the area?"

"Yup. The lack of transportation is important for sure. And though no one speaks about it, my guess is that developers won't build luxury buildings in mixed neighborhoods because people with money won't buy there."

Before Parker could process this information, they arrived at the address on Van Brunt Street. To their disappointment, it was a UPS store tucked into a retail area lined with stores, coffee shops, bars and restaurants.

"Shit," Parker said. She'd been shamed out of swearing by her uncle as a child so she rarely swore, but she was getting more comfortable with it lately. Sometimes cursing could communicate exactly what you were feeling. "I'll take this one."

They left the car at the curb and went in to see what they could find out about Deep Dig Excavation Services. The tall, heavyset black man wrapping a box behind the counter reminded Parker of Jessie, her almost adoptive father. "Are you the manager?"

"No. But if you'll settle for the owner, I'm Tyler Wilson." He curtsied, which was funny for a guy his size.

Parker smiled in spite of herself. "Nice to meet you."

He stopped wrapping and examined the shields and ID they displayed. "How can I help you?"

"We're here about one of your customers. We'd like to see the application for box 201 and whatever mail is in it."

"Sorry. No can do." Wilson looked apologetic.

"Do you recognize this man?" Parker nodded at Corelli and she displayed the photos of the victim.

Wilson's eyebrows shot up. "Is he...dead?"

"He was murdered last night. We believe he's the owner of Deep Dig Excavation Services and identifying him will help us move quickly to find his killer." Parker gave him a few seconds to absorb that. "Don't make us waste time getting a warrant."

"He's Ned Rich, that investigative reporter at *The Daily Post*. He said his company was about data, not dirt." Wilson chewed his lip. "How about a compromise? I'll show you his application and answer your questions but you get a warrant for whatever mail is in the box."

It wasn't exactly what she wanted but she'd take it. "Fine. Let's see the application."

"Give me a minute." He came out of the back room and handed Parker two documents, a copy of the application and a copy of Rich's driver's license. After a quick scan, Parker passed them to Corelli. "Do you know where Thirteenth Street is, Mr. Wilson?"

"Yes, it's over in Gowanus off Third Avenue. You can see by the note I made that I checked to be sure it was a valid address. That's my standard practice. I also called the cell phone number he listed and he answered."

If she couldn't get the actual mail without a warrant at least she could get some information. "How much mail did Mr. Rich receive?"

"Um." Wilson thought about the question. "Not a lot. Maybe eight to ten letters a week."

"How often did he come in?"

"A couple of times a week."

So the mail was important enough to make a couple of trips a week. "What was he like?"

"Always pleasant but not particularly friendly. It was, you know, hello, nice day. But he paid the rent on time and in cash."

"Thank you, Mr. Wilson. Someone will come in with a warrant to get the accumulated mail but please continue to hold any mail that comes in. And don't close the box until we tell you it's okay."

"Now we know who he is but I'm starting to feel like Gretel following a freaking trail of breadcrumbs," Corelli said when they were out on the street.

Parker snuck a peek at Corelli as she slid into the car. She was frustrated too but it was part of the job. "The Thirteenth Street address may be real or just another breadcrumb but let's check it out. In the meantime, give our favorite detective, Dietz, a call about getting the warrant for the mailbox."

CHAPTER THREE

The entire four-story building at the Thirteenth Street address housed the Brooklyn Office Mart, a shared twenty-four-seven office space company that provided desks, offices, conference rooms and business services. The guy at the desk didn't recognize Rich's name or face but confirmed on his computer that Deep Dig Excavation Services rented a lockable, one-person, private office space plus several locked cabinets. Now they were getting somewhere.

Though the manager on duty had not tried to keep them from entering, Corelli called the station house and asked Dietz to get a warrant for the office, send a team to search it and retrieve the files from the four locked file cabinets and the locked desk. While Parker figured out which keys on Rich's key ring opened the file cabinets, the desk and the office, Corelli retrieved the yellow police tape from the car. They placed the keys in an envelope provided by the manager, put it on the desk in the office, then sealed the office with police tape. After warning the manager that it was off-limits to anyone except the police officers who would come with a warrant and boxes to clear it out, they left.

"What's next?" Corelli asked.

"Let's see what we can find out at *The Daily Post*."

Parker crossed the Brooklyn Bridge into Manhattan and headed up the East River Drive to *The Daily Post* office on Thirty-ninth Street and Second Avenue. It was the tail end of the morning rush hour and traffic was still heavy. Forty-five minutes later they arrived at a dreary brown brick high-rise dwarfed and humbled by the glistening steel and glass towers surrounding it. Parker pulled into a nearby loading zone, flipped down the On Duty placard and hoped they wouldn't be ticketed and towed by an enthusiastic NYPD tow truck.

After informing security they were there about the death of an employee, they were escorted to the office of the Vice President of Human Resources, Ms. Terrie Garcia. She smiled pleasantly. "Please have a seat." She examined the cards they'd handed her. "Homicide? How can I help?"

Parker didn't hesitate. "Edward Rich was found dead this morning. He was murdered. We need whatever you can tell us about him."

"Murdered?" Garcia's smile faded. "That's terrible." She tapped her fingers on her desk, then pulled her keyboard close and typed something. She confirmed Rich's date of birth, length of service, that he was an investigative reporter at an annual salary of $55,000 plus bonuses for stories that lifted sales.

"What about next of kin?"

"Lisa Puglisi. Bergenfield, New Jersey." Garcia jotted down the information and handed the paper to Parker.

"Any idea of their relationship?"

"It says friend."

"Thanks." Parker handed the slip to Corelli. "Does he live at that address?"

"Let's see." Garcia scrolled down her screen. "No. He lives in Red Hook, Brooklyn." She read off the address.

"That confirms the address we have," Parker said. "Is it current?"

"It should be since it's where we send his paychecks."

A rented mailbox. Interesting. "We'd like to look through his office."

Garcia sat back. "Reporters don't have offices. If you don't have any other questions, I'll take you down to Josh Krupke, his editor. He can show you his desk."

Garcia led them through a large noisy room filled with desks separated by waist-high dividers. People stood and stared. They seemed to drag silence with them. Since some of *The Daily Post* staff were intent on destroying Corelli's reputation, Parker assumed they were surprised to see her here, and curious about her presence. Corelli, on the other hand, might have been strolling in a garden with nothing on her mind but flowers. She appeared to be unaware of the disturbance they created. Parker admired Corelli's strength, her ability not to let the hate and unfounded accusations spewed about and at her get her down, her dedication to doing the right thing no matter the consequences, and her self-confidence. Parker hadn't verbalized it even to herself but she liked and cared about Corelli.

Garcia ushered them into one of the small offices along the windows, introduced them to Josh Krupke, informed him Rich was dead and let him know he was free to share the reporter's information. As the door closed behind her, conversations on the floor started up again.

Krupke was not the pudgy, bald, cigar-smoking newspaper editor the movies had led Parker to expect. He was tall and thin, had wild hair and a bushy beard and looked like a grungy mountain boy. He was shocked to hear that Rich was dead, even more shocked to hear he was murdered.

Parker dove right in. "What was he working on?"

"I don't know exactly." Krupke shifted his gaze from the window to Parker. "He was usually researching a couple of story ideas but he didn't like to talk about them. When he hit one that looked like it had a payoff, he ran it by me for approval and I took it to legal and the brass. A couple of weeks ago he said he was on to something explosive but he wouldn't be specific. I was curious and pushed a little. Is it sex-trafficking, money laundering, embezzlement, rape, kidnapping, or what? He said, 'It's or what. A threat to our democracy.'"

Democracy. Could it be any more political? Parker glanced at Corelli. Was she also remembering her comment about no high-visibility vics, nothing political? "So that would have been mid-February? Did he express any fear or give any indication that he might be in danger?"

"You think the democracy story got him killed?"

Even if Parker knew, she wouldn't tell anyone in the media, especially anyone at *The Daily Post*. "We've just started the investigation. It would be helpful to know whether he felt threatened by anyone from a current or previous investigation."

"If he did, he didn't share it with me. Every now and then he backed off stories he felt were trouble. I don't know if that meant he felt threatened." Krupke looked up something on his computer. "That talk with Ned was the first week in February."

Parker realized that though Rich had discussed it a month ago, he'd probably been working on the story for a while. Had he stumbled on something dangerous or did something else get him killed? "Did you feed him ideas for stories or did he generate them himself?"

Krupke tugged on his beard. "He either generated them himself or he took off from a lead he got from our tipster line."

"Tell me about the tipster line."

"It's a daily feature in our paper. You must have seen it." He glanced at Corelli. "Oh, I guess you're not regular readers." He reached behind him for a copy of *The Daily Post*, thumbed through it, folded the paper to a sidebar and handed it to Parker.

Corelli leaned in and they read it together:

REWARD

$500 reward for any tip that leads to a story by Ned Rich, The Daily Post's famous investigative reporter. This is your opportunity to expose a crime or a person with a dangerous secret. Your name will not be revealed at any time so don't be afraid to say something if you know something that someone is hiding.

Call 1-800-post-tip and leave your name, address, telephone number and a hint about your tip. For example, Congressman X is cheating on his wife or the CEO of xy company is stealing money or the police in zz precinct are taking bribes. We're interested in hearing about whatever you think is a crime or whoever is deceiving the public.

"How did Rich get the tips?"

"Tipsters leave a recorded message on the 800 line that rings on my assistant's desk." He tilted his head toward a middle-aged woman outside his office. "Alice takes them down and passes them on to Ned." He picked up his phone. "Alice, please come in my office and bring a copy of the latest tip sheet."

Krupke introduced them and waved her to one of the other chairs in the room. "Explain the tip system to my visitors."

"Sure. Callers leave their name, address, phone number and a brief description of the tip they're calling about. The incoming calls are recorded and each day's recordings are maintained as a separate file on our computer. Every morning I listen to yesterday's recording, print out the list and email a copy to Ned. If he's interested, he might ask me to send him the file with the day's actual calls to get a sense of the caller but I never know which tips he follows up on. If he decides to go ahead with a story he puts in a request for a five-hundred-dollar reward for the person that gave him the lead." She handed the current list to Corelli.

Parker glanced at the page in Corelli's hand. It had three entries. "Can you give us paper copies of the lists for the last year before we leave?"

"No problem. I'll take care of it right away."

After Alice left, Parker turned her attention back to Krupke. "Do you know anything about Rich's background? His finances?"

"Just resumé stuff, like he went to Rutgers and worked at a few newspapers in New Jersey. The only thing I know about his finances is that he makes a decent salary and gets bonuses for stories that boost sales. He got twenty thousand for a recent story exposing some shenanigans in Albany."

"Did he work in the office?"

"He worked from home. Once a week he'd check in by phone and give me a vague status report. I can show you his desk but there's not much in it."

"We'll take a look before we leave. Do you know his home address?"

Krupke stared over Parker's shoulder, frowning. "You know, I can tell you a lot about these people"—he waved his hand in the direction of the desks behind the detectives—"age, where they live, own or rent, wife's name, number of kids…but I just realized I don't know a damn thing about Ned."

CHAPTER FOUR

The desk was a bust, just a few pencils, a blank, yellow legal-size pad, and a couple of office notices in his in-box. Corelli sat and pulled the computer keyboard toward her. "Do you know his password?"

"Whoa." Krupke put his hand over the keys. "You'll need a warrant to search the office computer." He swiveled to check the nearby desks. All were empty and none of the clusters of people were close enough to overhear. "But check his laptop, he probably downloaded his email to read at home."

Right. Krupke had no idea they hadn't found Rich's laptop, nor where he lived and worked, and Parker was not about to clue him in. "Thanks for your help. We'll see ourselves out."

"Wait," Krupke said, "I'm going to run a story on his death. I'll get something from my police reporter but is there anything you can tell me other than he was murdered?"

Damn. They'd better inform his next of kin before she reads it in the paper. "We're in the very early stages of the investigation so there's nothing we can share at the moment." Parker handed him a card. "Call me if you remember anything. We'll send a team in later to interview the staff."

Krupke's assistant caught them as they headed for the elevator. "Here are the tip sheets you asked for. Let me know if you need anything else." She handed Parker a letter-size manila envelope. "I hope Ned's not in trouble." Krupke said he would announce the death after they left so Parker ignored the implied question.

The elevator was crowded and the street bustling, so they didn't speak until they were back in the car. "We need to notify his next of kin before the story hits the newspaper. Please put Lisa Puglisi's address into the GPS. If she isn't his next of kin, maybe she can direct us."

Corelli pulled out her iPhone and typed 115 Bugler Street, Bergenfield, New Jersey into Google Maps. "Ironic. His job was exposing people to public scrutiny but if Krupke is any indication, Rich wasn't into sharing anything about himself with acquaintances. Or given his secrecy, with anyone. Hopefully his friend Lisa can help us figure him out."

Traffic on the East River Drive, the George Washington Bridge and Route 4 was relatively light, leaving Parker's mind free to review what they knew. "What do you think of Ndep's theory that he was killed somewhere else and his body was dumped in Penny Park in the middle of the night?"

"Lividity indicates the body was turned so Ndep is probably right." Corelli shifted a little to face Parker. "I'm guessing he was into blackmail. Think about it. His job was digging up information on people who had something to hide. Some people might be willing to pay to protect their secrets."

"Or kill to protect themselves." The GPS announced they'd arrived at their destination and Parker pulled over. They studied the small green bungalow, one of many in a neighborhood of neat, older, well-cared-for homes, each with a small mowed front lawn and trimmed hedges separating them from neighbors on both sides.

"Modest," Corelli said. "Maybe because I'm thinking he lived here and was into blackmail I was expecting something more elaborate."

"Why don't you take this one?" Parker said, as they approached the front door.

A frazzled looking woman with a small child on her hip and another wrapped around her leg, responded to the bell. "Hi, can I help you?"

"I'm Detective Corelli and this is Detective Parker. Are you Lisa Puglisi?"

The woman frowned. "No. I'm Donna Little. My husband and I bought this house from Lisa two years ago."

"Do you have a forwarding address or telephone number for her?"

The woman shifted the baby to her other hip. "No. I've never met her. We dealt with the real estate agent and then her lawyer represented her at the closing."

"I see. Do you remember her lawyer's name?"

"Let me think. It was Polish but it made me think of the Kawasaki motorcycle I used to ride in the good old days before I had children." She shifted the baby again. "Only kidding. Um, Wysoki, Bart Wysoki. His office was either in Teaneck or Hackensack."

"Thank you. Sorry to bother you."

Parker didn't want to seem condescending by micromanaging Corelli but she seemed happy to let her make the decisions so maybe she was overthinking it. "Let's see if we can find this Wysoki guy and get an address for Puglisi. Hopefully, she lives relatively close."

Corelli took out her iPhone and searched for an attorney by that name. "Got it." She grinned. "How did I ever live without my smart phone?"

Parker smiled, remembering their first day working together on their first case when Corelli angrily proclaimed that her antiquated flip phone did everything she needed. But after her college-age sister, and nephew, showed her that FaceTime would allow her and Brett to see and talk to each other when Brett traveled, she'd converted immediately.

In minutes Corelli was explaining to Lisa Puglisi's attorney why they needed to speak to her. He disconnected to call the station and verify her credentials and her story with Dietz. Seconds later Corelli's phone pinged an incoming text. *Lisa Puglisi 3400 Lakeshore Drive, Parsippany, NJ. Works from home. Will let her know to expect you.* "Okay, we're good to go as soon as I put the address in the GPS."

Just under an hour later Corelli rang the bell of the modern wood and glass house snuggled in a stand of trees on the shore of Deer Isle Lake. It was quiet, no traffic sounds, no boat sounds. A few other houses were visible but nothing very close.

"Not a bad place to live but it might not be so peaceful in the summer." She rang the bell two more times before the door opened. The woman standing there was not dressed for visitors, unless she usually entertained in bare feet wearing red pajama pants with flying cats on them, a T-shirt featuring a vampire with blood dripping from its mouth, and rainbow-streaked hair that looked as if she styled it by putting her finger in an electric socket. "Lisa Puglisi?"

"Yes." She made no effort to hide her annoyance.

"NYPD Detectives Corelli and Parker. We were told you were expecting us."

Puglisi frowned. "Was that today?"

"It was. Can we come in?"

"Oh, sorry. Sure." She turned and they followed her into a large living room with a stone fireplace on one wall and a huge picture window that overlooked the lake on the opposite wall. It was comfortably furnished with two easy chairs facing the lake and a matching sofa and loveseat in front of the fireplace. Built-in bookcases lined the rest of the room. Though it smelled vaguely of charred wood it was clean and neat, a contrast to its rumpled owner. Puglisi perched on the loveseat and waved them to the sofa. "Please sit. Sorry for my appearance but I've been working all night picking at a problem. My attorney said you want to talk about Ricky."

"Ricky?" The detectives exchanged a glance. "We actually wanted to talk about Ned Rich," Corelli said.

"Yeah, that's Ricky." She laughed. "Taking Rich as his last name is his private joke. Richard Hawley is his real name but he uses Ned Rich for his job and other nefarious undertakings." She picked up a pack of cigarettes and tamped one out. "Mind if I smoke?"

"Actually, Detective Parker is allergic to smoke." Corelli lied, not wanting her to be too comfortable.

Puglisi removed the cigarette from her lips, inserted it back in the pack without comment and threw the pack on the end table.

"What kind of work keeps you up all night?"

Puglisi seemed surprised by the question. "I'm a computer security analyst for the Department of Homeland Security and since the recent hacking is public knowledge, I can tell you that I'm one of hundreds trying to figure out how they did it and how to prevent it. I work remotely so I make my own hours. Unfortunately, I got sucked in last night and couldn't let go." Her hand hovered over the pack of cigarettes but then dropped them into her lap. "What kind of trouble is Ricky in?"

"What makes you think he's in trouble?"

"Why else would two NYPD detectives drive out to the sticks to chat with me about him?"

"What's your relationship with Ricky?"

"Nonexistent. We used to be friends. He and I bonded in junior high school because we were both computer nerds. We went to Rutgers together, majored in computer science and became experts in computer coding, security and research, but the older we got, the more our paths diverged. In college Ricky loved digging up stuff on people, especially classmates. At first he did it for laughs. He would threaten to expose students to their parents unless they bought him beer and pizza. But then he decided to use his expertise to dig up dirt on people and get them to pay him to bury it. To protect himself he used his considerable computer skills to create a new identity, Edward Ned Rich, with a life history that would look real to anyone but the most talented hacker. He took that job at *The Daily Post* as a cover and a way to get paid for researching to find people he could extort."

"Did you ever report him to the police?"

She shrugged. "Not my job. I tried to talk him out of it but he wouldn't budge so I refused to have anything more to do with him. I hadn't spoken to him in maybe ten years and then he called me late one night about a year ago. I could hear the music we used to listen to playing in the background. He sounded drunk. He said, 'I miss you. I just bought a spectacular duplex apartment in Brooklyn Heights and there's no one else I'd rather share it with. Cost me three million. You're gonna love it. Let's hang out like old times.'

"He really pissed me off. Like I should be happy he stole enough money to buy a multimillion-dollar apartment. I said, 'Have you changed? Because I'm still not interested in being friends with a crook.'" He hung up on me. I felt sad for him. Obviously he didn't have any friends and had to call someone who dumped him ten years ago. Over the years I'd see his stories in the paper and wonder how many other stories never made it into the news. Based on the cost of that apartment, I would guess a lot."

"And yet he had you down as his next of kin at *The Daily Post?*"

"Pretty pathetic. That surprised me when my attorney called. But it made sense when I thought about it because in college good ole Ricky had transferred all his parents' money out of their bank accounts into an offshore account he'd set up. They knew but either didn't want to or didn't have enough proof to nail him but they disowned him and refused to see or talk to him. It was around that time I broke off with him too."

"Nice guy."

She removed a cigarette from the pack but didn't attempt to light it. "You know, he *was* a nice guy at one time but something in him got twisted. He saw himself as a kind of Robin Hood, justified what he did by saying he only took from people who deserved it but he forgot the part about using the stolen money to benefit someone other than himself."

"Do you have an address for the Brooklyn Heights apartment?"

"I didn't ask." She met Corelli's gaze. "I gather NYPD has caught up with him but you still haven't told me why you're talking to me. I don't know much about his current life."

"I'm sorry but Ricky, as you know him, was murdered last night."

Puglisi paled. "Oh, geez." She blinked, jammed the cigarette in her mouth and reached for the lighter but she seemed to go inside herself as she absorbed the news. She removed the cigarette and gazed at Corelli. "Was it one of his...? He was playing with fire. I guess it was inevitable that somebody would fight back."

"Where were you last night?"

She put the cigarette and the lighter on the table. "As I said earlier, I've spent the last twenty-four to thirty hours in front of my computer. You know, ten years ago when I cut him out of my life I was angry enough to kill him but I walked away instead. He hasn't meant anything to me in a long time and I have absolutely no reason to kill him now. But if I'm a suspect, I'll give you contact information for my boss. She can trace the activity on my computer and confirm I was working."

"Give me her name, title, department and telephone number."

She got up and dug around in a messenger bag hanging near the front door, returning with a business card and a pen. She wrote on the card and handed it to Corelli. "The card contains my

contact information and I've added my boss's name and number."
She picked up the cigarette.

"We'll only call if we need to. But for now we need information
on his family. Do you know where his parents are? Does he have
any brothers or sisters?"

"There's nobody. He was an only child and his parents died in a
car accident a couple of years ago."

"So will you be responsible for burying him?"

She stood and walked to the window, twirling the cigarette in
her fingers. "I never thought it would come to this but I will, for
old times' sake."

CHAPTER FIVE

Traffic going toward Manhattan was heavy. But not nearly as heavy as the stop-and-go of the cars in the lanes heading out of the city toward towns in New Jersey. "I'm glad we're driving against rush hour traffic," Parker said. "How about giving Dietz a heads up on tracking down the address of Rich's Brooklyn Heights apartment? And we should probably have someone check to see if he has any offshore accounts."

"Let's wait on the offshore accounts. Maybe we'll find something in his apartment."

Inching along on the long slow approach to the Holland Tunnel, Corelli's stomach gurgled. Parker grinned. "Hungry? Want to swing by Chinatown before we go to the station? I know a hole-in-the-wall restaurant on Pell Street that has great food."

"Sounds good." Corelli's stomach gurgled again. "Better make it fast."

Being hungry when ordering resulted in a feast of dishes covering the table: hot and sour soup, fried pork dumplings, pork fried rice, General Tso's chicken and orange-flavored beef.

Corelli watched the waiter place the various dishes on the table but waited until they were alone to speak. "At least now that Puglisi confirmed our theory that Rich was a blackmailer, we have a thread to pull to find his killer."

"You probably have to be a blackmailer to afford to live in Brooklyn Heights." Parker sipped her water. "I've been looking for a new apartment and I can tell you Brooklyn Heights is pretty pricey even to rent a two-bedroom apartment." She forked some spicy beef into her mouth.

Corelli's hand stilled halfway to her mouth. "I didn't know you were looking for an apartment. A couple of my tenants are leaving in the next few months. If I remember correctly, I'll have one two-bedroom and two three-bedroom apartments available."

Parker concentrated on spooning fried rice onto her plate. Rents in the trendy Manhattan Meat Packing District where the building Corelli owned was located, were way above her pay grade. She met Corelli's gaze. "Manhattan rents are too high. I'm looking in the outer boroughs."

"You and Ndep? Or just you?"

"Gloria and I...are far from moving in together. We'd just started dating right before the sex-trafficking case and when I was so freaked out by...events...she stepped up to take care of me. But we moved too fast, I think, and became a couple before we were really there. It'll be just me for now, but I want space and light and I'm looking for a two or three bedroom."

"Take a look at the apartments in my building. My supers, either Rosie or Karen, can show them and discuss rents. I never intended to be a landlord and Uncle Genaro left me a good amount of cash along with the building, so I keep rents reasonable. Besides, you qualify for the partner discount."

"Partner, huh?" Parker made no attempt to hide her surprise. She wasn't sure but this might have been the first time Corelli referred to her as her partner in the full sense of the word. She signaled the waiter for the check and met Corelli's gaze. "Thanks, that's a generous offer but I don't want to feel...um, obligated."

Corelli laughed. "You think I'll use it as a hammer. Raise your rent when you do something I don't like? Or worse, evict you?"

Parker blushed. "I know you wouldn't do those things." She grinned. "Brett wouldn't let you. But you're my boss. It could be problematic."

"You don't work for me. And remember. We're partners. Some partners are friends."

Parker stared at Corelli trying to gauge whether she was serious. Corelli's close friendship with her former partner, Jimmy, had ended badly when he went rogue, so Parker assumed Corelli would always keep her at arm's length. Yet since she'd saved Corelli's life they'd been creeping toward friendship. Hadn't they? But given Corelli's mood swings she feared this sudden friendliness was just another side effect of her PTSD. Parker didn't want to hurt her feelings, but she didn't totally trust the impulse behind the offer. "I appreciate the offer, but I'd like to think about it." She'd discuss the idea of renting an apartment in Corelli's building with Jessie and Annie. And maybe Brett. "Time to head back to the office to consider what we have and what we need." Parker tossed two twenties on the table.

Corelli sat back as Parker swung the car onto Canal Street toward the Hudson River and West Street to go uptown to the station. "This case may not be as straightforward as I originally thought. You still up for lead?"

"I am if you still think I can handle it."

"Oh, yeah. You're as capable of dealing with a little blackmail and a threat to our democracy as anyone I know."

Parker blushed at the praise and quickly changed the subject. "Maybe the Thirteenth Street files have the answers we're looking for. But we're going to need help and a workspace to deal with sorting through them."

Corelli nodded. "If we're right about the blackmail, which I think we are, we'll also need additional people to interview potential suspects."

Dietz pounced on them the second they emerged from the staircase into the squad room. "Watkins got the info on the Brooklyn Heights apartment."

"Whoa." Parker put her hands up. "Down, boy." She grinned. "Thanks, Dietz. Is the captain in? We're going to need a murder room and some more help on this case."

"He's in. But I already figured that out based on the warrants you requested and the fact that you suspect blackmail. You have me, Watkins, Kim, Greene, and Forlini plus the big conference room for the case."

"I'm impressed." Parker punched Dietz in the shoulder. She was happy to have him. He was an excellent detective who probably should have retired but was a great asset working in-house to support investigations. "I'll talk to the captain later and take back all the bad things I said about you the other day. Hopefully, he'll change his mind and keep you."

"Har, har, hardy har har." Dietz waited, then getting no reaction, he shook his head. "I guess you're too young to get the reference but it means I'm not amused. I know you adore me and would never bad-mouth me to the captain or anyone for that matter." He paused. "Corelli, on the other hand…"

"Blah, blah blah." Corelli clamped a hand on Dietz's shoulder. "Let's get to work." The three of them walked down to the large conference room. Technicians were busy installing computers and telephones on multiple workstations along three walls. A tall evidence safe was in a corner along with a table with two drip coffee makers, one for tea, one for coffee. A large rectangular conference table and twelve chairs dominated the center of the room.

Watkins looked up from the computer he was working on. "Hey, Richard Hawley's Brooklyn apartment is on Columbia Heights Street near Clark Street. I drew up a search warrant and I'm on my way to Judge Miller's chamber to get it signed."

"That was fast work."

"The apartment was in his real name so it popped immediately. I prepped our standard warrant for everything and anything."

"Call us after you get it signed. We'll meet you there." If Watkins or Dietz was surprised to hear Parker respond instead of Corelli, they didn't show it.

No sooner had they settled down when high-energy Detective Hei-ki Young Kim bounced in. "Hey, boss." She saluted Corelli as she always did. "I picked up Rich's mail at the UPS place. He had four letters."

Parker extended her hand for the evidence bag. "So, Kim, how would you like to make some calls?"

"What did you have in mind?"

Parker handed her an envelope. "This is a list of people who called *The Daily Post* tip line to report something they thought Rich should investigate. Speak to each one, get more information about their tip, find out whether Rich spoke to them and whether he seemed interested. *The Daily Post* paid five hundred dollars for the tips he thought were potential stories. We're looking for something that might lead to blackmail, and anything related to um, a threat to our democracy."

"Really? What exactly does a threat to our democracy mean?"

"I'm hoping you'll know it when you see it."

Parker pulled on a pair of nitrile gloves, used nearby scissors to slit one of the envelopes, and carefully pulled out the contents. It contained ten one-hundred-dollar bills and a copy of an invoice like the one they'd found in his pocket, which Parker assumed identified the victim sending the money. Two of the other three envelopes held twenty one-hundred-dollar bills and the last one held thirty one-hundred-dollar bills. "Eight thousand dollars. Not bad."

Corelli watched Parker stuff each stack of money with its invoice or paper with the number on it into the proper envelope. "We've come a long way since this morning, Parker. We've identified him, confirmed our blackmail theory, found his hidey hole and his real name and address. I suspect we'll find something in the files coming in and who knows what we'll find in his apartment?"

"Kim, please enter these in our evidence log and have Dietz lock them in the safe." Parker tossed the nitrile gloves in the wastebasket. "We've also confirmed the invoice in his pocket was used in his blackmail scheme." She stood and paced. "So maybe Rich finds a blackmail target, meets with them in some dark place, shows them the goods and when they agree to pay, he gives them an invoice with an account number, the fee, and the mailing address of the box in Red Hook. If it didn't appear he was murdered somewhere else, that scenario would explain why he was in Penny Park in the middle of the night. What do you think?"

Corelli considered the question. "You're right. It probably doesn't explain why he was in Penny Park but it may be a good summary of how he did business."

Parker sat again. "All right, Corelli, let's get started on reports while we wait for the warrant."

An hour and a half later, Watkins called. "I'm on my way to Brooklyn Heights. I'll wait for you to enter the apartment."

Parker stood and stretched. "We'll be in the Brooklyn Heights apartment if anyone needs us, Dietz."

"Hey." Dietz held up a hand. "Before you go, Forlini and Green will be back with ten boxes of files. What'll I tell the analysts to look for?" He was looking at Corelli but Parker answered.

"Proof of blackmail, hopefully a book with names and amounts plus anything in the files that could result in criminal charges. And of course, anything that the analysts think is relevant. They should keep a list of the people mentioned and a brief description of each file or loose document." Parker turned as she walked to the door. "We're particularly interested in knowing what he was working on currently."

Corelli put a hand on Parker's arm. "You know, we probably could use some help with the search."

Parker nodded. "Dietz, when Forlini and Greene get back, have them and Kim meet us at the Brooklyn Heights apartment with boxes."

Rather than pay the toll for the Battery Tunnel, Parker swung east to the Brooklyn Bridge and thirty minutes later they were in Brooklyn Heights, a charming upscale neighborhood with tree-lined, cobblestone streets, blocks of restored row houses, and a limited number of high-rise buildings facing Lower Manhattan across the East River. Its proximity to Manhattan, its wonderful water views and historic waterfront promenade made it a desirable, and therefore expensive, place to live.

They drove past Cranberry, Orange, and Pineapple Streets and turned onto Clark where they found a legal spot close to Rich's Art Deco building, the only high-rise in the middle of the mostly attached ivy-wrapped brick row houses, brownstones, and other low-rise buildings.

Watkins was chatting with the doorman when they arrived. "Detectives Corelli and Parker, this is Jorge. You just missed the building manager. She couldn't stay but she wanted to see the warrant before she would allow us to go up to Rich's tenth-floor apartment. We're good to go."

Once they were in the elevator Watkins spoke again. "Jorge confirmed Rich lived alone, was friendly but kept to himself. He parked his car in the building's garage. I examined the visitor's sign-in book and unless I missed an entry, Rich didn't have any visitors. On the other hand, any friends he brought up to his apartment from the garage wouldn't have signed the book."

They donned booties and gloves before entering the apartment. Parker didn't think she had any preconceptions, but the elegant splendor of the apartment bathed in the late afternoon sun streaming through floor to ceiling windows shocked her. The beautifully decorated duplex, with four bedrooms and three baths on the lower level, and a large kitchen, large dining room, large living room, medium-size office, full bathroom and huge terrace overlooking the river on the upper level cost millions, but at least it was gorgeous. The décor reminded her of her uncle's house, formal and cold. She preferred warm and comfortable like Corelli's loft and Brett's apartment.

After walking through the whole apartment with Watkins, they left him to start in the master suite—the bedroom, sitting room and bathroom with a large glass-walled shower, a whirlpool bath for two, and a two-sink vanity. All three had windows facing Lower Manhattan and the water.

Parker and Corelli went upstairs to the office. His desk was orderly. The two neatly aligned folders on top, Bills To Be Paid, and Bills Paid, both contained mortgage statements, apartment maintenance, tax, electric, Verizon cell phone service, Verizon Fios Internet service, and garage bills, but neither contained anything helpful for the investigation. He had separate files in his desk for payroll stubs, JP Morgan Bank statements and extra checks, a Mercedes file that contained the title, registration and receipts for maintenance, and a miscellaneous file with receipts for purchases including a super expensive espresso maker. Everything was in the name of Richard Hawley.

There was a folder with photographs that looked to be family, but Lisa Puglisi and some guys around their age appeared in many of them. Based on the dates written on the back, none of the photos were recent. The top drawer of the desk contained a driver's license, car registration, bank ATM card, several credit cards, a gym membership card, and a password protected cell phone. The cards were all in his real name. Other drawers held supplies, pens, pencils, notebooks, pads, envelopes, and stamps.

His laptop computer was on the credenza behind the desk. Corelli opened it but it was also password protected so she put it aside for the professionals to deal with. She sat back. "Pretty run-of-the-mill stuff, nothing at all helpful. The good stuff must be in the boxes from his Thirteenth Street office or on his computer."

Parker sighed and stretched. "I need some air."

Now standing on the large deck-like terrace waiting for the team of detectives who would do a complete search, Parker looked out on the gorgeous view of Lower Manhattan and the Brooklyn Bridge in the dusk. "It might almost be worth becoming a criminal to live in a beautiful apartment with water views. Imagine sitting out here in the warm weather."

Corelli laughed. "You don't have to resort to crime, Parker. Many apartments in my building have views of the Hudson River, just like mine. And, there's a rooftop area for tenants. And a private one for me, which you're welcome to share."

"It's tempting but like I said, I need to think about it." Parker turned her back to the view. "I hope you're right that all of Rich's blackmail files are in the stuff from his Thirteenth Street office or on his computer. But my gut tells me he would want important things like the list of his victims and their payments here where he could look at them whenever he wanted. I'm betting there's a safe." She noticed Corelli was shivering. "It's cold, let's go inside."

They moved into the apartment. "His blackmail victims are the obvious place to look for his killer, but I don't want to assume anything. I'm thinking we should interview everyone he worked with at *The Daily Post*." She looked toward the hall door. "I hear Forlini and friends."

Corelli glanced at her phone. "Are you up for dinner at Gianna's house? Brett is driving to Brooklyn to spend time with the girls and Gianna texted me inviting you and me to join them. You could leave Watkins to supervise."

Normally Parker would jump at the chance to spend time with Gianna's family, especially the three fragile girls between six and eight years old she and Corelli found hidden in a closet during their last big case. Fearing the girls were in danger and would be vulnerable in the city's overburdened child protection services system, they brought them to Gianna, knowing she would not only shelter but nurture and give them the tender care they needed. And she had. In a little more than three months Crissy, Maria and Teresa were more related and unguarded than anyone expected. And now Gianna and her husband, Marco, were in the process of adopting them. "I'd love to but I want to stay with the team. Why don't you go?"

Corelli touched Parker's arm. "Are you sure?"

Parker wasn't sure whether she was asking about not staying to search the apartment or driving somewhere without her. "If Brett picks you up here and you drive into the garage when you get home, I think you'll be safe."

CHAPTER SIX

At seven thirty in the morning, Parker, Corelli, Dietz, Watkins, Forlini, Kim, and Greene gathered around the table for their first meeting on the case. The four analysts at a table on the other side of the room had already started sifting through the ten boxes of files brought in last night.

Corelli put her coffee cup down. "Listen up, people." When she had their attention she said, "You may have sensed this but I'm making it official. Parker is the lead on this one. And I'll be part of the team." She sat back.

All eyes shifted to Parker. She shuffled the papers in front of her, giving them a couple of seconds to absorb the change. When no one ran screaming from the room, she cleared her throat. "All right, let's start with Watkins, then Forlini, and last, Kim."

Watkins smoothed the pages of his black leather notebook. "As you know, we found a laptop, a cell phone and lots of bills, bank statements and receipts, plus documents for the apartment but we didn't find anything of immediate interest. We have people working on his computer and the cell. We didn't find a safe. According to his neighbors, he was quiet and polite, but not friendly. The search of his car in the garage turned up nothing. We'll go through everything again and hopefully something will pop up." He pointed to Forlini.

"Yeah, pretty much the same for us. The Thirteenth Street rental office is paid up for another couple of months so we sealed it in case we want to take another look. We didn't find anything other than the ten boxes of files we brought back. Four analysts"—he pointed to the group in the corner—"are sorting through them as we speak. We got the same story from the staff and the other tenants who were around. He was pleasant but not friendly. Paid the rent in cash and tipped well."

Kim waited a beat before beginning. "I managed to speak to all but two of the twenty-three tipsters who called *The Daily Post* in the last four weeks. Everyone said Rich called them back personally and asked a few questions. Apparently seven of them called to tip him off about an NYPD police detective running brothels but they called the day after the story broke on the news and he told them they were too late. He told the other fourteen he would look into their tips and call back if he found anything of interest. I checked out some of his articles and it seems to me that Rich liked to blow the lid off things. These tips seemed run-of-the-mill, stuff like garbage not being picked up every day, a neighbor who had loud parties, someone who seemed to be selling drugs outside of a school. My guess is he ignored them." She waved the tip sheets. "I made notes on the sheets if you're interested."

"Maybe later." Parker looked around the table to be sure she had everyone's attention. "Let me bring you up-to-date on what we know so far. Richard Hawley, thirty-eight and single, also known as Edward Ned Rich was brutally beaten and strangled to death. It appears he was killed somewhere else and dumped in Penny Park in the middle of the night. He had more than three hundred dollars in his pocket so it was probably not a robbery. There was no visual indication of sexual activity. As Rich, he was an investigative reporter for *The Daily Post* and according to his friend, a blackmailer. He had no identification on him when he was found but an invoice crumpled in his pocket enabled us to get an ID at the UPS store in Red Hook, where he rented a mailbox in the name of Deep Dig Excavation Services. We think it was his last blackmail invoice. We've recovered some of what we assume are his blackmail payments from the UPS mailbox. It appears he assigned his victims a number and instructed them to mail cash with that number, no name, to that box. He picked up his mail a couple of times a week. We assume he recorded payments in a ledger of some sort, maybe a computer spreadsheet that cross-references numbers to names, but we haven't found it. He was known as Ned Rich at *The Daily Post*. The mailbox and the Thirteenth Street office were in the name of Edward Rich. The Brooklyn Heights apartment and everything in it is in his real name, Richard Hawley." She stopped to take a breath and give people a chance to absorb everything.

"Our current theory is that his death is related to the blackmail. A reasonable assumption is that he met with someone he planned to blackmail and they killed him. But so far we have no information about who he was blackmailing. Three things before we finish up: I want to keep his Hawley identity confidential so no discussing it outside our team. The same is true for the blackmail. Unless you get a hint of it, don't bring it up. The detective who taught me about homicide investigations"—she glanced at Corelli—"always said every idea or thought about what thread to pull in an investigation is important. So, I encourage you to share any thoughts on direction or threads to follow." She hesitated but no one offered anything.

"And talking about threads, Forlini and Kim, we need to interview the staff at *The Daily Post*. Start with Rich's editor, Josh Krupke, and work your way around the office. Hopefully somebody will know something. Watkins, see whether you can find any offshore accounts under either name and check with Hawley's bank about whether he has a safe deposit box. Greene, pick up the tip calls where Kim left off. Corelli and I will dig through the stuff we got from his apartment." She gazed at Dietz. "And you, my man, will oversee them"—she tilted her head toward the two men and two women going through the file boxes—"and keep the rest of us on track."

Watkins moved to a computer. Kim discussed the tipster list with Greene and then she and Forlini left the room. Corelli retrieved one of the boxes from the Brooklyn Heights apartment and brought it to the table. "How should we do this?"

Parker didn't hesitate. "Dump everything on the table and as we review things we can put them back in the box."

Dietz walked back into the room. "Have you seen today's *Daily Post*?" He put it on the table between Parker and Corelli.

A picture of Rich covered most of the front page. The headline blared: **Ned Rich, Investigative Reporter for *The Daily Post* Murdered.** Corelli turned to the story.

Reporter Murdered

The Daily Post is mourning the death of reporter Edward "Ned" Rich, thirty-eight, who was murdered in Lower Manhattan's Rockefeller Park yesterday.

Mr. Rich, a native of New Jersey, lived in Red Hook, Brooklyn, and was employed by *The Daily Post* as an Investigative Reporter. Over his more than ten years with the *Post*, Ned Rich fielded tips from readers and fearlessly delivered explosive exposés of corruption involving little people and the high and mighty.

The police are speculating that his death might be the result of his latest investigation, which he characterized as having to do with a threat to our democracy.

No funeral arrangements have been announced.

Parker grinned. "Well, at least it's not totally made up. They got his age, place of birth and place of employment correct. Good picture, too."

Corelli narrowed her eyes. "Was that sarcasm, Parker?"

"Hmm, I suppose it was." She pulled a stack of documents to her, then seeing no movement from Corelli, looked up. "What?"

Corelli met her gaze. "Give the girl a little power and she undergoes a personality change."

Parker leaned across the table. "You ain't seen nothing yet, sista."

Corelli shook her head. "Exactly what I'm talking about." She reached for the pile of documents.

CHAPTER SEVEN

Three hours later, Greene dropped into a chair at the table. "Geez, I think some of these people call in a tip just to have somebody to talk to. I made it through almost four weeks and I haven't heard one tip that interests me. I need a break. I'm going out to pick up lunch at the Halal truck. Can I get you anything?"

"Oh, yeah, I'm starving," Corelli said. "Get me a falafel platter with rice, salad, lots of hot sauce and a pita. And if by chance you stop for coffee, I'll have a large black, no sugar." She threw a twenty on the table. "Tip the guys on the truck and the barista."

"That sounds good. I'll have exactly the same." Parker placed a twenty on top of Corelli's bill. She tossed the documents she'd been reviewing into the box on the table. "We're through the three boxes they brought back from Brooklyn Heights and we haven't found one helpful thing. Let's see if the Thirteenth Street files have anything."

Parker and Corelli approached the four analysts. "Detectives Parker and Corelli," Parker said. "What are you finding?"

One of the analysts stood. "Everything we've reviewed appears to be backup documentation for the investigative pieces he published." She picked up a group of folders held together by rubber bands. "Each story has multiple folders and the folders are arranged the same way. The story name and its publication date is written on every folder related to it and the first folder in each story contains a copy of the actual newspaper article, any articles or letters to the editor that resulted from it, and in many cases a copy of a request for five hundred dollars to be paid to the individual who provided the tip. Subsequent story folders contain names of sources, transcripts of interviews, handwritten interview notes and documentation of his research, either printouts or a list of links. It's pretty tedious but we're checking the links to be sure they relate to the subject." She held up a sheet of paper. "We're also compiling a list of names that appear anywhere in the folders, cross-referenced to the article they relate to."

Parker listened carefully. Rich's filing system should make it easy to spot anything unusual. "He sounds very organized. Have you found anything that's not tied to an article, something that might be blackmail material?"

Her eyes widened. "Not so far. But we'll keep our eyes open."

"Thank you." They returned to the conference table. "I'll bet all of those boxes contain documentation of the articles he published. Another dead end as far as the case goes." Parker stared into space reviewing what they had so far. "What are we missing?"

"You know, Ms. Former Assistant District Attorney, not all cases are solved."

"I hope you're not saying we should give up, Corelli, because my gut tells me this is a big one, but I can't find a thread to grab."

"I agree we seem to be up the creek without a paddle, as they say. But let's see what we get from the lines we've tossed into the water." She stood and grabbed a bag from Greene. "But the good news is our lunch has arrived."

Corelli handed each of them a container of coffee while Greene distributed the lunches. "Falafel with rice, salad, pita and extra hot sauce." She placed a takeout container, plastic utensils and a stack of napkins in front of each of them, then unwrapped her own lunch, a falafel sandwich. She sipped her coffee. "Do you think we'll find the killer in the tip files?"

Parker glanced at Corelli who seemed totally involved in her lunch. "Not the killer. The tipster who led Rich to the killer." She took a few bites of her lunch. "Um, this is good. Thanks, Greene." She put her fork down. "It just occurred to me that if a tip led him to the killer, he would have spent months doing research, digging up dirt, building his blackmail case before approaching the victim." Both Corelli and Greene nodded in agreement. "So maybe we're starting at the wrong end of the tip lists. We asked for a year's worth of tip sheets. Maybe you should start with the oldest rather than the most recent." Parker sipped her coffee. "Or even better, call Josh Krupke at *The Daily Post* and get the names of everyone who was paid for a tip they submitted going back, um, say two years."

"That's brilliant, Parker." Corelli looked…proud? Maybe the hot sauce had singed her brain. Or maybe she really was changing. Whatever the reason, Parker preferred it to being attacked or dumped-on.

"I agree, it's brilliant. I'll call Krupke and get started." Greene balled up the wrapping from her sandwich and tossed it into the bin designated for food waste and left the room.

"Something smells good." Watkins sat at the table. "I set the inquiries about offshore accounts in motion. Now we wait." He stood. "Unless you have something else for me, Parker, I'm going to grab some lunch at the truck. I'll check with the bank later."

"Go. But I might need you to go to Brooklyn Heights with us. The more I think about Rich, the more I think he has a safe somewhere in that apartment."

Suddenly energized, Parker scanned the room for Dietz. He was talking to one of the officers answering calls on the police tip line. She waved him over. "We need to do another search of the Brooklyn Heights apartment. Can you get our favorite safecracker, Detective Paulie Massetti, and two or three of his Burglary cohorts to help us? If they're available, give them the address and have them meet us there."

He frowned. "Cohort? What's a cohort, Parker? You remember we talk English here?"

"Yo, Dietz, wouldja understand better if I said homies? Or posse?" She glared at him. "Maybe coworkers does it for youse?"

"Ah, homies. Gotcha. Let me see what I can do." Dietz walked over to a desk with a phone.

"So we're not so stuck?" Corelli said.

"It seems that way." Parker considered whether to share her thinking. It was always tricky with Corelli but she really did seem to be changing. "Thanks to you. I did that thing you do of turning something around and looking at it from another angle."

"I do that?" Corelli sounded surprised.

"Do what?" Dietz looked from one to the other and not getting a response, shrugged. "Massetti will meet *youse* there in about an hour with a couple of his...um"—he grinned at Parker—"cohorts."

CHAPTER EIGHT

They had just entered the apartment when Paul Massetti arrived with three other Burglary detectives. After introductions, Parker explained the situation. "Rich was a meticulous organizer and he covered his trail very well. This apartment is the only thing we've found in his real name, and we stumbled on it accidently. I'm guessing this was his secure place and there are things I would expect him to have here that we haven't found. I'm also guessing our people missed a safe in their first pass, and I'm depending on your experience with this kind of thing to help us find it."

Parker gave the group a quick tour of the upper and lower floors, then assigned Massetti and one of the Robbery detectives to work with her and Corelli on the upper floor while Watkins and the remaining two Robbery detectives checked the lower floor.

Four hours later, seven frustrated detectives gathered in the living room. Massetti joined Corelli at the sliding glass doors and stared out at the lights of Lower Manhattan twinkling in the dusk. "Nice view," he said. His eyes widened. "I'll bet that balcony, or should I say deck, could hold at least a hundred people. Did you search it?"

Corelli turned her gaze to Massetti. "Duh. There's nothing out there except tables, chairs and umbrellas."

"Duh, back at ya. It sounds like the perfect place to hide something. Where are the lights for the deck?" Massetti spoke out loud as he ran a hand over the wall adjacent to the sliding glass doors.

Parker walked to the wall on the other side of the glass doors and hit several switches, lighting up the outside deck. "Is that enough light to search or do we need to call for some support, Massetti?"

Instead of answering, Massetti stepped outside and strolled around the deck. Parker, Corelli and the other detectives watched from the doorway. "We can do it. It's chilly so we'll need coats." While they pulled on jackets and coats, Massetti studied the area. One of his guys handed him his coat. "We'll work our way from the building to the outer edge and examine the deck in sections to be sure we cover every single inch."

Using the pattern of the wooden flooring he paced off a section and assigned a detective to search it. "Look for something that might trigger the flooring to move, maybe a button or maybe an unusual space between boards. Use your phone flashlight if you need more light." He did the same for each of the detectives but left himself free to supervise.

They worked in silence. As a section was finished, Massetti assigned another. Forty-five minutes in, one of the Robbery detectives shouted, "I've got it."

Everyone stopped. Massetti put a hand up. "Keep searching. There may be more than one." He knelt with the detective and together they unlocked the safe but didn't look inside. He then assigned the detective another sector.

They only found the one safe. After Parker thanked Massetti and company for their help and sent them on their way, she, Corelli and Watkins peered into the safe. It contained stack upon stack of hundred-dollar bills, a safe deposit box key pasted to a piece of cardboard, a rental document for a safe deposit box from Maritime Bank in Manhattan, a small manila envelope, and a ledger book. While Watkins emptied the contents into a box, Corelli and Parker opened the ledger. "Bingo." Corelli snapped her fingers. "The blackmail ledger has the names, addresses, account number, payment amount and frequency, plus a box number for each. I'm assuming the box number is related to documentation for the blackmail."

Corelli stored the box on the back seat of the car then settled in the passenger seat. "Good call, Parker. What made you want to go back?"

"I was thinking about how we wouldn't have known about the apartment if Puglisi hadn't told us about his calling her when he bought it. I realized it didn't make sense that someone so careful wouldn't have a secure place to hide things he used frequently. Then Massetti, our favorite safecracker, popped into my mind. I needed confirmation one way or the other."

"Do you want to go over it tonight?"

"I thought we'd lock it up at the station and go over it with fresh eyes in the morning. Why, you want to go to another group or yoga?"

Corelli looked at her phone. "Not tonight. Brett will be home in about a half hour."

Parker raised her eyebrows. "Home, huh? Are you two officially living together?"

Corelli frowned. "I…not officially, though since we got back from our New Year's sailing trip, we've spent every night at my apartment except when she's traveling. The other night was the first time we slept at her place. Want to join us for whatever it is she's bringing for dinner? She always buys enough for an army and you know she loves to see you."

Parker smiled. "She knows we're usually starved by the time we get done. After spending last night with *la familia*, I'm sure she's looking forward to having you all to herself. And my weary brain needs a little quiet space so I'm going to skip tonight."

CHAPTER NINE

The elevator door creaked open and Corelli looked up from her love fest with her two kittens and pulled them off her shoulders. Brett stepped into the room, flashed her heart-stopping smile, and balancing her briefcase and two bags of takeout food, made a beeline for her. They met halfway. Corelli took the bags of food and they kissed, a gentle, loving welcome home kiss.

Corelli leaned into Brett, buried her face in her long golden hair and inhaled the scent that had rapidly come to mean love and home. When they separated, Chiara moved to the table and began to unpack the food.

"Hard day?" Brett dropped her briefcase near the sofa she usually sat on to work after dinner, hung her coat and went into the kitchen to wash her hands and get plates, silverware, glasses and napkins.

"Every day is hard when I don't see you. I missed you."

Brett stopped short. "Is everything all right, Chiara? You sound sad."

"Not sad. I've just been thinking. And that's not always a good thing." Corelli laughed. "Let's talk while we eat."

They helped themselves to roast chicken, mashed potatoes, gravy, carrots, broccoli, and dinner rolls. Chiara poured the wine. They were quiet for a few seconds as they chewed their first bites.

Chiara knew Brett would wait until she felt able to talk so she took a minute to think about what she wanted to say. "Parker told me she's looking for a bigger apartment but not because she and Gloria are moving in together and it got me thinking about us." She focused on cutting her chicken. "I love being with you. I love the time we spend together, whether we're doing nothing, hanging with family or on a great adventure like our sailing trip. I'd like to live with you. And I would love to have you move in here." She looked up, feeling shy, not sure what to expect.

Brett was at her side in an instant. She placed a hand on either side of Chiara's face and kissed her deeply. "I love you, Chiara, and I would love to live with you. Here. Or wherever."

Chiara took a deep breath. "I love you too." This was a huge step. She'd had lovers over the years, Marnie was the most recent and the most serious, but she hadn't lived with any of them. She and Marnie probably would have moved in together when they returned from Afghanistan, but Marnie hadn't returned. The takeaway from that experience, as she'd learned in her PTSD group, was the future isn't guaranteed and grab happiness when you can. And though it had taken time to let go of the guilt about loving someone other than Marnie, she had let go. Marnie would always be in her heart, right next to Brett. "Well, that's settled. Let's eat."

Cuddling on the sofa later that evening, they talked about the details. "Are you sure you're okay moving in with me?"

"I am. As much as I love my apartment, it's filled with memories of Em. This"—she gestured to the enormous living space—"is you. You've breathed life into this humongous loft using color, art, furniture selection and imagination. It's warm and homey and comfortable. I would love to live here with you. And, if you agree, I'd love to hang some of Meg's paintings here."

Brett had purchased a number of paintings from her close friend Meg Lerner, a world-class artist, and she'd inherited more when Meg was murdered the previous year. "You know I'm a big fan of Meg's work. If I hadn't been priced out of the market when the art world discovered her, I would have many more than that one." Corelli tilted her head toward a small painting of two women staring into each other's eyes. "Will you sell your apartment?"

Brett leaned back into Chiara's arms. "Its value is still increasing so I'll probably hold on to it for another year or two. Do you think P.J. would want to rent it?"

"I don't think she could afford it."

"Hmm. I'd love to have someone I know and trust in there. I don't need the money and I might be willing to set the rent just high enough to cover my basic costs. I'll talk to my accountant."

CHAPTER TEN

On arrival at the station house, Parker and Corelli counted the cash they'd retrieved from the safe in Hawley's apartment, then returned the nearly one million dollars to the evidence safe. After they settled at the table again, Parker flipped through the blackmail ledger. "The entries go back ten years and it looks like many are still active." She passed the ledger to Corelli. "It means interviewing a ton of people but, hopefully, we'll find his killer's name and address in there."

Feeling optimistic that they were at last moving forward, Parker put the safe deposit box key and the ledger aside for later, then pulled out the last thing in the box, a manila envelope. She undid the clasp and spilled the contents onto the table. "Well, well, look at this." She showed Corelli the photos of Lisa Puglisi standing next to Hawley. They appeared to be selfies of them on the deck of the Brooklyn Heights apartment. "Looks like Lisa might have misremembered the last time she saw Ricky Hawley." She turned the pictures over. As she expected given Hawley's attention to detail, they were dated. "It seems she actually did visit the apartment."

Corelli tapped her fingers on the table. "It might be better to question her here if we can get her to come in voluntarily. Why don't I call her and tell her we found something for her in his things but she has to come to the station to get it?"

Parker considered the suggestion. "Sounds like a plan. And ask Dietz to get someone to dig into her background before we see her."

While Corelli went to make the call, Parker thumbed through the messages that had come in on the police tip line last night. There were, as usual, a few confessions to the murder and a couple from people who had talked to Rich when they'd called in a tip. The one that caught her eye was from an Anthony Messner, who claimed he was the attorney of the man whose picture was on the front page of yesterday's *Daily Post*. He requested a meeting with the detective in charge of the case. Great. Maybe he could provide something useful. She glanced at her phone. Eight thirty a.m. A little early to call an attorney. She put the message aside for follow-up and read the last few, but nothing else popped out.

Kim and Greene came in, coffee and takeout breakfast sandwiches in hand and sat at the table. Dietz, Forlini, and Watkins followed. Everybody seemed low-energy this morning. Not a good sign. It usually meant the investigation was losing steam. Corelli returned and Parker asked her to bring the others up-to-date. "Earlier Parker and I went through everything we found in the safe in Hawley's apartment. Besides a million dollars, we found a lockbox key and a book with the names of all the people he was blackmailing. We also found a couple of photos that contradict Lisa Puglisi's statement that she never visited the apartment. She's coming in this afternoon to discuss the discrepancy."

Parker handed the blackmail ledger to Watkins. "This has the names and addresses of Rich's blackmail victims. We're guessing the list includes his killer so keep that in mind when interviewing. Also, get an ADA to look at anyone being blackmailed for committing a crime. Forlini and Kim can work with you on this. Let me know if you need more bodies."

Forlini reported next. "Me and Kim interviewed the staff at *The Daily Post* but we didn't get anything of interest. Rich didn't socialize and no one seemed to know much about him. A couple of the women said he hit on them, usually after tossing them a lead from the tip line. None of them admitted to dating him. The conclusion seemed to be that there was something a little off about him. A couple of people mentioned a shouting match between him and another male reporter. The guy said he and his girlfriend ran into Rich in a bar in Brooklyn Heights. He introduced them and while he was in the bathroom, Rich tried to convince her to leave with him. He has an alibi for the time of the murder. Besides, he's about the same size as Rich was and I doubt he could do the kind of damage done to Rich." He looked at Corelli and then caught himself and gazed at Parker. "We can go back and try to shake something loose or start to work with Watkins."

"You can go back to the *Post* later if needed. I'd rather have you two work with Watkins." Parker shifted her attention to Greene. "Anything?"

"I'm waiting for the *Post* to email the list of callers who were paid for their tips, but I followed up on another month of tip calls. They all seem as boring as the others but I'll pick up where I left off."

Parker pushed the piece of cardboard with the key and the papers from the bank toward her. "The bank confirmed Rich has a safe deposit box and we found the key in his safe, so take somebody with you and go empty it."

"Forlini? What's the status on the review of Rich's files?" Parker tilted her head toward the analysts working on the Thirteenth Street files. "Have they turned up anything?"

Forlini followed her gaze. "They've just started on the third box and so far all they've found is more meticulous documentation of the investigative stories he published. Nothing current."

"Thanks." Parker turned to Dietz who was waving a document. "The autopsy report on Rich a.k.a Hawley, came in a few minutes ago. Lots of premortem bruising, his right arm had two breaks, one close to the wrist, the other farther up the forearm. COD was asphyxiation from strangulation. And livor mortis indicates he was moved after death. They found cat hair and some gold flakes on his clothing."

Ndep, the consummate investigator had pretty much figured all that out, but none of them had noticed the cat hair or the gold. Parker forced herself to focus on the discussion rather than Ndep. "Anything specific? On the cat hair? Or the gold flakes?"

Dietz checked the report. "It's gold plating, not real gold. And just your common house cat, probably a tabby. That should narrow it. Not."

"Right. We should be able to zero right in on the killer."
Parker waved the tip sheet. 'We got a message on the tip line from
someone claiming to be Richard Hawley's attorney. Corelli and I
will follow up this morning." She stood. "Thanks everyone, see you
back here later." She checked her phone. "It's still a little early but
some attorneys work long hours." She keyed the number he'd left
and after a few rings, a woman answered. She quickly confirmed
that Messner was in the office and had instructed her to show the
detectives in whenever they arrived.

CHAPTER ELEVEN

As usual, morning rush in Manhattan was impossible and even with the siren it took almost an hour to arrive at Fifty-second and Third Avenue. Once again Parker pulled down the On Duty sign and chanced a ticket.

They were stopped in the lobby of the modern glass building where Walters, Messner & Shonfield had their offices but immediately after displaying their shields and IDs, they were cleared through security and directed to the correct elevator for the fourteenth floor. A woman waiting in the reception area when the doors opened introduced herself as Messner's assistant and escorted them into his office.

He stood to greet them and after introductions, invited them to sit. Once they were settled at the conference table in a corner of his office, he started speaking. "I hope I haven't brought you here on a wild goose chase, detectives. I tried to explain it to the person who took my message when I called, but I realized it was too complicated." He held up a copy of yesterday's *Post* with Hawley's picture on the first page. "I believe this man is my client but my client's name was Richard Hawley, not Ned Rich." He looked from Parker to Corelli. "Everyone in the office agrees with me."

Corelli, as they'd agreed, led the interview. "What did you do for Mr. Hawley?"

"I wrote his will. And my partner did the closing on his apartment in Brooklyn Heights. Is it the same man?"

"What can you tell us about your client?"

Messner considered the question. "Let's see. He saw my partner's name in a news report about her closing on an apartment for a celebrity client and was impressed, so he engaged her to close on his apartment. That was a little over a year ago. Then about six months ago he came in to have his will drawn up but Meredith was on maternity leave so he settled for me." His attempt at looking modest failed. "He was always casually dressed but he seemed to have money. He intimated that he was a tech entrepreneur but didn't provide any details about his work. He was relaxed and related, friendly to the office staff as well as the attorneys. His will was simple enough that he signed it on the second visit. The only unusual thing was the letter he left to be delivered to his only beneficiary upon his death."

Corelli glanced at Parker. She tipped her head confirming the direction in which Corelli intended to go. Interesting how well they knew each other. "We can confirm the dead man is your client, Richard Hawley. Ned Rich was a pseudonym he used for his investigative reporting. We'd like a copy of the will and the letter."

"Since he was murdered, I don't have a problem with providing the will." Messner retrieved an envelope from his desk and handed it to Corelli. "As you'll see, his whole estate goes to Lisa Puglisi, a childhood friend. And the letter he left was for her. Unfortunately, I can't give you a copy of that because it's sealed and only she can open it. You'd have to get a warrant."

"I think I have a solution," Corelli said. "We're expecting Ms. Puglisi at the station this afternoon around three. Would you be able to deliver the letter to her there around four?"

"Let me check." He walked to his desk and picked up the phone. "Mina, what does my schedule look like this afternoon, say from three on?" He listened. "Please reschedule those two for this evening or tomorrow." He ended the call but didn't put the handset down. He turned to them. "I'll be there. And unless you have other questions, I'd like to take a client's call."

"We're good."

"Just leave the address with Mina on the way out."

In the car, Corelli slit the seal on the envelope and flattened the document she pulled from it. "Last Will and Testament of Richard Hawley. It's dated six months ago." She waved it so Parker could see the title page, then scanned the short document. "As the man said, Puglisi inherits everything, including an apartment we didn't know about in Boca Raton, Florida. Seems like a good motive for murder to me. Rutgers University Computer Science Department inherits if Puglisi predeceases him."

CHAPTER TWELVE

She was late of course. And snarky. But judging driving time into the city was difficult and just getting through the Holland Tunnel in the middle of the day could put a person in a bad mood, but Parker thought it was more than traffic. More like anxiety. And if she was anxious now…

They joined her in the claustrophobic interview room Corelli had requested and watched her fiddle with her phone, twirl her hair, and dab at her nose with a tissue while they took their time settling.

"Thank you for coming in, Ms. Puglisi—"

"Did I have a choice?" She was going to be testy. So be it.

"There's always a choice but most choices come with consequences. As I'm sure Detective Corelli told you, we have some additional questions."

She looked at her phone. "I have an appointment at five so let's get this over with."

Parker unclasped the envelope with the photographs and placed them in front of Puglisi. "When and where were these taken?"

She leaned forward and studied the two photos. Her face lost color. "I don't recall. Where did you get them?"

"Why don't you tell us where they were taken?"

"Sorry, I don't remember."

"Let's see if I can refresh your memory." Parker turned the photos over. "They're dated last year. About the time Ricky bought his apartment in Brooklyn Heights. Maybe you should look again."

Puglisi made a show of examining the photos. She shrugged. "Sorry."

Parker picked up one of the pictures. "The background reminds me of the view from the deck of Ricky's apartment. What do you think, Detective Corelli?"

Corelli studied the picture. "I agree. It certainly looks like Ms. Puglisi lied to us about shutting down Ricky because he was still stealing from people." She placed the pictures in front of Puglisi. "It makes me wonder what else she's lying about. And it makes me wonder, given their history, if she murdered her old friend."

The detectives were silent, putting pressure on her. It didn't take long. "I know what you're doing here but I didn't murder Ricky. Why would I?"

Parker held up the research report that Dietz had pulled together earlier. "Let's see, you were childhood friends as you said but you forgot to tell us you were a couple and you lived together at Rutgers. And, oh, you were both expelled for attempting to blackmail a professor. Although charges weren't brought, you lost your scholarships and shortly after, you enlisted in the Army. You did very well in all aspects of boot camp including fighting and shooting, but your excellent computer skills meant you ended up working with technology. You left the service at the end of your enlistment and worked at a software company until you were recruited by Homeland Security." She looked up. "How am I doing so far?"

Parker continued without waiting for a response. "Based on periodic large deposits in your bank account, it appears you continued to work with Ricky for a couple years while you were in the Army."

Was the deep red of Puglisi's face due to embarrassment or anger? "You have no right to investigate me." She spat the words, leaving no doubt it was rage.

"Being the prime suspect in the murder of Richard Hawley gives us the right to examine every detail of your life." Parker let her sit with that.

Puglisi's complexion shifted from fiery to white. "Why would I kill him after all these years?"

"You've lied before. Why should we believe you now?"

Puglisi took a deep breath then leaned on the table as if trying to get close to the detectives. "I lied because I assumed you'd arrested him for blackmail and I wanted to distance myself. It's true he was depositing money in my account. But if you dig deeper, you'll see I closed that account and contributed the money to a charity that works with underprivileged children."

"Why don't you tell us about the last time you saw him."

Puglisi closed her eyes, maybe picturing that last visit, maybe trying to figure out if this was a nightmare. "Like I said, we hadn't had any contact in years and he called."

She pushed a breath out between her lips. "He seemed so happy I thought maybe he'd changed. I went to his apartment in Brooklyn out of curiosity but over dinner I realized he wanted an audience, someone to brag to about how much money he'd accumulated. If you really look at those pictures, you'll see I wasn't happy about him snapping selfies of the two of us. I asked him to delete them. The lying bastard said he did. You'd think I'd know better than to believe anything he said. Anyway, that night I told him we were done, asked him to not call me again and then I left. I really had no reason to kill him."

"What about this?" Parker passed the copy of his will to Puglisi.

Seeing the cover page, she looked up with a question on her face. "What does this have to do with me?"

"Read it."

Puglisi reached into her bag on the floor, took out a pair of glasses and put them on. Parker and Corelli watched her read the three-page document, then read it a second time. "I didn't know about this. I really didn't. That fucker. If I'm the only person he had to leave anything to, he was more pathetic than I thought." She tossed the will onto the table. "I still don't want his money."

Corelli's phone pinged. "Messner is here." She left to bring the attorney in.

While they waited, Parker explained, "Mr. Messner was Richard Hawley's attorney. He wrote that will and he has a letter Hawley left for you. We'd like you to read it and then share it with us."

Corelli brought Messner in. "Ms. Puglisi, this is Anthony Messner, Richard Hawley's attorney." She leaned against the wall and pointed to the free seat. "Please take a seat, Mr. Messner."

Messner took his time opening his briefcase. He removed a letter-size envelope and the snapping of the lock as he closed the case seemed loud in the silent tension of the room. "I'd like to see a picture ID, if possible, Ms. Puglisi. A driver's license would be perfect."

Looking stunned, Puglisi dragged her large purse from the floor, pulled out her wallet and handed him the license.

He looked from her to the license and back, and apparently satisfied, handed the license back. "I understand you've already seen Mr. Hawley's will. I'd be happy to go over anything you don't understand." He handed her his business card and the envelope with her name hand-written on it. "Mr. Hawley stipulated that you receive this after his death."

Corelli straightened. "Thank you, Mr. Messner. Unless you need to be here while Ms. Puglisi reads the letter or she wants you to remain, I think you can leave."

Puglisi shook her head. "I have your card and I'll call to figure out what to do with this." She lifted the will from the table. "Could I have privacy when I read this letter, Detective Parker?"

"Certainly. Just knock on the door when you're ready." They left Puglisi and while Corelli escorted Messner out, Parker slipped into the connected room to observe her through the two-way mirror.

Puglisi stared at the envelope a few seconds then used her nail file to slit the flap. She smoothed the pages on the table, put her glasses on again and began to read. She read it, seeming unfazed, then she read it again. This time her body softened and tears ran down her face. She used the back of her hand to wipe the tears, then dabbed her face with a tissue. She stared at the wall, lost in thought. They gave her a few minutes before knocking and entering.

Puglisi looked up but didn't comment as they sat facing her once more. She pushed the letter across the table to Parker. "You're all right with us reading it?"

She shrugged. "You'll read it one way or another. So have at it."

Parker placed the three handwritten pages between them so they could read it at the same time.

Dear Lisa,

If you're reading this letter, I'm dead. I hope I've died peacefully in my bed at some respectable old age but I fear that's not what happened. You always said my delving into people's secrets would get me in trouble and this time you're right.

To avoid the danger you worried about, I've always been careful to protect my identity from the people I blackmail. But this time I landed a big fish. Remember the one I always dreamed about who has so much to lose and so much money they'll pay anything to protect themselves?

Ironically, the danger I'm facing is not from blackmailing them. I learned some critical information about them through the tip line and while doing more research, I uncovered something about a group they are associated with.

I know you don't have respect for the person I've become so you may not believe that I couldn't ignore a threat to our country. But it's true. Even though they are dangerous, I feel compelled to put on my Superman costume to investigate and expose them. Of course, I'm not totally altruistic. It's a big story and rather than bring it to the FBI, I'm pursuing it myself so I can get the glory. Some things never change, right? I'm not telling you what it is or where to find my research materials because I think it would put you in danger.

I'm sure you're surprised and probably a little pissed that you're my beneficiary but I meant what I said when you came to see my apartment. I love you, have always loved you and there's no one else in my life that I care about. I wish I could have been a different person, the person you used to admire, but somewhere along the way money and the power of controlling people led me astray. You were right. It didn't make me happy. I've been lonely and friendless since we split and I spent a lot of years longing for you. Stupid me.

Of course everything I leave is derived from, as you insist on calling them, my nefarious activities, and knowing how you feel about the money, I'm fine with you keeping or selling the apartments and doing whatever you deem with the money. Perhaps contribute it to a group that helps poor kids like us. But that's up to you.

Now to the nitty-gritty. There's a safe hidden on the deck of the Brooklyn Heights apartment. It's under a low block that serves as a table. Move the table and feel around until you find a small hole that your finger fits in. Pull up and the decking will lift to expose a safe. The combination is 09-13-23-43-15. It will contain a ledger with the names and addresses of the people I've been blackmailing, about a million dollars in cash, plus a safe deposit box key for the Maritime Bank on Fortieth Street in Manhattan. You'll find more cash at the bank and hidden in the Boca Raton apartment.

Unless you want to continue to collect the blackmail money, send anonymous notes to everyone, telling them to stop sending money. Close out my rented mailbox in Red Hook and terminate the lease on an office in Brooklyn where I store the backup materials for my legit investigative stories. Both the mailbox and the office are in the Edward Rich name, details are included below.

I guess that's it. Sorry to dump this on you but if you don't want to be bothered, turn everything over to the police.

Right about now if we were in a movie, Whitney Houston would swoop in singing your favorite song, "I Will Always Love You," loud and strong.

I will always love you,

Ricky

The letter made it clear that Puglisi wasn't involved in Hawley's schemes. Parker looked at Puglisi. "Is there anything you would like to share with us, Ms. Puglisi?"

She shook her head. "What a waste. He could have done great things. Could you find the safe and notify the people he was blackmailing? And I'm not sure what happens with the money. I assume the city gets it?"

"We've already found the safe, the safe deposit box, the mailbox and the office he mentioned. We'll let Mr. Messner know when you can terminate the rental agreements and begin to dispose of the property. I assume we have your permission to search the Boca Raton apartment and remove anything related to the investigation?"

Puglisi nodded.

"We'll be informing his blackmail victims that they're off the hook. Sometimes NYPD takes possession of the cash and distributes it to the divisions involved in recovering it. But I'm not sure what happens with this much money and property. You might want to have your attorney involved." Parker handed the letter to Corelli. "Please make a copy of this for Ms. Puglisi."

When Corelli returned with the copy, Parker stood. "I think we're done here, Ms. Puglisi. We'll be in touch."

Puglisi put the copy in her purse and stood. "Do you know what he meant about a threat to the country?"

"We're working on that."

CHAPTER THIRTEEN

Parker drummed her fingers on the table as she and Corelli rehashed the interview with Puglisi. "You know, the more I think about it the less I believe one of his blackmail victims killed him."

"Why?" Corelli asked.

"First, he was so careful to keep his identity a secret. Second, he was cautious and I get the impression that he never met his victims face-to-face so it's unlikely they actually knew who he was. And then there's the..." She made quote marks with her fingers. "...'threat to our democracy' thing. He felt threatened enough to make a will and leave that letter for Puglisi. I trust his instincts. But given his usual caution I don't get why he decided to deal with the threat himself rather than go to the FBI? Was he planning to blackmail whoever was involved? Or did he think he could infiltrate the group and be the hero who exposed the threat?"

Corelli punched her shoulder lightly. "You ask good questions but we may never know what he intended. Are we overlooking evidence of this threat?"

Parker had gone over and over what they knew and she was sure they hadn't missed anything. "Any ideas about how we figure out what this threat could be?"

Corelli shook her head. "None. I can't imagine how he would stumble on a threat, something like a spy ring or a plot to blow something up."

"What about one of those *Daily Post* tips?"

"Nothing I've seen so far screamed threat to America. What about you?"

Parker smiled. "You're right. They all looked boring. Kim and Greene thought so too."

"Excuse me, Detective Parker." The woman supervising the analysts examining the files from the Thirteenth Street place stood at the foot of the table. "I thought you might want to know that we'll be finished reviewing all the documents by the time we leave tonight."

"Please sit." Parker indicated a chair. "Did anything interesting turn up?"

She settled with her hands folded on the table. "No. Just more of the same. In the next day or so I'll submit a report listing the stories and the folders for each, plus the list of names that appeared in every document, cross-referenced to each box in case you need to retrieve anything. Detective Dietz knows where to find me if you need me."

Parker stood. "Thank you for getting it done so quickly."

As she walked away, Parker sighed. "No clue to the big threat there. Are you ready to leave?"

Corelli stretched. "Can you drop me off at my yoga class?"

"Sure. Need to stretch with the other warriors tonight?"

Corelli slugged Parker's arm. "Yoga for Warriors involves more than stretching, I'll have you know."

Greene burst into the room and dashed to the table. "I think I have something." Seeing she had their attention she continued, "I called a tipster who received a payment but her phone transferred the call to her nephew's cell. According to him, his aunt was murdered in her house in Queens about seven months ago. Whoever killed her stole her computer and all the genealogical files she was working on but left the relatively new TV and jewelry. He thought the murder was related to the tip she gave Rich but the police didn't take him seriously. He's agreed to meet me at her house in Queens before going into his office. It's on my way in so I made an appointment for eight tomorrow morning."

"Great work." Parker patted Greene's arm. "This could be the break we're looking for. Give Corelli the address and we'll meet you there."

CHAPTER FOURTEEN

When Parker and Corelli arrived at the small two-story house on 183rd Street in Jamaica, Queens, Greene got out of her car and joined them on the porch. A slender, light-skinned black man wearing a three-piece suit answered the door. He extended his hand. "Franklin Jefferson. Thank you for coming." He ushered them into a neat bookcase-lined room with doily-covered furniture. "Please have a seat." He studied them, probably trying to figure why there were so many and who was in charge.

"Good morning, Mr. Jefferson, I'm Detective P.J. Parker. Detectives Chiara Corelli and Charleen Greene are here to observe. Tell us about your aunt..." she hesitated.

"Magnolia Walker," Greene filled in quickly.

"Yes, sorry. Tell us about Ms. Walker's genealogical studies and what makes you think her murder is connected to her calling the tip line?"

Jefferson's gaze went inward. "Aunt Maggie was a librarian. When she retired a couple of years ago, she became obsessed with tracing our family's roots. Our ancestors were slaves and many in the family are light-complexioned, so she was determined to to think there was a reason. But that's not a great neighborhood and maybe the robbers saw an old woman and thought she'd be an easy mark."

Walker's neighborhood consisted of small homes owned by black middle and working class families. Parker was pretty sure there wasn't a lot of crime there. But she wasn't surprised that the two old white detectives would use the black neighborhood as the reason for the crime. "Did you speak to Ned Rich about Walker's murder?"

"Yeah. Her nephew seemed to think there was a connection. We called Rich and he said he hadn't had a chance to check her research yet. He didn't have any idea why she was murdered. Nothing Rich said changed our conclusion that Walker was killed because she fought the robbers who'd followed her into her house."

"You didn't interview Rich in person?"

"It didn't seem that important."

"Did you request copies of the research Walker gave him?"

"No. What would we have done with it?"

Parker bit her lip to keep from saying what she thought of their so-called investigation. "I assume you've read that Rich was murdered. Did you consider calling us to let us know about a possible connection?"

The two guys exchanged a look. "Nah. We'd already investigated and didn't find a connection so why waste your time?"

Parker stood. "We'd like a copy of the murder book." She told them where to send it and they left. She grumbled as they got into the car. "Just another little old black lady murdered in her home and lazy white detectives who take the easy way out."

Corelli snapped her seatbelt into place. "You think it's that simple, Parker?"

"Yeah, I do. All we can do for a murder victim is bring the killer to justice. But sometimes it seems that for every detective like you, there are two who don't think it's worth investigating a black murder."

CHAPTER FIFTEEN

Watkins joined them in the conference room. "We've interviewed six recent blackmail victims and brought in three of them. Based on the short description of the reason for the blackmail, we suspect they were being blackmailed because of criminal activity. None of them admits to knowing who was blackmailing them. In fact, they all seemed surprised when we told them it was no longer necessary to send money."

Parker frowned. "Rich referenced a box number on every blackmail record in the ledger. It would make sense to create a file for the evidence he collected to support the blackmail. And I'll bet the box number is a pointer to the documentation. It's frustrating that we haven't found where he stored those boxes. Maybe we should begin checking storage units in Brooklyn."

Watkins straightened the sheaf of papers he was holding. "Do you want to interview the three victims, or should I do it?"

"Corelli and I will take two. Why don't you do the other one?"

Parker glanced at the summary Watkins provided for Dan Holland. The fifty-one-year-old owner of a large Bronx-based construction company had been paying Rich six thousand dollars a month for five months. The reason column in the blackmail ledger said "violations." She passed the page to Corelli and sat in a chair facing Holland. Corelli leaned against the wall. It was hard to judge his height but he was wearing a collared polo shirt with Holland Construction embroidered over his heart and she could see his well-developed upper body and muscular arms. Definitely a man strong enough to easily beat and strangle Ned Rich. He eyed them warily but didn't comment. "I'm Detective P.J. Parker and this is Detective Corelli. Thank you for coming in this morning, Mr. Holland."

"I didn't know it was optional. This outrageous. I can't waste time sitting around here. I've got a company to run." The louder his voice, the redder his face became.

Parker ignored his outburst but noted how quickly he'd escalated from wary to enraged. "As you know, we're gathering information about the activities of the blackmailer you've been paying six thousand dollars a month. What kind of construction does your firm do?"

He relaxed at the softball question. "We provide equipment like cranes and personnel to operate them to other construction companies in the tristate area."

"It's lucrative, I imagine?"

"There's a lotta construction going on so it's a profitable business."

Parker took a guess. "Even with the cost of insurance? Haven't there been several crane accidents in the past few years? I remember a crane toppling off a high-rise because of some violations of New York City regulations."

He shifted in his chair. "There have been a few."

"And was your company involved in any of those?"

He turned fire-engine red. "You know I thought blackmail was a crime, not being blackmailed by some dirt bag. I've had enough." He stood.

Parker gazed at him. "You can stay and answer our questions or we can arrest you and detain you until you do. It's really up to you."

"Arrest? Based on what?" The veins in his neck bulged but he managed to keep his fisted hands at his sides. He glared at her, opened his mouth, then seemed to think better of it and sat.

Parker was glad he hadn't had a stroke. "We know you were being blackmailed because of violations. Was it crane accidents?"

"Yes."

"Tell us about the blackmailer. Did you meet in person? What information did he provide to convince you to pay? How did you pay him?"

He brushed a hand over his eyes, took out a handkerchief, blew his nose and then pushed air through his lips as if trying to relax. "I never saw him. I'm not even sure it's a man. I got a call on my private cell phone. No one but my wife and a few close associates have that number. The voice was disguised. He told me he had information about me bribing city inspectors and that I would receive a package with proof. I could choose to pay a monthly retainer, he used that word, for his silence or he would expose me. He said instructions for payment would be in the package."

"When did you get the package and what was in it?"

"It was delivered by the post office that afternoon. He had several pictures of me paying off an inspector. He also seemed to have information about the violations that could only come from a worker, maybe a former employee I fired. The payment instructions were to send six thousand dollars in hundreds every month to Deep Dig Excavation Services at an address in Red Hook and to include a slip of paper with the account number assigned. Nothing inside or outside the envelope should reveal my name or the company name."

Now that he'd put the information out there he seemed to relax. "How long did you wait to check out the Red Hook address?"

He appeared surprised by the question. "Two days. But they wouldn't tell me anything. They wouldn't even confirm that they accepted mail for Deep Dig Excavation Services. I watched the place for two weeks after I sent in the first payment but I didn't see anyone who looked suspicious."

"Did you ever try to meet with the blackmailer?"

"Yeah. I called the number he'd called my cell phone from but there was no answer so I figured it was burner. And I put a note in the first payment but he or she ignored it."

"So where were you Tuesday night?"

He frowned. "Tuesday? Um, I was home with my wife in Teaneck, that's New Jersey. We had dinner and watched some TV.

I went to bed about nine because I usually get up at four to be in the office by five thirty in the morning."

"Are you the only one there or are others in early too?"

"Jerry, Sammy, and Tommy are in then, getting ready for the day."

"Do you have a cat in your office?"

He looked at her like she was crazy. "A cat? No, I'm allergic."

Parker stood. "Thank you. You're right that paying blackmail isn't a crime but bribing an inspector may be. Sit tight. I'm going to send an assistant district attorney in to talk to you. She'll make the call about whether you should be prosecuted, so I suggest you use the wait time to think about what you can give her about the inspectors who take bribes." He was still ranting as the door closed behind them.

As they walked, Corelli was on the phone bringing ADA Natalie Brooks up to speed on Mr. Holland. She ended the call. "She'll be here in about an hour."

"What do you think?" Parker asked.

"Blackmail is always a motive. He looks strong enough to beat and strangle someone like Rich. Good question about the cat. He could have killed him and kept him in the office then dropped him in Penny Park late at night. Or, he could have left home a little earlier than usual to meet Rich in the park and killed him there, except neither scenario accounts for the cat hair. But it seems Rich was careful to avoid any contact with his victims and he made the terms of the blackmail clear so I would be surprised if he went out of his way to meet him. Unless we come up with something concrete, I would say no."

Dietz appeared in the hall. "Watkins set up Dr. Lauren Fitzroy in room three. He thought you might want to see the summary sheet before you go in."

Parker read it to Corelli. "TV personality hawking vitamins and supplements. Fake doctor, fake supplements. Seven thousand dollars a month. You got this one."

The detectives glanced at each other seeing the extremely thin, small woman sitting with her hands folded on the table. She certainly didn't appear to be capable of beating and strangling Rich, but she could have hired someone. Corelli stepped her through the questions. Her anger and her answers were pretty much the same as Holland's. Corelli got her to admit that Rich had discovered she was neither a legitimate medical doctor, nor a PhD. And he had somehow gotten into her lab computers and found reports that indicated most of her products didn't accomplish what she claimed they did. She wouldn't admit to fraud and claimed that her staff had never given her the negative reports. They left her waiting for Natalie Brooks to determine whether a crime was committed.

Watkins met them in the conference room. "Councilman Erik Tomlin was being blackmailed because he's cheating on his wife. He's been paying a thousand dollars a month to Rich, but in my opinion he isn't a killer. Once we find Rich's files we might find there's something more there, but I don't see a crime now so I told him we might be back to him. We're bringing in another three tomorrow and we've be in touch with four more. Should we interview them or do you want to be involved?"

"Why don't you take them. If you find someone who looks like a good candidate, we'll interview them."

Watkins left and Parker turned to Corelli. "We need to find those files and the genealogical documentation that Walker gave him."

"Puglisi didn't seem to know much about Rich's life but let me touch base with her just to be sure he never mentioned another place." Corelli left the room.

While she waited for Corelli, Parker thumbed through the messages that had come in on the police tip line last night. Someone would follow up with all of them, even those from the usual crazies who responded every time the department put out a request for information. She placed the three callers who reported seeing Rich in their Brooklyn neighborhoods on top of the pile and indicated they should be contacted immediately.

"Parker." She looked up at Dietz. "There's a lady here who wants to talk to the detective in charge of the Rich case. Should I bring her in?"

"Yes." She handed him the tip sheets. "I reviewed these and marked the ones I think are important." She stood. "Let's turn the board with the murder pictures around before you bring her in."

Dietz introduced the middle-aged white woman as Doree MacDonald and left them to it. Ms. MacDonald made no attempt to hide her curiosity about the activity in the room and Parker was glad she'd turned the murder board to the wall. "Thank you for coming in, Ms. MacDonald. I understand you have information about the death of Mr. Rich?"

"Well, I think so." She opened her rather large purse and pulled out a copy of *The Daily Post* with Rich's picture on it. "This man rents a two-bedroom apartment in one of the apartment buildings I own in Bushwick. His name isn't Rich but if it's not him, it must be his twin brother."

Parker's senses went on high alert. Could this be the break they were waiting for? "What was his name?"

Corelli slid silently into a seat at the table but didn't interrupt. "Richard Hawley."

Parker shot Corelli a look. "How long has Mr. Hawley rented the apartment?"

The woman didn't hesitate. "Eight years."

Parker tamped down her excitement. She needed to be sure. "Did he actually live there?"

The woman looked puzzled. "I assume so. He said he was a writer and worked from home. Though I don't live in that building, I'm often there fixing things or collecting rent and I run into him from time to time. Why would he rent an apartment and not live there?" Her eyes opened wide. "Do you think he was selling drugs or running a meth lab?"

Parker smiled to alleviate the woman's anxiety. "No, I don't think so. We have another address for him so I'm trying to clarify how he used the apartment. Have you been inside, seen what it looks like?"

"I haven't had any reason to go inside since he signed the lease. He was a good tenant, no problems, never late with the rent. In fact, he paid cash and dropped it off at my apartment around the corner, on or near the first of the month. I'm worried. I've knocked on his door several times since that story came out and he doesn't answer. And the other tenants don't recall seeing him going in and out as usual."

"Detective Corelli, would you see how quickly we can get a warrant?" Parker turned to MacDonald. "We need to enter the apartment, but to be sure we do it legally we're getting a warrant. I'd like you to go there with us. Can you wait for Detective Corelli to return?"

"I have a book and I took a subway so I can wait."

"I'll send somebody out for lunch and then set you up somewhere to eat and read."

It took Corelli just under three hours to get the warrant signed. Parker hadn't expected a problem since the premises appeared to belong to a murder victim but sometimes it was difficult to find an available judge who was willing to sign. But a warrant limited the possibility that any evidence they found in the apartment would be thrown out.

With MacDonald in the back seat of the car, Corelli spoke softly as she keyed the address into the GPS. "By the way, Puglisi didn't know of any places other than those listed in the letter he left for her."

Parker kept her eyes on the street as she headed east to West Houston Street and the Williamsburg Bridge. "Hopefully the missing records are in this apartment."

MacDonald kept up a running commentary on the state of the roads, the traffic, and city politicians as they made their way to the apartment. "You know Bushwick is an upcoming area. It used to be mainly industrial but warehouses are being converted to apartments and rents are low. Artists have moved in and there's lots of artwork and music. Restaurants and galleries are opening every day. It's a great place to live. I shouldn't have trouble renting the apartment."

When they arrived, MacDonald demanded to enter the apartment with them and refused to hand over the keys. Parker couldn't tell whether the woman was concerned for her property or just nosy, but she was losing patience with the stream of demands and pleas. Seeing Corelli near erupting, Parker interrupted. "Ms. MacDonald, you've seen the warrant. This apartment is part of a murder investigation and no one other than NYPD officials will be allowed inside until we've thoroughly searched and inspected it. If you don't give me the keys I'll call for backup with a battering ram and we'll smash the door down. Do you understand?"

MacDonald sputtered then stepped back. "I assume you'll let me know when I can have access to *my* property?"

"Certainly." Parker held her hand out for the keys. MacDonald slammed them in Parker's hand then clumped down the stairs. They drew their weapons.

"Thank you for that. I was ready to strangle her." Corelli knocked. "POLICE SEARCH WARRANT! OPEN THE DOOR!" Hearing no response she knocked and repeated the warning.

A neighbor across the hall opened her door but seeing the guns, closed it quickly. After Corelli knocked a third time and repeated the warning, they entered. The room was dark and Parker quickly closed the door behind them so as not to be a target in the light from the hall. They separated. And listened. But the only sound was the faint echo of traffic outside and footsteps overhead.

Parker switched on her flashlight. Corelli followed suit. They cleared the large room and moved into the kitchen then down the hall. One room, clearly used as a bedroom, contained a single bed, a dresser with socks, underwear, T-shirts and sweaters and a closet with shirts, pants, sneakers and work boots. A second room was filled with neatly labeled bankers' boxes stuffed with documents. The bathroom contained the usual toothbrush, toothpaste, razor and blades, shaving cream, shampoo, soap and towels.

When they'd cleared every room, they holstered their weapons and went back to what should have been the living room but seemed to be a sort of war room. The two windows were covered with plywood. There were long tables on three sides of the room, each with a chair behind it. A sofa with side tables and lamps, an easy chair with a hassock in front of it and a small table with a reading lamp and several books next to it sat in the middle of the floor on top of a shaggy area rug. Computer monitors, printers, modems and routers covered one of the long tables and six huge CPUs were underneath. A laptop sat on the middle table along with several yellow legal pads, a box of colored markers, three rolls of masking tape, several file folders and a large flipchart easel pad. Books and piles of papers were strewn over the other tables. There was no easel but sheets of flipchart paper were taped to the walls. Two large whiteboards, one on each side of the doorway were covered in notes and drawings.

"Well, it looks like we found his workspace. At least I hope we have." Corelli stood in the middle of the room and spun to take it in. "Get Dietz on the phone. We need people to do a thorough search, then transport all the boxes and the computers to the station.

Meanwhile the two of us will focus on what looks like the current project, the books, loose papers, the stuff on the walls. You—"

"What the fuck, Corelli? Now that we've found what we need to solve this case, I'm no longer the lead?" Parker was aware she was screaming but she was so angry she wanted to punch the wall. Or Corelli. She couldn't believe it. Or maybe she could. She should have known better than to trust Corelli.

As if she could read Parker's violent thoughts, Corelli put her hands up in front of her. "Hey. Hey. Calm down, Parker. I'm sorry. I was so excited I reverted to old behavior. I apologize. You're the lead and nothing we find will change that. How do you want to handle it?"

Parker walked away and took some calming breaths. Corelli had automatically reverted to her role as lead detective. Parker understood it was the excitement of discovering what looked to be what they needed to solve this case. She should have trusted Corelli. "No, I'm sorry I jumped to the wrong conclusion. I can't think of a better way to handle it. Given what we know about Rich, we need to look for a safe and carefully sift through everything here. I'm wagering that the blackmail records are in those boxes or on those computers, and hopefully, a lead to his killer is somewhere in this mess. She eyed the blinking lights on all the computers. We'll need a team of computer experts to figure this out. Why don't you call Dietz then we can determine how to tackle it."

Parker studied Corelli while she was talking to Dietz. Then, hoping she hadn't screwed up the relationship they were building, Parker moved to the wall and scanned the first page taped there. "Holy shit."

Corelli ended the call and moved next to Parker. "What's up?" She stepped closer and read the newspaper clipping, then read the next. It took a few seconds for it to register. "It looks like documentation of white supremacist terrorism, the Sixteenth Baptist Church bombing by the Ku Klux Klan in 1963, and the Greensboro Massacre in 1979."

They moved on to the next article. "A 1981 lynching in Alabama and the 1985 murder in Seattle of a family mistakenly thought to be Jewish communists, and the 1994 murder of a Florida abortion doctor. The 1995 Oklahoma City bombing has a whole sheet of

in the bedroom and any other boxes you've filled to the station tomorrow morning."

A few minutes later Massetti and another Burglary detective arrived. Just as Parker finished briefing them, Detective Debbie Maynard entered with two detectives in tow.

Maynard made a beeline for Corelli. "Detective—"

"Parker is the lead on this one, Maynard." Corelli smiled as Maynard pivoted.

She grinned and offered a half-salute. "Detective Parker. I've been assigned as the lead tech. Detectives Moses Stringer and Alex Menendez are working with me. What do we have here?" Maynard ran her eyes over Parker's body as if peeling back the suit she was wearing. She made no attempt to hide her appreciation. Parker flushed, feeling a mixture of embarrassment and anger.

Right after Corelli almost died from a murderer's gunshots, Parker was on leave being investigated for shooting the killer of three who'd shot Corelli. During that time she'd dated Maynard for a little more than a month. Maynard spent a lot of time bitching about Parker being too white. And once Maynard realized Senator Aloysius T. Parker was her uncle, she didn't let up so Parker ended it. They'd worked together on Parker and Corelli's recent big child sex-trafficking case when Maynard was part of the team assigned to review the computers involved. She'd flirted then but Parker ignored it. But the flirting felt different this time. It was brazen and disrespectful.

Parker met her insolent eyes. She was in charge and she would be professional, as always. She walked to the table with the computers. "Our victim was an investigative reporter and a blackmailer. We need to understand what was on his computers. It appears from what Corelli and I have reviewed so far"—she waved her arm to include the room—"that he was looking into white nationalism but I don't want to limit you. I want to know what he was looking at, who he was emailing and everything he was doing. So pack it up to go to the station."

Maynard smirked. "Yes, ma'am." She put an arm over Parker's shoulder, leaned close and whispered, "Anything for you, baby." Though the words may have been muffled, the deep raspiness of her voice and her closeness to Parker sent a false message of intimacy. The two male techs exchanged a look. Parker stiffened but chose to ignore it rather than lose her temper with the techs standing there. "Get to work." She left them.

While the three techs discussed their approach, Parker resumed looking through the file folders strewn on the tables. Corelli didn't comment but Parker knew she'd seen Maynard's intimate move and picked up on the tension in the air between them. That meant questions later. Out of the corner of her eye she saw Corelli place a thick folder on top of the charts they planned to take with them.

By two a.m. the apartment had been thoroughly searched and everything was packed to go. The computers and associated equipment had been inventoried and the setup recorded so it could easily be reconnected at the station house. Two uniforms were assigned to remain in the apartment until the team returned in the morning to transport everything to the station house.

"What was in the folder you took?" Parker asked, as she drove through Brooklyn heading to Manhattan.

"You noticed? Rich's research on the Davenports, both Harrington and his mother, Philippa. I didn't want anyone to wonder why it was there, but mostly I thought we could use a little background." Corelli cleared her throat. "What's with you and Maynard?"

Parker kept her eyes on the road. Maynard had all but announced they'd slept together. She knew Corelli wouldn't let it pass and neither would she if their positions were reversed. "We dated for about a month when I got back on the job after the shooting. I'm sure you got the message that we slept together a few times. But she was always needling me about being too white, about having gone to Yale and then Harvard Law and having been an ADA. I knew it was her own insecurity but seeing you and Brett together made me realize I wanted a positive, loving partner, not someone who was always running me down. So I ended it."

Corelli seemed lost in thought for a moment. "Clearly it's not over for Maynard. Her behavior reflects badly on you and I don't think ignoring it is enough. She seems smart and ambitious but her unprofessional conduct could also impact her career. You need to talk to her. Or, if you'd rather, I will."

Corelli wasn't saying anything she didn't know. "I'll do it but if she doesn't hear me, I might ask you to back me up."

Corelli shifted slightly so she was facing Parker. "I trust that you have my back. Trust that I have yours." She shifted again and rested her head on the back of her seat, ending the conversation.

But it wasn't over in Parker's head. Maybe it was going to Yoga for Warriors or maybe it was her PTSD group, but Corelli had changed in the last few months, for the better. From the beginning she'd trusted Corelli with her life, but recently she'd begun to trust her with her feelings.

CHAPTER SIXTEEN

The next morning while the apartment was being emptied, Corelli and Parker interviewed tenants in the building as they were leaving for work. Several acknowledged knowing Hawley and knowing he was a writer. The consensus was he was polite and not particularly friendly. The older couple across the hall agreed.

At the station later, Parker asked Maynard to join the team at the conference table. "I want to be sure everyone is clear on their assignments. Since you've been focused on the blackmail, Watkins, you and Greene review the files to see if the documentation supporting it is there." She moved her gaze. "Forlini and Kim try to get an overview on the type of files included. Dietz, get them help to organize it all so we know what we're dealing with." She met the computer supervisor's impertinent gaze. "Maynard, as I said last night, I'd like to know who he was emailing, what he was researching, and anything else you find that might help us understand what got him killed. Corelli and I will continue to work on the white nationalism angle. Any questions?" She gave it a few seconds. "All right, let's get to work."

Two hours later, Parker threw the article about Philippa Harrington Davenport on the table. "This is nasty shit. Or should I say she's a nasty piece of work?"

Corelli grinned. "Is nasty shit a technical classification you learned at Yale? Or was it Harvard?"

"Actually, I learned it on 133rd Street." Parker was referring to the time before she was six when Jesse Isaacs took her under his wing. Her father was unknown, her mother was murdered, her addict aunt overdosed, and her well-educated, rising star attorney uncle was nowhere to be found. So the social worker placed her with her alcoholic grandmother in Harlem and that meant she was pretty much on her own, out on the streets, filthy, in rags and digging for food in trash bins. Parker stood and stretched. "How would you describe it?"

"In Bensonhurst some of us would say, they're batshit crazy. Unfortunately, some of us would agree with what they believe."

Parker leaned on the back of the chair. "My uncle made such a big deal about racism and white supremacists that it was like background noise all my life and I didn't think much about it. But these people are unapologetic Nazis. They hate Jews, women, immigrants, people of color, Democrats, and anyone who isn't of Nordic or Aryan descent. Philippa, the mother, has been a raging Nazi for years but until the last eight or nine months her son, Harrington, didn't have much to say about any of it. Do you think he started alluding to white nationalist leanings because he was going to run for the Senate? I don't know which is worse, a true believer or someone willing to sacrifice principal for power." Parker paced. "I need a break. I'm going for a walk. But when I get back, let's visit Mr. Davenport, see if he's as bad as he sounds. Need anything from outside?"

"Yeah. How about lunch? My favorite falafel platter from the truck, and coffee."

"You got it."

It struck Parker that lately Corelli actually seemed to enjoy eating. When they started working together last August, she used to mostly push the food around on her plate after a few bites. Was it the result of dealing with her issues in the PTSD group or being in love with Brett? Whichever, it was nice to see. Parker strode over to Maynard. "Take a walk with me."

Maynard's gaze swept Parker's body and settled on her face with a knowing smile. "I'll follow you anywhere."

Once they were outside Parker steered them toward a quiet street with little foot traffic, then stopped and faced Maynard. "What happened just before we left the house is exactly why I asked you to take a walk."

"What—"

Parker put her hand up. "Your blatant flirting and aggressive behavior toward me make me uncomfortable and are inappropriate in a professional workspace. And others are noticing, including Corelli. She thinks if you don't stop, you'll get a rep that could impact your ability to move up and make you less in demand as a team member. She was going to speak to you about it but I said I would."

"I just—"

Parker put a finger over Maynard's lips. "Would you listen for a change? I like you, Deb. You're smart, witty, and fun to be with. But your wit is sarcastic and cutting, at least toward me."

"Is that why you dumped me?"

"I stopped dating you because your relentless commentary on me being too white or trying to be white, and your ridiculing the way I talk and dress and comport myself was unpleasant and hurtful." She started walking. Parker needed Maynard to understand. "I wasn't even seven when my uncle started making fun of me, the way I spoke, the way I liked to dress, what I felt. He and the private school he sent me to were constantly on me to stand straight, to act the way they thought a lady should act, and to speak properly and dress a certain way. They made me repeat words and sentences over and over until they decided I'd spoken correctly. It was exhausting. Some days I refused to speak at all. Luckily I had the love and support of Jessie and Annie Isaacs, people without any pretentions who loved me and taught me to love myself and be the best I could. They never saw the approval of white society as necessary and neither do I. What you see when you look at me is an educated black woman, confident in her intelligence and her place in the world. You mistake being educated, speaking properly and dressing conservatively as wanting to be white. A lot of people make that mistake.

"But you don't realize how insulting that is to me as a proud black woman, to imply that being who I am means I'm pretending to be someone else, someone you think is higher on the social scale than a black woman. Your attitude is actually racist."

"I acknowledge that I've had a privileged life." Parker could feel Maynard's agitation but she was determined to say everything that was on her mind. "But you know in all my years in predominantly white schools starting with the private school I attended from first grade through high school, then Yale and Harvard, not one person ever saw me as white. I was a black girl in a sea of white, struggling to learn where I fit and how to be. I was lucky. I'm intelligent and I learned quickly so I was able to fit in academically. Socially was harder, especially before college, but I managed to have friends, white and black, some still in my life."

Parker stopped again and faced Maynard. She locked on to her eyes. "I want you to stop treating me like a piece of meat. It's disrespectful to me and it makes you look bad. But most important, I want you to carefully examine your internalized racism. If you see me negatively for being educated and having accomplished the things I have, I wonder how you see yourself."

Maynard looked away. Parker thought she saw tears but maybe it was just the glint of the sunlight. "I'm sorry. I didn't realize."

"I'm not looking for an apology. Nor do I want you to feel bad. I want you to think about what I said and examine your behavior and your motivation. I want you to change how you relate to me and how you see yourself and all accomplished black women." Parker started walking. "And, Deb, if you can't change your attitude, I'll have no choice but to replace you on the team."

Maynard nodded but didn't speak until they neared the Halal truck near the station house. "I hear you. I'm sorry I've made you feel bad and even sorrier that you think I made myself look like an ass. But I don't think teasing makes me a racist. You know my history. You know I've worked hard to get where I am. I don't want to screw up my future so even though I don't agree with everything you said, I promise I will think long and hard about it."

Parker eyed Maynard. She could see she had shaken the usually overconfident detective but it was clear she was reluctant to see that her beliefs and her behavior were unacceptable. Well, she'd done what she could, now it was up to Maynard. "Let's get some lunch."

Parker and Maynard were laughing when they returned to the conference room, both carrying plastic bags from the Halal truck. "Join us for lunch, Maynard." Parker placed a bag and a cup of coffee in front of Corelli and sat at the conference table with the two detectives.

Corelli took the lid off the coffee and sipped, then unwrapped her falafel platter. She sniffed before taking a bite of falafel and some rice. "I love these Middle Eastern spices. While you were out, I called Davenport's Park Avenue office and was told he isn't in today."

Parker chewed the bite she'd just taken. "He lives on the Upper West Side. It might even be better to talk to him at home."

Maynard sipped her soda. "Rich was into some deep shit, trolling the dark web, even participating in some racist groups using a different name."

"What name?" Parker and Corelli spoke simultaneously.

Maynard laughed. "Ah, I see why you work so well together, you think alike. Ellis Hyde. Have you come across it?"

"No," they spoke at the same time again. The three of them burst out laughing.

Parker chewed slowly, thinking about the ramifications of another name. "Damn, I hope he doesn't have another hidden apartment somewhere filled with more files and books and papers to review."

Her mind wandered to Maynard's comment. Did she and Corelli work well together? She hadn't thought about it but despite all the ups and downs of dealing with Corelli's PTSD, they were a good team, different enough to bring opposing perspectives to the same issue, alike enough so they didn't go off in different directions. And they'd been successful on the big, hot potato cases as well as the day-to-day murders and the few cold cases they'd tackled in the seven or so months they'd been together. What did it say about her that her longest and most successful relationship was with her work partner, who tortured her for a good part of the time they were together? Parker tossed her garbage in the bin. "Ready?"

"It looked like it went well with Maynard," Corelli said as they drove up the West Side Highway.

Parker glanced at Corelli trying to ascertain whether she was really interested. "It did. She was shocked that I find her flirting and implying something between us that isn't true demeaning. Thank you for encouraging me to speak to her. I think she and I both learned something today."

"I get what she learned. What about you?"

Parker hesitated. She trusted Corelli. Mostly. But... She tapped the steering wheel.

"You don't have to answer that."

"It's funny. Jessie and Annie showered me with love and praise that mostly canceled the coldness, condescension and mocking from my aunt and uncle, but a part of me still expects to be ridiculed so it's hard for me to talk about my feelings. I learned today that even if it's scary, sometimes you have to share your feelings to change the situation."

Corelli's response was interrupted by the ping of an incoming text on her phone. She looked at the screen. "It's Watkins. Dietz told him where we were headed and he said he'd just come across Harrington Davenport's address in Rich's stuff. He lives in the Village on West Tenth Street between Fifth and Sixth, not the Upper West Side."

"How did I miss that? I'll turn as soon as I can. Do you agree that Davenport is responsible in some way for the death of Rich a.k.a Hawley a.k.a Hyde, and Magnolia Walker?" She made a right turn onto Forty-sixth Street and then a right onto Ninth Avenue and continued downtown.

"You're getting ahead of yourself, Parker. Let's see Davenport and then figure out how or if he ordered the murders. This simple case I assigned to you is getting more and more complicated. I ask again. Still want to be the lead?"

"You bet I do. But I'm wondering, if he lives in a townhouse in the Village, who lives in the mansion on the Upper West Side?"

"According to Watkins, his mother, Philippa Harrington Davenport."

CHAPTER SEVENTEEN

Parker pulled up next to a fire hydrant, the only available space near Davenport's well-kept brownstone on a lovely tree-lined street of brownstones in Greenwich Village. Other than two women walking arm in arm, a dog walker with six large dogs on a tangle of leashes, and the swoosh of the occasional passing car, the block was quiet.

They were about to exit the car when a gray-haired man arrived and climbed the eight steps to the front door. He pressed the bell. Rocking back and forth, he swiveled, looked up and down the street, then pressed the bell again. A few seconds later he knocked on the door. Waited. Pressed the bell, then leaned over and tried to look in the window. He typed into his cell phone, stared at the screen then put his ear to the door. He yelled, "Harry, it's me, open the door." He shifted from foot to foot.

"He's getting agitated," Parker said. "Maybe we should see what the problem is."

The man fingered his phone again, then shouted at whoever answered, "I'm ringing and knocking and calling but he's not opening the door. What should I do?" With the phone to his ear, he removed a key from his pocket and yelled, "Harry, I'm coming in." He turned the key and the door swung open.

Parker and Corelli were out of the car and up the steps before he could enter the house. Eyes wide, he flattened against the building. She could hear someone yelling on his phone. "Abel, Abel—what are you—"

Realizing he probably thought they were going to mug him Parker displayed her shield and ID. "Sorry to frighten you. We're here to interview Mr. Davenport. Is everything all right?"

He ignored Parker but spoke into his phone. "The police are here. What s-s-s-should I do, Mrs. D-d-davenport?" He listened, then handed his phone to Parker.

"Mrs. Davenport, this is Detective P.J. Parker. We're here to speak to Mr. Davenport. Is something wrong?" Parker listened carefully, trying to decipher her heavy drawl. "Do we have your permission to enter?" She handed the phone to the man and turned to Corelli. "She's worried. She's been trying to get in touch with her son since last night but he hasn't responded."

"Mrs. D says it's okay for you to go in and check on him." He spoke slower and with less confidence than the woman but his drawl was just as heavy.

"Please remain out here until we make sure it's safe to enter the house."

They drew their guns, entered and cleared the rooms off the narrow hall as they encountered them. Harrington Davenport was in the living room at the back of the house, sitting in an easy chair with the TV blasting one of the daytime conservative talk shows. His head hung forward touching his chest. Parker checked for a pulse in his carotid arteries. He was dead.

They moved on and when they'd cleared the other three floors of the house, they returned to the living room. After putting on booties and gloves, Parker stood in front of Davenport looking for a wound or blood or bruising of the neck. Corelli moved behind him. "I've got it, Parker. Gunshot to the back of the head. Might be a professional hit."

Parker moved next to Corelli and studied the bullet entry point. "Shot, not strangled like our two vics. What do you think? A coincidence or related to our murders?"

Corelli pretended to be shocked. "Didn't I cover that in Homicide 101? There are no coincidences in a murder investigation."

Parker rolled her eyes. "So you say." She focused on Davenport. "A gunshot to the back of the head, no sign of forced entry and judging by the state of the room, no fight. It's unlikely he'd let a stranger stand behind him so I'm guessing he knew his killer. What do you think?"

"Parker?" Corelli pointed to her phone. "We need to get this show on the road."

"Right. I'll bring the guy in to identify him."

She found him rocking back and forth on the top of the steps where they left him. I'm Detective Parker. What's your name, sir?"

"A-a-abel C-c-c-clemson."

"Mr. Clemson, I'm sorry to inform you that Mr. Davenport is dead."

He stared at her, his face blank, as if he couldn't understand what she'd said. "Oh."

Damn, she hoped he wasn't going into shock. "Do you think you could identify him for us just so we're sure?"

"You mean l-l-look at him and say who he is, like on T-T-TV? I can do that."

Parker escorted Clemson into the room. He paled, stared for a second then started backing away. "T-t-that's Harry. He's dead, right?"

"Yes, he's dead." He seemed ready to run so Parker grabbed his sleeve and led him out to the kitchen. She pulled out a chair for him.

Parker needed to confirm the identification. "You're sure the body in the other room is Mr. Harrington Davenport?"

"Y-y-yes, ma'am." He put his head in his hands.

She stepped back into the living room where Corelli was waiting. "It's Davenport. Would you call it in? And call Dietz, too. We need help and search warrants for this house and his law office. Remind Dietz that we might need a special master lawyer to oversee our search of his office to be sure we don't step on attorney/client privilege. I'm going to call Mrs. Davenport to break the news. Then I'll ask Clemson a few questions."

Corelli threw a quick salute. "Got it."

Parker returned to the kitchen. Clemson was still sitting with his elbows on his knees and his head cradled in his hands. "Please give me Mrs. Davenport's number so I can inform her of the death of her son." Instead of the shocked face or tear-filled eyes she expected, he was dry-eyed when he looked up. His hand shook as he passed his phone to her. She scrolled though his few recent calls and typed the number into her own phone.

Philippa Harrington Davenport picked up immediately and spoke quickly. "Is Harry all right?"

Normally Parker and Corelli would have conveyed this news in person but since Mrs. Davenport was waiting to hear about her son, Parker wanted to inform her before Clemson could. "I'm sorry to have to tell you this over the phone, Mrs. Davenport, but Mr. Davenport is dead."

There was a sharp intake of breath but no sudden sobs or hysterics on the other side of the call. "Was it a heart attack?"

Parker gave her the bare facts. "No. I'm sorry but it appears he was murdered." No response. But being a homicide detective dealing with violent death up close had taught Parker that everyone deals with bad news in their own way. "Please accept my condolences, Mrs. Davenport. I'll visit you later today when I have more information."

Parker dropped her phone into her pocket. Corelli came into the kitchen as she turned to Clemson. "Are you related to Mr. Davenport?"

"N-n-no. We're friends. I've worked for Mrs. D since I was seven years old so I've known Harry all his life." He dragged his sleeve over his forehead.

Parker was puzzled. "You've worked for her since you were seven? How could that be?"

"They pu-put my mama away because she was a d-d-defective so Mrs. D took me in. I worked to earn my keep. It was a long time ago and that's how things was done then."

Defective? Parker glanced at Corelli. Though she seemed shocked at the language, too, Clemson seemed unaware of their dismay.

Realizing she was off on a tangent, Parker got down to business. "When was the last time you saw Mr. Davenport."

"Um, yesterday. He needed food stuff so I shopped for him. He was eating breakfast when I got here. I think it was about ten."

"How did he seem?"

"He was…" Clemson rubbed his temples. "He was kinda sad, not joking like usual. But he was reading and we never talked when he was busy. I put the food away, washed the dishes, made his bed and left."

"Was Mr. Davenport married? Did he have children?"

"S-s-separated. He had two girls and two boys but Harry Two, his oldest son, died a few years ago."

"Where is his wife now?"

"Don't know. Maybe W-w-west V-v-virginia."

"Can you give us the names of his friends? Or enemies?"

He shrugged. "Mrs. D knows."

The three of them looked up at the sound of the doorbell. "I'll get it," Corelli said.

"Thank you for your help, Mr. Clemson. You can go but first give me your address and telephone number."

She recognized the Riverside Drive address. "You live with Mrs. Davenport?"

"I have my own apartment in her house."

Parker wrote down the phone number he dictated. "I can have a police car drive you home if you'd like."

"No thank you. Mrs. D gave me m-m-money to take cabs both ways." Parker walked him to the door and watched him make his way carefully down the stairs to the street. She was getting a weird vibe from Clemson.

CHAPTER EIGHTEEN

Parker joined Ndep and Corelli in the doorway of the living room. Ndep had already donned protective gear and she and Corelli were sketching the scene as Serena Lopez, the crime scene unit photographer, took pictures.

"Good afternoon." Parker smiled at MLI Gloria Ndep. The smile Ndep returned was friendly and professional as always, but once again Parker sensed her distancing herself, denying the intimacy they'd shared. A murder scene was not the place to discuss their personal issues. But lately that seemed to be the only time they saw each other. She really needed to make a date to get together with Gloria to discuss their relationship.

Lopez lowered her camera. "Okay, I've got all I need in this position so he's all yours."

Corelli looked up. "A couple more minutes."

When Corelli closed her notebook, Ndep offered her first impressions. "No sign the victim struggled." Maybe because English was her second language or maybe because she was meticulous about her work, Ndep always used proper language rather than cop shortcuts. She made notes on her iPad and turned to Corelli. "Any sign of forced entry?"

Parker felt slighted even though there was no way for Ndep to know she was the lead on this one. "There's no sign of forced entry, though I'll have all the doors, windows, and the sliding glass doors checked to be sure."

Ndep looked at the two detectives, then widened her eyes, apparently realizing that Corelli sketching meant Parker was taking the lead. "All right. I'm ready to examine the body, whenever you are, Detective Parker."

Corelli attempted to hide her smile, but Parker noticed and elbowed her as they moved into the room. "He was Harrington Davenport."

Lopez gasped.

Ndep's eyebrows shot up. "The white nationalist who's going to run for the Senate? Well, *was* going to run."

"The very same. And there's a connection to the last victim we shared, Ned Rich."

"Interesting. How did you link them? Was Mr. Davenport beaten and strangled too?"

"No, he was shot." Parker considered how much to reveal. She knew she could trust Ndep but she didn't want to share more than she would with any of the other MLIs or the ME. "We believe Rich recently interviewed him for a story that involved a third person who was murdered in Queens. We actually came here to talk to him about Rich but we bumped into someone his mother had sent to check on him since he wasn't answering his phone. His mother gave us permission to enter the house."

Ndep walked around the chair studying the body then stopped behind him. "Yes, a bullet to the cerebellum." She raked the hair on his head with her fingers, looking for wounds. "Here's another bullet entry point on the side of the head and, oh, another in the back of the head. So three bullets."

"Three?" Parker looked at Corelli. "We only saw one and were thinking a professional hit but three changes that. What are your thoughts, Gloria?"

"One shot might not have killed him so two makes sense. Three seems emotional, angry, to me. Whoever did it wasn't leaving anything to chance." Her fingers parted the hair on the side of his head opposite the bullet entry point. "There appears to be an exit wound on this side. You might want to have the CSI techs look for the bullet. Let's get him on the floor."

The three of them eased the body off the chair onto his back.

Ndep dug into Davenport's front pockets. "A few singles, some change, a dirty tissue and a cell phone." She dropped everything into the evidence bag Corelli held, then unbuttoned his shirt and checked his chest and neck. "Upper body clear." She checked his hands. "Nothing obvious under his fingernails which supports the idea that he didn't struggle with his killer." She held his hands so they could see, then covered them with paper bags. "I'll scrape under them at the morgue just to be sure." She unbuckled his belt and they eased his pants down. "No wounds on the front of his stomach or legs and no sign of sexual activity."

"Help me roll him over, Corelli." When he was on his stomach, Ndep checked his neck, back, buttocks and legs then took an anal temperature reading. "No wounds or sexual activity that I can see." She dug in his back pockets and came up empty. "No wallet, no phone. Not unusual if this was his home."

"So it appears two bullets lodged in his brain and the third exited. Probably a small caliber gun."

Parker moved closer. "Interesting. Maybe he knew his killer and was comfortable enough to let him or her stand behind him, or, maybe he was given a date rape drug to make him compliant so let's include that in the drug screen."

"If you think he might have imbibed a date rape drug, you might want to ask CSU to test the contents of that glass." Ndep pointed to the table next to his chair.

Parker examined the table with the glass on it. A razor and a short straw were there along with papers that Davenport was likely reading before he was killed. She moved the papers aside and revealed a mirror coated with a light powdery substance. "Or, it seems, he may have been high on cocaine."

Corelli came to check it out. "Well, well. I wonder what his followers would think about that?"

Parker turned to watch Ndep finish her examination, enter her observations into her iPad, then snap a couple of pictures. She realized she liked and respected Gloria, but the spark she'd felt when they first got together had dimmed, so it seemed both their feelings had changed. She'd learned today that talking about your feelings could help clear up misunderstandings so after they cleared this case she would talk to Gloria.

Ndep put her iPad in her bag. "If you are done with Mr. Davenport, I'm ready to take him to the morgue." She pulled out her phone.

Parker put a hand on Ndep's arm. "Can you estimate the time of death?"

"Based on body temperature and rigor I would guess somewhere between ten last night and four this morning." Ndep typed into her phone. "I just texted the morgue guys to come in for the body. We'll be out of your way in a couple of minutes."

As the morgue techs rolled the body out, Parker turned her attention to the room. It was nicely furnished but with its tan leather sofa and chair, simple wooden side tables, and plain brown, tan and gray rug, it had a sparse, masculine feel. She'd noted earlier that the bedrooms and the office/conference room seemed utilitarian. And though the kitchen was modern and seemed well-equipped, the takeout containers on the table and stuffed in the tall kitchen garbage can indicated Davenport wasn't much of a cook. The house had the feel of a bachelor pad and she assumed he moved here after he separated from his wife.

Parker's musings were interrupted by Corelli's announcement from the doorway. "Crime scene techs and our team have arrived. And I checked his cell phone and it's password protected."

The CSU team filtered in and immediately got to work. Corelli told them about the bullet, pointed out the glass and mirror, watched as they were bagged and labeled, then observed the collection of evidence.

Parker met with the uniforms and detectives in Davenport's conference room, brought them up-to-date on the murder, then made assignments. "Greene, call Dietz and tell him you need another detective to work with you, then take Hernandez and Shaunton to Davenport's law firm. Lock down his office and his secretary's desk and remain there to ensure no one removes anything from either place. Once we have a warrant for the office and a Master assigned, we'll conduct the search. In the meantime, interview his secretary and others in the office to get their alibis, identify Davenport's enemies, and find out what he was involved in politically and legally that might have led to his death. I'd particularly like to know whether either Magnolia Walker or

Ned Rich had an appointment with him or spoke to him on the telephone. Forlini and Kim, canvas the neighbors. Watkins, oversee the CSU search of the crime scene and when the warrant arrives, search the entire brownstone with Kim and Forlini. Corelli and I are going to talk to Davenport's mother."

CHAPTER NINETEEN

Corelli checked addresses as they cruised up Riverside Drive. "That's it. The corner building."

Parker slowed then made a quick U-turn, pulled into an empty spot on the park side of the street and gazed at the building. "I didn't think there were any private homes left on Riverside."

Corelli leaned forward in the passenger seat to get a better view. "Most of these old mansions are divided into apartments so don't jump to conclusions. Actually, didn't that Abel guy say he lived in an apartment in her building?"

They got out of the car, stood on the curb and studied the impressive, large, four-story red brick and marble building. Six marble columns separated the three windows on the second floor. The entire first floor was marble but it was the heavy wooden door set in the arched entryway that caught Parker's attention. That plus the two marble lions guarding the entrance and the marble balustrade that enclosed the attached garden reminded her of a fortress. And though no weapons were visible, the Army fatigue-wearing, muscled woman and three burly men watching warily from the steps of the building, appeared to be guards. "Are you sure this is the place?"

Corelli checked her notes. "Yes. And the welcoming committee confirms it."

Not sure what to expect, Parker unbuttoned her woolen coat for easier access to her weapon. The sound of Corelli unzipping her down coat confirmed they'd had the same response to the group waiting for them. "I wonder whether they're here just for us?" Parker stepped into the street and waited for a break in the traffic.

The pseudo-military group closed ranks to block the entryway.

"Bastards," Corelli said under her breath.

"Please state your business." The woman directed the command to Corelli in an accent similar to that of Mrs. Davenport and Abel Clemson.

"Who's asking?"

Parker heard the tension in Corelli's voice. She could easily fly off the handle and turn this into a confrontation. Corelli's hand moved to her Glock. Parker touched her arm. "Let me take care of it."

"We're detectives. Mrs. Davenport is expecting us." Parker stepped forward and displayed her shield. She elbowed Corelli and she displayed her credentials.

The woman sidestepped to address Corelli as one of the men moved to block Parker. "What do you want with Mrs. Davenport?"

Parker glared at the aggressive man and raised her hand, prepared to shove him away if necessary. "Unless you're looking for trouble, I suggest you step back." She turned her attention to the woman. "And you are?"

"Friends of the Davenport family here to keep the riffraff out." The woman acted as if Parker was invisible and directed her response to Corelli.

Corelli stepped around Parker and was toe-to-toe with the woman. "Really. How ingenious. Using the riffraff to keep the riffraff out."

Parker touched her arm, trying to calm her, but Corelli shook her off. "Are you armed?" The hostility in Corelli's voice unsettled Parker. But Corelli's anger and the quick movement of her hand to her Glock alarmed the four would-be guards. The woman put her hands up in front of her as if to surrender. Two of the men did the same but the aggressive guy pushed the woman aside and moved into Corelli's personal space.

"Get back, Everet." He hesitated but followed the woman's order. She glared at Corelli. "We're not armed. We're not licensed to carry."

They were on Davenport's property so unless she had a problem with the group, there was nothing to be done. Parker had to defuse the situation before Corelli did something they would both regret. She put her hand over Corelli's to ensure she couldn't draw her Glock. Corelli tensed but didn't do anything to extricate her hand.

Parker met the eyes of the woman, the leader of the group. "Show us your ID."

The woman looked uneasy. "We provide protection for Mrs. Davenport but we don't work for a security company. We can show you our drivers' licenses."

"That would be fine." Parker responded.

As they reached in their pockets, Parker removed her hand from Corelli's then moved her coat aside and placed her hand on her own weapon. She was pleased to see four sets of eyes widen as they followed her hand and then jumped to Corelli's hand, which was still resting on her gun. "Detective Corelli, please record their licenses."

Corelli glanced at Parker, took a breath, and retrieved her iPhone. She took pictures of the licenses of Taryn Smoltser, Everet Collins, DeWayne Johnson and Phil Craddock. The licenses were issued in West Virginia, but they all claimed to live at the same address in Fort Lee, New Jersey, not far over the George Washington Bridge.

When Corelli pocketed her phone, Parker moved forward. The four separated but as Parker walked between two of the men, the aggressive one bumped her. She placed her hand on her weapon again and turned so they could see it. "The next time you come close to either one of us, I will arrest you." The men retreated and Parker and Corelli walked to the arched doorway.

Corelli leaned in close. "Sorry about that. Their fatigues and pretending to be soldiers triggered a memory of some of the Afghani police we were training when Marnie was killed. I flashed back to Afghanistan for a couple of seconds."

Parker was relieved that Corelli acknowledged what had happened. "You haven't had a flashback in a while. Are you all right now?"

"Yes." Corelli rang the bell. One of the four muttered, "Fucking turd" and this time it was Corelli who put a hand on Parker's arm. "Let it go or I might have to kill them. They're not worth the bother and the paperwork."

Parker rang the bell. A minute later an attractive blonde in her late thirties or early forties opened the door. Seeing Parker, her eyes widened. "You, again! Go away." She swung the door.

Parker jumped back. "What the...?"

Corelli stuck her foot in the doorjamb, short-circuiting the woman's attempt to slam the door in Parker's face. The woman yelped and retreated as Corelli forced the door open. She stared at Parker, then shook her head. Her anger seemed to drain away and her focus shifted to Corelli. "Sorry. For a minute I thought...um, sorry. Um, you surprised me." She shivered. "How can I help you?"

Parker spoke as Corelli stepped aside. "Mrs. Davenport is expecting us."

The woman frowned. "You're the detective?" She sounded shocked and made no effort to hide her contempt. Parker sensed Corelli tense again.

"And you are?" Parker mentally kicked herself. She should have anticipated this. A black woman with power would not be welcome in the home of a prominent, unapologetic racist like Philippa Harrington Davenport.

It looked like the woman wasn't going to answer but then she spat out her name. "I'm Heather Harrington, Mrs. Davenport's niece."

"Well, Heather, you can tell Mrs. Davenport that Detective P.J. Parker, the lead detective investigating the murder of her son, and Detective Chiara Corelli are here to see her."

"Wait here and I'll see if she's available." She pushed the door, apparently intending to shut them outside, but Parker's hand shot up and held it open. "We'll wait inside, thank you." Parker half expected Davenport to tell her niece to send her around to the back door and she wasn't going to give her the opportunity to try it. Corelli closed the door behind them.

"Hey, you can't just..." Heather glared at them then scurried down the hall. Words like "uppity," "bitch," and "cops" drifted behind her.

Corelli grinned. "Taking no shit, I see."

"It was a gut reaction. I've experienced my fair share of racist micro-aggressions but never anything so blatantly racist. Should I have ignored it?"

"Absolutely not. Not under any circumstances. And certainly not from these...white nationalist Nazis." Corelli lowered her voice. "Stick it to her. You're the lead detective on her son's murder case. She has no choice but to deal with you on your terms." After a few minutes Corelli pointed to several chairs farther down the hall. "Looks like we'll be waiting a while so we might as well be comfortable."

Parker peered into the two rooms they passed on the way to the chairs. "Fancy but shabby. Wow, look at the ceiling." Corelli followed her gaze. The blue and gold octagon-patterned ceiling must have been gorgeous back in the day but clearly it had been neglected and one area looked dangerously close to falling. "If the rest of the house is as badly maintained as what we've seen so far, it may collapse around Mrs. Harrington Davenport one day soon. Having her four faux-guards paint and plaster the place would be a better use of their time and her money, supposing she pays them."

Fifteen minutes later they were summoned and followed Heather up a lovely wooden staircase to a room with lots of windows facing the garden. The pale plum walls looked freshly painted, the elegant furniture appeared new and the plums and pinks and lavenders in the patterned rug pulled it all together. Filled with sunlight and the gentle vibe of the understated colors, the room had an airy feel, quite unlike the hallway and the rooms off it.

Philippa Harrington Davenport sat in a throne-like chair with the windows behind her. The diffused light softened everything—her features, the lines and color of her fancy, clingy purple dress, and the faded red of her upswept hair. The picture she presented brought to mind the many romantic paintings Parker had seen in museums. The skeptic in her wondered whether Philippa had required the fifteen minutes to set the scene.

"Please sit, detectives." Given her imperious tone, the twang in her voice was jolting. She waved them into chairs facing her and the windows. "I'm sure you understand how difficult this time is for me." She directed her comment to Corelli.

Ignoring the instruction to sit, Parker moved to stand directly in front of Davenport and extended her hand with her card. Davenport flinched. "Detective P.J. Parker and my partner Detective Corelli."

Davenport stared at the card. Or was it her black hand she was staring at? Did she expect to get cooties or worse from touching something of hers? Parker used the time to study the woman. Her dead son was sixty-five years old so she had to be in her eighties. She must have been beautiful at one time but basing your life on hatred seemed to take its toll. Close up, her dyed red hair and heavy makeup emphasized the coldness of her eyes, the thinness of her lips and the hard lines of her face. There was nothing romantic, warm or cuddly about this mama.

"Parker? Sounds familiar. Are you related to *that* Senator Parker?" Davenport made a question sound like an insult. She didn't wait for an answer, just took the card and looked beyond Parker to address Corelli. "What can you tell me about my son's murder?"

Parker dragged one of the chairs closer and slightly to the right of Davenport so she could see her face without the glare from the windows. Corelli shifted so her chair was behind Parker, out of Davenport's line of sight. "Do you know whether your son had any enemies?"

Davenport glared at Parker. "Surely you know who my son is?"

"Why don't you tell me?" As an ADA, Parker had learned to keep her emotions out of her voice so there wasn't a trace of anger or sarcasm in the question.

Davenport shifted slightly to the left, trying to make eye contact with Corelli. Parker glanced behind her. Corelli's head was down over her notebook, as if she was reading something engrossing, ensuring the woman couldn't engage her.

"Any *intelligent person* would know but of course *someone like you* might not..."

If Parker was confident about anything it was her intelligence so she let the insinuation hang, but she wouldn't make it easy for the bitch. "Someone like me might not...what?"

Philippa hesitated. "Might not be aware. Harrington Davenport is—was—the preeminent conservative Republican man in America, head of the most prestigious conservative law firm in the country. He was preparing to announce his run to replace Charles Schumer..." She made a face as if just saying the Democrat's name made her sick. "...as the United States senator from New York state." Trying to understand the thick accent, Parker listened carefully while Philippa extolled the virtues of Harrington Davenport. The accent wasn't soft like someone from the south but more like Parker's idea of how a hillbilly would sound. Abel Clemson, the woman outside, and based on the few words she had spared them, Heather, sounded the same. It must be how West Virginians talked.

"You think he was murdered because he was a conservative? Or because he was planning to run for the Senate? If so, who do you think is behind his murder?"

Davenport peered around Parker. "What do you think, Detective Cardelli?"

Corelli raised her head and met Davenport's eyes. "I'm only here to take notes. Detective Parker is the lead on this case. Rest assured, you're in good hands. She graduated from Yale and then Harvard Law School and was an assistant district attorney before joining the police department. She is more than capable of handling all your questions and some you haven't thought of yet." Corelli lowered her head again.

Davenport's eyes narrowed. She seemed to understand Corelli's words as the criticism they were and she wasn't happy about it.

Parker almost burst out laughing. Sock it to her, Corelli. She didn't speak until Davenport looked at her. "Surely a man living in a strongly democratic city and state and involved in the white nationalist movement had many enemies. And unless I've misunderstood, you also are a major, um, figurehead in that movement so I would expect you're well aware of the threats."

Parker would surely have been dead if the arrows shooting from Davenport eyes were not figures of speech. "I am *not* just a figurehead." The words sounded as if they were ground out between millstones.

"Really?" Parker took a minute to decide how to phrase what she was about to say, which she knew she shouldn't, but she thought it might shake the woman a little. "I'm surprised that in a movement run by white males who believe women and black or brown people are less than them, you think you're not a figurehead." Parker turned toward the gasp. She hadn't realized Heather was still in the room.

When she turned back, Davenport was looming over her. "Despite what some believe, I am the brains behind this movement. I am the leader. It wasn't my husband or my son, it was, is, and will be me, until I decide otherwise."

Mission accomplished. Woman enraged.

"As a woman and a person of color, I don't pay a lot of attention to the hate spewed by your...movement, but I'll bet there'll be a reckoning now that your son is dead. How will you handle that?"

Davenport sneered. "There will definitely be a reckoning, but I assure you there won't be any question about who is in charge when it's over."

"Amen." Parker swiveled to look at Heather again. Her eyes seemed to glow with pride. Or maybe it was anger.

When she turned back, Philippa was in her chair again with her hands folded in her lap. "You're right about threats. We do get them, too many to worry about."

"Is that the reason for the...what shall I call the ragtag group outside? Security?"

Davenport frowned. "It is. You can make fun, but my ragtag security, as you call them, has been very effective at protecting me. Like Heather," she said, acknowledging the presence of her niece for the first time, "they moved here from West Virginia because they're dedicated to taking their country back and dedicated to me because they know I'll lead the way." She clamped her lips closed as if she'd said more than she intended.

Something in her tone and the perceptible increase in her breathing raised Parker's antennae. Was taking back their country alluding to the threat to democracy Rich had feared? "Do you know if Mr. Davenport met with a woman named Magnolia Walker? Or Ned Rich, a reporter?"

Philippa's gaze flicked to Heather but then settled on Parker again. "I've never heard of that Magnolia person, but isn't Ned Rich the reporter who was murdered recently?" Her laugh was dismissive. "Harry would never give an interview to a legitimate reporter at *The Daily Post* and certainly not to a muckraker like that one."

Since Rich had probably approached Davenport, not as a reporter, but as someone with information that could ruin him, Parker wouldn't take her word for it. Time to pour a little oil on the fire. "Interesting. I believe Walker and Rich had discovered something in the Harrington family history that would have been of great interest to him. Even shocking. And to you as well."

Philippa studied Parker for a few seconds. "I can't imagine what information a *black person*"—Parker heard it as the insult it was meant to be—"and a slimy reporter could have about my family that my son and I don't already know."

Gotcha. Davenport had just confirmed she knew who Walker was. Parker didn't want to make any accusations she couldn't back up with proof, so she changed the subject. "Did Mr. Davenport have security?"

"He was supposed to have round-the-clock security." Philippa met Parker's gaze. "We've had so many murders in the family that I made him promise he'd always have someone with him, even in his house, but like most of his gender, he thought he knew better."

Parker leaned forward. "Other murders?"

For the first time, Davenport looked like a grieving mother. She blotted her eyes with a tissue from the box on the table next to her and obviously struggled for control. "With Harry gone now, four of my six children and three of my grandchildren have been murdered in the last twenty years. It was done to hurt me. They were all my favorites."

Parker hadn't expected this. It put the murder in a different light. "Were they all murdered in New York City?"

Davenport shuddered. "Only Harry. Phoebe, Elliot, Albert, Willa, Harry Two, and Fiona were all murdered in different parts of West Virginia."

After she and Heather provided the last names, locations, and approximate dates that Parker requested, Philippa seemed exhausted and a little disoriented.

Despite her feelings about the woman, Parker took pity. "Mrs. Davenport we need the name of your security company, the names of some of your son's friends and contact information for his ex-wife. Maybe Heather or Abel can help us?"

"Abel doesn't know anything about anything." Philippa rang the small silver bell sitting on the table. "I'll have to look up the name of the security company, but my ex-daughter-in-law Katharine lives on Fifth Avenue. Meriwether Davis, Harry's best friend since college, lives in Westchester and Lena Wood and her husband, Walter, live in Brooklyn."

"Meriwether Davis is a cable TV personality, but should I know Lena Wood?"

"Unlikely." Davenport's sneer was back. "She blogs about the beauty of marriage between whites, motherhood, being a homemaker and serving your husband and family."

"You rang?" Abel Clemson appeared older, less assertive than he had earlier. He said he'd known Harrington Davenport since he was a boy. Finding his body must have taken something out of him.

"Bring me my Rolodex." Abel walked the four feet to the desk and placed it on the table next to Philippa. He stood head bowed, shoulders rounded. Clemson was white but she used the same tone for him as she'd used for Parker, condescending and almost nasty. He'd used the word defective to describe his mother. It made sense that a racist like Mrs. Davenport would be a eugenicist so why would she have taken him in as a boy? The more immediate question was why hadn't she asked Heather to fetch the Rolodex?

Parker hadn't seen one of those old fashioned, pre-electronic contact maintenance devices in a long time and wasn't aware they still sold them and the cards they required. No need for a search. Philippa spun the wheel and immediately pulled out a card. Despite what she'd said, she knew the name of the security firm. She looked at Corelli. "Michele Benson Security Services, Inc., same Park Avenue address as my son's law firm. Do you want the office telephone number or Michele's cell phone?"

"We'll need both," Parker said.

Davenport ignored Parker and continued to focus on Corelli as she dictated the numbers. "Now I'm tired. Show them out, Abel." She waved her hand toward the door and closed her eyes. She was done and she left no room for discussion.

"Thank you for your assistance, Mrs. Davenport. It's likely I'll have more questions as the investigation unwinds." Davenport didn't open her eyes or give the impression that she heard, but Parker had no doubt she was listening. "Let's go, Corelli."

Seeing the so-called security outside irritated Parker. She faced Clemson. "Do you know anything about Benson Security?"

"It's M-m-michele Benson. I know her since she was a little girl." He chewed his fingernail. "Harry likes her but Mrs. D doesn't because of white s-s-supremacy."

"You look uncomfortable. Is it being surrounded by white supremacists? Or is it NYPD?"

He rotated his wristwatch round and round his wrist. Parker had asked about NYPD to ease his tension but it seemed to have the opposite effect. Finally, he looked in Parker's direction but not quite at her. "Not you. I don't like their beliefs even though I'm white."

The admission surprised Parker. After all these years she would have guessed he was brainwashed. "Why do you stay?"

His jaw hardened. "The Davenports took me in. Mrs. D. raised me. She's like a mother. They are my f-f-family. Where would I go? What could someone like me do?"

Parker took a breath. Her job was to find the killer or killers so no matter how sad this man's life made her feel, it was not her business. But… "Do they abuse you verbally or physically? We can help if they do."

He stared at her as if she was crazy. "No, ma'am, they take care of me."

Sure. Time to change the subject. "Are the security people outside employed by Benson Security?"

He gazed at the four people standing outside. "B-b-brandon Lester takes care of them, not M-m-michele. I think they work for free."

"What's the name of Lester's company?"

"Um, I don't know. He works for Mrs. D."

According to Rich's notes, Lester was ex-military and one of Philippa's most loyal henchmen. "Did Mr. Davenport have professional security?"

"M-m-michele took care of him, not Brandon."

"Do you know why he didn't have security with him last night?"

He seemed to dig deep looking for the answer. "He promised Mrs. D because she nagged but he lied. He didn't like having them in his house. I'm not sure why."

"He had an alarm but it wasn't set when we arrived earlier. Did you have the code in case it was set?"

"I know the code because I did stuff for him, like stock the refrigerator, pick up his dry cleaning or serve drinks and dinner when he had private guests."

"Private guests? Can you explain?"

He blanched but scanned the hallway and the nearby room before lowering his voice. "He wanted the white nationalist vote so he had to meet the leaders from hate groups but he didn't want to be seen with them."

Parker sensed he was holding back something. "Were these social or political meetings?"

Clemson laughed. "He wouldn't socialize with the trash. But he wanted to get elected so he met with them to get them to like him."

"Were some of these private guests women he was interested in?" Clemson pulled back as if she'd hit him with a hot poker. His reaction was so intense Parker decided to take a chance and push him. "Or men?"

A tic in his right eye began to pulse. He stared at the floor as if expecting to find an answer or a secret trap door to escape.

Parker watched him struggle with the question but based on his response, she was pretty sure she'd guessed right and Corelli's thumbs-up from behind Clemson confirmed it for her. Davenport was a closet homosexual. The only sounds in the dim hallway were Clemson's increasingly fast breaths and the laughter from outside.

After a minute he pivoted to scan the hall and the nearby room again. "How did you know? The white nationalists would never accept a h-h-homosexual so there was no way he could admit he desired men, especially very young ones. So I brought boys to him at a small apartment he rented near his house. He didn't hurt them but they had to agree to sex with someone wearing a mask. The boys only saw my face."

"Do you have any names?"

He shook his head. "I find them around Times S-s-square but I only hire a boy one time. I pay them in cash. I use a fake name and they only use first names."

"So you pimped for him?" Clemson whirled to look at Corelli.

He shrugged. "He takes care of me so I do whatever he needs me to do."

"Does that include murder?"

He spun back to Parker, his blue eyes wide, his already pale skin now ashen. "N-n-nothing even close. Wh-what are you t-t-talking about?"

"Did you meet Ned Rich or Magnolia Walker when they visited Mr. Davenport?"

"N-n-no."

"Did he ever mention them to you?"

"N-n-no. He didn't discuss his visitors with me. He just u-u-used me to do things for him."

"And he never asked you to kill anyone for him?"

"No. N-n-never."

CHAPTER TWENTY

The four guards stepped back as Parker and Corelli walked past them on the way to the car. Parker considered questioning them again but decided to go to the security firm to get answers. She'd have them picked up later if it seemed necessary.

Settling in the car Parker turned to Corelli. "Damn, if this detective thing doesn't work out you could always go on the stage. I barely controlled myself when you did your I'm just the dumbass sidekick, she's the boss lady, routine. I almost expected you to shuffle when we left Davenport."

"Ah, you liked that?" Corelli laughed. "I refuse to let that bitch pull me into her games." She hesitated. "And I wanted to shove your superior credentials down her racist throat. You did a great job dealing with her...disdain."

"Disdain? I'd call it condescension and blatant racism. In a way it felt very familiar. When I was growing up my dear Uncle Aloysius would ridicule, try to humiliate and make me feel of no value, if I didn't conform to his idea of who I should be. I learned that if I pretended it didn't hurt, it took away some of his power over me." *And now I'm oversharing.* Parker relaxed her fists. "I really do appreciate your support."

"Hey that's what partners do."

There it was again. Partners. It did seem that way more often than not lately. But her reaction to Corelli's mistake at the Bushwick apartment made it clear she didn't totally trust Corelli. Yet she'd just bared her soul to her. Time would tell but Corelli deserved the benefit of the doubt.

Corelli stared out the passenger window, then turned to her. "I'm sorry, Parker, that bastard really abused you in so many ways. And if it was possible, I'd beat him to a pulp."

She appreciated Corelli's concern but she didn't want to be seen as a wounded soul. "Thanks, but that was a long time ago and I only mentioned it to explain why I was able to handle Philippa's disdain, as you called it, racism, in my opinion. Our energy is better spent trying to connect the murders of Magnolia Walker, Ned Rich, and Harrington Davenport. Philippa conveniently confirmed she knew who Magnolia Walker was. We know Magnolia Walker met with Davenport and immediately after he pooh-poohed her, she contacted Rich and then was murdered. And according to Rich's records he verified her genealogical research and came to the same conclusion: Walker and Davenport had a common black ancestor on the Harrington side of the family. And knowing what we know about Rich, I assume he met with Davenport. But if Davenport ordered the murders of Rich and Walker, who murdered Davenport?" And how do the murders of the other Davenport family members fit in? Parker put the car in gear. "Let's go talk to Michele Benson."

Driving downtown on Riverside Drive Corelli stared at the barren trees in Riverside Park and beyond at the Hudson River. "There are lots of violent people involved in these groups, people who think the rule of law doesn't apply to them. They're fanatics about ridding America of non-whites, Jews, Muslims and those, like us, who identify with a letter on the LGBTQI spectrum. We've discovered two flaws in Davenport's credentials as the spokesperson for the white supremacists, black blood and his predilection for young men. I'm positive there are many in the movement who wouldn't hesitate to kill him for deceiving them on either of those two counts."

"Who other than Abel Clemson knew about the boys? And who knew about the black blood?" Parker turned onto the West Side

Highway heading downtown to Benson's midtown offices. "What's your take on Abel and Philippa?"

"I get a weird vibe from Clemson. From what I saw earlier, Philippa treats him like a servant, not a member of the family, yet he seems to have her on a pedestal. He said he and Harrington were friends and he seemed to accept Davenport's need for young men but maybe he's homophobic. And the *grande dame* gives me the willies. She's a fanatic. And she definitely was making a veiled threat at the end of our meeting. Whether it's true or not, she believes she's the Big Kahuna, not just a sidepiece. She's scary. I could see her ordering Walker and Rich's murder without blinking an eye but not her son's. And talk about an unlucky family. Are you going to have someone check out the murder of her children and grandchildren?"

Damn. Corelli was walking on eggshells now. She knew they needed to check out these other murders but didn't seem to trust she could just state the obvious without another blowup. "Absolutely. Given the family politics it's not so surprising but still it's not normal for so many in one family to be murdered." She glanced at Corelli. "This so-called simple case has so many arms it looks like an octopus. Would you call Dietz and ask him to follow up on the murders?"

"You have to admit it seemed simple at first. But you're up to the challenge even if I made the wrong call." Corelli took out her phone and her notebook. "Dietz, we need to get police reports on some murders going back a few years." She dictated the names of the victims and the cities in which the murders occurred. "Yes, they are related to the Rich/Davenport murders."

Michele Benson was a surprise. Maybe it was seeing so many crazy, disheveled screaming women in tight T-shirts with offensive slogans, making crude gestures on the news and then meeting the rigid racist Philippa Davenport, but the classy, laid-back, attractive blonde in her high thirties or early forties, dressed in a tailored navy pantsuit with a white button-down shirt was not at all what Parker expected. And she certainly hadn't expected to be attracted to her.

As she moved from behind her desk to greet them, Benson's gaze swept over the two detectives. She shook hands with Corelli who was closest, then took Parker's extended hand. Parker jerked at the jolt of electricity. Benson smiled and tightened her grip. *Had Benson felt that little shock when their hands touched?*

Benson's piercing blue eyes locked onto Parker's. *Holy hell, Michele Benson was flirting with her.* "Philippa called me earlier about Harry's murder and again right after your visit to rant about the lead detective." Her soft voice with slight traces of Philippa's heavy West Virginia accent, and the warm, sexy vibe she exuded pulled Parker in, made her want to flirt back. That had never happened with someone they were interviewing. Parker extracted her hand but felt the loss.

"Please sit, detectives."

Did Benson always sway like that or was it for her benefit? She didn't dare look at Corelli. Parker forced herself to focus on the business at hand. She'd realized that Philippa's seemingly vague recollection of the name of the security firm was an act, but it puzzled her. Not only had she called Benson after she found out her son was dead, but she'd also called as soon as they left her house to share her outrage that her son's murder investigation was being led by an uppity black detective.

Philippa wasn't a normal grieving mother. She was a woman driven by her politics and she would use her son's murder to her political advantage. No doubt the white nationalist network was telegraphing the murder right now. And it would soon hit the national news. Damn, they had to get out in front of the rumor mill. Parker whispered to Corelli, "See if Dietz can schedule a news conference this afternoon."

"Excuse me." Corelli stood. "I need to make a call." She left the office.

Parker placed her card on the desk in front of Benson.

"I know who you are, Detective Parker. And I read the papers, so I know Corelli is usually the lead. After Philippa's call complaining about the detective being black, I called one of my sources in the department and he assured me that you were leading the investigation before Harry's murder, that it was not an attempt to antagonize those in the movement who believe blacks should be subservient."

That someone in Benson's position had sources in the NYPD didn't surprise Parker but Benson's frank acknowledgement of the racism did surprise her. "And what do you believe, Ms. Benson?"

She flushed. "I believe my source about your assignment. And other than that, I don't think my beliefs are relevant to the murder of Harry Davenport." She met Parker's gaze. "But what does Ned Rich's murder have to do with Harry?"

She gave a direct answer. "In the course of investigating Mr. Rich's murder we found a connection to Mr. Davenport. As a matter of fact, we were on the way to interview him about the other murder when we encountered Mr. Clemson outside Davenport's townhouse, trying to contact him. Corelli and I actually found his body."

"Intriguing. Can you share anything about the other case?" Benson took Parker's card and slid one of her cards in front of Parker.

"Sorry. I'm sure you know that's not possible."

Benson made a note on a pad on her desk. "So how can I help you, Detective?"

"I understand you provide security for Harrington Davenport and his mother. Unfortunate that he died on your watch." Parker hadn't meant for that bit of sarcasm to slip out but it had and she wouldn't apologize.

Benson tipped her head as if to acknowledge the dig. "It's not unusual for clients, especially men, to hire us for our expertise and then ignore our advice. Harry's politics upset plenty of people and rumors of his coming senatorial run heightened the level of rage directed at him. I planned to have an agent with him twenty-four-seven as Philippa requested, but he thought he knew better and ignored my advice and hers." She lifted her shoulders, as if to say "Men, what could you do?" "But you were misinformed. I don't provide security for Philippa."

"Have there been any specific credible threats against Mr. Davenport recently?"

"Nothing that stood out to me." Benson watched Corelli slip into the chair next to Parker, then moved a thick file to a spot on her desk between Parker and Corelli. "Those are the threats he received in the last six months, some came through the mail and some are printouts of emails. We followed up on the local ones and asked affiliates in other parts of the country to check out the others. Some of the senders are your run-of-the-mill crazies and others disgruntled citizens. In every case, we decided they weren't the type to act but we let them know we'd be watching them."

"Were you close to Mr. Davenport?"

Benson slid her chair back and tented her hands in front of her face, taking a few seconds before responding. "My daddy and Harry grew up together in West Virginia, so I've known him and Philippa my whole life. We were friendly, not friends. We hadn't discussed white nationalism in many years but he knew where I stood on the issues." She met Parker's eyes and smiled slyly. "Could you protect someone whose ideas you didn't agree with?"

Parker didn't hesitate. "Yes. Protect and Serve. It's my job." Was Benson hinting she wasn't a white nationalist? "What about Abel Clemson?"

"What about him?" The question seemed to surprise Benson. "He's been part of the Davenport family since long before I was born. Rumor has it that he's Wilfred Davenport's bastard, but that might be people trying to explain them taking him to live with them. According to my daddy, Abel was responsible for taking care of Harry when they were kids and was always with them. If Harry got into trouble or got hurt, Abel was the one who got the beating." She frowned. "Though I've always thought he was a little off, he's uneducated but observant. He adores Philippa but most of the time she treats him like he's an idiot. But the way her children and grandchildren are dying, it looks like Philippa will be left with only Abel in the end."

"What do you know about the other murders in the family?"

"Only that they occurred. Harry's is the first that I've been close to."

Parker glanced at Benson's business card. "Tell me a little about how you came to security and who your customers are."

"I served twenty years in the Marines, mostly as an MP, and did tours in Afghanistan and Iraq. When I retired three years ago and decided to go into security, Harry was my first client. He even gave me free office space until I could afford the rent. Now I have fifty employees, all ex-military, many I served with over the years."

"How does Brandon Lester fit in to your organization? Did you serve with him in the military as well?"

"You've been misinformed again, Detective. Brandon *is* ex-military, but we didn't serve together. And he doesn't work for me. Our only connections are Philippa and that we come from the same part of West Virginia." She hesitated as if maybe she'd said enough but then continued, "In fact, Philippa wanted me to hire him, but there's no room in a legitimate company for someone like Brandon." Benson shrugged. "Philippa expects everyone to obey her so she was royally pissed and even tried to get Harry to dump me when I refused to hire him. She did get Meriwether Davis to cancel his contract but so be it." Benson twisted a paper clip, straightening and bending it until it snapped. She closed her eyes and rubbed her temples. Maybe she was nervous that she'd revealed too much. "The West Virginia crowd is like an extended family. And you know how family is, fighting one minute and partying the next."

Parker really didn't know. She'd only recently met her birth father and her knowledge of her mother's family ended at her alcoholic, always-drunk grandmother. She didn't know her grandfather's name or if her grandmother knew it, forget about any relatives before them. "And your other clients?"

Benson aligned some files on her desk and gazed out the window. She took a breath. "Most are CEOs you see in the business pages of newspapers every day, and because of my association with Harry, some of them are closet white supremacists." She met Parker's gaze again. "No offense meant, Detective."

"None taken." Parker held her gaze. "After all, this is still the free country you fought for, the one whose constitution you swore to uphold and the reason we can all hold any beliefs we choose. And you certainly don't need my approval for your clients."

Benson had the grace to look away.

"Do you have any ideas about the murder that you'd be willing to share with us?"

"Nothing other than those." She pointed to the letters. "Harry's increasing popularity made him a likely target for his enemies. But being shot somewhere in public by radical left crazies would fit that scenario better than him being murdered in his own home. You haven't said anything about a break-in or forced entry so I assume it was personal or at least connected to his personal life."

"No enemies on the radical right?"

"Touché. It's true that other men who saw him increasing his hold over the white supremacist, um, crowd might be tempted to take him out. But I would guess most of them know, even if they won't admit it, that Philippa is the real power and removing Harry wouldn't change that."

Parker decided to see what she knew. "Do you think his proclivity for boys is the reason behind the murder?"

For the first time Benson seemed thrown. She moved a pen into a drawer, straightened some folders, and then looked up. "Good work, Detective Parker. I guess it's a possibility, but I'm pretty sure he never let the boys near his townhouse. Did you mention this to Philippa?"

"Does she know?" Parker was not about to answer Benson.

"She may. Brandon does a bit of spying for her so he may have discovered it. But she'd never reveal something that would diminish Harry and by association, her, in the eyes of her followers. I found out accidently. As I said, Harry was my first client and I could tell he was filtering what he told me. I staked out his townhouse and followed him for a couple of weeks and figured it out. When he mentioned he was thinking of running for the Senate I confronted him about it because I thought it could be a problem." She met Parker's gaze. "He insisted that he was discreet, that the boys had no idea who he was or even what he looked like."

Parker had gone to see Philippa to gather information that might help solve her son's murder. Instead, she walked away with uneasy questions. "Hypothetically, how far do you think Philippa would go to stop someone from revealing information that could destroy her standing with white nationalists?"

If Benson was surprised by the question, she didn't show it, but she didn't respond immediately. Rather she seemed to be giving it some thought. "Hypothetically, I think she'd do whatever was necessary to eliminate the threat." She took a breath. "In real life, I'm not sure."

"Thank you for your honesty." Parker picked up the file of threatening letters. "Unless you want to make copies of these, I'll take the file and return it after we've reviewed it."

Benson stood. "After Philippa called I figured you'd show up and I made that copy for you. It includes every single threat he received. At least the ones he shared with me. As I said, you never knew how forthcoming Harry was being."

Parker stood and Corelli followed. "How do the volunteers fit into your organization?"

"Volunteers? Oh, you mean the group that hangs outside of Philippa's mansion. They don't fit at all. They're Brandon Lester's people. It's hard for normal people to understand but Philippa and Harry are icons for various factions of the rather disparate groups of white nationalists. Many people idolize them and are willing to risk their lives for them, and I suppose, for the cause. In professional settings, I provided experienced security guards trained to detect threats to protect Harry. But when he was at a rally of...like-minded white nationalists, he preferred to use Brandon Lester's rough, untrained volunteers for security. Harry loved firing up the white nationalists with his rhetoric and sometimes his security ended up brawling with the crowd. He said it made him feel powerful, like he had his own army. But..." She frowned.

Parker waited but Benson left it hanging. "But what?"

Benson's smile was sweet. "Sorry. I just realized that recently he seemed to be backing off from his normal rabble-rousing, his speeches were less fiery, more about getting out the vote."

"That makes sense since he was planning to run for office."

"It does but I can't put my finger on it now, but something was bothering him."

Before the Rich case, Parker had been vaguely aware of the Davenports and their followers but hadn't paid much attention since they didn't seem relevant to her life. Maybe Debbie Maynard was right. Maybe thanks to her uncle, the senator, she was too white-identified and didn't see the threat. What else could have blinded her to the danger of the racists who didn't make any attempt to hide their agenda? "Was it about his army?"

Benson ran her fingers through her close-cropped hair. "I've heard some crazy rumors, but I don't plan to spread them so don't ask."

CHAPTER TWENTY-ONE

Corelli broke the silence in the car. "Did you know racists came in the form of sexy babes? I got a lesbian vibe from her. Did you?"

So Corelli had felt it as well. "My guess is they come in all sizes, shapes and personalities. But if you had asked me that yesterday, I would have denied it was possible. And yes, I got the vibe. At one point I thought she was flirting with me." *And I wanted to flirt back in the worst way.*

"You got that too? People like her are anti-LGBTQI so I thought I was making it up. On the other hand, though Benson is a white, blue-eyed blonde, she's far from their ideal of the homemaker wife serving her white man and pumping out beautiful white babies. She served in the military, has her own business where she bosses men around and worst of all, she's not married, nor, if our gaydar is working, does she seem interested."

Parker swerved to avoid a bus pulling into traffic. "Against my better judgment I liked her. What do you think about this private army and rumors she's heard?"

They were almost at the station when Corelli answered. "It brings the threat to democracy to mind. On the one hand I think a private army is a stretch, but on the other it sounds like Philippa thinks she can mobilize one." She grinned. "But Benson seemed to like you so maybe if you ask her out, she'll confide all her white nationalist secrets in a moment of postcoital togetherness."

Parker gave her a dirty look.

"Oops, don't tell Ndep I said that." Corelli stepped out of the car, zipped up her down coat and walked with Parker to the station house. "If this is too intrusive, just ignore me. Have you ever dated someone white?"

"It is intrusive. And yes, I have." Parker opened the door but didn't enter. "You know, Maynard contends I'm more white than black. Maybe that's why I've had just as many cultural issues with Ndep and Maynard as I had with my white dates. Although we're all black, their backgrounds are very different from mine. Ndep's parents brought her to the U.S. from Nigeria when she was eleven years old and she has one foot in the U.S. and one in Nigeria. She still lives with her parents and is so family-oriented that I doubt she'll ever come out of her very tiny closet. And Maynard grew up poor, with a single mother in a rough neighborhood in Philadelphia. She fought her way out through sheer willpower and determination. It's hard for me to relate to either of their lives. And, though I've had the same middle-class, private school upbringing as my white dates, the fact is, I'm black and it was hard for each of us to understand the other's experience." She gazed at Corelli. "I hope that answers your question." She walked into the station, ending the conversation.

Corelli seemed lost in thought as she followed Parker to the conference room. Marnie, Corelli's ex-girlfriend who died in Afghanistan, was a black detective from a religious family. Perhaps Corelli was thinking about cultural issues between her and Marnie. *Or maybe I'm the only one with cultural issues.*

Dietz greeted them. "I was afraid you weren't going to make it. You've got ten minutes before the press conference."

"I'd like to meet with the whole team after we finish with the media. Ask everyone to be ready to report on what they're working on and what, if anything, they've found. I need a minute in the ladies' room then I'll be ready to go. What about you, Corelli?"

"I'm with you." Corelli lowered her voice. "You okay doing this?"

Am I? She'd saved Corelli during flashbacks at press conferences, so she was sure she could depend on her if she needed help. "My interactions with the media as an assistant district attorney weren't as contentious as the ones between detectives and reporters but I'll be all right. Feel free to jump in if I seem to be stumped or you think I'm talking too much or giving too much information."

Winfry was waiting when they stepped onto the stage for the news conference. "Ready for your first media fencing match, Detective Parker?"

"As ready as I can be, sir. And Corelli promises to back me up."

"As will I." He stepped to the microphone and the room went quiet. "Good evening, I'm sorry to announce the death of highly regarded conservative attorney Harrington Davenport." He gave them time to express their shock to each other. "Mr. Davenport was murdered sometime last night. Detective P.J. Parker, the lead on the investigation, will take a few questions. Detective Parker."

Parker scanned the room. She recognized most of the attendees, noted the few who tried to mold the news and inevitably attacked Corelli, the professionals here to get answers to legitimate questions, and happily, their friends Darla North and her camera person, Bear Murray.

Parker replaced Winfry at the podium and Corelli moved next to her. She took her time adjusting the height of the microphone to steady herself while they absorbed the fact that she was the lead. "Good evening. As you probably know Mr. Davenport was getting ready to enter the primary race in hopes of becoming the Republican candidate for the U.S. Senate from New York. His death is a big loss for his family and the Republican party. His body was discovered at his home earlier today."

Philip Melnick, a reporter for *The Daily Post* who had been close to Parker's uncle was on his feet with a question almost before she finished the sentence. Was he in touch with his friend now? "Detective Parker, I heard you were the lead detective on the murder of my coworker Ned Rich but now you're leading the Davenport investigation. Does this mean NYPD is pushing the little guy aside to take care of the important, rich people? And aren't you still in training to be a detective?"

Parker felt Corelli shift forward, ready to attack. She put her hand on Corelli's arm. "If you're worried about my credentials, Mr. Melnick, let me remind you that I am a Harvard Law graduate and

I was an assistant district attorney in the New York City District Attorney's office before I became a police officer. I served on the streets for eight years and was promoted to detective after saving a family of five from a crazed killer. Detective Corelli"—she turned to Corelli—"one of the top closers in the department, has been training me to be a NYPD homicide detective. And as you can see, Detective Corelli is at my side and we are working together." She stopped to consider what she wanted to say about the other part of his question. "One of the things Detective Corelli has emphasized is that the NYPD treats every murder victim equally. There are no important or unimportant murders to us. It is the media that considers some murders more significant than others. You can rest assured that Mr. Rich is not forgotten. We believe the two cases are related so I'm leading both and I promise we will follow each and every lead."

The room exploded as reporters jumped to their feet and threw out questions. She pointed to Jodi Timmons, reporter for WNYZ, a TV station. "Ms. Timmons."

"Can you discuss that connection? Was Ned Rich doing an exposé of Mr. Davenport?"

"It's very early in the investigation, Jodi, and I really can't comment on that." She pointed at Jen Wiley, a reporter for New York One. "Ms. Wiley."

Wiley was relatively new on the police beat but she was usually fair. "Detective Parker, there are lots of rumors floating around about the Davenports encouraging their followers to take violent actions. Are you investigating these rumors and do you think they're the reason Harrington Davenport was murdered?"

"NYPD homicide detectives don't investigate rumors. We investigate murders, which is why our focus is on the deaths of Mr. Rich and Mr. Davenport. Of course if we find something that ties back to a rumor, we'll follow up on it." She noticed Darla waving her hand. "Ms. North."

Darla stood. "First let me congratulate you for taking the lead on these important cases. The juxtaposition of the two cases is interesting. I can see Mr. Rich being murdered for exposing something about Mr. Davenport but I can't see how that relates to Mr. Davenport's death. Are his white nationalistic views involved in his murder? Are you thinking it's political?"

"Sorry, Darla, as I said, we're in the early stages so I can't comment on our thinking about the murders." Parker raised her eyes and scanned the room. "In fact, ladies and gentlemen, there's not much more we can tell you at the moment but we'll keep you posted."

The team greeted Parker with applause when she and Corelli returned to the conference room. She flushed and managed a bow in acknowledgement.

"Good job, boss." Watkins patted her on the back.

That meant a lot coming from Watkins. Referring to her the same way he did Corelli affirmed his acceptance of her leadership. And if he did she knew the rest would follow.

"Thanks. And thanks for hanging around. I want to get a sense of where we are in this monster of a case to be sure we're all on the same page." She looked around the table. Everyone had a piece of the puzzle but she and Corelli had the entire puzzle in their heads. "Why don't you give us an overview of where we are, Corelli?"

"Sure. What started as the simple murder of an unidentified male, became less simple when we learned he was Ned Rich, the investigative reporter for *The Daily Post*. And it got more and more interesting as we followed Rich's breadcrumb trail and uncovered the multiple IDs, and the cloak and dagger stuff with multiple addresses, multiple apartments, and his life as a blackmailer. The investigation took on a new dimension when Greene found a black woman who had left a tip on Rich's *Daily Post* tip line. She'd been murdered after sharing with Davenport and Rich that she had found a blood connection between her family and Harrington Davenport's family."

Hearing the collective gasp, Corelli stopped. She allowed the team time to absorb that bit of information. "The fact that a leading white nationalist family is not as white as they and everyone believed, is just between those of us at this table for now." She gazed at Dietz, then slowly moved her gaze to the others—Watkins, Forlini, Maynard, Greene, and Kim. "And, it all got even more complicated when Parker and I went to Davenport's townhouse to question him about his connection to the murders of Walker and Rich and found *his* body. Magnolia Walker was strangled. Rich was brutally beaten, his right arm was broken in two places and he was strangled from behind. Davenport was shot. We can figure out why

Davenport would have wanted the other two dead, but how does him being murdered fit? We haven't come up with an answer. But it turns out that Harrington Davenport is not the first in his family to be murdered so we're gathering information on those cases from West Virginia." She looked at Parker. "Did I forget anything?"

"If all of that isn't challenging enough," Parker laughed, "Rich told his editor he was working on something that was a threat to our democracy. And in a letter he left for his beneficiary, he said he was working on something that was a threat to our country. Since, as you know, Davenport was a white nationalist with a big following, and since Rich had been digging into white nationalism, it's probable that any threat he found would come from those groups. And there are rumors floating around about possible violent actions."

Corelli tipped an imaginary hat. "Oh, yes, that."

Parker smiled. "Yes, that. In that regard, you all heard Jen Wiley say she's picked up rumors of violence. Could someone follow up with her?"

"I've got it." Kim made a note.

"Thanks, I think that covers the broad outline of what we're working on." Parker checked to see whether they still had everyone's attention. "Watkins. You want to go next?" Like Parker, Watkins had a financially comfortable childhood and a good education. He was adopted as an infant by a white family and had grown up in a predominantly white social network on the Upper West Side in Manhattan.

Watkins offered his easy smile. "Sure." He looked at his notebook. "We're reviewing Rich's detailed blackmail files to determine whether the blackmail was being paid to cover an indiscretion or a crime. We've turned three cases over to the ADA for criminal charges. All the other files we discovered in Bushwick seem to be related to investigations Rich did that went nowhere, no blackmail, no newspaper report." He glanced at his notes. "The key we found at the Brooklyn Heights apartment opened the safe deposit box at Hawley's bank. It contained another million dollars in cash but nothing else."

Watkins checked his notes. "That's it on Rich. The search of Davenport's townhouse didn't turn up anything of immediate interest but we'll start digging into it tomorrow."

"Greene, you're up."

"We secured Davenport's office and his secretary's desk. The warrant came through late in the day but the Master assigned to watch us isn't available until tomorrow. Davenport's two partners and his secretary said he seemed normal the day before and none of them had any ideas about enemies or threats. As you asked, I had his secretary check his schedule. Neither Walker nor Rich had an appointment or met with Davenport. She also showed me his telephone log and there was no mention of either leaving a message or speaking to him. I left Hernandez and Shaunton there and their replacements will stay overnight to ensure no one gets into his desk or his computer files before we start work tomorrow. I'll need help searching."

Parker waited a couple of seconds, then assuming Greene was finished she looked around the table. "Maynard."

Maynard sat up. "Yeah. Watkins has printouts of Rich's emails and we should have printouts of Davenport's emails in the next day or so. Don't worry about Davenport's office computers. It appears that Rich was doing a nightly download of the entire system to one of his servers. I was thinking of turning it off so we can't be accused of hacking and that would leave us with the files as of the day Davenport was murdered."

"Good thinking, Maynard. Turn it off. Anything else on the computers?"

"As I mentioned earlier, Rich was surfing the deep dark web and participating in far-right groups using yet another pseudonym. We'll spend some time tracking what they're saying and maybe find out something about this threat to democracy."

"Forlini. Kim? Who wants to report?"

Kim raised her hand. "We didn't turn up anything canvasing Davenport's neighbors, but we need to go back to catch a few who weren't home." Kim took a drink of water. "We got the murder book for the Magnolia Walker murder this afternoon." She shook her head. "Those guys didn't waste much time investigating before closing it as a house invasion gone wrong, so it's pretty thin. I know they told you she was strangled but that wasn't the whole story. In fact, after reading the ME's description of her injuries and manner of death, we concluded that her killer and Rich's are one and the same."

Corelli sat up straighter. "Whoa. Are you sure?"

"Yup." Kim passed the autopsy report to Corelli. She read it, pursed her lips and passed it to Parker.

Parker skimmed the report. "I'm going to write them up. A little initiative on the part of those two and we'd have known this right away. I presume you two have checked NYPD files for similar murders." Forlini and Kim nodded. "Okay. Work with Greene to search Davenport's office tomorrow. Corelli will ask the FBI to do an expedited search of their database for similar cases."

CHAPTER TWENTY-TWO

Corelli and Parker spent the morning researching Katharine Davenport, Lena Wood, Walter Foster, Meriwether Davis and Brandon Lester, the five associates of Davenport they planned to interview later.

When they appeared at the door of her tenth floor, five-bedroom condo in a luxury Fifth Avenue high-rise overlooking Central Park, Katharine Davenport barely glanced at their identification. "Ah, yes, the detectives." The attractive blonde dressed in lilac slacks and a lilac sweater flashed a warm smile. "I've been waiting for you. Please come in." She led them into a spacious sun-filled room beautifully decorated in gold and blues. It felt welcoming and comfortable rather than stiff and formal like her former mother-in-law's house. Her view of the park was fabulous. She gestured to one of the sofas and the three of them sat.

Parker took the lead. "You don't seem surprised to see us."

"Well, let's see, ex-wife involved in contentious divorce negotiations with a stingy husband who is found shot to death." Katharine flashed that smile again. "I read crime fiction, Detective, so I know I'm a suspect. I would have been more surprised had you not come."

"I'll get right to it then. Where were you the day before yesterday between nine p.m. and five a.m.?"

Katharine didn't hesitate. "Home alone reading one of said novels. I went to bed around midnight."

"Were you in contact with anyone during that time, a friend, the doorman, a delivery person?"

"No. As I said, alone, then asleep."

Katherine's offhand attitude intrigued Parker. "You don't seem upset by your husband's murder."

"I'm not. I..." She seemed at a loss. "We were madly in love when we were younger. He'd joined the Army as soon as he turned eighteen because he couldn't tolerate the racist hate Philippa and his dad, Wilfred, spewed at home. When we met at twenty-one, he was sweet and loving. He became a good husband, a good father, and an honest lawyer. We were happy until Wilfred developed early onset dementia. The Davenport family had been a moving force in the West Virginia eugenics movement and his dementia was an embarrassment so Philippa used it as an excuse to move to New York City where she could easily keep him hidden. But she really came to get Harry to front for her. She was like an earworm constantly saying how powerful he could be, how he could be a senator and someday the president. In the last year or two he slowly began to drop veiled hints about her crazy ideas, the same hateful things he'd run from. He was a lot more subtle than Philippa but the racism and hate was there in the subtext and he knew the white nationalists would get the message.

"Our children and I got it as well. It caused us to separate and our children to pull away from him. It's what drove our son, Harry Two, to West Virginia where he was murdered. I'm positive Harry didn't believe the crap he spewed but he was seduced by the power. Rumor has it that he recently realized Philippa and her little band of warriors are insane and was trying to back away from them." She stared out the window. "You know, I've been so angry at him that I haven't allowed myself to grieve the loss, not of the hateful man who was murdered, but the loss of the good, kind man I loved." She reached for a tissue and dried her eyes. "Sorry, I didn't mean to go there."

Parker paused as Katharine pulled herself together. "I understand you're quite handy with a gun. Do you have a gun registered in New York City?"

"I left my guns with my parents in West Virginia, but to tell you the truth, the threats from thugs in that movement have been getting worse and I've been considering moving back to West Virginia because of the open carry laws. I expected the threats to escalate if Harry was nominated. But even with him dead I'm afraid I'll be a target."

"Why has your divorce been so bitter?"

"The white nationalist craziness. You know their women are supposed to be subservient, stay home, have babies. That's not me. Never has been. I have a career. I'm an artist and my work is in demand. He always supported my independence but with this run for the Senate I think he needed to demonstrate how manly he is, was, and make it look like it was my fault he was cheating on me. I have my own family money plus the income from my art. I don't need Davenport money but I feel entitled to a reasonable alimony for all the years I put my life on hold for him. I planned to put the alimony into a trust for our grandchildren."

"What will happen now?"

"I don't know. I guess it will depend on whether he changed his will. I was his beneficiary while we were married. And before you ask, I have no idea if he gave it a second thought. I doubt he expected to die." She raised her hands palm up, signaling helplessness. "I guess that gives me a really good motive for murdering him."

Parker agreed but was careful to keep a neutral face. "Can you think of anyone else with a good motive?"

"I would imagine there are those in the movement who objected to his rise and will be happy that he's dead." Katharine hesitated a moment. "I hate to say it, but if he was turning against Philippa, some of her crazy followers might have killed him thinking they were protecting her. Even his friend Meriwether Davis, the TV host, had recently begun to attack Harry, not directly, but by bringing on guests who criticized him for not being white nationalist enough. It's ironic because they're old friends and they were both strongly against the whole white nationalist 'take back our country from everyone who's not a white male,' propaganda. Harry was drawn to the power. But Meriwether, who grew up poor, is drawn to the money and the power and the farther right he goes, the more of both he acquires."

"You think Mr. Davis would be willing to murder to obtain more money and power?"

"I don't know how far he would go but money and power are an aphrodisiac for men like him." The harsh tone and the rigidity of her jaw left no doubt how Katharine felt about such men.

Parker needed the dots connected. "But how would murdering his old friend help him?"

"I don't know what it was but Harry had something on Meriwether. Maybe he threatened to expose him."

Parker waited for Corelli to finish writing before she continued. "Anyone else?"

Katharine sneered. "That good little Nazi, Lena Wood. Ms. über wife and mother, darling of the...what was the name Hillary used? Ah, the deplorables. She's power hungry. She tried to seduce Harry but women didn't interest him as he got older, or maybe he just stopped repressing his desire for boys." She took a minute for that to register. "Do you know that about him?"

"And you think Ms. Wood was angry enough about being rebuffed to kill him?"

"There was something but again, I don't know details. Harry used to keep files on people, not for blackmail, but for control. Though now that I think about it, control is blackmail. Anyway, I'm almost certain he had a file on me. If you find those files, I think you'll find a list of people with good reason to kill him beside me. And now you'll have to excuse me. Talking about this is exhausting."

As they closed the door behind them, Corelli scanned the hallway. She elbowed Parker and tipped her head toward the security camera at the end of the hall. When they got down to the lobby, Parker requested a copy of the security tapes for the past seventy-two hours.

Careful not to discuss the interview in a public place, Parker followed the doorman to oversee the copying while Corelli keyed the Scarsdale address of Meriwether Davis into the GPS on her phone and then, taking advantage of the break, checked her email. Twenty minutes later they were in the car with a copy of the tape. Parker drove south to Sixty-second Street to get on the northbound FDR Drive. Once they were speeding along the highway, she turned to Corelli. "Call Dietz and have him tell Maynard, Greene and anyone going through Davenport's papers to be on the lookout for his blackmail files."

Corelli completed the call and turned to Parker. "It's obvious Katharine is still in love with him or the man he was when they got married. But a woman scorned is an angry woman and an angry woman with access to guns is definitely capable of murder. And let's not forget about the will. I'll bet there's plenty of money involved."

At the gate to Meriwether Davis's estate they were asked their names and business by a guard who seemed a little rough around the edges. He called up to the house and then instead of pointing them to a road on the right that looked well-used, he sent them left on what turned out to be a winding road designed to hug the shoreline and show off the estate's beautiful setting overlooking the Hudson River. The road ended at a large rambling house with the river on one side and acres of pine trees on the other.

Davis opened the door himself and led them to a plant-filled room with floor-to-ceiling windows on three sides and a view of the water. "Please take off your coats and sit." He glanced at his phone. "I wish you'd called ahead. I'll be driving into the city in about fifteen minutes and we could have met there."

Corelli smiled. "Then we wouldn't have seen your lovely house. Quite impressive."

He leaned toward them. "I gather you're here about Harry. I'm devastated by his death. We go back a long time. But I'm not sure how I can help you."

He seemed more nervous than devastated to Corelli. "You can start by telling us where you were between nine p.m. and five a.m. the night he was murdered."

"I came home directly after my show finished so I left the city around nine thirty and then I was at home the rest of the night. You can check with the night guard."

"We'll need his name and contact information. Which security company do you use?"

"Brandon Lester. He'll be able to tell you which guard was on duty and when." He opened his phone and read off a cell phone number.

Corelli keyed the number into her phone. "I understand you've been using guests on your program to attack Mr. Davenport. What happened between the two of you?"

He paled. "Nothing happened. We were still friends but I do a news show so I need to have balance. I can't favor friends."

Corelli gazed at him. "News? Really? I had the distinct impression that your show was somewhere between entertainment and...opinion."

He stood. "I really must go."

Corelli watched him fidget. The fact that she and Parker remained seated rather than obey his indirect request, seemed to confuse him. "And speaking of opinion, do you know Lena Wood and her husband, Walter?"

"Of course. I know all the key players in the white nat...the alt-right movement. And Lena is a very popular figure. Why?"

"We gather there was bad blood between them and Mr. Davenport. Can you think of any reason either of them might want to kill him?"

His eyes widened. He sat again. "You know, Harry could be an arrogant asshole so it's possible he alienated them but I can't think of any motive for murder unless he was..."

Corelli shifted forward. "Unless he was what?"

"Unless he threatened them in some way. Harry liked to control people so perhaps he had information that would hurt them politically or financially. But it would have to be something really bad to motivate them to murder him." Davis shrugged. "I have no idea what that could be."

"I understand you were also friends with Mr. Davenport's wife, Katharine. What is she like? What was their relationship like?"

"I envied Harry when he married Katharine. She was wonderful, deeply in love with him, and very supportive both emotionally and financially. I was on my own but I basked in the warmth of their friendship. We had many good times together. But Katharine didn't approve when Harry, then I, got involved with the alt-right. She stayed loyal and continued to play the happy wife but the marriage wasn't so great. I'm not sure what precipitated her leaving, but they've been battling through their lawyers for a while now. I've been surprised at the bitterness of the divorce. Katharine is wealthy in her own right so it's not about money." He put his hands out. "He changed so much from the man she married. Maybe she felt betrayed by him. But I can't see her murdering him because underneath it all, I think she still loves him." He stood again. "I really must go prepare for my show."

Corelli and Parker stood. They grabbed their coats and followed Davis to the door. Corelli stopped as if noticing the sleek green Jaguar parked next to their department-issued vehicle for the first time. "Nice car, Mr. Davis. Do you drive yourself back and forth to the city or does a limo pick you up?"

His eyes flicked to his car. "No limo for me. I prefer to use my own car."

"If I had that car, I'd drive myself too." Corelli strode over to the Jaguar, walked around looking at it from all angles and peering into the windows, before waving goodbye to Davis and sliding into the passenger side of their car. She jotted something down as Parker turned the key.

They traveled down the long, winding driveway leading to the country road that would take them to the highway, Parker glanced at Corelli. "What the hell was that? Since when are you all starry-eyed over a car that you certainly could afford if you wanted one?"

"Just checking to see whether he has E-ZPass and getting his plate number in case it's not registered in his name. He does have the toll pass, so we should be able to verify the time he left the city."

"Excellent. We might be interrupting her dinner preparations but put Lena Wood's address into the GPS. I want to see how this paragon of womanhood lives. Also, see if you can set up a meeting with Brandon Lester."

"All set for Wood." Corelli selected the number Davis had provided for his security firm. She frowned. "But I'll have to leave a message for Lester since he's not picking up."

A cigarette dangled from the lips of the tall, burly, unshaven, unsmiling man who filled the doorway at the Brooklyn home of Lena Wood. "Yeah?"

Parker took the lead. "NYPD Detectives Parker and Corelli to see Walter Foster and Lena Wood." They displayed their shields and ID. "Are you Walter Foster?"

He rubbed his beard. "Yeah."

"We'd like to talk to you and your wife."

"She's busy. What do you need to talk about?"

"We'll wait." Not anticipating an invitation, Parker stepped toward him. Though she half expected to be stopped by his bulk, her move seemed to surprise him and he reacted by stepping back. "Hey, you can't…"

She plowed ahead with Corelli right behind. "Where do you want us?"

It was clear he didn't want them at all. "The living room, I guess."

"Who is it, Walt?" a woman's voice from somewhere in the house called out.

"The police want to talk to us. Where should I bring them?"

"I'm in the kitchen."

They followed him down a hall through a very messy living room and into an even messier kitchen. Takeout containers, dirty coffee cups, half-filled glasses, and overflowing ashtrays sat on most of the available counter space and part of the table. The garbage can overflowed with takeout containers. The floor might have been eat-off-the-floor clean once, but not this month.

The blue-eyed, porcelain-skinned blonde at the table with a cigarette dangling from her mouth was a stark contrast to the squalid clutter surrounding her. Her hair was in a neat bun, her face lightly made up and she was wearing a high-necked, long-sleeve white dress with a lace collar and lace-trimmed cuffs. She was neat and clean and looked like a woman in a late nineteenth or early twentieth-century photograph. The perfect white nationalist wife and mother, although Parker didn't see or hear any signs of children.

"Lena, these are detectives, uh—"

"Detectives?" The woman sounded surprised. Parker assumed she hadn't heard her husband's response to her question about who was there.

"Yes, Parker and Corelli." Parker handed her a card. "We're here about the murder of Harrington Davenport."

Wood's skin pinked. Her gaze went to Walter who was standing just behind and to the side of Parker. She pushed a napkin off a plate and ground her cigarette out. "Yes, we heard about Harry. A terrible tragedy. Philippa must be devastated. But why do you want to speak to us?"

Parker knew from their research that Wood and Foster were from Idaho but since everyone they'd interviewed today had traces of West Virginia in their voices, she was surprised by Wood's softer accent.

Wood's gaze settled on Parker. She stared at her for a second as if really seeing her. "Oh, my, where are my manners. Please sit, detectives."

"No thanks, we won't be long." Judging by the rest of the kitchen, the chairs would probably be sticky and ruin her pants. Besides, having to look up at a black woman might make Wood uncomfortable physically and psychologically. Parker moved closer to the table. "How did you know Mr. Davenport?"

Wood tilted her head to see Parker's face rather than stare at her waist. "We were friends. Harry was an important figure in our…um, circle and we met often at meetings and gatherings. We also socialized some with him and Katharine before they split." She hesitated and then added, "Katharine is lovely but I hear their divorce has been nasty. Unfortunately, she doesn't understand the role of a good wife and she feels entitled to alimony and half his assets because she supported him while he was in school and getting started. My word, that's a wife's duty. She's so full of hate."

Parker had to repress her smile at the irony of this woman who represented a movement based on hate, accusing a woman who opposed the hateful beliefs of being full of hate. "You don't think a wife is entitled to share in the wealth accumulated during forty years of marriage?"

Wood sat up straighter. "I don't believe in divorce. I believe it's up to a wife to keep her husband happy so there's no need for divorce, and therefore, no need for alimony and division of assets."

Wow. Parker wanted to debate that statement on so many levels but it was irrelevant to why they were here. "We understand things haven't been so friendly between you and Mr. Davenport lately. Why?"

"I don't know where you heard that but it's absolutely not true. In fact we attended a meeting at his house last week. You can ask the others who were there. Right, Walt?"

Perfect. Parker was hoping to find out who attended the secret meetings Abel Clemson mentioned. "All right. Give us some names and we'll check it out."

Realizing what she'd done, Wood paled. "Well, I don't recall any last names, do you Walt?"

"I don't think anybody used last names."

Wood shot her husband a look that would wither most people but he just shrugged it off.

"Really? A clandestine meeting? Interesting." Corelli made a show of opening her notebook and clicking her pen, ready to write. "Give me the date and location. I'm sure the attendee list is in his meeting file along with the transcript of the meeting."

"Transcript?"

"Oh, yeah, he was meticulous about recording the meetings and then having them transcribed. We haven't had a chance to go through them yet but if you give me the date, I'm sure I'll be able to find it easily enough."

Corelli sounded so reassuring, Parker had to look away to keep from laughing. It occurred to her that Corelli was more fun to be around lately. Probably another benefit of her PTSD group.

"Do you remember, Walter?"

"Nah."

"There probably weren't too many meetings last week. I'll check." The click of Corelli's pen sounded loud in the tense silence of the kitchen. "But you have Detective Parker's card so you can call her if you remember the specifics."

Now that Corelli had given them a reprieve, the tension in the room dissipated and Parker moved on. "We know that Mr. Davenport kept files on many of his acquaintances as a way of controlling them and we've been told your names are included. What did he have on you?"

"Nothing." Lena's denial was too loud. "We have nothing to hide. What you see is what you get. I post a weekly video blog about the beauty of marriage, being a homemaker, motherhood and family."

Wood didn't seem to notice the discrepancy between extolling the role of the homemaker and the disaster that was her home. Parker wondered whether there were similar inconsistencies between her talk and her actions in the other qualities of a virtuous woman she spouted. "You mean marriage between whites, don't you?"

Wood lowered her head, not brave enough to look a black woman in the eye and defend her racist beliefs. "Yes, my vlog is targeted to white women and that's what I talk about."

"And how did your attempts to seduce Mr. Davenport fit into your picture of white marital bliss?"

"I never." Her lip curled. "You must have talked to that jealous bitch, Katharine."

Parker threw a little oil on the fire. "Katharine is beautiful, elegant and artistic. From what I've learned about Harrington Davenport, I doubt he'd settle for less. Competing with her for his attention would be difficult, I imagine."

Wood shot a venomous look at her. "I'm really surprised someone like you has such a good fantasy life." She pushed back from the table. "I have to prepare dinner for my family now so unless you're going to arrest us, I'd like you to leave. Please show them out, Walter. And don't answer any more questions."

Corelli was laughing as they drove away from the Wood/Foster household. "You really zinged her, Parker. And you made her angry enough to hit back and show her true colors at the end. I'll bet she could kill if she was angry enough."

CHAPTER TWENTY-THREE

They checked in with Dietz then spent an hour documenting and reviewing the interviews they'd completed that day. Parker yawned and stretched. "Even though we didn't get anything solid, we poked a few hornets' nests and I have a feeling something will shake out." She pushed her chair back. "You ready to go?"

As Parker fastened her seat belt she turned to Corelli. "Your apartment? Or do you have your PTSD group or yoga tonight?"

"My apartment, please. Brett instructed me to bring you home for dinner." Corelli's eyes twinkled. "But I thought we should have fish instead."

Parker stared at her, not quite getting that she was cracking a joke, then doubled over laughing. "Well," she said, drying her eyes, "I'm glad I have other plans tonight. I'm having dinner with Jessie and Annie."

"Great. Like most parents, Jess grumbles about not seeing you enough. How often do you go there?"

"Not as often as I should because, you know, this crazy boss of mine makes me work late every night when we're in the middle of a hot case. But about once a week recently." She glanced at Corelli. "Gloria has dinner with her family most nights and because she's not out to them or even considering coming out, I've never been invited. It brings up old feelings of not being seen. Annie and Jessie have always seen me and loved me for who I am, while encouraging me to be the best I can. Being with them reminds me I have my own family." Damn. That had just slipped out. And now she'd made herself vulnerable to Corelli again.

"I hear you." Corelli touched her arm. "Marnie wasn't out to her parents either and it bothered me too. Not just because I felt excluded but because I felt I had to hide who I am. She was okay being affectionate sometimes, like when we met Jessie and Annie at Hattie's Bar, but other than that, we had to be cool. It didn't feel good."

"How did you deal with it?"

"Occasionally, I pushed. Mostly I ignored it because I knew her parents were religious and would likely reject her when she told them. Then, after a couple of days in Afghanistan, she realized life is too short to let someone else decide how you live it. She promised she would talk to them about being a lesbian when we got home from the training mission. Two weeks later she was dead." Corelli turned her gaze to the passenger window. Parker couldn't see her face but she could hear her distressed breathing.

Parker assumed talking about it brought back the memory of seeing Marnie blown up by one of the Afghani policemen she was training, so she didn't intrude. But she was relieved Corelli had made herself vulnerable too. "Thanks for sharing your experience with Marnie. It helps to know I'm not the only one who has ever faced this situation."

Corelli turned and gazed at Parker. "Speaking of sharing. How are you dealing with the implied and voiced racism of these white nationalists? I'm kind of blindsided by the blatant bigotry. I can't imagine how you feel."

Parker froze. Her gaze drifted to the front window. The racism was fundamental to this investigation and if she didn't figure it out, it could skew her decision making. "Like any black person, I've encountered racism in my life but it's always been subtle. This is so in my face that on the one hand, I think I must be misinterpreting what they're saying. And on the other hand, as much as I'd like to say it doesn't bother me, I'm in a rage. I know it's childish but

I'm enjoying taking every opportunity to rub their faces in my superiority. I need your help to ensure I don't screw up because of it." Had she exposed too much?

Corelli touched Parker's shoulder. "You're handling the investigation fine. It's kind of nice to see another side of you. But I'm worried about you, your feelings and how much of this bullshit you internalize. You *are* superior to them, Parker. Your intellect and your education raise you above them. But even more important is your humanity, who you are and what you bring to the world. Talk to me. I can't change them but I'm with you one hundred percent." She took a deep breath and smiled. "If I haven't freaked you out talking about having you for dinner and then about death and racism, you're still welcome to come up and have dinner with me and Brett."

"I'm not freaked out. But I promised Annie, so I'll take a rain check." She drew her weapon and stepped out of the car. That was the agreement when they started working together, and unlike Corelli, Parker believed there were still police out there who would like to see Corelli dead for exposing the ring of dirty cops. "See you in the morning."

Parker scanned the area and watched Corelli enter the lobby and walk into the elevator. When the elevator door slid closed, she slipped her gun into the holster and got back into the car. She glanced in the rearview mirror as she turned onto the West Side Highway going north. A car turned with her and seemed to tail her. She kept her eye on it but when they merged onto the West Side Highway it fell back and she shook her head. "C'mon, P.J., you're getting paranoid." Her mind drifted back to the discussion with Corelli.

The food was good and the company enjoyable but the sense of being loved, of belonging, was even better. Parker slipped out of one warm embrace into another. Jessie and Annie weren't blood but they were her family and had been as long as she could remember. She couldn't imagine what her life would've been like if Jessie hadn't rescued her five-year-old self. She smiled thinking about the story he liked to tell of him as a new police officer in Harlem, seeing her little legs sticking out of a garbage can. She'd been stuck headfirst because she was looking for food. That was the beginning. Then Annie came along. If it wasn't for them she would have been left with her alcoholic, always drunk, grandmother, fending for herself on the streets. Her grandmother officially had custody but she lived with them. It wasn't until they tried to adopt her that they learned upcoming Harlem attorney Aloysius T. Parker was her uncle. He fought for legal custody and won. Jessie and Annie were granted limited visiting rights. Happily, it turned out her blood relative didn't really want her and as long as she did well in school she was free to stay with Jessie and Annie whenever she liked.

She kissed Annie's cheek. "I'll try to make it again next week. I love you both."

She took a few seconds on the front porch, inhaling the crisp March evening air, trying to hold on to the warmth of the visit. Coming here was always the right thing. She pulled her keys out of her coat pocket and headed to her car at the curb. But before she could click the remote to open the car doors, something hit her hard from the side, throwing her down on the ground. She was yanked up, punched in the stomach, then in the face. She gasped for air.

"Uppity black bitch."

There were two of them, heavily muscled bruisers with masks. *Bastards.* She grabbed a fist coming at her, pushed away the arm it was attached to and not realizing she was still grasping her keys, swung her fist.

"Fuck. The bitch stabbed me." He stumbled away.

Taking advantage of the distraction, she kicked the knee of the other man standing there. He swore as he went down. She unbuttoned her coat but before she could draw her Glock, an arm wrapped around her neck from behind and jerked her off her feet. *Fuck.* He was huge and her feet were dangling. She kicked back but couldn't seem to connect. She grabbed his arm with both hands, trying to free her neck to breathe but he easily pulled her right arm down between them. *Go for his eyes.* She raised her left arm, trying to scratch his eyes but he tipped his head back and her nails scraped his face and neck.

As he slowly cut off her air, he pulled her right arm up. The pain was unbearable. She tried to scream but no sound came out. She heard a snap. She was losing consciousness. She was going to die but she'd leave evidence. She let go of the arm around her neck and with the last bit of energy she could muster, forced her left arm up again and reached for his eyes. He cursed as she dug her nails in as deep as she could. She felt a jolt, as if a car had hit her. Everything went black.

Strong arms embraced her. Annie's voice begged God to let her baby live. Gasping for air, she opened her eyes. Everything was blurry. She tried to smile but her face didn't respond. "Officer down, officer down." Jessie's voice. He must have saved her. Sirens and voices. Annie stroking her hair was soothing, comforting. She tried to stay awake. "We got one of them but the other two got away." Jessie. Probably talking to officers from the precinct. She heard scraps of conversation. "Big. Almost as big as me. White. Blood."

"She's got blood on her hand and her clothes but I can't see where she's hurt." Annie was crying.

"I don't think it's hers. Detective, Detective Parker." The voice was insistent. She opened her eyes. An EMT. She looked familiar. "How are you feeling?"

She opened her mouth and forced out a sound. "Fine." Her throat hurt like hell and the word didn't sound right.

"Fine?" The EMT laughed. "You cops are all alike. I'll bet you feel like shit. I'm going to put an oxygen mask on you and start an IV and then we're going to splint this arm." The two EMTs moved quickly. She closed her eyes, felt the mask being put on and sucked in the air. She opened her eyes. The IV bag was hanging above her. "I'm going to splint you now. Sorry. It's going to hurt." Pain shot through her body as the EMT straightened her arm and quickly fastened the splint. "Sorry, Parker, but it would have hurt more being loose in the ambulance. Chiara will kill me if I don't take good care of you."

"Here's the gurney, Allegra."

The fog cleared a little. Right. Corelli's friends Julia and Allegra, EMTs who'd helped with the kids on the child trafficking case. "Allegra?"

"Ah, good you remember me. What can I do for you?"

"Fingernails. Scratched his face."

"I'll bag them. Are you riding to the hospital with us, ma'am?"

"Damn right. No way my baby is going anywhere without me."

half-sister, rushed in. Brett, Annie and Jessie followed a few minutes later. Thoughts of Gloria were pushed away by the love filling the room.

A half hour later, Brett stood. "You know folks, P.J. has had a tough twenty hours so why don't we let her rest? And you two"— she looked at Jessie and Annie—"have been here all night and should get some sleep."

As they shuffled out, Parker lowered the bed and lay back with a sigh. The next time she opened her eyes Corelli was sitting next to her. "Please thank Brett for getting everyone out of here. I love them all but I am exhausted."

"That's to be expected after the beating you took. And the surgery."

After a few minutes of silence, Parker decided to ask the question that had been on her mind for a while. If Corelli got mad she would blame it on the drugs. She cleared her throat. "Is it my imagination or have you been different lately?"

Corelli put her phone in her pocket and gazed at Parker as if deciding how much to say. "It's not your imagination. I have changed. The PTSD group and the occasional private session with Dr. Magarelli have helped me work through some of my issues. Although I'll never forget the horror of seeing Marnie blown up, talking about it with my group of women war vets has helped ease the guilt. I'm sleeping better, or should I say, sleeping more than two or three hours a night, and I feel more at peace. The nightmares and the anger are happening less frequently. I'm more myself, more relaxed and happy, like before we went to Afghanistan. Without the anger, my feelings are accessible and it's easier for me to express them." Corelli smiled, something that was happening more and more frequently. "I hope I'm a better partner."

She must have dozed again because when she opened her eyes Corelli was gone. In the semisilence of the hospital, Parker's thoughts wandered to her feelings about what Corelli had shared and her own feelings about their partnership. The short burst of voices in the hallway pulled her away from the personal. Which officers did Jessie trust enough to have stand guard at her door overnight? Was she going to be off the case now, stuck at home until her arm healed? Why had she been attacked? Who had ordered it?

She was dozing again when Corelli whispered her name. Parker opened her eyes and glanced at the wall clock. It was near eleven p.m. Corelli had been here almost twenty-four hours. "Sorry to wake you but I thought you might like an update on the guy we have in custody. He made his call but he's still not talking. It looks like we'll have to file charges for him to grasp the seriousness of his situation. I've asked ADA Brooks to take a run at him tomorrow. Also, I forgot to tell you, Gianna has called every couple of hours to check on you. She sends her love but with the three little ones at home, she doesn't think she'll be able to visit. Amari and Kelly called and asked that I let you know they're thinking of you. And Darla and Bear stopped by for a while earlier today. They send their regards."

"Gianna sent flowers." Parker pointed to several large colorful bouquets on the floor near the window. "And so did Amari. You missed the excitement earlier when her flowers arrived and the nurses realized Amari DeAndre, the famous singer, is a friend of mine. I'm going to have to ask her to sign some CDs so I can give them to the staff to thank them for the good care I'm getting."

"Our not so famous old friend, Ben Fine, Assistant Director in charge of the New York FBI Office was here to see how you're doing. Jessie told him we think white nationalists are behind your attack and Fine asked if we want FBI help with the case. I told him to talk to you."

Parker appreciated that Corelli had truly handed over the lead on the case. Except for her slip in the Bushwick apartment, she'd stepped back and let Parker direct the investigation. She pressed the bed control and sat up. "I should have expected that."

"Well, I guess it got lost somewhere between finding the body and almost being beaten to death. We're dealing with white nationalists who we know can be violent, but we have no proof that it was them and not just a random attack. It's up to you whether or not to bring the Feebies in. Maybe rather than bringing them in as partners, we can get them to share what they know about these people."

"That's a great idea. Do you think the brass will let me work the case?"

"Captain Winfry was here overnight when you were in the recovery room and I got him to agree that once the doctors say it's okay, you and your monstrosity of a cast can come back. He'll call it limited duty but there's no reason you and I can't continue to work the case like we've been. But you'll have to lug that cast and foam thing around and you'll have to put up with my driving. I suggest you evaluate the risks and decide."

The dread Parker was feeling eased. She should have known Corelli would understand her need to keep working the case. "Hmm, on the job with you driving or stay home?" She pretended to think about it. "It's a difficult decision but I'll risk letting you drive."

"Good choice. Have the doctors said when you'll be able to go home?"

"The surgeon is releasing me some time tomorrow. I'm supposed to take it easy for a couple of days, and then as long as I'm just *detecting*, her word, not mine, I should be able to return to the job. Annie is adamant that I move in with her and Jessie so she can help me shower, dress, cut my food and do anything that requires two hands. I hate to admit it but she's right, so I'll go there from here. You'll need to pick me up but other than driving and writing, I can handle almost anything around the job. Except I'll no longer be able to protect you."

Corelli grinned. "You know I don't consider that a problem, right?"

"I'm well aware but it's my job. Or it was. If someone comes after you, I'll be helpless to stop them."

"Don't fret. Winfry and Jessie decided we both need to be guarded so Winfry is putting two guys in an unmarked car on us whenever we leave the office. So now you'll know how it feels to be babysat."

Parker was relieved. "I know you hate it but I feel better knowing you're being protected."

"Speaking of protecting. Did your attackers give you any clue as to why they were beating you up?"

"Not that I remember." Parker closed her eyes, picturing the scene. "Wait. One of them called me an uppity black bitch but that was it. The one in custody is the one with the broken knee. What about the one I wounded?"

Corelli leaned forward. "The one with the bloody nose?"

"I think it was more than that. I had the car keys in my hand and when I punched him in the face, he screamed that I stabbed him. I assume the key punctured his cheek or maybe his eye. Sorry I didn't mention it sooner."

Corelli laughed. "Sure. I can see you sitting up on the operating table saying, 'Stop the surgery. We need to check emergency rooms.'" She stood. "It's getting late so I'm going home but I'll get something out to hospitals in the city tonight. If it's not too serious he may try to fix it himself, but maybe he'll need a doctor. By the way, they did get skin from under your nails and it was sent to the lab. When we find the guy, we can do a DNA comparison."

Corelli walked to the window and peered out. "The press is still out there and they're clamoring for information. If we don't feed them, they'll camp outside Jessie's house. Are you all right being seen on camera or would you rather I do a brief press conference tomorrow with Jessie or Winfry? If I do it, I'll go over your injuries and the surgery but stress that you'll be back on the job in a couple of days. What do you think?"

The last thing Parker wanted was to stand in front of gaggle of reporters and photographers with her face looking like a battered old basketball, trying to pretend her arm wasn't in a humongous cast and she didn't need this foam thing to lug it around. But she worried about Corelli dealing with the flashing lights without her there. "Maybe Winfry should do it so you don't chance a flashback without me there."

She braced for a nasty retort but instead, Corelli nodded. "I hadn't thought about that. Winfry and Jessie can do it. And I'll sneak you out the rear entrance while they're in front of the cameras."

CHAPTER TWENTY-FOUR

After being fussed over for two and a half days, Parker was more than ready when Corelli came to pick her up. Annie helped her ease into the passenger seat then gave Corelli a list of things she needed to do to take care of her. At the stop sign, Corelli glanced at the large wedge of blue foam that encased Parker's hand-to-shoulder cast. "I didn't realize they'd send you home with that foam thing. It looks like a pain in the ass."

Parker sighed. "It is. But you know what? Given that my arm is bent at the elbow in a shoulder-to-fingers cast and the doctor wants me to keep it elevated to prevent swelling, it's even more of a pain in the ass to move if it's not resting on the foam cushion. You should try sleeping with it."

"I'd rather sleep with Brett, thank you."

"Smart ass." Parker liked it when Corelli teased her. "To tell you the truth, given a choice, I'd rather sleep with Brett."

"Ooh, I'm going tell Brett you said that."

"Go on, she'll have a good laugh." Parker was sure Brett wouldn't be offended. "Thanks for keeping me updated on the investigation. It makes reentry easier." Her good hand went to her face. Her eye was open and the bandage was off but now the swelling and bruising were visible. "I wish I didn't look so horrible. Everyone will assume I'm worse than I am."

"Don't worry about the team. They'll ooh and aah but they're professionals. Just don't moan too much and it'll be fine."

"I'll try to control myself but feel free to kick me if I dive into self-pity."

"Right. Then you tell Annie I kicked you and I'll end up with my own cast and foam cushion." Corelli glanced at Parker. "How are you feeling mentally and emotionally? Don't tell me fine. I've been there. Being attacked and injured like that leaves you feeling vulnerable. At least that's how it left me. Even you, Ms. ADA, police hero, can't walk away from three brutes beating and trying to kill you without some lingering emotional pain."

Parker's jaw stiffened. Showing weakness was an invitation and she'd learned early on, primarily in dealing with her uncle and the mean girls at school, never to flinch or back down. She didn't know what to make of all this sharing of feeling she and Corelli were doing, but Corelli was right. She was feeling shaky. "I've been anxious. I keep asking Jessie whether the doors and windows are locked. And I'm having nightmares."

"As I thought. Those feelings are natural after an attack like that."

"Jessie said that exact thing."

"But if they continue, you might want to zip in to see Gil Gilardi. Our lovely department psychologist could help you work through it."

"Ha. You didn't think she was so lovely when you had to see her after being shot. But tell me what happened to you? Did you see a psychotherapist about it?"

"Nope. And it was a huge mistake." Corelli kept her eyes on the road. She took so long to answer that Parker was sure she'd said all she was going to about whatever incident she was referring to. And then she took a deep breath. "A couple of days after Marnie and I got to Afghanistan, two American soldiers dragged me behind a building, intent on raping me. I fought them but they were big and I was tiring. Luckily Marnie came looking for me and heard the scuffle. She pulled them off me and screamed for the MPs. But they got away. Their faces were covered so we couldn't identify them. They'd beaten me badly and I spent two days in the base hospital. The attempted rape left me with PTSD and for a long time every man on the base felt like a threat. Marnie was helping me work through it but ten days later she was killed. Seeing her blown up magnified my anxiety and anger and hopelessness. And even though I was somewhat better by the time I came home, being undercover stoked the PTSD fire."

"I'm sorry. I didn't know."

"How could you know? Other than Brett, you're the first person outside of my PTSD group I've ever told. Don't make the same mistake I made, Parker. Pay attention to your feelings and do something if the anxiety continues. I'll be watching."

"Oh, great." She smiled, wanting Corelli to know she appreciated her concern. And her sharing. "What's happening this morning?"

Corelli hesitated, then went with the change of subject. "You need to see the captain so he can give you the 'you're on limited duty' speech. And I figured you'd want to check in with the team. After that I suggest we drop in on Michele Benson. Maybe she can give us some background on the guys who attacked you."

"You found the other two guys?"

"The one who broke your arm and tried to strangle you is still out there but we got the one you clobbered. An emergency room doctor at Bellevue Hospital saw the notice I put out and called. You hit him so hard the key punctured his cheek and he had to go to the emergency room for surgery to repair his face. The ass used his real name at the hospital but I recognized him even with his bandages. He's one of the faux-guards we met outside of Philippa's house, Everet Collins. I was thinking Benson might be able tell us more about Lester's group and maybe help us figure out whether he or Philippa sent them after you."

"Why talk to Benson? Why not Lester? Why not Philippa Harrington Davenport? She's the one funding these thugs."

Corelli studied Parker. "A couple of reasons. First, we haven't found Lester. Second, our goal is to identify the killer and I think Benson is more likely to help us with that. Third, even if Philippa didn't order the attack, I doubt she'll do anything to help bring down the person who did. Fourth, it's your first day back after the attack and I expect you're anxious and emotionally fragile, not the best place to be when dealing with Philippa's blatant racism. Losing your temper and accusing her of something we can't prove won't help us figure out who attacked you and why. Or solve our murders."

Parker knew Corelli was right. She really wanted to shove this cast and the foam in Philippa's face and get her to admit she'd ordered it, but Philippa would stonewall. "Okay."

Corelli looked pleased. "I planned to go up to Davenport's office after we talked to Benson, but Greene wrapped up the search."

"Did the Special Master work with them?"

"Greene let him know we didn't plan to look at Davenport's client files so he reviewed what they removed to be sure it wasn't client related and said to call him if we changed our minds."

"What about the office server that Rich downloaded?"

Corelli smirked. "If we stumble on the information by accident, I don't see how we can be held responsible for reading it. But Rich provided more than enough other information to read so I figure we'll just skip the client data unless we find a reason to examine it."

"It sounds like you've taken care of it all." *The team really doesn't need me.*

"Nah. Everything was already set in motion so I just kept the team moving on their tasks. But I've actually been spending most of my time trying to track your attackers and figure out how they fit into the picture."

Parker realized her insecurities were showing. "Thanks, it'll be easy to slip back in unless you're planning to fight me to keep the position of lead?"

"No way." Corelli patted Parker's cast. "You'll bop me on the head with this monstrosity and I'll have a traumatic brain injury. No dueling for me. It's all yours."

"Just so you don't think I've been a lazy bum, I did work on the case between naps. I ended up with a lot of questions."

Corelli glanced at her. "Care to share?"

"Magnolia Walker was murdered after talking to Davenport. Rich was murdered after talking to her, doing his own research and then talking to Davenport. The way they were beaten, had their arms broken and died from being strangled from behind, indicates the same killer. So how does Walker fit with Rich being killed by one of his victims?" When Corelli didn't answer Parker continued.

"Davenport was shot. How do the murders of Walker and Rich relate to Davenport's murder? And it seems that the person who killed Rich and Walker came after me. But why? Because I'm a black female detective in a position of relative power dealing with people who hate people like me? I probably offended some of Harrington Davenport's white nationalist friends when we interviewed them. But did hinting to Philippa Davenport that I knew what Rich and Walker knew about the Harrington family spur her to action?"

"All good questions," Corelli grunted as she turned into the lot at the station house.

"Look at that, we made it to the station and you didn't kill us." Parker made a joke to cover her discomfort at needing help getting out of the car.

Corelli opened the passenger door. "Okay, tell me how to help you."

Parker took a breath. She knew Corelli wouldn't make a big deal out of this so she needed to forget her pride or freeze her ass off in the car. "I'm going to hand you the foam with my arm on it. You just hold it and move with me as I swivel and put my feet on the ground. Once I stand, I'll take it."

"Got it."

Corelli followed her instructions and in a few seconds Parker was standing in the parking lot cradling her arm. Corelli held the station house door open for Parker. She was glad they weren't going upstairs to the squad because she wasn't sure she could manage on the narrow stairway. Greetings flew at her from every direction as they walked back to the conference room. Had Corelli warned people not to tease? Probably, because there were no jokes about the cast and the foam.

The team cheered when they entered, then gathered to greet her. Corelli helped her take off her coat. Everyone seemed happy to have her back. Maynard didn't get close but smiled shyly when she caught Parker's eye. *What's with that? Am I more aware or am I giving off some kind of sex pheromone?*

"All right, guys, this monstrosity is awkward and kind of tiring and I have to see Captain Winfry before we have a team meeting." Parker surprised herself by being honest. She turned to leave and Corelli followed even though it wasn't necessary for her to be in the meeting. Parker's first instinct was to object but then she realized Corelli was looking out for her.

Corelli had called it. The captain gave her the "limited duty" speech, mentioned that two detectives in an unmarked car would follow and protect them whenever they were out of the office, then told Corelli to keep Parker safe and dismissed them. Parker bristled at the idea that she couldn't take care of herself, but the awkwardness of the arm she was carrying on a cushion, as if it was the Queen's crown, reminded her of her helplessness. She felt a pang of sympathy for Corelli and understood in a visceral way why she resisted being seen as needing a bodyguard.

Corelli discreetly put her hand under the foam, taking some of the weight, to make it easier for Parker to lower herself into a chair at the table where the team was already assembled. "Thank you, Corelli, this thing is a bitch."

She looked around the table. She didn't think anyone noticed the assist because they were all avoiding looking at her arm. Maybe it was time to address the elephant in the room. She could see she would need help and Corelli might not always be around. "This unusual cast"—she lifted it slightly—"is necessary because of the nature of the two breaks, one disconnected my hand from my arm and the other snapped my forearm. They put in two plates and twenty screws to fix them. I need to keep the arm elevated to prevent swelling and this foam monstrosity makes that a little easier. But it's like carrying a fifty-pound bag of potatoes with one arm so it's awkward and tiring. Don't be surprised if I ask you to hold my arm when I sit or stand."

The laughter seemed to ease the tension, but Parker could see the hundred questions on their faces. She was pleased that Watkins took the lead. "So, boss, how did the attack go down?"

They listened attentively as Parker described what she remembered of the attack. After answering a few questions, she asked Corelli to update them on the status of the two men in custody. "So far, neither is giving up who and why, but we know they're white nationalists involved with a group affiliated with the Davenports. Parker was able to break the knee of one and rip a hole in the face of the other so both needed surgery. ADA Natalie Brooks will question them once their surgeons clear them. The bad news is that the one who broke Parker's arm and tried to strangle her is still out there. We know he's tall and husky, and white like the other two, but that's it. The good news is that despite being battered, bruised and strangled and despite the pain from having her arm broken, Parker managed to scratch her assailant and then tell the EMT to check her fingernails for DNA. So when we find him we have proof."

Parker wanted to make it clear she was back so she immediately took charge. "All right, we're ten days into this investigation and I've missed the last four, so how about you bring me up-to-date on what you're working on. Do you have anything, Dietz?"

"The tape from Katharine Davenport's hallway shows her leaving her apartment at 10:19 and returning just before 11:45 p.m. Want her picked up?"

Parker glanced at the clock. "Bring her in late this afternoon."

Dietz started to stand.

Corelli put a hand up to stop him. "We have a full plate today. Why not have her brought in tomorrow?"

Parker realized once again that Corelli was taking care of her by putting limits on what she attempted to do on her first day back. "Right. Tomorrow morning then, Dietz."

The knock on the conference room door was unusual and all eyes went there.

Watkins jumped up and opened it. He immediately stepped back. Louden Warfield III entered. Parker glanced at Corelli but she looked surprised too. Warfield, the criminal defense attorney feared by police testifying and prosecutors opposing him, had no reason to be here since they had no one in custody. She hoped he wasn't going to defend her attackers.

Wearing his characteristic navy suit with a blue shirt the color of his eyes and red suspenders he strode to the table and took Watkins's seat. "Detective Parker, sorry for interrupting, but may I have a private word with you and Detective Corelli?"

"Yes, of course." Parker looked at the team. "Give us a few minutes, please."

When they were alone, Warfield, or Deni as he'd asked them to call him, leaned in close. "I was angry to hear about the attack. I came by to see for myself that you are doing okay and to let you know that if either of you decide to kill or seriously injure the bastards when you find them, I will represent you in any legal proceedings, gratis."

Parker grinned. "Thanks, Deni. As you can see, I'm encumbered but I'm alive and well. And though it's not the plan, if either of us lose control when we get them, I assure you we will definitely take advantage of your generous offer."

He grinned, patted her good hand and stood. "Take care of her, Corelli." He strode out.

As the door closed behind him, Corelli laughed. "Since the cop-killing lawyer is willing to come over to what he considers the dark side should we commit murder, it might be worth murdering them just to turn him."

The team streamed back in. Parker could see they were all curious about Warfield showing up here but if he wanted to make it public he wouldn't have asked for privacy. "Okay, folks, let's get started. Ready, Watkins?"

"Sure." Watkins glanced at the black leather notebook open in front of him. "We're still going through Rich's blackmail files. But truthfully, I doubt one of his victims killed him. Most of them have been paying him off for years for things like affairs or other nonviolent offenses. Even the crimes of the four we're charging are nonviolent, things like paying off city inspectors, taking bribes, pimping, and embezzling from partners."

Parker was glad Watkins had come to the same conclusion she had. "Great minds. I've been thinking the same. Rich was cautious. His victims didn't know his name or what he looked like. Also, his blackmail victims certainly had no reason to kill Magnolia Walker or to attack me and it's clear the same man who murdered Walker and Rich was the one who attacked me. Dietz, please talk to Captain Winfry about which unit should handle the blackmail investigation and turn over everything we have. We need to focus on the murders and the alleged threat to democracy." Obviously relieved to get rid of the drudgery of the blackmail cases, Watkins looked like he'd just hit the lottery.

"Anybody have anything else?"

"Yeah," Dietz spoke. "We're getting information back from our queries about the other murder victims in the Davenport family. Should I hold it until we get reports on all the deaths or give it to someone now?"

"Some of them were shot, right?" Forlini asked. "Were the bullets tested?"

Dietz ran his finger down the list in front of him. "Yeah, it looks like most, maybe all, were shot but you'd have to look at the reports they sent to see whether they found and tested the bullets."

Forlini turned to Parker. "It's really odd that so many people in one family, even a kooky family, were murdered. I think we should get whatever ballistics tests were done and request they be done on any others if shells are available. It's crazy but maybe it's one killer, one gun."

Parker tried to move back from the table to shift the position of her cushion and Corelli was immediately behind her helping her slide back. "Thanks. Okay, Forlini work with Dietz on getting this done. And you and Kim review the reports."

Kim put her hand up. "I met with Jen Wiley from New York One about the rumors she mentioned during your press conference the other day. She couldn't give me anything or anyone specific, but she mentioned picking up slogans like 'white is right, white is might' and words like 'army,' 'attack,' 'take over.' I agree with her gut feeling that something violent is being planned."

"That fits with Rich's belief about a threat to our democracy and with the rumors Benson mentioned. We'll press Benson on the rumors." Parker looked around the table. "Maynard?"

"We've searched Davenport's home computer and printed copies of all his emails for the last twelve months." She pointed to a huge pile of paper on the table. "We can go back farther if you need them. We've also spent a lot of time diving into the deep web on Rich's computer using his alias, Ellis Hyde. We've found a lot of chatter about TAB and TBA but we don't know what they mean. There are also ongoing discussions about whether Davenport's death will be a problem, who's in charge, weapons, dress, communicating and figuring out assembly points, which could relate to those rumors."

"Thanks, Maynard, keep digging." Not wanting to make eye contact with Maynard and encourage her, Parker turned to Greene. "What about you, Greene?"

"We've examined everything we took from Davenport's office and his safe. These"—she slid a stack of folders to Corelli—"appear to be the files he kept on his associates. Other than that, we haven't found anything that seems pertinent."

"Good work, team." Parker took a breath. She hadn't expected to tire so quickly. "All right. Maynard, if Davenport had separate folders for client and personal emails in the file that Rich downloaded from Davenport's office server, print out the personal emails. If they're lumped together don't bother."

Maynard hesitated a second. "Sure. I'll have one of the guys check it later."

Parker turned back to Greene. "Continue going through what you have, then dig through Davenport's emails. Watkins, Forlini and Kim can assist as time permits. Corelli and I will review Davenport's files on his associates. Watkins and Kim, I'd like you to take a shot at interrogating my two attackers when they're alert. Thanks, everyone."

When they were alone at the table Corelli spoke softly to Parker. "I see you're fading. Your body is telling you to slow down. Would you consider going back to my apartment for a nap? I can take the files and whatever else we might need to start a review, and we can work there for a while. After we see Benson, I'll drive you to Annie and Jessie's house."

Parker opened her mouth to issue a denial but her droopy eyes convinced her Corelli was right. "A half hour, an hour tops, then you have to wake me."

"Just let me gather what we need. Davenport's files, Walker's research, Rich's charts repeating Walker's research, Rich's emails and a couple of files on white nationalists." She piled everything into a box. "Anything else?"

"Not that I can think of." Parker yawned.

As they put on their coats, Forlini approached. "How about I carry the box out to the car, Corelli, so you can assist Parker with her, er, arm."

CHAPTER TWENTY-FIVE

The kittens were nowhere to be seen so Corelli assumed they were asleep on her bed downstairs. She took Parker's coat and helped her lie down on a sofa with her arm and foam resting on a hassock next to it. Within two minutes she was dozing.

Corelli curled up on the sofa she and Brett usually sat on to work after dinner and started reading through the stack of Rich's emails. The kittens arrived shortly after and started their usual rub, purr, and knead routine. She scratched their heads and they snuggled together on her lap.

"Hey, how long did I sleep?"

Corelli checked her phone. "Almost an hour. Need some help?"

"I think I do."

Corelli lifted Parker's arm and she sat up. "I think the table is the right height for you to comfortably rest your arm and put whatever you're reading in front of you."

"Sounds good." With a little help from Corelli, Parker stood and settled at the table. "So how far did you get while I napped?"

"I went through Rich's emails but nothing jumped out at me. I thought we'd start with the documents that Walker gave Rich.

Maybe do an hour or so and then head up to talk to Michele Benson?"

"Walker's research seems to be the beginning, doesn't it?"

They stepped through Walker's genealogical research and Rich's verification of her work, then reviewed Walker's notes. Parker jotted a couple of things on the pad in front of her, trying to get her thoughts in order. Though she was using her left hand and the notes weren't legible, the process helped her focus. "Walker's research turned up a mutual black ancestor in the Harrington and Walker families and both Walker and Rich noted they'd called Harrington Davenport. We've been assuming that meant the son but his office had no record of him speaking to either. Do you remember what Philippa's niece Heather said when she opened the door and saw me standing there? 'You again? Go away.' She seemed shaken. My guess is that she doesn't really see black people, that we all look alike to her and for a moment she thought I was Walker coming back." Parker gave Corelli a few seconds to think about that. "What if both Walker and Rich contacted Philippa, not her son?"

"Interesting. I hadn't picked up on Heather's thinking she recognized you. And it makes perfect sense. Walker was only interested in the family connection, so of course, she would have gone directly to Philippa. And either Walker told Rich when they met or he made the same logical assumption. You're saying Heather recognized Walker? So it's likely Philippa ordered the murders of the two of them."

"Heather looked like she'd seen a ghost." Parker gazed out the window. "Acknowledging even one drop of black blood would destroy Philippa's life, everything she's built. It's the last thing she would want out there in the white nationalist hate sphere. So I do think she ordered the murders. And the attack on me." She met Corelli's gaze. "Proving it might be difficult, though. She obviously didn't kill them herself."

"Philippa would only use trusted resources for murder. Would it break your heart if Michele Benson is involved, Parker?"

"Sure. But I'll live. Benson has ex-military loyal to her on her payroll, and I would guess some are also white nationalists who might do whatever is necessary to advance the cause. I can see her ordering the murders." Parker wrote a reasonable facsimile of

'Benson,' underlined it a couple of times, then tapped her pencil on the paper. "Yet, I can't. And it has nothing to do with how attractive she is. It has to do with my gut. Let's tread carefully when we meet with her later."

Corelli jumped up. "I'm going to make us some lunch. I'm thinking mozzarella and prosciutto sandwiches with tomato, fresh basil, vinegar and olive oil. Is that okay? If I cut yours into small pieces will you be able to manage?"

"Sounds delicious. Yes, I can manage with my left hand. Are you serving coffee with it?"

"But of course." Corelli set up the coffee then pulled the sandwich fixings out of the refrigerator. She warmed some rolls, made the sandwiches, cut one for Parker then served them both coffee and sat across the table.

"I'm seeing new sides of you, as an actress, now as a chef." Parker took a bite. "Yum. I'm not sure how much endurance I'll have today so let's start on Davenport's files while we eat, then head out to see Benson."

"That reminds me, I've been meaning to tell you. I've been trying to get in touch with Brandon Lester, originally to discuss the guards at Meriwether Davis's house but now about the two men who attacked you. He isn't answering his cell. I've called Davis and Philippa but they claim they don't know where he is."

Corelli opened the first file in the pile. She frowned and placed a sheet of paper in front of Parker. "Why do you suppose Davenport had this with his private files?" They both stared at the short list.

> TBA
> * Statue of Liberty
> * Museum of Jewish Heritage
> * Ellis Island
> * African Burial Ground National Monument

Parker put her coffee down. "Except for the fact that there's nothing dedicated to women, these places represent everything white nationalists hate. Maynard mentioned seeing TBA and TAB in the chatter on the hidden white nationalist websites. If they're planning violence, maybe this is the hit list."

"I'm thinking the FBI must have some insight into what's going on in these groups. Are you up to meeting with FBI Director Ben Fine today?"

"I hate to admit it, but I think I'll need to go to Annie and Jessie's place after we meet with Benson." Parker picked up another piece of her sandwich.

Corelli looked thoughtful. "Since Jessie and Fine are old friends, we could ask Fine to meet us there this evening after you've had time to rest. I can either work on the files there or leave and come back later, whichever seems better to you."

"The hour nap earlier seemed to work so if you're willing to stay we can discuss what you get through while I nap and then work on the rest together."

Corelli doffed an imaginary hat. "Yes, ma'am, I'd be happy to stay."

Parker smiled. "While you call Fine, I'll call Annie to tell her you'll be staying for dinner and to let her know Ben Fine is coming later as well."

Calls made, they finished lunch and got back to work. "Okay. Here's the file on Meriwether Davis." Corelli moved to sit to the left of Parker so they could look at the documents together.

Parker paged through the documents and photos. "Davenport's file goes back more than thirty years. He describes five accusations of rape against Davis, seven encounters with prostitutes, and five cases of threatening witnesses. According to Davenport's notes, he squashed every single one of these charges and Davis kept his law license. That's disgusting."

"Disgusting is right. And look at this list of payments Davis receives from prominent white nationalist millionaires to speak lies to his viewers. Interesting that Harry Davenport cut off his payments but Philippa continues to pay him." Corelli pushed the pages and photos into the folder and threw it in the box. "I need a break. Ready to go see your girlfriend, Michele?"

"Give it up, Corelli." Parker attempted to stand. "Benson may find me attractive, but I doubt she'd choose to be seen in public with me. I don't need another girlfriend who has that problem."

Corelli helped Parker lift her arm and get to her feet. "I didn't realize Ndep was like that."

"She was fine in the beginning when we were mostly at home or with my family and you and Brett, but once I was back on an even keel and wanted to go out to dinner or to a club to dance, she started to back off. The fact that she's texted me a couple of times since I was in the hospital but has made no attempt to see me is pretty telling, don't you think?"

Michele Benson looked up from her computer as Parker and Corelli were ushered into her office. Her eyes widened and she jumped up. "What the fuck happened, Detective Parker?"

Benson made a beeline for Parker but Corelli intercepted, took Parker's arm and eased her into the chair. Benson took the hint and returned to the chair behind her desk.

Parker took the lead. "You didn't know? I thought you white nationalists had a high-speed grapevine. Besides it was all over the news. At least the real news stations."

Benson looked down at her desk. Parker couldn't tell whether she was framing her response or controlling her anger. "Many of my clients lean that way but despite what you think, I'm not tuned in to the white nationalist network. And lately the news has been too exhausting to watch so I've been skipping it." She stared at Parker. "Are you saying it was white nationalists who did that to your face and your arm?"

"I am. And I was hoping you might be able to help us understand their affiliations."

"You caught them?"

Corelli jumped in. "Two of the three are in custody because Detective Parker incapacitated them. We know for sure one of them is part of Lester's group and we assume the other one is as well. The third one got away. Would you be willing to look at their pictures?" Corelli stood with her iPhone ready.

"Of course."

Corelli moved around the desk and brought the first picture up. "He looks familiar but with that bandage covering half his face it's hard to tell."

"That's Everet Collins." Corelli switched to the next picture. Benson's breathing sped up and she pushed back from the desk. "I believe his name is Andy Topping. He's one of Philippa's unofficial guards, one of the ones outside her house. They're all members of her group, OurAmerica, and she must be paying them because as far as I know, they don't have any other jobs."

"What is OurAmerica?" Parker knew but wanted to hear Benson's description.

"Philippa's husband, Wilfred Davenport, grew up a staunch white nationalist in a wealthy family whose history was interwoven with the eugenics movement. In his thirties he formed OurAmerica, a group for white men who felt their birthright was being eroded by the progress of blacks, women and other minorities. Their goal was, and is, to take over the country and turn back the clock. Stop me if you know this."

Parker waved her on.

"Wilfred married Philippa when he was thirty-six. She had just turned sixteen. She adored him and wanted to be part of OurAmerica but she was shut out because of her sex. Wilfred introduced her to Nazism and after several years of being the ideal white wife, producing six perfect white children, she formed her own group, FolkWomen. Then when she was in her mid-thirties and Wilfred was in his mid-fifties, he started showing signs of early onset dementia, a mental condition that would be anathema to the eugenicists and others who believe in the superior white race. Other than an occasional picture with the family, she managed to keep him out of the public eye but pretended he was still in charge. She has run OurAmerica for years, though not all the members or members of other white nationalist groups know, and many would balk at a woman leader. Though he never spoke about it directly, Harry let people in the movement assume he was running the group. He was the ideal front for Philippa because he really had no interest in doing the work. He only wanted the adoration and the glory. I'm not sure what she'll do now that he's dead."

"You know a lot about them."

"I believe I told you, my family is close with the Davenports, and Philippa and Harry have been fixtures in my life since I was born."

Parker considered how much to tell Benson. She was being forthcoming but that didn't mean she wasn't on Philippa's side or her payroll. "We have two murder victims related to this case. Their back ribs were broken, their right arms were broken in the same two places, and they were strangled to death from behind. I was attacked by three men. I was able to fight off two of them though they managed to damage my face and bruise the front of my body. The third man broke my arm while he was strangling me from behind and if my dad hadn't interrupted, he would probably have broken my ribs and killed me too."

She gave Benson a minute to absorb that. "Except for the frontal bruising from fighting off the other two assailants, my injuries are exactly like our two victims. Unfortunately, the killer got away because my dad was more interested in making sure I lived than making an arrest."

Parker leaned forward. "Do you think Philippa sent three of her boys to kill me? And do you have any idea who the other one might be? The one who almost killed me is a well-built white man, about six feet, two inches tall who seems to favor breaking an arm and strangling his victims from behind."

Benson's gaze went to the window. After a few seconds she focused on Parker again. "White nationalism is Philippa's life, though given that most white nationalists think women are lesser, just like blacks and other minorities, I don't pretend to understand it. But I can't see her ordering a killing, even if her position was threatened. Are you focused on her because she's a blatant racist? If being black was a reason for her to order a kill, the streets of New York would be littered with bodies. Do you have any proof she was involved?"

Parker wasn't ready to share the information about Harrington's black blood with Benson. "Nothing concrete. Yet."

"As for your other attacker, I have no idea. There are many in the white nationalist movement who might take it upon themselves to eliminate someone they see as a threat to Philippa. And many who fit the description of your attacker, including Brandon Lester."

"Do you know how we can reach Lester?" Corelli asked.

"Have you tried his cell?"

"He's not answering."

Benson chewed a nail. "If Brandon is running, he may have gone back to West Virginia. There are lots of places to hide and lots of people who would protect him there."

"We found this in Harry's files." Corelli passed her the paper with the four monuments listed.

Benson stared at it for a few seconds. "I believe I mentioned I've heard rumors. This is the first proof I've seen that they're real. They're planning something. It must be important because this stuff is usually broadcast all over the hate websites and I haven't seen a word."

"Where did you hear about it?"

Benson chewed her lip. "Actually, Harry hinted at something bad going down. I felt he wanted to talk about it but when I pressed, he laughed and said I shouldn't worry. He would make sure it never happened. I've tried to find out what he meant but no one is talking. At least no one is talking to me, which shouldn't be a surprise because Philippa doesn't trust me and I assume from Harry's comments that she's involved."

CHAPTER TWENTY-SIX

"What did you think?" Parker asked once they were settled in the car.

"Benson seemed genuinely concerned about you and though I don't agree with her assessment that Philippa wouldn't order a murder, I thought she was pretty forthright when talking about her. And about Brandon Lester."

Parker rested her head on the foam block in her lap for a few seconds. "Lester disappeared right after I was attacked so I'm not surprised Benson suggested he might be my attacker. If he doesn't turn up soon, we'll contact the police in the West Virginia town they all come from."

Corelli made a face. "The way things go in these small hick towns the police are probably all Harringtons or Davenports but it's worth a try."

Annie was out so they were able to slip into the house without a lot of explanation and while Parker napped again, Corelli spoke to Dietz. "Anything new?"

"Yeah," Dietz said. "We received the police report from the shooting of Phoebe Davenport Young in West Virginia. They had a shell they'd never tested because they never found a gun. I gave them our FedEx account number and they agreed to overnight the shell to us."

"Great. Can you get Maynard and Watkins to dig deep on Brandon Lester and Michele Benson, both ex-military and both originally from West Virginia. While we don't want to break any laws, we do need military records and anything else they can dig up." Corelli knew Dietz would understand and communicate the message as she intended—be careful but go where you have to go to get the information we need.

"You got it." Dietz lowered his voice. "How's Parker doing?"

Corelli knew Dietz had a soft spot for Parker so she gave him the truth. "She tires easily, which is not unusual when your body has taken the kind of abuse hers did, but otherwise she's in top form. I'll call if we need anything else. Talk later."

By the time Annie arrived home to start cooking dinner, Parker and Corelli were at the dining room table getting ready to read Davenport's blackmail files. She fussed over Parker, remarked that she was pleased to see her looking quite fresh after a day of work and headed off to the kitchen. Corelli winked at Parker. The naps were working.

"Since Annie invited Ben Fine for dinner, we have limited time before he shows up so let's get started." Corelli pulled the files closer to her. "I'll start with Lena Wood and Walter Foster. She's forty-five, grew up in Idaho in a religious home with an abusive father, was into the drug scene, was a staunch feminist with a lot of casual sexual partners until her late thirties when she got involved with an alt-right talk show host who converted her to his way of thinking. He would bring her on his show as a guest and she became the perfect Nazi woman. At least it seemed that way but according to Davenport's notes she continues to sleep around, uses birth control and has had two abortions, the most recent two years ago. Though she talks about the joys of being a wife and mother and homemaker, she and Walter are not legally married and have no children.

"Walter also grew up in Idaho and is still married to a woman he left there with three daughters and no support. He was a member of an Idaho militia, talked big but had no power or status in the group. Davenport included nude pictures of Lena and pictures of Walter having sex with another woman whose face was in the shadows." Corelli shifted the photos so Parker could see them.

Parker covered her eyes. "Please, seeing them once was enough. What a sleazy group of people. Except Katharine, it seems. Her unwillingness to support the white nationalist agenda and her desire to be her own person with her artistic work are the only things he documented. I wonder if he still loved her."

"Philippa, his mother, didn't fare so well." Corelli tapped the papers in front of her. "She came from a poor family but she was smart and beautiful and ambitious. I don't know how he would know this but Davenport claims Philippa set out to marry Wilfred, lingering near his office and flirting until she caught his eye. Once she landed her rich husband, she did her duty by having six children. But she had no interest in them so the children and Abel, her husband's bastard son, were left in the care of people she considered intellectually and morally inferior."

Corelli thumbed through the box of papers. "Ah, here it is. I thought I saw this when I looked through the box earlier today. Davenport had Abel's DNA tested secretly and confirmed he was Wilfred's son." She returned to the page she was reading. "He details Philippa's self-involvement, her ruthlessness, the way she used his dad to take over leadership of their hate group, and how she placed attaining and keeping power above everything, even her children. He documents occasional affairs with leaders of other white nationalist groups and one long-term affair with Tommy Lester, the dad of the illusive Brandon Lester."

Parker jumped in. "And speaking of Brandon Lester, Davenport got access to his sealed youth arrest records and young Brandon had numerous charges brought against him for car theft, burglary, multiple assaults, and drug usage. He was dishonorably discharged from the Army for aggressive sexual and physical behavior, including nearly beating his female commanding officer to death. He was deemed psychiatrically unfit to serve. He's the leader of a white nationalist militia group in West Virginia and has a few hundred followers, some who came north to work for him. He and his followers provide security for Philippa Harrington Davenport. She funds him and his group."

"Your girlfriend, Michele Benson's, file isn't too bad. There are a number of photos of her with women in restaurants, lesbian bars, and other places where she's pretty open about being a lesbian." Corelli handed Parker the photos.

Parker took her time looking through them. "Interesting that her circle of friends seems to include women of color." She handed the pictures back to Corelli.

Corelli slid the photos into Benson's folder. "Let me know if you want a blow up of a picture of her."

"Stop wasting our time, smart ass." Parker made a go-on motion with her hand.

Corelli grinned. "Besides suggesting that she was a lesbian, the investigator noted she had lots of books in her apartment that were not what he would expect from a dedicated white nationalist and recommended she not be trusted despite her family background. Brandon Lester was the investigator but Davenport added and initialed handwritten notes at the end of the report. "Michele's sexual orientation and non-acceptance of white nationalism are irrelevant. Her excellent military record, her excellence at running her business and her loyalty to me are what's important."

"So Benson and Katharine are the only two who come out looking good." Corelli stacked the folders and put them back into the box. "I guess it's a matter of how much the person fears they'll lose and just how far Davenport tried to bend them to his will. Other than Katharine, any of the people in these files, including his mother, could have a motive."

Parker sat back. "I don't totally agree. It seems to me that while the information he collected on his friends and relatives could incriminate them, the behavior and actions of the leaders of white nationalist groups he catalogued might have given him leverage over them but it would probably just be embarrassing. Color me jaded, but I don't see Gregory Landers cheating on his wife, Tom Dolan embezzling from his group, or Elliot Harris being arrested for exposing himself, as drastic enough to incite them to murder Davenport to keep it from coming out. On the other hand, since our last encounter with a reverend, I'm suspicious of the Reverend Samuel Twigs. Judging by Davenport's records Twigs has a great deal to lose. His congregation is huge and lucrative enough to provide him with a huge estate, a private plane, and expensive vacations, so his penchant for young girls might be enough to damage him where it hurts. Let's bring him in."

Parker took a long drink of the water Corelli had placed beside her. "What a repulsive man Davenport was. Keeping files on your enemies is one thing, but keeping files on your mother, father, siblings, wife, and friends is really beyond the pale."

When the doorbell rang, Parker braced herself for a touchy-feely response to her battered face and her awkward, scary cast and its cushion, but Ben Fine cursed and asked for details of the attack. He listened carefully, agreed it was likely related to the case, then dropped the bomb. FBI agents had found four murders with the same MO as Walker and Rich, body bruising including broken ribs, a broken right arm and death by strangulation. The table went silent as Parker, Jessie, Annie, and Corelli took in that information and realized how close to death Parker had come.

Corelli recovered first. "Do you have any idea about the identity of the killer?"

"No. But I had my guys put all the information we have about each of the four cases in a binder so you can review them yourselves." Fine picked up his fork, then put it down and addressed Parker. "We've been working this white nationalist angle for quite a while and though they speak of it as a single large movement, the reality is that it's small pockets of like-minded people who are usually not connected with other groups. In fact, we've determined that the biggest danger is from lone wolves inspired by all the hate rhetoric to take violent action."

Parker had been imagining a large-scale conspiracy. Maybe the danger was more local. "Thanks, that's helpful. What do you know about the Davenports and their group?"

Since Fine owed his position as Director of the FBI's New York Region to Parker and Corelli, he no longer hesitated to share information with them. "It's been around for years so it's bigger than some, but when you really look, it's mostly old white men who were part of the original group, which was kind of a gentlemen's club. They were loyal to Wilfred and his son but our guess is they'll fade away now that Philippa is the obvious leader. She's a piece of work, isn't she? However, she does have a small group, maybe twenty-five to fifty younger, militia types who for some reason pledge allegiance to her."

"Is Michele Benson loyal to her?" That an attractive, obviously intelligent and most certainly lesbian woman in her thirties could be part of this white nationalist web of hate, sparked Parker's curiosity.

Fine hesitated. "She's part of the group we think of as the West Virginia haters, the Davenport family, Meriwether Davis, Brandon Lester, Bo Waters and others who have taken root in New York City. She provides security for some sympathetic to white nationalism but we don't know much about her except she manages to straddle the line between reality and the hate-filled lies espoused by the white nationalists."

Was she reading something into Fine's hesitation or was it an indication he wasn't sharing everything they had on her? "Corelli and I picked up lesbian vibes from her. Do you have anything on her personal life?"

"She's not on our white nationalist radar. Except for her familial connection to the Davenports and the fact that Harry helped her start her business, we haven't found anything to tie her to the movement. And other than her military records, which are unimpeachable, much of what we have on her is from public sources."

Parker knew Greene had interviewed Bo Waters but she had no idea he was part of the West Virginia group. "What do you have on Waters, Ben?"

"His mother is a Harrington, so he's related. Went all through school with Harry, then when Harry enlisted in the Army, Bo went to law school at West Virginia University. Married into a prominent, wealthy family and set up a law practice in West Virginia. When Harry started his firm, he and Bo became partners and merged their practices. They put a younger Harrington cousin in charge of the West Virginia office and Bo moved his family to New York City. Bo doesn't seem to have any connection to white nationalism."

Corelli pushed her plate aside. "What do you know about Brandon Lester?"

Fine took a few seconds to consider his answer. "He came to New York from West Virginia to support Philippa Davenport. He runs his own off-the-books company using military misfits to provide security for Philippa and several other white nationalists."

"One of the three men who attacked Parker is on his payroll and we're assuming the other two are as well," Corelli said. "Do you have any idea where he is?"

"I didn't know he was missing. But whether it's him or someone else, I'm afraid you and Parker are still in danger. I'd like to assign a couple agents to provide additional protection." Fine glanced at Annie and Jessie. "What do you think, Jess?"

Annie answered. "I think it's a wonderful idea, Ben."

Jessie put his hand over Annie's. "That's a great offer but it's really up to P.J. and Chiara to decide. How do you see the guys fitting in?"

Annie frowned but didn't comment.

"The two women would report to Parker and like any team members, she would decide what they do." He gazed at Parker, then moved to Corelli. "But to be honest my real goal is to ensure that you both have adequate protection any time you're out on the street, so that means where you go, they go."

Parker met Corelli's eyes. "Are those the two who have been shadowing us?"

Fine looked puzzled. "You made them?"

"Give us a little credit, Ben," Corelli said. "We understand the danger and we're being hypervigilant. But I'm guessing your agents didn't pick up the car with the detectives Captain Winfry assigned to go where we go." Corelli turned to Parker. "What do you think? Maybe one of them could drive instead of me?"

"Your driving has improved so I feel safe." Parker shifted her arm and its cushion, trying to get comfortable. "Thanks for the offer. But our people have it under control." She looked around the table, noted the slight lift of Corelli's chin, Ben's disapproving look, Annie's concerned face, and Jessie's struggle to hide his smile. She yawned. "Unless you have something else, I need my beauty sleep."

CHAPTER TWENTY-SEVEN

Her second day back and she was tired before they'd even reached the station house. Parker closed her eyes and rested her head on her foam cushion, hoping to nap for a few minutes on the way. A series of beeps signaling incoming texts interrupted the quiet in the car. Corelli swore under her breath as she fumbled for her phone. "It's not me." She stopped the car and put her hand out.

Parker extracted her phone from her coat pocket and passed it to Corelli. "Five texts. Darla, Watkins, Kim, Greene and Winfry. All warning that the press is waiting for us. Someone must have alerted them that you're back on the job."

Damn. Parker had assumed the press conference at the hospital would satisfy the media's thirst for information but she should have known better.

Corelli grinned. "We could avoid the station today but they'd be there tomorrow, or we could feed the beast, let them ask a few questions and take pictures. It's up to you."

Parker sighed. One way or another her picture would end up in the news. "I probably can't avoid them for eight weeks so let's get it over with."

By the time they pulled into the lot the media mob was being held back by several uniforms. The reporters and camera people were silent as Corelli helped Parker out of the car. Parker was grateful Corelli had positioned herself so they couldn't see her hand Corelli her arm and cushion while she swiveled to stand.

Maybe her cast and blue cushion scared them, maybe they were sympathetic or maybe it was the uniforms but the mob waited for them to approach rather than rushing and screaming questions as usual. When they got close enough for them to see the damage, there were some gasps and lots of camera action capturing her still swollen, black-and-blue face and her cast and foam companion.

"What happened, Detective Parker?" She didn't know who asked but the mob was respectful as she described the attack and her injuries. "Two of the three attackers are in custody."

Darla called out, "You're investigating the death of a white nationalist. Do you think they're responsible? Or was it a random attack?"

"We don't think it was random but we're still investigating. Thank you for your interest."

Corelli held her arm to keep her in place. "Detective Parker is too modest to tell you that she put two of her attackers in the hospital and both needed surgery. She also failed to note that she came close to dying by strangulation but was saved by her dad, Captain Jessie Isaacs. And finally, you should know that although the third assailant stood behind her, broke her arm and was choking the life out of her, she managed to reach up and scratch him. Let your readers know we're looking for a large white man with scratches on the left side of his face. And that's all, folks." Corelli steered her into the station house.

Parker watched from the conference table as Corelli pinned the photo of Harrington Davenport on the opposite side of the board from the photos of Walker and Rich. Underneath his picture she pinned photos of Philippa Harrington Davenport, Michele Benson, Brandon Lester, Katharine Davenport, Meriwether Davis, Lena Wood, and Walter Foster. They hadn't identified suspects for the Walker and Rich murders other than Harrington Davenport. Corelli drew lines from Walker and Rich to Philippa and Harrington Davenport. She also added Parker's photo and those of her two attackers in custody, Andy Topping and Everet

Collins, with a dotted line and a question mark pointed toward Philippa Davenport and Brandon Lester. She added the photos of the four white nationalist leaders in Davenport's files—Tom Dolan, Elliot Harris, Gregory Landers, and Reverend Samuel Twigs—on Davenport's side of the board. Next to each she wrote the main charge Davenport had recorded. It was busy but there was plenty of room on the large board.

As she worked, team members drifted over to watch and ask questions, then went back to work. Maynard greeted Parker then moved to check the board. Parker watched her scan the photos, then gasp. "Whoa. What's Chelle doing up there with those freaking Nazis?"

"Shelly who?" Corelli and Parker responded simultaneously.

Maynard pointed at Benson.

"You know her?"

Maynard sat next to Parker. Corelli joined them. "I've met her a few times."

Corelli dug into the box and retrieved Benson's file. She opened it and spread the pictures of Benson with various women and occasionally with a group of women in a bar.

Maynard took her time looking through the pictures, then pointed to a woman sitting with Benson. "That's her friend, Olivia. They grew up together in West Virginia and then joined the Marines together." She gazed at Corelli, then settled on Parker. "Why is she here?"

Parker wanted to get information, not give it. "Do you know what she does for a living?"

Maynard rubbed her forehead. "She's in security."

Corelli jumped in. "And Olivia?"

"They work together, I think. What's up with this?"

Parker smiled. "Be patient. The women she's friendly with, what kind of jobs do they have? Does she know you're working on this case?"

"I doubt she or anyone else knows I'm a detective. I always just say I'm in computers because being police freaks some women. Even the friend who knows them only knows I'm in computers. As for the other women, their jobs run the gamut, a couple of teachers, a secretary, a programmer, a doctor, a nurse and that's all I can think of now."

CHAPTER TWENTY-EIGHT

"I finally caught up with one of Davenport's neighbors," Forlini reported at the morning meeting. "She remembered two unusual things from that night. First, a fancy green car was parked in front of a fire hydrant near Davenport's house. It pissed her off because her house is next to his and she has a thing about fires. And second, she noticed the older man she pegged as Davenport's lover because he was in and out of the house at all hours, standing in the shadows across the street watching the house."

"How could she be so specific about the night?" Watkins asked the question before Parker could get it out.

Forlini smiled. "It was her fifty-ninth birthday and she was coming home from a celebratory dinner with friends at 9:47."

"That's pretty specific." Parker locked eyes with Corelli. "I'll wager that Abel Clemson is the old guy. And I'd say a Jaguar qualifies as fancy wouldn't you, Corelli?"

Corelli pretended to think. "Why yes, I think I would."

"Like many a good citizen these days, Grace Tomlin took a video with her phone that's date and time stamped." Forlini held his phone so Parker and Corelli could see the image. The video started with the license plate then moved slowly around the entire car, front to back, both sides. And standing on the other side of the street, his face illuminated by a light on the building he was leaning against, was the alert figure of Abel Clemson.

"Good work, Forlini. Let's get Meriwether Davis and Abel Clemson in here today, Dietz." Parker glanced around the table. "Anyone else have anything new?"

Dietz took a seat at the table. "Katharine Davenport is in room two."

Parker closed her eyes trying to recall why they'd brought her in. Oh, the security tape in her hall. "All right, let's see what Katharine Davenport has to say about her little lie."

"Ready?" Corelli was at her side. She allowed Corelli to lift her arm enough so she could stand and manage it herself.

Katharine Davenport's eyebrows lifted to her hairline when Parker entered. "My lord, what happened?"

"Three of your husband's buddies tried to murder me. I put two of them in the hospital, but the third, the one we believe murdered two people related to this case, got away."

"But I saw you after Harry was murdered so he couldn't have had anything to do with it."

Corelli helped Parker settle her arm on the table. "If not him, who do you think ordered the hit?"

Katharine frowned. "Maybe Philippa or one of her minions? I really couldn't say. But why am I here?"

Parker took a guess. "We know you were at your husband's house the night he was murdered. Why did you lie about it?"

"Oh." Katharine looked down at her hands. "I lied because, you know, the spouse is always the murderer."

"You were on bad terms. Why were you there if you didn't go there to kill him?"

She raised her eyes. "Harry called me in a panic that night. He said he needed someone sane to talk to and begged me to come. He even promised to settle our divorce."

"You went for the money?"

"No. I went because he sounded desperate. And he was in despair about his mother, as usual." She seemed to be waiting for a question but when neither detective spoke, she continued, "He's dead so I guess I can just say it. Philippa is involved in some crazy scheme to terrorize the country and incite all the various groups unhappy about the government...or whatever...to unite and take over the country. At first Harry thought it was just her usual crazy talk but then he realized she'd managed to pull in other crazies around the country. They actually have a plan to attack monuments and museums on the Fourth of July."

Parker interrupted. "Did he show you the plan?"

"No. But he said Meriwether, Brandon, and Heather were working with her. He met with the four of them and the few leaders he could get to come to New York, three days earlier, hoping to convince them to drop the plan and concentrate on getting him elected to the Senate. He figured by that time they would have cooled down. But there was an ugly scene with Philippa over unleashing the violence and she and those who agreed with her stormed out of the meeting." She smiled with tears in her eyes. "He admitted I was right, that he was wrong in thinking he could control the pockets of militants around the country. He also said he had started pulling back on the white nationalist rhetoric and once he was elected, he would come out against the white nationalist philosophy."

Finally, they had confirmation that there *was* a plan to attack democracy. Parker needed to know what else Harry Davenport had told Katharine. "What did he want from you?"

Katharine shrugged. "He just needed a friend. He said I was the only one he trusted to talk through how to deal with Philippa and Meriwether and the others involved. He knew I would never side with their hate and that I'd find the thought of violence repugnant. I think he wanted confirmation of what he knew in his heart he needed to do, even though his mother was involved. He said he would report them and their plot to the FBI in the morning. But of course, he didn't have time."

Parker studied Katharine. Did she see her ex clearly or was she blinded by her love for him? "Are you sure he wasn't involved in the plot to overthrow the government?"

"Absolutely. He has always been against violence and I don't think he ever took the violent aspects of white nationalism seriously. His relationship with Philippa was complicated but he respected her passion and her drive. The fact that he was willing to report his mother to the FBI is proof that he thought she'd gone off the rails and was really going to order the destruction of national monuments."

"Why didn't you go to the FBI with this information or at least mention it to us when we interviewed you?"

Katharine folded her hands on the table. "I had no evidence. I could only tell the FBI what Harry told me and I thought they'd write me off as the crazy ex-wife looking for revenge on her crazy ex-mother-in-law. I didn't tell you because I was afraid if you knew I'd been there you'd arrest me and stop looking for his killer. You are still looking, aren't you?"

"Do you think Philippa is capable of ordering her thugs to kill him?"

Katharine paled. "She's a hateful woman and they've had their differences over the years, but I can't believe she'd hurt Harry."

"When you left Mr. Davenport's brownstone, did you notice anyone across the street?"

"No. Harry apologized and said he would always love me, so I was very emotional and focused internally when I left."

Parker signaled Corelli that she was ready to stand. "You can go but don't leave the city. We may have more questions."

Katharine stood. "How did you find out I was there?"

"We have our ways," Corelli answered as she assisted Parker. "You need to read better mysteries, the ones where the detectives know what they're doing."

Parker sighed as they sat at their conference table again. Damn, she was starting to tire. She chewed her lip. "Ideally, we'd get a search warrant for Philippa Davenport's entire house but a judge will want something more concrete than the hearsay testimony of the ex-daughter-in-law." She sighed. "For now, we keep digging." She looked at Corelli. "Do you think we should get the FBI involved?"

"I agree that all we have are suspicions and Katharine's word. Fine would have told us if the FBI had an inkling of a plot like this so I think we should wait until we have something definite."

Corelli eyed Parker from across the table. "Dietz, when are we expecting Davis and Clemson to arrive?"

He looked up from what he was reading. "We're still tracking Clemson down and Davis will be in between four and five this afternoon."

"Okay, Parker, I suggest we go to my apartment and while you take a quick nap, I'll pick up lunch for us."

Parker yawned. "Sounds like a plan to me. Do we need to alert our escorts?"

"They should be outside. I was pretty sure you'd need a break about now so I arranged for them to meet us."

With Corelli's assistance, Parker lifted her arm and the cushion. Damn this was going to be a long six weeks. "Do we need to take anything?"

"Just ourselves."

CHAPTER TWENTY-NINE

Meriwether Davis was annoyed. At least that's what Parker decided watching him through the two-way mirror. For the last fifteen minutes he'd been in constant motion, sitting, standing, sitting, standing, tapping fingers, huffing air, and checking his phone. "Let's go, Corelli. I don't want him to call his attorney."

His eyes went to her cast with its lovely blue cushion, then lifted to her battered face. He didn't seem surprised. He didn't comment. "Please take a seat, Mr. Davis. Sorry to keep you waiting but you know police interviews can go for hours."

His eyes narrowed but he sat across from them. "What was so important that I had to come all the way down here?" He made it sound like they'd asked him to drive to South Carolina to speak to them.

Corelli took the lead. "We were wondering why you lied to us?"

"Lied about what?"

"You know that lovely green Jaguar is very distinctive. People notice it."

He smiled at the mention of his pride and joy. "It is, isn't it? But what has that got to do with my being here?"

Corelli didn't answer so he moved his gaze to Parker but immediately looked away.

Corelli opened her notebook. "Let's see." She slowly thumbed through the pages. Then she stopped, gazed at him, looked down at the page again. "When we spoke to you at your...estate, you said the night your dearest friend, Harry Davenport, was murdered, you'd gone straight home after your TV show ended."

"You don't have to be sarcastic. He was my dearest friend." He managed to sound angry. "And I did leave the studio and go home."

"Really? Then who double-parked your fancy green Jaguar at a fire hydrant in front of Mr. Davenport's house at 9:47 that night?"

He showed the barest sign of surprise. "You're mistaken." He glared at Corelli. "This is a waste of my time," he said, rising.

Corelli blocked the door. "Before you go, let me share a video with you." He backed up and sat. Corelli put her phone in front of him. "Note the date and time stamp." She pressed play.

He paled. There was no denying it anymore. He shifted in the chair. They could almost hear his brain riffling through its file of excuses to come up with one that would cover his lie. Seconds ticked by. Sweat appeared on his upper lip. He leaned forward.

"Harry called me before my show that evening. He said he needed to talk privately and begged me to come to his house after the show. He sounded as if he was having a breakdown, so I went. When I got there, he had calmed down. He said he'd solved the problem that was bothering him so we talked for a few minutes about the movement. He asked my advice about his campaign for the Senate and I left. I swear he was alive when I left. I lied because I didn't want to be a suspect."

"We heard he was at odds with you and Philippa about something."

"Me?" He swallowed. Perhaps mentioning Philippa brought up some bile. "I don't know who told you that but I have no idea what you're talking about." He forced a laugh. "Being at odds with Harry is nothing new. He loves you when you agree with him but feels betrayed when you don't. I've known Harry for more than forty years and he always has had some problem or another with Philippa. And he's been unhappy with me recently because I've had guests on my show who don't agree with him. As I said, after he asked my advice on when and where to announce his run for the Senate, I left. I was there less than a half hour."

Corelli gazed at him but didn't speak. So far they only had Katharine's word on the plan and his role. Better to wait until they had concrete proof than to bring it up now and alert Philippa and her merry band. Meriwether snuck a peak at Parker but quickly looked away again.

He wasn't a suspect in Harry's murder because Katharine had seen Harry alive after he left, but maybe she could shake him up. Corelli slammed her fist on the table. "You've done nothing but lie to us. Why should we believe you when you say he was alive when you left?"

"Because I had no reason to kill him. Our jobs put us at loggerheads, but he was my best friend."

"That you were friends at one time is probably true. But that you had no reason to kill him is probably a lie. We know you've been receiving illegal payments from a number of right-wing people and groups."

"Hey, my finances are private information."

"Your bestie Harry didn't seem to think so." She opened the file Davenport had kept on Davis and placed a document in front of him. "That's information your friend Harry kept on the illegal payments deposited into one of your offshore accounts. Are you claiming all those monthly deposits, including five thousand dollars each month from Philippa, aren't real?"

She held up another page. "He also had copies of your taxes and it appears as if you didn't report any of this income. This is just a small fraction of what Harry collected about you, and it plus the rape charges sure seem like a good motive for murder to me. Did he threaten you?"

"No, none of that is true."

"It's all here"—she held up the folder—"in ugly black and white detail. Any one of the stories in here could ruin your career. That's a motive for murder if I ever heard one. What do you think, Detective Parker?"

"I agree. And did you notice that he didn't even have to ask what happened to me. I'll bet he knows exactly who tried to murder me. Makes him an accessory after the fact, doesn't it?"

"I want my lawyer."

Corelli stood. "You're free to go. But you might want to think about what information you have that would be of interest to us."

Dietz entered with a uniform. "Get him out of here."

Meriwether looked dazed as the uniform led him out of the room.

Dietz handed Corelli a piece of paper. "Clemson is in interview three."

"Thanks, Dietz." She handed him the folder. "Hopefully we'll nail Davis on his involvement with the plan, but in the meantime, make copies of the financial stuff in here and turn it over to the financial crimes team."

Corelli stretched and yawned. "If you're up for interviewing Clemson, I'll bring him here so you don't have to move."

"Yes, but then that's it for me. And I'd love some water if you don't mind."

"Anything for you, partner."

Abel Clemson shambled in with a puzzled look on his face. At first sight of Parker his eyes widened. "Are you all right, Detective Parker? That looks bad."

"You hadn't heard?" Parker wanted to give him an opening to talk if he knew anything.

He shook his head. "No." He adjusted his tie. "Um, why did you want to talk to me? I already told you everything I know about the day we found Harry."

Parker let him sit with his anxiety for a moment. "You also lied to me that day."

He looked alarmed. "What did I say?"

"Tell me what you see on this video." Parker nodded to Corelli.

Corelli put her phone in front of him then keyed the video. She played it twice.

Parker's voice jerked his attention to her. "I would swear that was you standing across the street from the green car at 9:47 the night Mr. Davenport was murdered."

"It was me." He moved his hand back and forth over the table. "Harry called and asked me to come. Sometimes when he was feeling bad, he liked me to keep him company." He looked up at Parker. "But when I saw M-m-meriwether's green car, I knew he didn't need me because they always talked and drank for hours."

"How did you get there and back?"

"S-s-subway."

"Can I see your Metro Card?"

"I don't have it. I don't use the subway too much so I buy a c-c-card when I need it and then throw it away."

"That's convenient."

Parker's sarcasm seemed to go over Clemson's head. "It is. I tried buying a card with lots of trips because it's cheaper but I kept losing them or forgetting them home in a drawer, so a roundtrip works good for me."

"What subway station did you use?"

"I took the train at Broadway on Eighty-sixth Street to Twelfth Street."

"And to go home?"

"I was worried that maybe I should stay so I walked around for a while. I got confused and I don't remember where I took the train but I got off by Central Park."

CHAPTER THIRTY

Parker settled her burdensome arm on the table but her gaze was on Forlini. The usually serious, unflappable detective seemed hyped this morning. And the usually low-key Kim looked as if she was about to explode.

Once the team was seated, Parker turned to Forlini. "Am I correct in assuming you have something for us this morning?"

Forlini glanced at Kim. "We have reports on the bullets used in three of the other Davenport murders and all appear to be from the gun used to kill Harrington Davenport. We expect the others to follow suit. The likelihood that the seven members of the Davenport family were shot by the same person is extremely high."

Parker gave the team a minute to process this information. "This is a game changer. It means Davenport's killer has been in the Davenport family orbit for at least twenty years. Someone with a grudge. Or maybe vendetta is a better word. And it means we now have six additional murders to solve. The people in that family circle that immediately come to mind are Katharine Davenport, Meriwether Davis, Abel Clemson, Michele Benson, Bo Waters and

Brandon Lester, all from West Virginia, all close to the family. Did I miss anyone?"

"Heather?" Corelli asked.

"Right. Heather is younger than the others and is sort of in the background but she's Philippa's niece and definitely in the Davenport orbit. She may know something."

Maynard put up her hand. "I don't know about motive but if I have her history right, Michele Benson was in Afghanistan, Iraq or Germany for most of those years."

Maynard's loyalty to her friend was an admirable trait. Since their talk, Maynard had stopped teasing and flirting, leaving room for Parker to appreciate her and remember why she'd dated her in the first place. She forced her wandering thoughts back to the meeting.

"It could be one of the competing white nationalist leaders who have been around for years, but why?" Forlini looked down at his notes. "No note of any kind was found at any of the crime scenes, at least if the crime scene reports can be trusted. And Philippa Davenport says she never received any threat about killing her family members."

Once the others had offered their opinions, Corelli added her thoughts. "It could be someone we haven't encountered in the investigation, but it does seem more likely that it's someone close to the family. However, while I can see a motive for Katharine to murder her ex, murdering her son and all her in-laws would be stretching it, I think. And we've already cleared Davis of Harry's murder."

Maybe it was her injuries or the difficulty of doing even the simplest things like tying her shoes or buttoning her blouse, but Parker was feeling worn out by this case. Too many threads and all they could do was pull on them and hope. "Let's bring Heather, Clemson, Benson, Lester and Waters in. Maybe we can flush the killer out. Anybody have anything else?"

Watkins spoke up. "Yes. I reviewed the FBI reports of the four murders where the victims were beaten, had their right arm broken and strangled." He held up the notebook Agent Fine had given Parker. "Two occurred in Idaho about three years apart, one in upstate New York and the other in West Virginia. We put a summary together so you could review it without having to wade through the reports they sent us." He slid summaries to Parker and Corelli.

Parker looked around the table. "You have anything, Greene?"

"We picked up Brandon Lester outside of Philippa Davenport's house at four o'clock this morning. Did you know he lives there? He says he'd just come back from West Virginia where his mom was in the hospital. I asked the local police to check out his story. I didn't see any trace of scratches on his face or neck, but I guess it depends on how deep you dug. He's in room two."

Parker felt a surge of hope. The name of the night guard at Meriwether Davis's estate was no longer an issue, but maybe bringing him in was a sign. Maybe they would solve the murders and hopefully stop the destruction outlined in the plan, if it was real, not just a fantasy. "Anything to add, Maynard?"

The computer guru looked at Parker. "Nothing new."

Parker felt her eyes drooping. Corelli stood. "Okay, folks, let's get back to work. Keep us posted."

Parker waited until they were alone at the table. "Thanks. I've never tired so easily. I don't know whether it's my injuries or the sheer breadth of this investigation, but I almost dropped off."

"Your body was battered, Parker. It demands the rest it needs to recuperate. We have two options. Since you seem to recover with a short nap, we can either go to my apartment or we can go to an empty interview room and you can take a nap using our coats as cushions. The sofa at my place will be more comfortable but it's your decision."

When Parker lifted her head off the table in the interview room, Corelli looked up from the report she was reading and glanced at her phone. "Thirty-two minutes. Not too bad. How do you feel?"

Parker yawned. "Much better. Have you learned anything from the summary of the FBI reports?"

"I have," Corelli said. "There are some variations in the description of the injuries by different coroners and medical examiners, but the basic methodology in each case seems to be the same or close enough to be attributable to the same man. They confirm our assumption that the killer of these four also killed Walker and Rich and almost killed you. I did learn one new thing

Legacy in the Blood   195

that will interest you. Walter Foster was a person of interest in the second case in Idaho about ten years ago. We need to bring him in but first let's get our computer people to track his whereabouts around the time of the Upstate New York and the West Virginia murders."

"Son of a...Walter Foster. I should have guessed. He's huge and he's part of Philippa's circle. Give me a hand, please. I need to stand and move a little."

As they walked back to the conference room Parker made a decision. "Have Maynard get right on the research but I want Foster brought in immediately so we can see whether his face is scratched. But even if he's healed, we should be able to get a DNA sample to compare to my nail scrapings. Did they find any evidence in the four previous cases?"

"The only DNA or other forensic evidence collected at the scene of any of the six murders was the gold flakes and cat hairs on Rich." Corelli put a hand on Parker's arm and faced her. "You don't realize what a feat it was that you reached up and scratched your attacker while he was breaking your arm and choking you to death, especially after you had already fought and badly injured two other assailants."

Parker's face heated. "You would have done the same, Corelli."

"I certainly hope so. But back to business. Lester has probably worked up a nice sweat waiting for us. After we talk to Maynard, should we take him on?"

Would Corelli think she was so brave if she knew that she was feeling fear at the idea of confronting Lester, possibly her attacker? "It's ironic. We no longer need the name of the guard on duty at Davis's estate the night Davenport was killed, but now Lester is a suspect in the multiple murders in the Davenport family, the murders of Rich and Walker and the attack on me. He's also a suspected leader of the elusive plan."

They headed for the conference room. "You probably know this, Parker, but don't be surprised if you feel anxious seeing Lester. He's supposed to be a big guy and whether or not he's the one who attacked you, he will remind your body of the attack."

Damn. Was that the voice of experience or was Corelli a mind reader?

Corelli was correct about Lester. He was agitated when they entered the room. But she was wrong about Parker. Seeing him enraged her. He glared at her but didn't show any surprise at her arm baggage or the bruises on her face. "Why am I here? You have no right to arrest me."

They had the sitting maneuver down pat so it was probably not apparent that Corelli was assisting Parker with her arm unless someone was focused on their movements. Parker bit back her anger, let him be the one to lose control. "This is a murder investigation, and while you're not under arrest, you are a suspect, so we have every right."

"What murder? And what does it have to do with me?"

"Actually, multiple murders. And we think it has a lot to do with you. Are you not aware that your friend and sometime employer, Harrington Davenport, was murdered? And that a number of members of his family have been murdered in the last twenty years."

"I heard Harry was murdered but I didn't kill him. And of course I know about other members of the Davenport family. Why would I murder him or the others?"

He was tall and muscular, probably a weightlifter, and could well be her attacker, unless he actually did leave New York City Saturday morning. She scrutinized the left side of his face and neck, but as Greene said, no sign of scratches. "And then of course there's the attempted murder of me."

His gaze flicked from her face to her cast and back. "Why would I try to kill you when we've never met before?"

"That's a great question. But you're here to answer our questions. So, where were you between eight p.m. and four a.m. the night Mr. Davenport was murdered, one week ago today?"

"How the hell would I know? I hardly remember what I had for dinner last night."

Parker was sure his belligerence had served him well in the past but she was not put off by it. "Maybe you remember when and why you left town so suddenly and why you were not answering your cell phone?"

"Yeah. My mama was rushed to the hospital last Saturday morning so I drove home to West Virginia to be with her. I turned my cell off while I was driving because I didn't want to be bothered talking to anyone and I had to turn it off in the hospital."

"You remember Saturday morning but you don't remember what you were doing Friday night?"

"Now I do. I ate supper with Philippa and then spent the rest of the night in my apartment watching TV."

"You live with Philippa Davenport?" Parker didn't attempt to hide her surprise.

"No way. There are several apartments in her mansion. I live in a two-bedroom that's totally separate from her and the other apartments."

"Hmm, I don't remember seeing any monthly rent payments in your financial records."

"Hey, what fucking right do you have to look at my financial information?"

Ah, her guess was correct. Parker poked the bear. "I'll say it slower so you understand. You. Are. A. Suspect. In. A. Murder. Investigation. Actually, multiple murder investigations so we have every right." Parker waited a few seconds.

"Is it that the Davenport siblings considered you white trash? Or are you greedy and want Philippa all to yourself? There are rumors about the two of you. But I'm trying to figure out what would drive you to kill so many members of her family?"

His face was blazing but he managed to maintain control. "You're crazy, lady. I have no reason to kill any of them. Philippa is my cousin and my friend, that's all." He unscrewed the top of the bottle of water on the table in front of him and drank half of it.

"Your cousin?" How had they missed this little tidbit?

He grinned. "Yeah. My mama is her first cousin. I'm a Harrington, if you can believe it. Besides, I like my women younger and...well, you know."

"What is your relationship with Michele Benson?"

He frowned. "I don't see—"

"Just answer the question." Parker leaned in.

"Michele and I don't see eye to eye on things so we generally avoid each other."

"According to Meriwether Davis you provide security for him. Are you licensed to provide security services?"

"Why is this your business?" He straightened. "Nothing says I can't have a side business."

"And how does Philippa Davenport's hefty monthly payment fit into your business? Does it have to do with the plan?"

The shock on his face disappeared quickly but it was there long enough to confirm she'd hit the target with that question. He put his hands on the table, leaned toward her and hissed, "I don't need to listen to this shit." He jumped up and quickly opened the door but stopped short when confronted by Detective Forlini, a formidable physical barrier even for someone as large as Lester.

"Sit. I believe Detective Parker still has questions for you." Forlini was soft-spoken but there was no doubt this was a command, not a request.

Lester fisted his hands, closed the door and sat again.

Parker changed direction. "Listen, Brandon, we know you collected information on Michele Benson for Harry. Do you know he collected information about you and your violent history? His files go way back to your sealed youth arrest records plus your dishonorable discharge from the Army for uncontrolled violence, which included almost beating your commanding officer to death."

His face went from red to blazing red.

"There were also the several cases in West Virginia where you nearly beat someone to death and Davenport managed to get you sentenced to community service rather than prison. And then there were the cases where your hired muscle assaulted people and in one case killed someone." Parker looked into his eyes. "Foster is one of your goons for hire, the one who kills on demand, right? Why did you order him to murder Magnolia Walker and Ned Rich? Why did you send Walter Foster, Everet Collins and Andy Topping to kill me?"

His face went from blazing red to white. "You don't know what you're talking about, lady." His jaw clamped shut and he sat, body rigid, hands in tight fists on the table, and stared at the wall behind the two detectives. Sweat rolled slowly down his face.

Parker sensed violence seething just under the surface. She could easily give him a shove over the edge but that wasn't her goal. His reaction to the question about Foster told her what she needed to know.

He glanced at the door, maybe remembering there was no escape there. He was shaking. "I don't know what game you're playing but if you're going to arrest me on some made-up charge, I want a lawyer." He sounded like a man desperate for a life preserver as he was going under. "Where's my phone? Don't I get one phone call?"

Parker held his gaze for a minute. "Save the call for later. You can go but don't leave New York City."

He sat for a moment, as if he didn't believe her. He glanced at the door, then back at her. He opened the door.

"This way out," Forlini said.

CHAPTER THIRTY-ONE

As Forlini led Lester away, the anger that had kept Parker focused was replaced by anxiety. She inhaled deeply, trying to steady her racing heart. Perhaps Corelli was right. Perhaps she was feeling vulnerable right now and her reaction to Lester's violent vibe was normal. She hoped so. "Did he freak when I mention Foster or did I imagine it?"

Corelli bagged Lester's empty water bottle. "You didn't imagine it." Corelli matched her pace to Parker's as they walked back to the conference room. She handed the bagged bottle to Greene. "Get this to the lab. We want the DNA compared to the DNA taken from Parker's attacker." She eased Parker into a chair. "I'll get us lunch from the Halal truck and then maybe we can take stock of where we are."

Parker swallowed the last bite of her chicken shawarma and rice and waited for Corelli to scoop up the last bits of falafel, rice and salad left in her dish. "Don't you get tired of eating the falafel plate every day?"

"No." Corelli gathered their garbage and tossed it into the designated bin. "But I only have it when we have lunch at the station, not every day. Ready to do some work?"

Parker moved a pen and her notebook in front of her. Corelli would produce a readable summary of their thoughts but the unreadable scrawls she managed with her left hand seemed to trick her brain into thinking. "I'll start. We now have verified that at least four members of the Davenport family were killed with the same gun, so we're looking for one killer and assume it's someone close to the family. All we need to do is find the gun."

Corelli wrote it down. "Who knows? Maybe we'll get lucky and arrest someone with the gun in his or her possession. I'll add, we now know that the man who tried to kill you has killed six people. And we believe he is Walter Foster, who is on the payroll of Brandon Lester, who is on the payroll of Philippa Davenport. And we're guessing that Philippa ordered the killings of Walker, Rich and you."

Parker scribbled a version of Foster's name in her notebook. "Where are we on picking up Foster?"

"I spoke to Dietz when he and I were at the Halal truck, and he's put a round-the-clock stakeout on his house. His wife has been going in and out but there's no sign of him."

"I doubt he'd do a runner without his darling Lena." Parker tapped her pen on the table. "Until we bring Foster in, we're in wait mode on the murders. And though we know a few of the people involved and a few of the monuments and other national treasures they're targeting, without a copy of the plan we can't take any action to stop it."

"Relax. We're stalled, not stuck." Corelli jotted a note. "Speaking of the plan, Dietz said that Samuel Twigs is waiting for us in interview one. Any ideas on how to approach him?"

Twigs? Parker remembered they'd brought the white nationalist leader in because the dirt Davenport had on him could destroy his life. "Now that we're thinking it's someone close to the family he's off the hook for Davenport's murder but maybe since he's here we can rattle him enough so he'll spill something helpful about the plan."

They took a minute to observe the Reverend Samuel Twigs as he waited for them in the interview room. Parker knew from the pictures that he was a fairly good-looking man in his late thirties with the blond hair and blue eyes revered by white nationalists. The way he was dressed, a blue pinstriped suit with a blue shirt that matched his eyes and a red tie, reminded her of criminal defense attorney Louden Warfield III. But the similarity ended at the clothing. Though Warfield defended criminals, he, unlike the creep sitting across the table, was an honorable and principled man.

Parker introduced them as they settled at the table facing Twigs and were immediately treated to the usual litany of complaints from the entitled about being forced to come to the police station and then wait hours to be seen.

When he quieted down and looked expectantly at Corelli, Parker opened the file with the incriminating evidence Davenport had collected and placed the six photographs of him having sex with minors in front of him. As his eyes shifted from one to the other, his face got whiter. He lifted his gaze to Corelli. "What is this?" His attempt to sound irate fell flat.

Parker's voice drew his eyes to her. "It's pretty obvious, at least to me, that it's pictures of you in the act of raping children. I think you meant to ask how we got the photographs."

He shifted his gaze to Corelli. "What has this got to do with Harry Davenport's death?"

Parker answered again. "Mr. Davenport collected these and other rather unflattering information about you. With these, he had the power to destroy your reputation, wreck your marriage, take away your church, your mansion, your private plane and so on. His possession of these pictures gives you a very good motive for murder, wouldn't you say?"

He half turned in his seat, attempting to ignore Parker, and extended a hand toward Corelli. "I'm not prepared to talk to this…this…woman. Do I have to, Detective?"

"Gee, I don't know." Corelli turned toward Parker. "Does he have to talk to you if he's not prepared, Detective Parker?"

"Definitely not, Detective Corelli. I'll have him moved to a holding cell until he feels prepared." She gazed at Twigs. "We'll be back tonight or at the latest tomorrow afternoon. When you feel prepared to talk to me, let the officer on duty know and I'll see you as soon as I can." She let that sink in. "Take him to the holding cell, Detective Corelli."

He put his hands in front of him as if warding off an attacker. "Just one minute. I will not wait until tomorrow afternoon to talk to you."

"Are you saying you're prepared to talk to me now?" Parker pointed to herself.

She could almost hear his teeth grinding. "If that's what it takes. But first I'd like to know what you're going to do with these pictures?"

Parker pushed the six photos over to Corelli, wanting to avoid seeing them again. "We're Homicide, not the Special Victims Division so we have no interest in them."

Parker ignored the smile he covered with his hand and a fake cough. "Since you didn't seem surprised to see me with my arm in this contraption and an obviously bruised face, I assume you have insider knowledge that I was beaten and almost killed by three of your white nationalist brethren."

He looked toward her but his gaze settled over her shoulder. "I hadn't noticed. But I assure you *I* do not approve of violence. And to that point, I don't know anything about Harry's murder so I'm not sure how I can help."

"We're interested in the meeting he held at his house a few days before he was murdered. We know it was about the plan."

His eyes widened. His breathing sped up.

Gotcha. Parker took advantage of his surprise. "Yes, Reverend, we know about the plan. What was the purpose of the meeting?"

"Harry wanted to make sure all the various leaders were on the same page."

"And what page was that?"

"I don't think I'm telling tales out of school, but he'd come to the conclusion that the best way for us to gain control of the country was to focus on getting out the vote to elect him senator. He wanted all factions, all groups that is, to agree to a non-violent election and transition to power."

"And if he didn't win?"

"We didn't discuss that. But I agreed with him. Violence is never the answer."

"Who else agreed?"

"Let me think. Gregory Landers and his White Boys, Tom Dolan and his Soldiers All, and Elliot Harris and his White Tops All."

Of course. He had files on them. "Who didn't agree, Mr. Twigs?"

"It's Reverend, please. His mother, Philippa Harrington Davenport, and her OurAmerica group, Brandon Lester and his White Freedom group. He has people here and in West Virginia. Trey Montgomery and his Texas Freedom Fighters, Eason McCormick and his Idaho Fighters Militia. There were several groups on the telephone. I don't remember who, but some agreed and others didn't."

"So more in favor of the plan than against? And Philippa Davenport opposed her son?"

"That insufferable woman shouldn't have been there. It's white men who will bring this country back to its former glory. Women have no place in our movement. It's bad enough that Philippa acts like she's important, but now that niece of hers acts like she's the heir apparent, offering opinions nobody asked for. They both should have been home like normal women. She and Harry pretended he ran OurAmerica, but everyone knows she's pulling the strings. She thinks she's smarter than any man, including her husband and son. I just don't understand why intelligent white men follow her." He stopped short, probably remembering he was talking to the enemy. "Oh, Lena Wood and her husband, Walter, were there too but at least she has the good sense to live the life of a proper white woman."

"What side was Lena on?"

He was silent. Was he praying? Had she pushed him too far? Then he smiled. "She didn't participate, only listened which was appropriate. But she and Walter followed Philippa out so I guess she was in favor of the plan." He took out a neatly folded white handkerchief and wiped his brow. Just when Parker decided Twigs was finished, he went on, his voice filled with loathing. "Philippa sees herself as a great warrior. She thinks we need to demonstrate our power and violence is the only way to get people's attention." He shuddered. "She and Harry had a bitter argument over it, right in front of all of us. It was embarrassing. But she refused to listen to reason. She said her militia has the bombs and weapons needed to destroy the monuments and no matter what Harry and others against the plan thought, the Fourth of July was set in concrete." He wiped his face again. "You know, Brandon Lester, her lieutenant, has a rather rough and dangerous group of armed followers."

Parker lifted her arm. "I know firsthand how rough and dangerous they can be."

Twigs looked like he wanted to throw up. Parker figured him for one of those people who liked to talk about revolution but left the dirty work to others. "Do they intend to go ahead with the plan now that Davenport is dead?"

He lifted his shoulders. "I'm not part of that circle so I can't be sure, but Harry's death has fired up some people who think the government killed him so I'd say it's likely going to happen."

He looked from Parker to Corelli, maybe waiting for another question but neither said a word. He stared at the folder in front of Parker. Even though Parker had said they knew about the plan he probably thought he could appear to cooperate by giving them more information and continued unprompted, "As far as I know, the definite targets are still the Statue of Liberty, the Lincoln Memorial, that gay Stonewall place in New York City and some museums in DC like the ones for Indians and arty women and African history. And if they can recruit enough soldiers, they'll probably include the Supreme Court and other targets around the country."

Pleased that they had tricked him into giving them the info on the plan, Parker pretended to make a note with her left hand, giving Corelli time to jot it all down. "Is there some special place on the Internet where the plan or things like it are discussed?"

"As I said, I'm not part of the violent group but Philippa mentioned it during the meeting. It sounded like one of those old TV comedy shows." He looked down. "I really don't know anything else. I'd like to go now."

Parker nodded. "Thank you for you cooperation. We may get back to you with other questions and please feel free to contact us if you remember something."

When Twigs stepped out of the room two detectives greeted him. "Samuel Twigs, you are under arrest for the rape of—" The detective read the names of six children.

As they spun him around to cuff him, he glared at Parker. "Liar." He spat the word at her. "You said you weren't interested in the pictures." He sounded hurt.

Parker stood. "We're not. But these two detectives are from the Special Victims Division, and they are."

As the detectives walked away with him, the sounds of the Miranda warning drifted back.

CHAPTER THIRTY-TWO

Dressing was getting easier. Annie had gone shopping for clothing that she could manage herself. She'd bought shirts with armholes wide enough to slip over her cast, knit cardigan sweaters with sleeves that stretched enough to go over her cast and the shirts, and a pair of loafers. Parker had developed one-handed techniques for pulling on socks, panties, and slacks, buttoning a shirt, and slipping into a sweater. Stepping into the loafers was easy. She still needed help cutting her food, getting in and out of the car and some other things but she was feeling more independent. And because she was feeling stronger physically, she no longer felt overwhelmed by her cast and foam cushion.

"What are you looking so happy about this morning?" Corelli said, as she helped Parker into the car.

"For the first time since I woke up in the hospital, I don't feel exhausted. And I didn't need Annie's help dressing this morning. Even though I'm lugging my arm around, I feel like myself again."

"It's a wonderful feeling, isn't it?" Corelli grinned. "The first time I was able to walk to the bathroom myself after the shooting, even with the walker, I felt like I'd won Olympic gold. Our bodies are resilient."

Dietz was walking back from the food truck with a container of coffee and a bagel when they got to the door. "Yo, Parker. We got Walter Foster in three and Lena Wood in two whenever you feel like chatting. The sneaky bastards were trying to make a getaway about three thirty this morning. Our guys watched them pack a van with all their belongings and grabbed them just as they loaded the last box. They took the van into custody too."

"You just made a good day great, Dietz. Please make sure he gets breakfast. You know, coffee, eggs and bacon and potatoes, and collect everything he uses so we can get a good DNA sample."

"Already done. Everything is on the way to the lab. They promised to put a rush on it. By the way, he has bandages on his hand, neck and face. All left side."

Parker and Corelli sat at the table and waited for the team to drift over. Parker felt wired with the excitement that usually came as they were closing in on the killer. She felt it in her bones, even the broken ones. And she sensed everyone else around the table was feeling it.

Dietz rubbed his hands together. "We're filling up this morning. Michele Benson, Bo Waters, Heather Harrington, and Abel Clemson are here waiting to be interviewed. Lester was reluctant to return so he's being escorted in."

It was a good thing she was feeling energetic this morning, since it was going to be a long day. Parker reviewed the list in her head. Foster would be the most challenging for her and potentially the most violent. "Forlini and Watkins I'd like you to observe when we interview Foster in case we need a physical intervention. Anyone else is welcome."

"Greene and Kim, why don't you take Bo Waters and Abel Clemson? Remember Waters is a Harrington and Clemson was raised by the Harrington Davenport family. The issue is the murder of multiple members of the Davenport family so find out what they know and whether they have a motive. Here's a list." She passed them a single sheet of paper.

PHILIPPA HARRINGTON DAVENPORT
FAMILY MEMBERS MURDERED

Harrington Davenport – son
Phoebe Davenport Worth – daughter
Albert Davenport – son
Elliot Davenport – son
Willa Davenport – granddaughter
Harrington Davenport II – grandson
Fiona Medford – granddaughter

"Corelli and I will take Benson and Heather Harrington later."
Parker took a deep breath. "You ready, Corelli?"

"I am. But since the man tried to kill you, it might be less stressful if I interview him with Forlini or Watkins and you observe."

"What would you do if he'd tried to kill you?"

Corelli ran her fingers through her hair. "I would interview him."

Just as she thought. She needed to confront her attacker. "Jump in if you think it's necessary but I want to interview him. Let's have him brought to us, though. I think that works because of the element of surprise. Watkins and Forlini, give us a couple minutes to settle in room one then bring Foster to us."

Forlini cracked his knuckles. "I observed him through the mirror this morning. He's big and he's cuffed but he looks ready to pop. I suggest I stay in the room, behind him, just in case."

"Let's take a look." Corelli led Parker, Watkins and Forlini to the small observation room. They stared at the sweating, wild-eyed man. "I'm thinking we should get a couple of uniforms to assist when you move him and I agree Forlini should stay in the room, with Watkins observing and the uniforms outside the door. But it's your call, Parker."

Parker stared at the man who almost certainly had almost killed her but she felt no fear. "He looks like a cornered animal. I wonder if he's claustrophobic. My guess is he would be less angry, more willing to talk if we remove the cuffs and give him a bottle of water so he feels respected. What's your take, Corelli?"

"It's risky but with Forlini in the room and Watkins plus two uniforms outside, it could work. Are you sure that's what you want?"

"Let's start that way and if he doesn't settle, we'll cuff him. But I've changed my mind. I think it would be more effective if we interview him in there. So as soon as we have two uniforms, the three of us can go in."

Ten minutes later Forlini returned with two husky uniformed officers and Parker, Corelli and Forlini filed into the room. Foster looked up as Parker sat facing him, then he did a double take. His eyes were wide. His gaze went to the door. Corelli put a cold bottle of water in front of him and sat.

"Detective, please remind the officers outside to bring water to Brandon Lester."

Parker didn't think Foster's eyes could open any wider but they did. Forlini held the door open so Foster could see the two burly officers standing there. He relayed the message that the officers would ignore because Lester wasn't even in the building.

Now that he knew he was outnumbered by men of equal stature and he thought his boss was also in custody, Parker put the last piece in place. "If you can control your temper, I'll have the cuffs removed." She waited for his response.

He stared over Parker's shoulder. "I can do that."

"Remove Mr. Foster's cuffs, Detective Forlini."

Foster sat quietly as Forlini unlocked and pocketed the cuffs then he stretched his arms and rubbed his wrists.

"We haven't met face-to-face in a while, Mr. Foster, so in case you don't remember, I'm Detective Parker, this is Detective Corelli and Detective Forlini is behind you."

"I'm not stupid. I remember." He sounded offended.

"And do you remember the last time we met?"

"I just said I did."

"Oh, so you remember when you came up behind me, broke my arm and tried to strangle me to death? Just the way you murdered Magnolia Walker and Ned Rich?"

He opened his mouth, then clamped it shut. "I don't know what you're talking about. I didn't murder nobody. I remember you barging into my house."

"I see. So where were you and Lena going in the middle of the night with all your belongings in that van?"

He took a minute to think before answering. "Home to Idaho. We don't like Brooklyn. We figured we'd avoid traffic by leaving early."

"Did you sell your brownstone?"

"No, that belongs to Mrs. Davenport, senior."

"What happened to your face and your neck?"

His hand flew to the bandages. "Cut myself shaving."

"Is that what Lena told you to say?"

"She don't tell me what to say."

"And what happened to your hand?"

His gaze went to his left hand. "Cat scratched me."

"Did you know that Harry Davenport kept files on you and Lena? He had some really good nudes of Lena and a few of you in bed with a woman, not the real wife you abandoned in Idaho or Lena, your fake wife." She pushed the pictures in front of him. He ignored them and stared at the mirror behind Parker. "Such good Christians. But it sure doesn't look like either of you were praying. But since, you and Lena aren't married, I guess it doesn't matter. Did Harry threaten to expose you and Lena, destroy her fake image as a pure white wife and mother?"

He flushed and fisted his hands.

Corelli leaned forward. "Is that why you killed him?" Forlini stepped away from the wall, ready to pounce.

"I don't even own a gun, bitch." The low, harsh tone of voice threatened violence as did the widened nostrils and raised upper lip that displayed his teeth, like a snarling animal.

"Oh, that's right, you prefer to kill with your bare hands."

He muttered and tried to stand but Forlini pushed him down. Parker continued as if she hadn't noticed his anger. "We know about the Idahoans killed in the same way as you tried and failed to kill me. Not to mention the ones in Upstate New York and West Virginia."

"I don't know what you're talking about."

"I'll bet those bandages are covering scratches made by fingernails. Mine."

He couldn't resist touching the bandages, but he didn't take the bait.

"So does Philippa Davenport pay you directly or are you just another murder-for-hire flunky on Brandon's payroll?"

"I work as a security guard for Brandon."

"Did I mention we have Brandon in custody and he's waiting to talk to an assistant district attorney so he can make a deal." Parker leaned in as best she could with her bulky foam companion and spoke softly. "You've been around, Walter. If he makes a deal, he's going to throw you to the wolves. We know you killed Magnolia Walker and Ned Rich and tried to kill me. I can't promise anything but I'll ask the district attorney to take your cooperation into consideration if you tell me who ordered you to kill the three of us."

Foster's jaw tightened as if he was afraid to let himself speak.

"All right, Detective Forlini, put him in a holding cell. We'll see whether Lena or Brandon makes a deal first."

Forlini flicked the cuff on one hand and quickly secured the second hand behind his back.

"You fucking black bitch, I'm sorry I didn't—" He cut himself off.

"You're sorry what, Walter? That you weren't good enough to kill me? Did you know I put your two accomplices in the hospital and both needed surgery? You broke my arm and strangled me, yet I'm here. A big guy like you could have fought my dad and finished me off. But faced with someone your size, you ran. You're a coward, Walter. You kill from behind because you're afraid to look your victims in the eye. I may be banged up but I'm feeling pretty good. I'm the black woman who beat three big ex-military men of the so-called superior white race."

Foster roared and tried to get to her but Forlini put his arm around Foster's neck and jerked him back. Choking, Foster writhed trying to get away. And the bandages on his neck and face came loose exposing the scratches. Forlini pushed him toward the door.

Parker stood. "Oops, your bandages fell off and I see the scratches I put there while hanging on your arm. Hard to breathe with that arm crushing your throat, isn't it, Walter? Feeling helpless?" Forlini pushed him out of the room into the arms of the uniforms waiting. She could hear him screaming about killing her as they dragged him to the holding cell.

CHAPTER THIRTY-THREE

"Well, that was fun." Parker glanced at Corelli, checking her reaction.

Corelli put her hand on Parker's shoulder. "You really got to him and almost got a confession out of the bastard but it would have been dicey if Forlini hadn't already cuffed him." She opened the door to the conference room.

Forlini strolled in a few seconds later. He dangled an evidence bag. "I found some bandages on the floor.

"Good job, Forlini. I hope he didn't hurt you." Parker pointed to the bag. "Did they really come off by accident?"

He wiggled his eyebrows. "When you have someone in a chokehold from behind sometimes your arm puts pressure on the side of their face so that's probably why they came off. I'll send them to the lab. Should I get someone to book him?"

Parker was 99.9% sure but why rush? She knew the DNA comparison would be a high priority in the lab so she would wait. "Not yet. But when we do, let's make sure we get some good pictures of those scratches."

Watkins joined Parker, Corelli and Forlini. "Heather Harrington must have heard the ruckus in the hall because she looked out, locked eyes with Foster for a few seconds and then she watched him shuffle away with the uniforms. Could be they just know each other because he works for Lester, but it seemed like more than a casual connection to me."

"That's interesting. Thanks for the heads up."

Parker and Corelli took a few seconds to watch Heather Harrington in room one. She seemed composed but her tapping fingers showed her impatience or perhaps her anger. Although Parker entered first, Heather ignored her and glared at Corelli. She didn't seem to notice Corelli slip her hand under the foam as Parker sat. "What was so important that I had to come all the way down here to talk to you? You know where I live." Yes, anger. Entitled anger.

"Since some of your folks tried to kill me, it's been hard to get around."

Her eyes steely, she focused on Parker. "Well, ain't you the sight." Heather glared at her. "If you can't do the job, darlin', you should be home in bed instead of inconveniencing the upstanding white citizens of this city."

"Unfortunately, we rarely get to interview upstanding white citizens." Parker turned to Corelli. "Do we?"

"None that I can recall on this case, Detective Parker."

Noting the flush of red on Heather's neck, Parker continued, "How did it feel to see Walter Foster in handcuffs?"

"Oh, was that who he was?" The flush deepened.

"Walter, Andy Topping, and Everet Collins tried to kill me. I put Andy and Everet in the hospital but Walter, the strangler, got away and was trying to get out of town with his pretty little wife. Do you know Lena?" Heather's nose wrinkled as if she smelled something bad. Parker kind of agreed. "Now all three are under arrest for murder and attempted murder and they're clamoring to make a deal. The first one to give us the name of the person who ordered the murders and the attack on me, will get the deal."

Heather fingered her gold necklace. "I've seen them outside the house but I don't really know them. I believe they do security work for Brandon." In her recent reading about white supremacists,

Parker had learned that the large gold "14" hanging off Heather's necklace was a numerical representation of the fourteen-word, white supremacist slogan, "We must secure the existence of our people and a future for white children."

Taking her touching the necklace as a tell, Parker decided to push it. "We believe the person who ordered the murders and the attack on me is someone in your circle. Any ideas?"

Heather lifted her shoulders. "No idea."

Parker wasn't convinced but it was time to throw Heather into the deep water. "Why don't you tell us about the night you murdered Harry Davenport?"

"What the hell, are you crazy? Harry was family. Why would I do such a thing?" The angry rapid-fire denial replaced Heather's slow West Virginia drawl.

Parker let her sit with silence for a moment. "How's this for a reason. You want to step into Philippa's shoes when she can no longer lead but since you're a mere woman without Philippa's history and stature, Harry was your competition. With him out of the way, the path for you to be her successor is clear."

"That's really stupid." Heather's tone was as close to a snarl as a human could get. "Harry wasn't interested in taking over. In fact, a couple of nights before he died he and Philippa had a falling out that made it clear he was washing his hands of anything to do with being a true white nationalist. He was committing political suicide. Why would I kill him?"

"Jealousy. Wanting to be Philippa's favorite. The same reason you murdered all the other members of Philippa's family." Parker wanted to keep her angry.

Heather stood. "I'm truly offended." She pointed a finger at Parker. "You're black"—the condescension in her voice was no accident—"so naturally you don't understand family connections, but you"—she focused on Corelli—"your name sounds I-talian so you should understand what family means."

"Sit," Parker commanded. It looked as if Heather might object but she slowly dropped into her chair. "I understand family. I understand that sometimes ambition overrides everything including love, loyalty and blood connection. And I understand your ambition to be number one, knowing you are as smart or smarter than Philippa. You're willing to pay your dues and serve

Philippa but you can't let her children or her grandchildren take what is rightfully your place. Murder is easy. Pick them off one by one, slowly but surely."

Heather's face whitened and she looked horrified. "You think I'm so ruthless that for twenty years I've been slowly eliminating the competition? My cousins? You are even more ignorant than I thought. You can't prove it because it isn't true. Just like you can't prove I murdered Harry because it isn't true." She held Parker's gaze. "But if I did kill anyone, you and your friends here"—she waved a hand to include the station—"would never figure it out because I'm smarter than all of you."

Parker believed the part about her not murdering Harry and the others, not the part about Heather being smarter than all of them. "What will you do about the plan now that Harry is dead?"

Heather's mouth opened and closed rapidly like a fish gasping for oxygen. She grabbed the bottle of water on the table in front of her, twisted the cap off, and drank half the bottle in two swallows. Her hand went to the necklace. "What plan?" Her voice was shaky.

As Parker intended, the question had caught her off guard. "The one about blowing up monuments. I would guess you wrote it, but as usual, Philippa and the men took all the credit."

"You're crazy. There's no plan." Heather's fingers closed around the cross.

"Really? That's not what we're hearing from others at the meeting."

Heather wrapped her arms around herself and clamped her jaw so tight Parker feared it would lock.

It was clear Heather wasn't about to give up anything on the plan so Parker changed direction. "I understand you and Walter Foster had an intimate moment when he was dragged down the hall toward the cells. Just how intimate are you?"

Heather's lovely white skin was a disadvantage when she was trying to hide something. Her face was on fire. She clutched her cross and looked down. "I told you I don't know him."

"Do you live with Philippa?"

Heather blinked. She probably hadn't expected the change in subject. "No. I have a separate two-bedroom apartment on the first floor of her house."

"Who else has apartments there?"

She hesitated. "Abel and Brandon and a couple of Brandon's old military pals who work for him. There's also a guest apartment for visitors."

"You never did tell us where you were between eight p.m. and four a.m. the night Harry was murdered."

"I was with…um, I was home with Philippa. I made us dinner, then we did some business and watched TV. We usually go to sleep sometime between eleven and twelve but I'm not sure exactly what time it was that night."

Parker touched Corelli's thigh to signal she wanted to stand. "You can go but we may have more questions so don't leave the city."

Parker stretched as they waited for Michele Benson to be escorted in. Maynard had asked to watch the interview and her reaction would be interesting. "Why don't you do Benson, Corelli?"

Corelli squeezed her shoulder. "I don't know. She really likes you so you might get more meaningful answers. But if you insist…"

"I insist." Parker didn't stand when Benson arrived, but she did greet her. "Sorry to keep you waiting, Michele, but we have a lot going on. Please sit."

"What's this about?" Benson addressed the question to Parker.

Corelli answered. "I'm sure you remember Detective Parker mentioning the murders of members of Philippa Harrington Davenport's family over the last twenty years. We've found something that connects them and the murder of Harry Davenport. We now believe we have a single killer for all."

Benson leaned forward. "That's interesting but I don't understand how it relates to me."

"You were in the Marines for twenty years. Where were you stationed during that time?"

Benson smiled. "You think I'm the killer?" She gazed at Parker. "I assure you it's not me." She looked up as if the answer was written on the ceiling. "Twenty-two or twenty-three years ago, I spent thirteen weeks in boot camp in Parris Island, South Carolina, then I went home to West Virginia for a couple of weeks. After that I reported to Law Enforcement Military Police training at Fort Leonard Wood, Missouri. I was there for about five months. Then I spent a little over a year in Camp Pendleton in Southern

California before shipping out to Iraq for a little more than a year, then I spent a couple of years in Germany, another year in Okinawa, then I did another tour in Iraq followed by a couple of tours in Afghanistan and then four years at the Pentagon in Washington, DC. In between tours I was home a week to ten days at a time usually. If you want exact dates and places, you'll have to request my military records because I sure as hell don't remember. But I'm puzzled. What motive do you think I have for killing members of Philippa's family?"

Corelli glanced at Parker and seeing what she took as agreement she leveled with Benson. "As I said, we've determined we have a single killer. And we believe the killings are personal, that it's someone who has been part of Philippa's circle for the past twenty years or more. You're here because you fit that profile. We will check your record but more important, we'd like your input on this."

"Sure, if I can help I will."

"Besides you, Katharine Davenport, Meriwether Davis, Bo Waters, Heather Davenport, Abel Clemson, and Brandon Lester fit the profile. Can you think of anyone else? Or can you think of a motive for one of them?"

"I really can't see any of her loyal followers wanting to destroy her family. You're assuming that because Harry was killed here that the killer must live in New York City. But the other murders occurred in West Virginia and I would guess there are people in West Virginia who would like nothing better than seeing all the Harrington Davenports eliminated."

"Shit, Benson, we want answers not complications." Corelli jumped up and paced in the tight space available. "Damn it. I can't believe I didn't think of that."

"Sorry." Benson looked from Corelli to Parker. "Since Harry was shot, I'm guessing the murders are connected by the bullets. In my opinion, the only possibility of solving this is finding the gun. I assume you don't have enough evidence to search everyone's houses?"

"No, we don't." Afraid Corelli's anger at having overlooked the West Virginia angle would change the cooperative tone of the meeting, Parker took over. "There is something else you can help us with. We understand Philippa has a plan for July fourth that involves destroying monuments like the Statue of Liberty. You mentioned rumors. Is that what you've heard?"

"Philippa? Christ she really is losing it. As I've said, Harry hinted at violence but nothing specific and certainly not that Philippa was involved. Are you sure? Have you seen this plan?"

"No. But Harry discussed it with others who told us about it. Apparently, he was trying to head it off and had a falling out with his mother over it. But all we have is secondhand accounts, which amount to hearsay."

"I would guess Brandon Lester and his volunteers are involved." Parker detected a bit of anger in Benson's statement. "Why?"

Benson's jaw tightened. "I'd appreciate it if you kept this part of the conversation between us, and Detective Corelli, of course."

Parker was curious but she couldn't promise. "Sorry, but if it's pertinent to the investigation—"

"I know if it's relevant you'll use it." Benson smiled. "But I meant in terms of revealing that you heard it from me."

"That I have no problem with unless we're making a case against you."

Benson laughed. "I think I'm safe then. Anyway, Lester and his group of followers consider themselves an army in the service of white nationalism. Philippa is their Hitler, if you will, and Brandon is her Hermann Göring, her general. She's quite wealthy, as I'm sure you know, and I believe he and the members of his group are on her payroll."

Parker studied Benson's face. "You're not kidding about her army, are you?"

Benson shook her head. "Unfortunately not."

A private army? Parker let that thought roll around in her head for a few seconds.

Benson reached across the table and covered Parker's good hand. "I've spent a lot of years separating from all the white nationalist hate. They don't let go easily, but when I was a teenager, I talked to Katharine and Harry about it and they encouraged me to pull away. In fact, that was why I enlisted. As a result, I'm not included on anyone's "must know" list so I really have nothing on this plan. I could put some people on researching it, but I assume you've already done that."

Parker extracted her hand. Benson's hand felt good but this was not the time or place to be holding hands with a potential suspect.

Corelli had stopped pacing and was watching them. Her lips were quirking but if she had to choose, she'd take Corelli's ribbing over her anger any day. She signaled Corelli and they stood. "Thanks for coming in, Michele. I'm sorry we kept you waiting but as you might expect, we've been busy."

Dietz joined them at the conference table. "Having fun yet, Parker?"

"You know, I think I am. We're close to figuring this out and we're going to nail the bastards." He laughed and walked away. Now that she had a minute to breathe, Parker realized she was hungry. She looked at Corelli. "Lunch?"

"Sure. Darla texted earlier. Do you want to meet her and Bear at Buonasola Grill or do one of the food trucks outside?"

"Do we have time to drive to the South Street Seaport to meet them?"

Corelli laughed. "If you're not worried about keeping our guests waiting, we have plenty of time and it might be good to get away from here for a bit."

Corelli was right. They needed to get away. Interviewing Foster had shaken her and it would be good to spend time with friends, which Darla North and Bear Murray were, even though they were members of the media. "Text them and let's do it. But don't let me blab about the case."

The hostess gaped at Parker's arm and the fading bruises on her face. "Detective Parker, I read about you being attacked but I didn't realize it was so bad. Do you need help?"

"Thanks, Macy, I'm not as bad as I look. Is our usual table available?"

Macy smiled. "Of course. Ms. North and Ms. Murray are already seated."

Parker entered the dining room and greeted Darla and Bear. In the summer their favorite table was outside on the deck but in cold weather they sat inside at a table against the wall so Parker and Corelli could sit facing the door.

Darla jumped up. "P.J., you look better than I expected but I'm going to skip trying to hug you."

Bear greeted Parker then helped Corelli move the table. Corelli settled Parker with her back to the wall and her right arm on the outside of the table, then moved around to sit next to her.

"Thanks for agreeing to meet us. We've been worried about you." Darla grinned. "And naturally we're hoping for the inside scoop. You have three murders and the attempt to murder you. I can't figure out whether Davenport's murder is connected to the other two or is related to the rumors about white nationalist violence."

Parker laughed. "You know there are no inside scoops. At least until we know what's happening."

"What rumors have you heard?" Corelli was the one asking.

Darla shrugged. "Unfortunately, nothing specific. According to the rumors the drums are beating all over the country about some planned violence but if it's true, they're doing a good job of keeping it secret. Bear has been trying to track down who started the rumors and keeps stoking them but no one seems to know."

"Or willing to admit it," Bear said.

Parker was surprised that Bear commented. She usually let the effervescent Darla carry the conversation. "We're looking into the rumors. And we're getting close on the murders, but we really don't have anything to share yet. I'm taking bets you've been digging into the white nationalist groups."

Darla nodded. "I've been trying to confirm the rumors but there's nothing on social media or the Internet."

Knowing they came here often and rarely studied the menus, the waitress arrived to take their orders. While Parker thought about what she could eat with one hand, Corelli ordered linguine with white clam sauce, Darla the gumbo and Bear her usual sliced steak sandwich. The waitress had already poured coffee for all. Parker decided on a sandwich that Corelli often ordered. "I'll have the grilled chicken sandwich with pesto, roasted red peppers and some sliced jalapenos. Please ask the kitchen to cut it into four pieces so I can manage with just my left hand." She turned to Darla. "So did you find anything for us?"

Darla pulled an envelope out of her bag. "When we leave, I'll give you this. It has some reports and articles you might find interesting. I've focused on New York groups and I'm kind of fascinated by Davenport's mother, Philippa Harrington Davenport. She's the only woman in a leadership role in any of the groups around the country and she's the most aggressive, pushing for white nationalists to run for office so they can take over the government, and recently urging violence. We've interviewed a few people who seemed like they might be in the know, but so far we've found nothing world-shaking. You probably know the only thing that unites the many unrelated small white nationalist groups around the country is the idea that white men are destined to rule and women, people of color and people they define as defective, that is anyone with a disease or physical issues, need to be controlled and in some cases eliminated. Some of the groups are anti-government of any kind. Others want to be the ones governing and making the rules. The groups have only been connected loosely in the past but the Internet and the deep dark web have made it easier for them to communicate."

Darla glanced at the nearby tables and then lowered her voice. "I did find something interesting. I came across a discussion about bombing the Statue of Liberty on one of the hate sites and as I scrolled through the thread, the site went down. When it came back up, the conversation had disappeared. I don't know what to think about it. Was it true and removed because it shouldn't have been public? Or was it removed because it wasn't true and the site was trying to avoid scrutiny?" She paused. "Then a little later a post went up reminding all concerned to post private information only to those sites set up specifically to discuss the plan."

Corelli and Parker exchanged a look and then Corelli asked, "Were the addresses of those special sites posted?"

Darla leaned in. "No. Based on that look, I'm guessing you know what plan they're talking about."

"Sorry." Parker reached across the table and touched Darla's hand. "We don't have anything we can give you, Darla. Did you note the site this occurred on?"

Darla shook her head. "This one-way thing we have going here is frustrating. I hope you'll give me a heads up when you can. And to answer your question, of course I noted it. It's in the package of information."

The waitress dropped off their lunches and to Parker's delight the conversation turned personal.

CHAPTER THIRTY-FOUR

The lunch break with friends had refreshed her. She knew in her gut that the DNA test would confirm Foster was her attacker. But someone had ordered him to kill Walker, Rich and her, and she was determined to nail that person too. The most likely candidates were Brandon and Philippa. All she needed was Walter Foster, Everet Collins, Andy Topping or Lena Wood to spill the beans. Hopefully, the threat of Brandon Lester making a deal would get one of them to talk.

She asked Corelli to check with Dietz about the setup, then called Maynard over. "What did you think about the interview with Michele Benson?"

Maynard frowned. "I didn't think she was involved so that part was okay." She looked around, then leaned closer. "I noticed she held your hand for a long time. Are you two...?"

Of course Maynard would notice. "Benson is a flirt, but I don't take it seriously. Besides, I would never get involved with a suspect." Parker wanted to be honest with Maynard but she didn't have to tell her she liked it. "I actually called you over because I want to harass a group of killers who hate strong women, especially strong women of color, so I'm organizing teams of two women to question them. Think you can handle it, working with Greene?"

"You bet." Maynard grinned. "This is great. I never get to interview anyone."

"We'll meet later to review things before we start." Parker watched Maynard saunter away and admired the unselfconscious sensuality of the woman. It had attracted her the first time. *The first time?* What was she thinking?

Corelli slid into a chair at the table. "What's up?"

Parker glanced at Maynard, now intent on her computer screen. "I'm pairing Maynard with Greene to give her some experience interviewing. I'm feeling great now but in case I tire midway, I want you to orchestrate this extravaganza."

"Yes, ma'am." Corelli tipped an imaginary hat. "Ah, there's ADA Natalie Brooks. I'll get everyone together to review our objectives and discuss strategy so we're all on the same page before we start. I've asked Graciela Cabrera, the new detective who transferred in the other day, to be our fourth."

Corelli called the four female detectives to the table. "Since these guys hate women and minorities, we hope our teams will offend them. We're pairing me and Parker, Greene and Maynard, and Kim and Cabrera. ADA Natalie Brooks will be available to talk deals if anyone is interested."

"Andy Topping and Everet Collins are under arrest for attacking Parker and we're waiting on the DNA comparison to confirm Walter Foster attempted to kill Parker and murdered Magnolia Walker and Ned Rich. Our goal today is to get one of them to give up the person who ordered the killings. Anything we learn about Philippa Davenport and the plan will be a cherry on the sundae. Any questions?"

Maynard put her hand up. "You're 99.99 percent sure Foster is the one who killed Walker and Rich and tried to kill Parker, so the goal with him is to get a confession and find out whether Philippa Davenport or Lester ordered the hit. And you want Lester to give up Philippa? Is that right?"

"Yes. Lester is in a leadership position in Philippa's orbit so he can give up Philippa, tell us why Walker and Rich were murdered, and give us insight to some of the other players and the plan. We're willing to make a deal with him if he gives us enough of what we want. I'm guessing he might be the one to ask for a deal. We want

Foster to go down for the murders he's committed and his attempt on Parker, so we're not interested in offering him a deal. Wood doesn't seem to be a big player but we'd like her to give up Foster and anything she knows about Lester and Philippa."

Parker was pleased to see Cabrera raise her hand. "How long will we have with each before we shift?"

Corelli turned to Parker. "Do you have a timeframe in mind?"

"This is your baby, Corelli."

"Okay, I'm thinking ten minutes first go, then meet in the hall and decide about the next round."

The six female detectives and the ADA stood to the side and observed the dance that Corelli had choreographed. Foster, handcuffed and surrounded by three large male uniformed officers, was the first one led into the hall outside the interview rooms. Male detectives and uniformed officers escorted the other four in, one at a time. They were kept away from each other, but the wide eyes and uneasy glances made it was clear seeing the others in custody unnerved them. When all five were stationed along the hallway, Parker gave them several seconds to absorb what was happening before she stepped up with a list in her hand. "Let's see, Wood, room one. Lena locked eyes with Foster then glanced at Lester as she was walked to the assigned room. Parker called out Topping, room two. He looked down as he shuffled into the room on his walker. Collins was defiant as he entered his room. Foster pretended he didn't hear her call his name but as Forlini and the guards pushed him into the room, he cursed her. When Forlini came out and reported that Foster was cuffed to the table, she signaled Lester's escorts. The attorney he'd demanded arrived just as he was being led into the interview room. Parker and Corelli followed them.

Olga Thorn, Lester's attorney, broke the silence. "Detective Parker, I was sorry to hear of the brutal attack on you. I've only spoken to my client on the phone for a few minutes, so perhaps you can tell me why you brought him in, let him go, then brought him back today? Sounds like harassment to me. Or a fishing expedition."

Parker glared at Lester and he dropped his gaze. "He's a suspect in the murder of Harrington Davenport and a string of murders in the Davenport family that go back over twenty years. Finally, we suspect that he ordered the murder of two people and the attempt to kill me."

"Oh, my." The attorney glanced at Lester. "And do you have evidence to support any of these charges?"

Lester looked up. "They don't have a damn—"

Olga Thorn put her hand up, cutting him short. "Brandon, you will only speak if I tell you to answer a question. You are not to volunteer any information or opinions. Got it?"

Thorn turned back to Parker. "Detective?"

Parker hoped making it sound as if they were about to sign a deal would freak out Brandon. "The three men who attempted to kill me are here and we expect them to give up Brandon in exchange for a deal."

Brandon stared over her head, acting like he didn't have a care in the world.

"Do you have any questions for Brandon that he hasn't already answered?" Thorn didn't attempt to hide her annoyance.

Damn an attorney always made things harder and since they really were on a fishing expedition, they'd have to back off. "We do," Parker said. "In what capacity does Mr. Lester know Walter Foster, Andy Topping, and Everet Collins?"

"You may answer, Brandon. And to speed this up, I'll tell you when I don't want you to answer."

"They work as security guards for me."

"And do you ever use these three employees for other tasks?"

"Sometimes they help me move things or deliver packages, things like that." He was relaxed and confident.

Time to shake him up. "When and where did you meet Magnolia Walker and Ned Rich?"

Lester flinched. "I never met them."

"But you know who they are?"

"I, uh, read about them in the newspapers."

"There was a front page photo and several stories about Rich's murder but as far as I know not one mention of Walker's murder. Do you remember where you saw it?"

He lifted his shoulders. "It wasn't important, so I don't remember."

"Were you aware that your three employees attacked and attempted to murder me?"

Lester took his time answering. "Not until you told me the last time I was here."

"Are you aware that Walker and Rich had information about the Harrington family that would not only be embarrassing but would also destroy everything Philippa has worked for most of her life?"

Lester frowned. "You're lying. Philippa is too powerful for any information to affect her position."

Olga Thorn eyed Parker. "What information is that?"

"We're not prepared to release it yet but let me assure you it gives the Harringtons including Mr. Lester, a powerful motive for murder."

"And how does that relate to the attack on you?"

"I'm an uppity black woman in a position of power who knows the secret and I hinted at it when I met with Philippa to discuss her son's murder."

"Any more questions for Mr. Lester?"

"Not at the moment."

Thorn tapped her phone. "You have one hour. And then if you aren't ready to charge my client, we're leaving." She removed some files from her black leather briefcase, put on her glasses and started reading, essentially dismissing them.

They'd been more than ten minutes and the other teams had moved on to their next interviews.

Corelli headed for Brooks who was leaning against the wall outside the interview rooms. "Either Lester didn't order the attacks or he's a really good actor."

Parker took a position next to Brooks. "I agree. But if not him, who? Philippa is the obvious culprit since I hinted to her that I knew what Walker and Rich knew and she has the most to lose if word gets out that she has black blood."

Maynard and Greene approached. Maynard looked pumped. "That was great. Foster was happy to answer our questions about the Harrington family murders and denied even knowing about them, but he clammed up or got aggressive when we pressed on the murders or the attack on you."

"Maynard did a good job questioning him but he didn't give us anything," Greene said. "I think he knows he's going down for the murders and a deal won't be much help. Topping implicated Foster but Maynard and I agree he doesn't know who ordered the hit on you."

"We got nothing," Kim said, as she and Cabrera joined them. "Lena Wood was all 'I'm just a simple white housewife dedicated to serving my nice white hubby and I have no idea what he does when he's not home.' It was kind of nauseating. And Collins said Topping invited him to go along for some fun."

"Well, this was a bust." Parker sighed. "We have nothing on Wood so I'm going to release her. We're wasting our time. We'll have to settle for nailing Foster for the murders and forget about who ordered them."

Corelli straightened. "Kim and Greene take care of Wood, let Lester and his attorney know they can leave, get Topping and Collins transported back to Rikers and send Foster back to his cell."

It had been a long, intense day and Parker realized her exhaustion was making her feel hopeless again. She gave herself a mental kick. If she didn't believe they'd close this case, the whole team would give up. She took a deep breath. "Okay team, back to the drawing board. We still have to find Davenport's murderer and let's not forget *the plan* is still hanging over us." As they walked back to the conference room, Maynard and Cabrera chatted with Corelli. Parker realized that though she hadn't accomplished what she wanted, Maynard and Cabrera had gained face time interrogating suspects, something they both needed.

Corelli waited until they were alone and spoke softly so only Parker could hear. "I think we should call it a day, Parker. How about a nap and a relaxing dinner with me and Brett, then I'll drive you to Jessie's house?"

"I'd love that but I don't like the idea of our escorts waiting outside for so long."

"We can dismiss them, then call for a patrol car to follow us when you're ready."

Refreshed by the nap, Parker welcomed a hug from Brett and realized she was starving. Corelli unpacked the Chinese food while Brett set the table and put out beer and wine. Parker used a fork instead of chopsticks but everything was in small pieces and eating was easy.

As usual with Brett, laughter and conversation flowed and it felt nice to be enveloped in their warmth. She wanted what they had. She just needed the right partner. Although Ndep was acting like they were done, she wanted a face-to-face conversation to formally end their involvement.

"P.J." Brett interrupted her musings. "Chiara and I have decided to live together. I'm going to move in with her."

Parker perked up. "Wow, congratulations. I can't say I'm surprised. When?"

A smiling Corelli put her arm around Brett. "We'll start moving her stuff next week."

Even though Corelli was smiling more frequently these days, Parker was still taken aback to see that Corelli, like Brett, had a beautiful smile, and though they were very different, Corelli, like Brett, was caring and loving. "What?" She'd missed what Brett said while she was mooning.

"Would you be interested in my apartment, P.J.? I'd like to hold on to it for another year or so. I know you're in no position to move right now but I would really love to have someone I know and trust living there. I need the tax deduction so the rent would be low, just enough to cover basic monthly expenses. I'd prefer to leave my furniture, but I could put everything in storage if that works better for you. The only negative I see is that you would have to find a new place in a year or so when I decide to sell it."

"Wow. I could never afford to live there on my salary but a year or so would give me time to figure out where I want to live. How high are the expenses?"

"I'll ask my accountant to figure it out but my guess is less than a thousand dollars a month."

"That's less than I pay now. I was planning to buy new furniture when I move. And having your things there would give me another year to save. Let me know what the accountant comes up with. In the meantime, can I think about it?"

Brett flashed a smile. "No rush. It's you or it stays empty."

Corelli laughed when she got off the phone with their escorts. "The regular guys decided to stay on duty and have dinner while they waited for us. They'll be outside in a few minutes."

In the elevator, Parker confronted Corelli. "Did you put Brett up to this?"

Corelli laughed. "Are you kidding? That woman is always one step ahead of me. I told her you were looking for an apartment but you moving into hers was totally her idea."

They stepped outside and in seconds they were confronted by a mob pushing them back against the building. A couple of men wearing masks pushed to the front of the crowd and started throwing punches. Parker struck out once or twice with her left hand but she needed it to hold up her cast. *She was like a turtle on its back, helpless to defend herself.* She was relieved when Corelli stepped in front of her. *Where the hell was their security team? Shit. Was that the glint of a gun in the streetlight?*

"Gun ahead," Parker shouted.

Corelli scanned for the gun while she fumbled with her zipper trying to get to her Glock. The crowd surged against them. Corelli kicked and punched wildly at the men surrounding her, forcing them to fall back. She unzipped her coat and drew her weapon. The crowd came forward again, forcing Parker against the door. She gasped at the pressure. Corelli pushed forward to give Parker space yet be close enough to protect her from being hit. "POLICE. GET BACK OR I'LL SHOOT!" Corelli screamed the command. Those nearest backed away, Corelli lifted her weapon.

Everything stilled at the sound of sirens approaching. Male voices shouted, "POLICE!" Parker tried to locate the gun, but it had disappeared. The pressure eased as the crowd dispersed.

Their two escorts rounded up the eight men who hadn't been fast enough to escape.

Corelli turned to Parker who was leaning against the door to the building. "Are you hurt?"

"No. Just shaken. And frustrated because I was helpless to do anything." Parker felt weak and sweaty. Her fear made her angry. Her desire to catch these bastards, which was already high, had increased exponentially. "Thank you for putting yourself between me and that mob."

Corelli hesitated, then put her hand on Parker's good shoulder. "You would do the same and more for me."

Parker knew that was true. That's what partners did. They protected each other. But being helpless was a bitch. "Are you all right?"

"Yeah, they didn't land many punches and with the crowd pushing from behind they couldn't really get much power into the swing. Do you want to wait in the car while I question these guys?"

Tempted, Parker glanced at the car. "No. I can help with the questioning at least."

The men weren't armed and claimed they were standing on the corner of Fourteenth and Ninth when a woman offered them twenty dollars each to crowd around two women, one carrying a blue foam thing, as they came out of this building. The white woman who was wearing a big hat and sunglasses, said it was a joke to surprise their friends and they should push close but not hurt anyone. They didn't know anyone had a gun.

Parker believed, and Corelli agreed, the white nationalists who were probably the ones doing the punching, and the one with the gun had run at first sign of police intervention, and the ones they'd caught were street people, there for the money. Four squad cars arrived within seconds of each other, and the eight men were cuffed and taken in to be questioned.

Their escorts apologized profusely for not being there earlier.

Parker was still shaking when they got in the car. Corelli didn't address Parker's fear directly but talked about her own feelings in similar situations. By the time they arrived at Jessie's house, she'd slowly talked Parker down. That's what partners do.

CHAPTER THIRTY-FIVE

Parker couldn't stop the smile. "Maynard, you're doing a happy dance in your chair. What have you got?"

"After you told me what that Twigs pervert said about their chat room, my team brainstormed a list of old comedy shows then played with them trying to come up with the name of their secret site. One on our list was *That Was The Week That Was* and it led us to their secret chat room. It's called TWW1776 and it's buried among a lot of historic sites. It stands for The White Way and the 1776 is obvious. The current chatter is about going ahead with the plan because the deep state is responsible for killing Harrington Davenport. We connected one of the addresses to Davenport's home computer and several to Philippa Harrington Davenport, and man, is she inciting the troops to violence."

Parker grinned. "I believe that's enough to get us a warrant to search her house. Terrific work, Maynard. Anything else?"

"Is it okay, Watkins?" Watkins nodded at Maynard. "Be my guest."

Maynard cleared her throat. "While reading through Davenport's emails, Watkins spotted a couple with attachments that we hadn't printed out." She held up some papers. "This was sent to Davenport by Philippa Davenport, his mother. It's upsetting but confirms what Rich said." She handed copies to everyone around the table.

Parker stared at the first page.

PLAN TO LIBERATE THE UNITED STATES OF AMERICA – POTENTIAL JULY 4th TARGETS.

Statue of Liberty, NYC
Lincoln Memorial, DC
Stonewall Inn, NYC
Holocaust Museum, DC
National Museum of the American Indian, DC
National Museum of Women in the Arts, DC
National Museum of African History and Culture, DC
?Supreme Court, DC
?Minnesota Women Suffrage Memorial
?Tennessee Women Suffrage Memorial
?Statue of Esther Hobart Morris, Wyoming
?Brooklyn Bridge, NY
?Pentagon, DC
?US Capitol
?White House
?Sears Tower, Chicago
?Golden Gate Bridge, SF
?Indian Museum
?Mother Mosque of America (Islamic Cultural & Heritage Center), IA
?American Moslem Society (Masjid Dearborn), MI
?Ohavi Zedek Synagogue, VT
?Synagogues
?State Capital buildings

"Holy shit." Forlini broke the stunned silence.

Parker turned to the next page.

DRAFT - Taking Back America Manifesto - DRAFT

Celebrating July 4th by ringing in a new order. Today, we, the pure white-blooded ~~men~~ people of the United States of America, have demonstrated our power to destroy the monuments erected in our country to honor false ideals and idols. We will try to avoid the loss of lives. However, this is just the beginning of the damage we will initiate through the United States if our demands are not met. The next round of attacks will aim to eliminate as many people as we deem necessary to communicate our power and our commitment to our ideals. The United States of America is our destiny.

All those of lesser intelligence and development such as ~~women~~, brown and black people, immigrants, non-Christians and those professing a false democracy must be removed from all and any position of power and influence including, but not limited to, politics, journalism, communication, engineering, computers and teaching at any level.

We reclaim America as the country of and for white ~~men~~ people only. We do not recognize the current government and its supporting institutions like the Supreme Court. Therefore, the current government of these United States will be turned over to those we deem fit to make decisions beneficial to whites, properly allocate resources, manage the undesirables and control the military.

Committee to Make America White Again

Proposed Monuments/Buildings/etc. To Be Destroyed
(Note: Committee will make final decision on order and whether to maximize casualties)

STATUE OF LIBERTY
Symbol of immigration
Located NYC
Use multiple bombs to bring it down (see specs)
Closed in evenings
White ~~men~~ people armed with AR15 rifles and bombs
Can be approached by boat from NYC and NJ

Find out if bags are checked when boarding boat, and if not, several people can plant bombs to go off remotely or on a timer. Set off after fireworks so it's clear that it's an explosion.

Parker didn't bother to read the specifics for each of the targets. She could imagine the devastation they planned. She placed her copy of the document on the table. "So Rich was right." She stared into space then pulled herself back from the awful images sparked by that horrible document. "This is a game changer. Watkins, go through Davenport's emails again and see if you can determine who else is in on this. It's the priority so use whoever is free. Maynard, focus on the addresses but keep digging on Harrington Davenport, the deep web, and especially Philippa. Let Dietz know if you need more resources. Thanks, everyone, let's get to work."

Parker was puzzled when Maynard and Watkins remained at the table. "What's up, guys?"

Maynard leaned in to speak softly. "We found something that we thought should be dealt with separately. We traced one of the addresses in the secret chat room to the desk of NYPD Deputy Chief Nick Contiro. He's posted lots of racist comments and is involved in the plan."

Parker sat back. Corelli swore under her breath.

Parker blew out a breath. "Are you sure? I assume you have proof?"

Maynard held up a sheaf of papers. "I've printed out everything I could. The computer is in his office and the posts were made during the workday. There's some stuff in the posts that ties back to what Watkins has been able to find out about him, so we're sure."

"All right. We'll take it from here. Good work." Parker scanned the papers Maynard handed to her. "I shouldn't be shocked to find racists in the department, but I guess I expect better of those higher up on the chain." She turned to Corelli. "You and I need to talk to Captain Winfry about this. And I think it's time to bring in the NYPD Counterterrorism Bureau and JTTF, the Joint Terrorist Task Force."

"The Counterterrorism Bureau?" The surprise in Corelli's voice tickled Parker. "Great idea. The JTTF will keep the NYPD in the loop. I'm impressed." Corelli made no attempt to hide her admiration.

The surprise for Parker was how good Corelli's praise made her feel. "It came to me one night when I couldn't sleep." She glanced around. No one was close enough to hear but she lowered her voice anyway. "I was hugging Henrietta and my mind was wandering and

I realized if we did find anything that was a threat to our city or the country, NYPD could handle it."

"Henrietta? You have a new girlfriend?" Corelli sounded hurt but thankfully she kept her voice down.

Parker laughed. "Oops, I didn't mean to reveal that I named my foam thing Henrietta. I'm always hugging her and we do everything together so I decided she needed a name."

Corelli doubled over laughing.

Parker couldn't help but laugh with her. "Are you laughing because I named my foam thing or because you think I'll never have another girlfriend?"

Corelli wiped her eyes. "Because you named…" She started laughing again.

"Okay, it's not that funny."

Corelli pulled herself together enough to speak. "As for not ever having another girlfriend, I think you're off the wall." She spoke close to Parker's ear. "Maynard is desperate to get back in your good graces. I thought she was going to punch Benson after she saw her holding your hand during our interview. And then of course, there's Michele Benson who really, really seems to have a thing for you. And those are just the ones we know about."

Why now? Parker was truly curious. Was it because she was attracted to both women and they were reacting to her? Or was it because she was emotionally and physically vulnerable and giving off pheromones in reaction to them being attracted to her? Was Corelli right that others would react the same way? Whatever, she needed to do a Scarlett O'Hara and think about it tomorrow. She'd never let her love life or lack of one affect her work and she wasn't about to start. "Enough. How did we get on to my love life? Let's see if Winfry is free."

Shaking his head, Winfry skimmed the copy of the plan Corelli had placed in front of him. "Damn, if this is real, we've got a problem."

Parker understood his unwillingness to accept what he was reading. This wasn't your everyday murder case. "It's real, Captain. We'd like to set up a meeting with Chief Octavia Clemente from the NYPD Counterterrorism Bureau to discuss bringing in the JTTF. If that's all right with you?"

"If you're sure, I'll give her a call and ask her to come here."

"I'm sure, sir. The team, especially Maynard and her two computer experts, has done a great job with this."

"Should I ask the chief to bring someone with her?" Winfry held her gaze and waited patiently while she considered the question.

"I'd suggest Chief Clemente bring whoever would head up the JTTF effort."

Winfry picked up the stack of papers. "I'll bring Deputy Chief Nick Contiro to the attention of Internal Affairs." He held Parker's gaze. "It's always a shock to find out someone you thought was a friend, is a racist hater but they're crawling out of the woods these days."

Parker sensed his sadness. Racism always cut deep but it was particularly painful when it was someone you thought you knew. Every day felt like death by a thousand cuts these days but getting caught up in the hurt, in the rage at the injustice of it would not help her bring down the bastards. "Captain, going to IA right now might lead to exposing our knowledge of the plan. I suggest we pass it on to Chief Clemente to deal with when it seems appropriate."

He rubbed his hand over his bald head. "What do you think, Corelli?"

"I agree with Parker, sir. I understand the impulse to destroy him immediately, but in the interest of taking down this operation we need to hold back for now."

Winfry stood. "So be it."

CHAPTER THIRTY-SIX

It took a day to arrange the meeting but now Parker, Corelli and Maynard stood as Captain Winfry, Chief Clemente and a man and a woman in street clothes entered the precinct conference room. "At ease, everyone," Chief Clemente said as her gaze briefly touched the faces of each of the three detectives. She sat and they all followed suit.

Winfry nodded at Parker. "I'm Detective P.J. Parker, the lead on the case that brought us here today. Normally I would stand to conduct a meeting but as you can see, I'm somewhat encumbered so if you don't mind, I'll remain seated. Starting on my right, let's go around the table and introduce ourselves."

"Detective Chiara Corelli, Parker's partner."

"Detective Deborah Maynard, manager of the computer team."

"Deputy Chief Jonathan Desoto, Co-leader of the Joint Terrorism Task Force."

"FBI Agent Tamara Day, Co-leader of the Joint Terrorism Task Force."

"Octavia Clemente, Chief of the Counterterrorism Bureau, and curious to hear what you have for us."

"Captain Jedediah Winfry, precinct commander."

Parker looked at the expectant faces, then started. "Thank you for coming. Our case began sixteen days ago with the murder of Ned Rich, the investigative reporter for *The Daily Post*." She traced the history of the case, noting rumors of planned violence, then getting confirmation from Katharine Davenport and Samuel Twigs and the subsequent discovery of the plan. The three counter-terrorism people slowly leafed through the copies of the document Maynard handed out.

Chief Clemente was the first to look up. "I don't believe we're aware of this plot." She looked at the two JTTF leads. "Are we?"

"No. We aren't." Deputy Chief Desoto practically levitated. "And to be frank, I'm having trouble believing they found something our people didn't find."

Oh, no. Parker was ready to scream. Maynard was pissed and looked ready to go for his throat. Before she could figure out how to respond, Corelli whispered something in Maynard's ear that defused the anger. Making a mental note to ask about those magic words, she turned her attention to the condescending man crapping on her team's ability.

She edged forward, needing to stand. Corelli read her body language and took the weight of her arm, giving Parker the leverage to stand. She looked down on the man. "Excuse me, Deputy Chief. I can't explain what you and your team didn't find but I can explain and demonstrate what my team did find. Perhaps you'd like to call your experts to come over so they can learn..." Parker hesitated, letting the word learn sink in before finishing her thought, "...what we did to uncover the plot?"

She glanced around the table hoping she hadn't totally screwed this up. Chief Clemente and FBI Agent Day both seemed to be repressing smiles, Captain Winfry was looking down but she would swear his lips were quirking and Corelli and Maynard were grinning. Only Chief Desoto looked unhappy. She was all right with that.

"We don't need to call anyone. FBI Agent Day and I are perfectly capable of understanding computer searches." He looked at his boss. "Chief, I suggest we look now before we waste any more time."

Chief Clemente gazed at Parker. "Is that all right?"

"Of course, Chief. We expected questions so Detective Maynard prepared a presentation to walk you through our process. Detective."

Maynard walked around the table, dimmed the lights, pulled down the screen, then brought her presentation up on her computer. Her voice was shaky when she started, but as she got into it, her natural confidence took over. They'd gone over her presentation several times making sure it was short on technical terms and long on a clear and thorough explanation of how they made their way through the Internet and the dark corners of the web. Maynard answered every question patiently. It took an hour but at the end when there were no more questions, she thanked everyone, shut her computer, turned the lights on and sat.

Parker was proud, proud of Deb as a friend and proud of her as a member of the team. "Thank you, Detective Maynard. That was excellent."

Chief Clemente chimed in. "I agree, Detective Maynard. You and your team did excellent work and your presentation and explanation of it was the best I've heard in a long time."

Maynard flushed. "Thank you, Chief. I have a great team and Detectives Parker and Corelli are great leaders."

Parker hoped Desoto had learned not to mess with her team but she had to ask. "Unless you have further objections, Deputy Chief Desoto, I'd like to proceed."

"No objections." He didn't look thrilled.

Parker cleared her throat. "This wasn't included in the presentation because it seemed best to keep it confidential but Detective Maynard's team traced one of the addresses in the secret chat room to the desk of NYPD Deputy Chief Nick Contiro. He's posted racists comments but more important, he's involved in the plan."

The silence was uncomfortable but Parker waited for everyone to look through the evidence Deb distributed. "We thought it should be handled during the takedown rather than letting the cat out of the bag before we're ready."

Chief Clemente met Parker's gaze. "Thank you for your discretion. We'll deal with this when the time comes." Holding Parker's gaze, Clement asked, "What do you think is the next step?"

Parker took a few seconds to process the question, not because she didn't know, but because she wanted to frame her answer properly. "Get a warrant to search the houses of Philippa Harrington Davenport, Meriwether Davis and the other leaders we've identified. Several of those are out of state. I suggest we coordinate the execution of all the warrants and just before, or as they are happening, we take all those involved into custody."

"You forgot to include a warrant for Brandon Lester," Desoto said, with a gotcha smile.

It pleased Parker to demonstrate how thorough they'd been. "No problem. He has an apartment in Philippa Davenport's mansion. We've confirmed she never registered converting the mansion into a multi-family building so the one warrant for the premises will give us the ability to search all the apartments in the building including those Brandon Lester, Abel Clemson and Heather Harrington live in and any others we don't know about."

Chief Clemente straightened the documents they'd handed out and slid them into the folder they'd provided. "Do you see your team involved as this operation goes forward?"

"I think it's evident that while my team is not usually involved in threats like this, we've worked hard to expose the insurrection. Perhaps your team would have caught it eventually, but we caught it in enough time to do a proper takedown. To the degree possible, I would like the three of us plus the eight team members not in the meeting to be included in planning the operation and as part of the search team. I realize that making the cases against and prosecuting those involved in the insurrection will be done by the JTTF, but we will need to be able to interrogate those who are also involved in crimes we're investigating. If you won't include all of us, at least take Maynard and her two computer team members."

Chief Clemente stood. "Agent Day, I'd like you to coordinate the operation with Detective Parker, making sure her team is involved. To begin with, put her team together with our people to get the warrants written. Deputy Chief, I'd like you to coordinate the operations with FBI offices in the other jurisdictions involved. That will require working with Detective Parker's team to identify all the participants. Finally, I will meet with this group"—she waved a hand around the table—"here, for a half hour every morning to review progress. Any questions?" She gave it a minute. "Remember we have a single objective and we need to function as a team. I don't want to hear anything about petty squabbles. Detective Parker, I understand your team is still wrapping up three murders and the attack on you but other than that, I expect all your attention to focus on bringing down those involved in trying to destroy America." She walked out.

Desoto extended his hand and said, "Sorry for being an ass." Parker shook it. "If you send me, and I guess the chief and Tamara, copies of Detective Maynard's presentation, I'll get a team looking for anything else we can find. Can we meet tomorrow after the morning meeting to sort out the out-of-state warrants we need?"

"Of course."

He left but Day remained. "As he just admitted, Jon can be an ass sometimes but he's a team player. Don't hold it against him." She stretched. "I've texted a couple of my team to join us so we can get started on the local warrants."

Back in their own conference room, Parker took Maynard aside. "What did Corelli whisper when Desoto was implying our work was shoddy?"

Maynard whispered in Parker's ear, "She said, watch and learn how a master destroys a big ego. And I watched and I learned. Embarrassing him in front of his boss, Agent Day and Captain Winfry was so much more effective than my screaming and cursing would have been. Lesson learned. I hope I can learn to control my temper."

CHAPTER THIRTY-SEVEN

Five-forty a.m. and still dark as the parade of vehicles silently crept up Riverside Drive and filled the street for two blocks above and the two below the Davenport mansion. Car doors clicked softly as agents and detectives flowed onto the pavement and waited for orders. Uniformed NYPD officers moved to both ends of the caravan of vehicles ready to divert traffic and keep curious neighbors away.

They'd worked nonstop for the last two days preparing warrants and planning for today. And Corelli was hyped. She was leading the search with FBI Agent Day. She felt bad for Parker but not knowing what kind of resistance they'd encounter, Day insisted it was too dangerous for Parker with her arm in that cast. Parker was upset and for a change she was the one dumping on Corelli. It was only when she reminded Parker of what happened when they were attacked by the mob that she reluctantly accepted her limitations and agreed to remain outside with Captain Winfry, Chief of Detectives Broderick and Chief Clemente until the building was secured.

Corelli glanced at Broderick. He looked disgruntled but she was ready to kill him. Instead of praising Parker for uncovering the plot and organizing the takedown, he'd dumped on her for not bringing him into the investigation before the Counterterrorism Bureau. Thankfully, since Parker had witnessed his attacks on her during previous cases, she took it for what it was, an insecure man who wanted to suck up the glory. Now they were all huddled in the morning chill, eyes on phones waiting for six a.m. when they could serve the warrant.

The team had settled on a knock and announce entry but depending on the response from within the house, they were ready to batter down the door. The air vibrated with tension and excitement. Planning for the search had been meticulous. They'd pulled whatever plans they could find for the building and had a pretty good idea about the inside of the residence. The agents and detectives going in to execute the search warrant knew exactly which floors and rooms they were responsible for searching and would sweep through the house looking in all the people-size places for anyone who might try to interfere with the execution of the warrant or pose a danger to the agents and detectives. Everyone inside would be rounded up and moved into Philippa's kitchen where they would remain while the search of the house continued. Once in the kitchen, Philippa Davenport would be given a copy of the search warrant.

Seconds before six o'clock, Corelli started a quiet count down. "Ten, nine, eight…" Parker gave Corelli a thumbs-up.

"Four, three, two, one and GO." At Corelli's shout, agents moved to the door and announced their presence. "FBI! SEARCH WARRANT! OPEN THE DOOR!"

They'd agreed to wait a few minutes to give someone time to get to the door. Her eyes on her phone, Day held her hand up, ready to signal the team to batter down the door. And then the front door cracked open. "Who's there?" Corelli recognized Heather's voice.

"FBI! SEARCH WARRANT! BACK AWAY. WE'RE COMING IN!"

The door swung open and the troops poured in, rushing in all directions like water from a broken dam. An agent escorted the stunned Heather to the kitchen. Corelli and Day had assigned themselves the areas they expected to find the key players so Watkins joined Corelli in the search for Philippa Davenport's bedroom. It was exactly where they expected it to be and apparently, she hadn't heard the ruckus.

Watkins shouted, "POLICE! SEARCH WARRANT!"
Philippa bolted awake, screaming in rage. Threatening them
with death, she pulled open the drawer of her bedside table. Corelli
grabbed her arm, extracted the gun from her hand, checked the
safety and slipped it into the pocket of her coat. Undeterred,
Philippa demanded they leave her house and ignored the request
to go to the kitchen with them. She refused to take the robe Corelli
had pulled off a nearby chair so they pinned her between them,
arms at her side to keep her from punching and scratching, and
carried her to the kitchen. Corelli handed her the robe and an agent
handed her a copy of the warrant. Ignoring both, she continued
screaming and cursing.

A member of JTTF and Maynard escorted Abel Clemson from
his apartment to the kitchen. Meanwhile, Forlini and Greene
herded Lester and the young girl in bed with him into the kitchen
as well. Heather Harrington embraced Philippa, calmed her down
and helped her into her robe. Heather read the warrant to her.
Philippa demanded to call her attorney. After two bulky male and
one female FBI agent arrived to maintain control of the people
in the kitchen, Corelli tagged Kim to bag Philippa's handgun and
then interview the young girl in another room. She was sure the
young woman was underage, and they could use a statutory rape
charge to hold Lester until they nailed him for the murders.

Corelli went outside to get Parker. Staying close enough to
protect her from agents and detectives rushing to do their jobs, she
briefed Parker as they walked to the kitchen.

Philippa Davenport rushed Parker as she entered, clearly intent
on doing damage. Corelli stepped between them and captured the
raving woman, interrupting the physical attack, but not the verbal.
"You, you black bitch, you did this. It's too bad you didn't die when
they attacked you. Get out of my house. You people have no right
to invade my house. I know my rights."

"I don't want to cuff you, Philippa, but if you don't control
yourself, I will." Corelli spoke over Philippa's head. "Heather, take
her and keep her away from Detective Parker or I'll cuff her to a
chair."

Heather dragged the red-faced woman to the other side of the
kitchen.

Parker stared at Davenport. This was too much pressure for someone her age. She might have a heart attack or go over the edge. She hadn't expected to feel a shred of empathy for her. And yet she did. Parker couldn't imagine the psychological stress of learning that one of her ancestors was black when she'd believed her whole life she was a purebred white woman and had built herself up, established a toehold amongst white males by spewing hate of blacks. And Parker had no doubt that Philippa was smart enough to see the writing on the wall, that her dream of being a white woman leading a takeover of the government by white men, was over. "Mrs. Davenport, when you've read the search warrant, you'll know we have every right to be here and to search every inch of your property. You can't stop it so I suggest you try to relax."

Surprisingly agile for her age, Davenport flew at Parker again. "You don't tell me what to do, bitch." Corelli got between them and took the punches the frenzied woman intended for Parker. It took two agents to wrestle her away and push her into a chair. Corelli cuffed one of Davenport's hands to her chair. "You've just added assault of an NYPD officer to the charges against you, Philippa. I suggest you drink some water and cool off until we transport you to the station house."

Understanding her presence was upsetting Davenport, Parker left the kitchen. Corelli was right behind. "Wow. I've never had such hate spewed at me. By her one drop standard she's as black as me but either she doesn't know she has a black ancestor or she hasn't absorbed it yet." Parker stopped to take in the activity around them. "I'd like to check out the house, Corelli."

They wandered through every floor. As they'd thought on their first visit, Davenport hadn't put much money into maintaining it. In many rooms the paint was peeling, the carpeting and drapes were dusty and stained, and the windows were dirty. The furniture was ancient as well. Agents and detectives were methodically searching every room, closet, and hallway, checking for loose floorboards, under rugs and in and under every stick of furniture. Boxes with files and any items that might be related to their investigation—like photos—were being carried out to waiting vans.

The warrant specified that any and all electronics, including phones, should be removed. Parker stopped to watch Maynard direct a team packing up Davenport's computers and related equipment. She was proving to be quite the leader. With her confident air and exceptional computer skills, agents and detectives seemed more than happy to follow her orders. When Maynard noticed Parker, she glanced around, winked and gave a half-salute.

Maynard caught up with Parker and Corelli as they were entering Lester's apartment. "Hey, you okay, Parker? I heard the old bitch tried to attack you."

"I'm fine, thanks to Corelli who stepped between us. You look like you're having fun."

"I've never been involved in something like this. It's great. I need to check on how this team is doing, but just so you know, we found a number of phones, four laptops plus video equipment and videotapes in here. I peeked at what was in the camera and it seems like our boy Lester likes to film himself with women so we have him with that girl he was in bed with. And while it's not in my wheelhouse, I'm told they found a gun hidden under a loose board under his bed, rifles and lots of ammo in that closet"—she pointed—"and the makings of homemade bombs on the kitchen table. I also heard they found cases of AR15 rifles and ammo in the basement."

"Thanks, Maynard."

Parker and Corelli moved on to the apartment they were told belonged to Abel Clemson. It was dark and spartan, and though the paint was peeling, neat. Or at least it was before the search. The bedroom contained only a double bed covered with an ancient floral white chenille bedspread, a dresser and a TV on a table facing the bed. The living room with limp tan curtains, a gray canvas sofa, battered coffee table, and worn brown recliner situated on a washed-out oval braided rag rug, was equally drab and uninviting. They observed the search in the living room for a few minutes and as they turned to leave, an agent in the bedroom called out. "Gun. And ammo."

Interesting. Abel seemed so timid Parker wouldn't have pegged him as the type to have a gun. "Let's take a look." The agent was on her knees in front of the dresser holding a drawer. The gun was taped to the underside.

Parker frowned. It looked old. "Do you know what make it is?"

The agent held the drawer up so Parker and Corelli could examine the gun. "I think it's an old Ruger but I'm not certain.

There's .22 ammo for it." She put the drawer down, photographed it, pulled the tape away from the wood and placed the gun and the boxes of ammo with the tape in a banker's box for removal.

Parker looked at Corelli. "Weren't the Davenports all shot with .22s?"

"Yes. It's pretty common though. I don't see a motive but it's worth checking out Maybe Abel is our killer." Corelli made a note in her phone. "When we meet with Agent Day, I'll make sure it and the gun I took away from Philippa are tested."

"She had a gun?" Parker didn't know why that surprised her.

"Yeah, she went for it intending to shoot me and Watkins, or maybe just to scare us into leaving her house. Hard to tell with these country gals."

Maynard stuck her head into Abel's apartment. "Parker, Corelli, there's something you need to see in Heather Harrington's apartment."

In comparison to Heather's apartment, Abel's was a monk's cell. Her living room had a muted blue and green color scheme, soft velvety living room furniture, crisp white curtains, and a blue ivory and green patterned rug. It was filled with plants, some flowering under plant lights. "Come into the room she uses as an office." Maynard led the way.

Parker peeked into the bedroom and was not surprised at the ultra-feminine décor or the messy room. The headboard, double dresser and night tables looked to be cherrywood. The unmade king bed had a lavender and pink bedspread over satiny-looking pink sheets. The only other furniture was a deep pink chaise longue near the windows overlooking the garden. Out of the corner of her eye she saw something dart across the floor. "I think I just saw a cat or a very large rat run across the room." One of the agents searching the room laughed. "It's a cat and it's not very friendly."

In the smaller room that served as an office Maynard pointed to a computer and a box full of paper files on the floor in the corner. "Magnolia Walker's computer and what I think is her genealogical research and a bunch of her other papers." Maynard lifted a clear plastic bag out of the box. "Ned Rich's wallet, press credentials, and I assume, his wristwatch, ring and cell phone." She tipped her head toward one of her team packing the computer on the desk. "That's Heather's computer. I opened it just to see if it was password protected. It wasn't so I did a quick scan of her email. She and Walter Foster have quite a few emails going back and forth. I didn't take the time to read them but I thought you should know."

"Thanks, Maynard. Mark her computer as a priority for review." Parker's mind was racing, fitting the pieces together. She turned to Corelli. "Are you thinking what I'm thinking?"

Corelli laughed. "Probably. What's the likelihood of Heather having the computer and paper stolen from Walker's house, Ned Rich's belongings and a close connection with Walter Foster?"

"Plus she has a cat. And cat hairs were found on Rich's body. Even though there wasn't any blood, I'm sure there would be DNA left if Rich was murdered here. Let's get the CSU to check out this apartment as soon as feasible."

Parker hefted her arm. "She was in the room with Philippa the day I dropped the hint that I knew what Walker and Rich knew. Hiding the Harrington's black blood would protect her future as well as Philippa's. So maybe Heather was the one who ordered the killings and the attack on me."

The search continued throughout the rest of the day into the late evening. They brought in food for the NYPD/FBI team and the house inhabitants being held in the kitchen.

By ten in the evening the search was completed. Heather, Lester and the young girl had been transported to the station house. In recognition of her age, Philippa would remain under house arrest until she could be taken to the station house in the morning. They had no reason to hold Abel and he was left with Philippa. Corelli, Parker, Chief Clemente, Chief Broderick, Captain Winfry, Agent Day, and other key players agreed to meet at the station house at ten in the morning.

CHAPTER THIRTY-EIGHT

The mood was jubilant as the team gathered in the large station house conference room. None of them had ever been involved in such a critical and extensive search operation like the one they'd help plan and execute yesterday and they were still elated. Helping themselves to coffee, tea, or a soft drink and a pastry or a bagel, they stood around rehashing events. Chief Octavia Clemente arrived, helped herself to coffee, introduced herself to each member of the team and thanked them individually for their part in the takedown.

Parker was proud of their work and enjoyed watching the team soak up the praise. But when her attention switched to her discomfort from supporting her arm she decided it was time to start the meeting. "Please sit and let's get started." Just as they had all settled, the door swung open and Chief Broderick entered. He greeted Clemente and ignoring everyone else, helped himself to coffee before taking a seat. Corelli elbowed Parker. "Asshole. He only has eyes for the brass. I'll bet he's been sitting in his car so he could make a grand entrance."

Chief Clemente made eye contact with every member of the team. "I'll be writing individual commendations for each of you but I also want to congratulate you for the remarkable teamwork that brought us here today. At some point we'll have a celebratory dinner, but right now, as you know better than I, we have a lot of work to do to process everything you found and build the cases necessary to prosecute those you exposed. You're all invited to attend the press conference later today. And now I'll turn the meeting over to Detective Parker."

Parker flushed with pride. She was the lead but they'd all worked intensively to wrap up the many aspects of the case. "Thank you, Chief. Let's start with Deputy Chief Desoto."

He looked down at the papers in front of him. "My team oversaw the execution of simultaneous warrants on leaders and groups in Texas, Idaho and West Virginia. Originally there were more groups participating, but after Harrington Davenport's death, the other five groups backed away from the plan. We confirmed this through tapping into the secret dark website your team"—he dipped his head to Maynard—"discovered and from FBI undercover agents embedded in the groups."

He took a sip of water. "In each group we searched, we found a list of members, copies of the plan including additional information on local or nearby monuments they were assigned to destroy, and an arsenal of weapons and homemade bombs. The leaders were arrested and members are being rounded up as we speak. I'll liaise with the lead FBI agents in each area as the investigations proceed. FBI offices around the country are following up on local groups even if they don't seem to be involved, to let them know we're watching. That's it for now."

"Thank you, Deputy Chief." Parker turned. "Agent Day?"

Agent Tamara Day cleared her throat. "I'd like to start by thanking Detectives Parker and Corelli and all of you. You did a terrific job and managed to uncover a plot that somehow slipped by the NYPD/FBI Joint Terrorism Task Force and the larger FBI terrorism group. Bravo to all of you, especially to Detective Deborah Maynard and her group." She glanced at the papers in front of her. "Detective Parker, since you wrote the report, why don't you deliver it?"

Parker was surprised at Day's generosity. "Thank you, Agent Day, though I wrote the report, we all know the takedown could not have happened without the combined effort of our team and the JTTF. We're in early stages of analyzing everything we found, so for today I'll just summarize the results of the search warrant.

"Probably most important, we interrupted the planned violence and arrested many of those involved including key planners Philippa Harrington Davenport, Heather Davenport, Meriwether Davis and Brandon Lester. Happily, we discovered ample proof to convict all of them, including numerous assault weapons and homemade bombs in the basement of the Davenport mansion and in Brandon Lester's apartment in that building. Additionally, the search of Meriwether Davis's Westchester property found a militia training camp, plans for several monuments scheduled to be destroyed and a cache of assault weapons and homemade bombs. All of Lester's people, including those camped out on Davis's Westchester property, are in custody.

"The search of Heather Harrington's apartment turned up information pertinent to the two murders related to the case and the attack on me. We also discovered three handguns in possession of the domestic terrorists and another in the apartment of Abel Clemson. We will test all four and hopefully prove one of them was the weapon used to murder Harrington Davenport and six other members of the Davenport family.

"Along with the JTTF we'll be sifting through everything recovered and hopefully, confirm our assumptions. JTTF is giving us first shot at interviewing those we suspect of involvement in our aspect of the case. We hope to solidify what we know about our murders and then hand the suspects over for prosecution on the domestic terrorism issues.

"Several days ago we received DNA confirmation that Walter Foster was the attacker who attempted to murder me, and we expect the evidence uncovered in the search to prove he and Heather Harrington were responsible for the murders of Walker and Rich as well." Parker looked at all the smiling faces around the table. "You've done a great job so far, so let's get to work and wrap this up."

Chief Clemente stood. "Good job, folks. I'll leave you to it. See you at the press conference."

Broderick rose from his chair. "Let me second what Chief Clemente said. Excellent job everyone. Thanks for your hard work." While the focus was on Broderick, Clemente and Desoto filing out, Corelli leaned in and rolled her eyes. Parker smiled. Corelli had used the blue cushion as a shield, so no one else saw the disrespectful but amusing action.

Captain Winfry waited until the door closed behind them. "What are your next steps, Parker?"

"First order of business is to interview Philippa Harrington Davenport, Heather Harrington, Meriwether Davis and Brandon Lester. Detective Maynard's team, working with the JTTF computer team, will analyze the contents of the computers of each of those four suspects plus the computers of Walter Foster and Lena Wood, which were retrieved from the van they'd packed to get away to Idaho. The rest of us will organize and analyze everything else we found."

Winfry stood. "I'm damn proud of all of you, of your hard work, of the teamwork that exposed this dangerous group, and your cooperation with the JTTF. Let me know if you need anything from me."

Bleary-eyed after three straight hours of reading emails and documents printed off the various computers they'd captured, Parker was happy for the interruption when her phone vibrated on the table. "Parker."

"Ndep here. Can we meet for lunch? We need to talk privately."

"Let me check." Parker put the phone close to her chest and tapped Corelli's foot with hers. "Ndep wants to talk over lunch. Would you be willing to drive me to Buonasola in about a half hour? If you get a separate table to give us privacy, I won't have to worry about her getting angry and leaving me stranded."

"Let's do it. Brett mentioned us having lunch today, so I'll text her and see if she can meet me."

Parker lifted her phone. "Gloria? I'll be there."

The four of them arrived at the same time so after greetings they were shown to separate tables in different sections of the restaurant.

Ndep touched P.J.'s hand. "I didn't realize you were so badly injured."

"He almost killed me, Gloria. If Jessie had come out a minute or two later, I would be dead."

The color drained from Ndep, leaving her face ashen. "I'm so sorry I—" She stopped when the waitress arrived. They gave their orders, then sat in an awkward silence for a minute. Parker hadn't meant to sound hostile but she was angry and it just popped out. She took a breath. "I'm glad you called, Gloria. We need to talk about what we're doing."

"This is hard." Gloria took a sip of water then raised her eyes to Parker's face. "I'm sorry, P.J., I can't be in a relationship with you."

"I got the message. I'm not surprised. I felt our original connection was fading but you didn't have to just walk away without a word. Even friends visit each other when they're in the hospital."

Tears filled Gloria's eyes. "I had planned to talk to you the day after you were attacked but then Chiara called and I didn't know what to do. I couldn't tell you when you were injured."

"So you let me guess that you were tired of me?"

Gloria's gaze rested on Chiara and Brett. They were smiling, holding hands on the table and talking to each other. She turned to P.J. "That's not it. I want what they have, what I hoped we could have." She wiped the tears streaming down her face. "But I can't have it." She put a hand up to keep P.J. from interrupting. "I've given notice at my job. I'm getting married in Nigeria in three weeks."

"Married? To a man?" Parker felt sucker punched. This was so outside her experience she didn't even know what to say. "I don't understand. Have you met this man or is the marriage totally arranged by your parents?"

"We've talked on the telephone three times. He sounds nice. He's a physician. He wants me to go to medical school so we can practice together and help our people."

She wanted to scream but she could see how difficult this was for Gloria. "What do *you* want?"

The tears kept coming. "I want to learn to love him, to make him happy. I want to have children and hopefully, to make myself happy. This is what my people do."

"That's what they do in Nigeria. But you're in America. You've lived longer in America than you did in Nigeria. Don't you feel American? Don't you want to choose who you marry?"

"It's true I've lived here more years than I lived in Nigeria but what you don't understand, P.J., is that inside my parent's house, in my community, it's as if we never left Nigeria. We speak the language, eat the food and live the same lives as if we were on Nigerian soil. I've always straddled two worlds. Sometimes I feel like a cartoon character. I put on my suit in the morning and go out into the world where I speak English, eat bagels and Thai and Italian food, where I'm seen as a strong, independent woman. Then at night I go home, shed those clothes, put on our traditional clothing—a loose fitting blouse, long wraparound skirt and headwrap—and become the dutiful daughter, sister, aunt, cousin. I have strong feelings for you but my family is my life. I lie to my parents, say I'm working overnight, when I stay at your apartment. I can't love you and have my family, my community. I would be isolated from everything I value."

Parker sat back. "I don't understand, Gloria. But I want you to be happy. I hope choosing that kind of life, that he makes you happy."

"Thank you, P.J. I appreciate you saying that. I've cried and prayed for the last three months and I'm reconciled to my decision. I want you to know that I will not forget you. Ever. I…" She threw a twenty on the table. "I have to go before I embarrass myself." She leaned over and brushed P.J.'s lips with hers. "I will miss you." She grabbed her coat and ran out.

Parker stared after her. She'd already let go of Gloria so it wasn't as if her heart was broken but she felt sad. How did she not know Gloria was struggling with such a momentous decision for the last three months? Was she insensitive? No, she had sensed it, sensed Gloria distancing herself, sensed their connection fading but never in a million years could she have imagined what was going on with her. She should have talked to Gloria. Instead, she'd avoided dealing with her own feelings and let Gloria struggle on her own.

A light touch to her hand brought Parker back to the restaurant. She was surprised to see Brett and Corelli at her table.

Brett was sitting across from her, with a sweet smile. "Can we help, P.J.?"

She shook her head. "I can't talk about it right now."

Corelli looked concerned. "Do you want to go home to Jessie's?"

"It would be better to focus on work and let my subconscious deal with it for a while, so let's drop Brett off and go talk to Philippa. That should lift my spirits." She grinned.

Brett took her good hand. "What about lunch?" She tilted her head. "Neither of you touched your sandwiches."

"I'm not hungry but I'll have it wrapped for later." While they waited for the sandwiches, Parker's mind kept going back to Gloria. Did all immigrant children feel pulled between the old customs and their new life? Did Gloria really have to choose between her family and her happiness?

When the sandwiches arrived, Corelli helped her up. On the drive uptown Brett and Corelli followed Parker's lead and avoided talking about the scene they'd witnessed between her and Gloria.

CHAPTER THIRTY-NINE

Parker acknowledged that Philippa would probably go ballistic again if she interviewed her and after some discussion, she agreed to let Corelli take the lead in questioning her.

Philippa eyed the two of them warily as they took the seats facing her. She was calmer today but she avoided looking at Parker. Perhaps her attorney, Bo Waters, sitting next to her, had warned her. As soon as they settled, Waters spoke. "I'd like an explanation of why you invaded my client's house, held her under house arrest and dragged her, an eighty-three-year-old woman, to the police station today."

Corelli glared at him. "I gather your client didn't show you the search warrant or tell you what we found?"

He looked at Philippa. "Did they give you a search warrant?"

She waved a hand as if brushing an insect away. "I don't know. They handed me some papers but I was too upset to read them. Heather looked at them."

His jaw hardened. "Sorry. Perhaps I should have led with what are the charges against my client? And what evidence do you have?"

Corelli assumed Philippa hadn't bothered to tell her attorney the truth. He was a relative and would defend her no matter what. But it appeared that Bo wasn't happy. "We're still sorting through the information obtained while executing the search warrant, but we found multiple copies of a plan, first handwritten by Mrs. Davenport, then on her computer, to destroy monuments like the Statue of Liberty and museums and mosques around the country. Not only was Mrs. Davenport the major author of the document, we have proof she was the leader of the effort to incite white nationalist militia groups around the country to participate. In fact, we know she and her son Harry argued about it. He was concerned enough that he concluded he had no choice but to report her and her associates to the FBI. Unfortunately, he was murdered the night before he planned to do it."

"That's not possible. Harry would never—"

"Philippa, I advise you to remain quiet unless I say it's all right."

She directed a withering look at her attorney, but she didn't speak.

Corelli watched the attorney make several notes. "We have her computer with multiple emails discussing the plan to cause chaos and demand control of the government."

Bo's jaw dropped. "That's insane."

Corelli grimaced. Was he already setting up her defense? "As I said we have extensive evidence supporting that charge, including the hundreds of AR15 rifles and ammunition, plus homemade bombs found in her home. In addition to that, we believe she ordered the murders of Magnolia Walker, Ned Rich and Detective P.J. Parker. We—"

"You're crazy." Philippa stood. "Why would I waste my energy or resources killing worthless people like that?"

Bo Waters glanced at Parker as he pulled his client down. "Sit, Philippa. You're not helping yourself."

Philippa brushed off his hand. "I demand to know. Why do you think I would kill them?"

Could it be she really didn't know? Corelli remembered Parker hinted that she knew it but she never actually stated what it was when they met with Philippa. They assumed she knew. "You know Magnolia Walker was black?"

"Yes, yes, Heather told me she came to see me." Philippa was impatient. "But I don't waste my time talking to ignorant black women." She glared at Parker.

Corelli didn't have to look at Parker to feel the rage the always cool, collected detective never allowed herself to show. "Ms. Walker came to see you because her extensive genealogical research on her family found she had a relative in common with the Harringtons, a black relative."

Philippa went from colorless to fire engine red in ten seconds. "No, no, no. That is a lie. She must have wanted money."

Her attorney took her arm. "Philippa, please sit, drink some water. Let me discuss this."

She sat but she wasn't calm. He took a deep breath. After all he was a Harrington, too. "I assume you have proof?"

"We have Walker's research which shows a common black relative. Her research was verified by Ned Rich, the investigative report who was murdered recently, and we think his murder was also ordered by your client. Ms. Walker's computer and the paper copies of her research that were stolen when she was murdered were found in Heather Harrington's apartment. As I said, we believe your client ordered the murders."

Philippa was shaking her head but it wasn't clear whether she was denying her black blood or the murders. "I do not have black blood. It's impossible." She leaned over and pointed at Parker. "You black bitch, you're lying, trying to disgrace me."

"Philippa." Waters pulled her down again. "Sit and be quiet."

She brushed his hand away. "And I never ordered the murders of those people."

He made a few notes. "I need some time alone with my client. And I would appreciate a copy of the search warrant."

Corelli put a hand under Parker's arm. "Just so you know, Mrs. Davenport will also be charged with attacking a police officer during the search of her home."

Parker was still vibrating when they stepped out of the interview room. "I hate to say it but I believe the racist bitch didn't know about her black relative."

"Either she didn't know or she's a great actress." Corelli steered Parker down the hall. "Why don't you take a few deep breaths while I get us some water. I thought you might explode in there and you need to relax before we talk to Heather."

Parker leaned against the wall, took some deep breaths and sipped the water Corelli provided. "From time to time I've been discounted and disrespected on the basis of my skin color. What black person hasn't? But I've never been face-to-face with such blatant hatred like that. And knowing that by her own standards, one drop of black blood makes a person black, she is herself black, makes it worse somehow. This will destroy her entire world and force her to deal with self-hatred. I should be sympathetic but I'm not."

As expected, Attorney Olga Thorn demanded to know why they were holding her client, Heather Harrington. Except for several side glances at Heather as Parker outlined the charges related to the plan that the counterterrorism unit was likely to bring, Thorn listened carefully and made notes.

When she finished and the attorney had no questions, Parker went on. "We will also be charging Ms. Harrington with conspiracy to commit murder. We believe and will prove that she ordered the murders of Magnolia Walker, Ned Rich and me, to prevent the public knowing that the Harringtons have a black ancestor and therefore are not the pure whites that white nationalists champion."

"A black ancestor? You're nuts, lady." Heather laughed but her voice was tight. "And who would I order to kill someone? It's not like I have a gang or anything."

Thorn frowned. "You have evidence of this, of the black blood? And the murders?"

Parker gazed at Heather as she responded to the attorney. "Magnolia Walker's genealogical research which was verified by Ned Rich clearly shows a common black ancestor. Magnolia Walker's computer and genealogical research which were stolen from her house when she was murdered and the personal belongings of Ned Rich, the other victim, were found in Ms. Harrington's apartment. We're developing additional evidence such as emails exchanged with the killer, as we examine her computer and other items removed during the search of her apartment."

Thorn looked at Heather, maybe expecting a protest, but Heather sat tight-lipped and white-faced. Her hand gravitated to the large gold number "14" hanging from her neck and her thumb rubbed up and down.

Parker felt a frisson of excitement. The tense movement of Heather's thumb was sending sparkling gold flakes onto the table and Heather's clothing. Her necklace must be gold-plated. Did Corelli see it? They'd have to get someone in here to collect it.

"Will you object to bail when she's arraigned?" Thorn asked.

"We will. We believe even without the murder charge she and her co-conspirators in the planned violence are a danger to the community."

The interview room was silent but the tension was crackling when they closed the door behind them.

Parker leaned against the wall. Back-to-back interviews were exhausting but she wanted to get them out of the way so they could concentrate on building the cases. Corelli had apparently seen the gold flakes and was on the phone with Dietz asking to have someone go in and collect the evidence tying Heather to Rich's death.

Parker waited until Corelli pocketed her phone. "I'm glad you noticed the gold flakes too. Let's take a walk and get coffee before we interview Lester."

Corelli yawned and stretched. "Coffee sounds good. Are you sure you're okay walking to Starbucks with the cast?"

"I'm stiff and I really need some air. It's only a block and a half each way so let's try. We can get a cab back if it's too much for me."

They put on their coats and headed out. "Let me know if you need me to boost your arm." Corelli offered to carry her arm as if it was a normal thing between friends. "Heather knows we've got her. I'm betting she's going to ask for a deal."

"Thanks for offering to help." Parker smiled. "And I agree, Heather is smart."

Parker was able to walk to the coffee shop and back with just a little help from Corelli on the return. Between the coffee and the exercise, her mind cleared and she realized there really was no reason to interview Brandon Lester. The counterterrorism unit would prosecute the domestic terrorism charges against him, Narcotics would handle the cocaine dealing, and Special Victims would pursue the statutory rape charge for the underage girl in his bed and his pornography business. While a part of her would love to rub his belligerent face in his future, she really didn't want to be that kind of person. She turned to Corelli. "I don't know what I was thinking. Let's not waste our time interviewing Lester."

Corelli smiled and gave her a thumbs-up.

Driving to Jessie and Annie's house at the end of the long day, Parker's phone chirped a reminder. She dug it out of her coat pocket. "Damn, I forgot the appointment with my surgeon tomorrow at eleven thirty. It's two weeks since the surgery and she needs to take X-rays to check that it's healing properly. Would you pick me up later tomorrow morning and drive me to the doctor before we go in?"

"Sure I could use a little extra time to hang out with my kitties. By the way, are you busy tomorrow night? I was planning on visiting Gianna and the kids. Want to join me?"

Parker grinned. "That's a wonderful idea. I haven't seen them in a couple of weeks." She owed Corelli big time. When she agreed to work with her, Corelli was persona non grata in the department and among their colleagues because she'd exposed a ring of dirty cops. Parker didn't want to work with the most hated detective in the department, but she accepted the assignment to gain entry to Homicide. She never anticipated it would give her something even more important: an extended family. The Corelli clan, Simone, and Gianna and Patrizia and their husbands and children had welcomed her. But after saving Corelli's life, the clan had pulled her close. And during Corelli's recovery when she was a vital member of her care team, Parker bonded with each of them and Corelli's recently acknowledged girlfriend, Brett. And now, Gianna, the most genuinely generous, kind and loving person Parker had ever met, was one of her closest friends. And Brett was the other.

"Do you think my cast will disturb the little ones?"

"Are you kidding. Those girls love you. If anything, they'll want to play nurse."

CHAPTER FORTY

Parker slept in then ate a leisurely breakfast prepared by Annie. They were chatting at the table when Parker decided to ask her opinion. "The lease on my apartment is running out in a couple of weeks. I'd started to look for an apartment and then this case took over."

Annie put her coffee cup down. "I could look for an apartment for you if you'd like, honey."

"Brett offered me her three-bedroom apartment in Battery Park City for a year or so at a very low rent because she wants to hold on to it for a while before she puts it on the market."

"But then you'd have to move again in a year? Wouldn't it be better to look now and move once? Will Gloria be moving in with you?"

Oops, she hadn't mentioned Gloria's story to anyone. And she wasn't sure she was up to talking about it yet. "Gloria and I are not seeing each other anymore. We met yesterday and ended our relationship." Not exactly true but close enough.

Annie peered over her coffee cup. "Are you all right, Peegee?"

Parker smiled at her use of the affectionate childhood nickname. "It was mutual so I'm fine." She put her fork down. "All my life

I've been focused on school, then my career and proving myself to Uncle You-know-who and I've never just let myself be. I like the idea of Brett's apartment because it will give me the time and space to figure out what I want and in some ways, who I am."

Annie gazed at her with love. "It's been a long time coming, sweetheart." Annie got her. She was so lucky to have had her and Jessie in her life.

P.J. blinked back tears. "It has but I'm ready. The good thing is that since Brett is moving in with Chiara, she's leaving everything except her clothing and personal things in the apartment. That means I won't have to think about furniture, linens, pots, pans, dishes, silverware, glassware or anything else for a year or more. I'm planning to move my clothing, books and other personal items and sell or give away everything else."

"Do it." Annie clasped P.J.'s hand. "When are you thinking of moving?"

Parker hadn't realized she'd made the decision about Brett's offer but it just felt right. She squeezed Annie's hand. "Right before my lease expires I'll move my things and unpack but I'll stay here until the cast comes off."

"You direct and I'll pack and unpack. How's that?"

P.J. squeezed her hand. "Perfect."

Making the decision to accept Brett's offer had lifted Parker's spirits. Corelli gave her the once-over as she eased her into the car. "You look, um, relaxed and happy. Something happen today? Or is it seeing your surgeon again?"

Parker was tempted to tell her she'd decided to accept Brett's offer but she wanted to tell Brett first. She laughed. "Winding down of this monster of a case, a little bit of extra sleep and a nice chat with Annie is all it took."

Parker hadn't thought about how they would x-ray her arm through the cast so she was skeptical when the technician said she was going to saw it off and watched in horror as she did just that. Her arm looked weird, skinny and hairy, and her elbow wouldn't bend. A part of her hoped she'd healed so fast she wouldn't need the cast. But after the technician took several X-rays, she wound a thin cotton padding around the arm and covered it with multiple layers of soaked fiberglass tape. She explained that the fiberglass would harden into a cast as it dried.

Parker held her breath while the surgeon reviewed the X-rays. "You're healing well. It's possible the cast could come off in four weeks rather than six. I'll see you again in two weeks."

The white national terrorist part of the investigation was no longer Parker's responsibility but Agent Day had shown up just after they returned to the station to give her an update. At least that's what she said, but after a brief summary, it seemed to Parker that Day was focused on singing Maynard's praises. She listened patiently to how much the JTTF members respected Maynard's talents and how crucial she had been to the work of exposing the plan, and then put a hand up to cut off the conversation. She looked into Day's eyes. "Why don't you get to the point?"

Agent Day blushed. "Sorry. I'm not usually so circular but it's rare that I want to poach someone from another team. I'd like to bring Detective Maynard over to the JTTF. Captain Winfry said it's up to you and Corelli whether I raise it with her. The FBI agent heading our computer team is transferring to Florida to be near his aging parents and I'd like to offer his job to Maynard. It would mean a promotion and a salary increase."

Parker sat back. Lose Deb? She was a valuable team member. And now that the tension had eased between them, she liked having her around. But most of their cases didn't require someone with her computer skills and the JTTF position seemed a really good fit for her talents. "We'd rather keep her." Corelli nodded, signaling her agreement. "But obviously we won't stand in her way if that's what she wants. Make the offer."

"Thanks. I'll invite her out for a drink this evening to discuss it." Day walked over to Maynard's desk.

Corelli stared after her, then turned to Parker. "That was a surprise, but not surprising. Maynard has proven to be a great asset. How do you feel about it?"

"I'd hate to lose her but she's a natural leader as well as a computer whiz so she deserves the opportunity to move up. On a personal level she wants another shot at a relationship and it might be easier to explore if we didn't work together."

Corelli's eyebrows went up. "You're considering getting involved with her again?"

Parker grinned. "I'm considering considering it. But she doesn't know that."

Dietz dropped into a chair at the conference table. "Hey, Parker, Heather Harrington and Olga Thorn, her attorney, are asking to speak to you and Corelli. Thorn didn't say why."

Parker looked at Corelli. "Why not? Maybe she's got something she wants to trade." Corelli eased Parker's arm up and they ambled down to interview room two. Heather was normally pale but now she looked gray and beaten. As soon as they sat, Thorn spoke. "My client is interested in a deal."

Parker frowned. "What does she have to offer? We have her on the terrorism charge. Finding Walker's and Rich's belongings in her apartment tie her to their murders. Her cat's hair and the flakes we collected after our last meeting match those on Rich's body and confirm his body was in her apartment. And her emails with Walter Foster discussing the plans to murder Rich and Walker and attack me, support the conspiracy to murder charges."

Thorn glanced at her client. "Heather understands the seriousness of all the charges and she's hoping if she tells you what happened to Walker and Rich, you might put in a word for her with the DA."

Parker considered the issue. They had enough to convict her but it would be nice to know how it went down. And although Philippa seemed to be uninvolved in the murders, it would be nice to know for sure. She glanced at Corelli and saw her agreement. "If we find the information credible and helpful, we'll mention her cooperation to the DA but that's all we can do."

"We understand." Thorn shifted to face Heather. "Tell them."

Eyes down, hands shaking, voice almost a whisper, Heather started. "I answered the door when that…when Magnolia Walker showed up. She said she had some important news to share with Philippa. I asked her to wait and gave Philippa the message. Philippa wasn't interested in anything a black person…had to say and she said I should get rid of her. I told the woman Philippa was busy but if she gave me the message, I'd pass it on. She said, 'It's private, about the Harringtons, so I'll come back.' I told her I was a Harrington and showed her my driver's license to prove it. She said, 'Well, you and I have a common ancestor way back.' She handed me a chart and pointed out that our common ancestor was black." Heather took a swig of the bottle of water in front of her. "I was shocked. She gave me a folder with the papers and wrote her name, address and phone number on the outside of it. 'This is a copy of my genealogical research and the family tree I've put together. I can see you're surprised,' she said. 'Call me when you want to talk.' It was weird, she seemed excited to share the information. I was enraged. How dare she accuse us of having black blood. I practically pushed her out the door and screamed at her, 'Don't hold your breath waiting for our call.'

"I looked at what she'd put together and it looked legitimate. If this got out, it would destroy our world, our work, our everything. I didn't want Philippa to know but I didn't know what to do or who to talk to about it. I asked myself, what would Philippa do? And then I got clear. I had to eliminate the threat. Walter Foster and I had been seriously involved for several months and he was supposed to spend the night. I knew he had killed before and I told him Walker was a threat to our movement and needed to be eliminated. He and I went to Walker's house about ten that night. We rang the bell. She looked out the side window and recognized me so she let us in. While I spoke to her, Walt grabbed her from behind and"—she drank again—"strangled her. Then we took things out of her refrigerator and closets and scattered them and grocery bags on the floor in the hallway and turned over some chairs and a table to make it look as if someone had pushed in after her. I took her computer and any papers I could find that seemed related to her research, we left the door partially open and the lights in the hallway on and walked out."

Heather was breathing heavily but she pushed on. "When a couple of days passed and I didn't hear anything, I thought we were in the clear and I was the only one who knew the secret. And then months later, Philippa got a call from that reporter, Ned Rich. I always answer the landline and he told me he'd discovered something important about the Harrington family and he knew about our plan. I panicked. I agreed to meet him outside on Riverside Drive across the street from my apartment. He told me about the black relative and when he started asking questions about the plan, I said I was cold and invited him to my apartment. Walt was there. He strangled him. We put him in my bedroom and moved him down to that park in the middle of the night."

Parker was still curious about Rich's intent. "Did he try to blackmail you? Or was he looking for information on the plan?"

Heather frowned. "I don't know because we never finished the discussion. His knowing about the black relative was enough for me. I just wanted him dead."

"And you…" She met Parker's eyes. "When you hinted at a Harrington secret, I knew I had to get rid of you. I drove the car with Walt and the other two and we followed you when you left the station. When you stopped and Walt saw your gun, he wanted to wait until you were alone. Later I realized you"—she met Corelli's eyes—"probably knew too but by then you always had a car following you."

Parker alternated between rage and sadness as she listened to Heather. How awful to be so filled with hate that you would kill three people to hide a black ancestor. "Were you the one who sent that mob to attack us?"

"Yes. I planned to shoot you both but I couldn't get a clear shot, and then the other cops showed up and I heard the sirens, so I ran."

"What part did Brandon play in the murders?"

"Brandon?" Heather narrowed her eyes. "Brandon is all for Brandon. He may be a Harrington but I don't trust him. I'm the one who stepped up to protect the Harrington name. It was all me and Walt."

"You're saying Philippa didn't order the murders of Walker, Rich or me?"

"I was afraid knowing we have a black ancestor would kill her." Heather blew out a breath. "I wish I'd never asked Magnolia Walker to give me the message for Philippa."

"Are you willing to put this in writing and testify in court if necessary?"

She didn't reply.

"Heather?" Thorn touched her hand.

"Yes, I'm willing."

"Then we'll expect a signed written statement. As agreed, we'll put in a good word and we'll let the ADA know you're willing to cooperate. It should help your defense." Parker and Corelli left them sitting in silence.

"It's sort of what we figured, but it's nice to know for sure and even better that she's willing to testify that Foster was the killer."

Corelli was quiet for a few seconds. "I guess it's normal to panic when you learn your whole life is built on a lie."

Parker shook her head. "But it's not normal to kill three people to cover up having a black relative a hundred-fifty years ago. It's the hate. Rather than black blood these white nationalists should worry about the hate that rules their lives, the hate that they pass to their children."

CHAPTER FORTY-ONE

Driving to Bensonhurst, Parker and Corelli discussed just how open she should be about her injuries with the younger four children. The bruises and swelling were mostly gone but she couldn't hide her cast. But when she walked in lugging her arm in its foam nest, the eight members of the Gianelli family swarmed around her. Gianna had already told the girls that a bad man had hurt Parker and based on what Chiara had told her, she described Parker's injuries so they knew what to expect.

They had a million questions about the cast and how it felt and why she needed the foam but none of them was particularly upset. Gabriella was learning to share so she didn't gobble up all the time and the three little ones took turns sitting on Parker and Corelli's laps, talking about their homeschooling, reading out loud to them, showing them the pages they'd written and bringing out their drawings for their approval.

Gianna was doing a great job bringing Maria, Teresa and Chrissy, the three abused girls she and Marco were adopting, up to their grade levels so they could start school in September. As

Parker read through the writings and looked at their drawings, she noted that Maria was writing Penelope on all her papers. "Hey, who's stealing my name?"

Maria lowered her eyes. "Me."

Parker was thrilled. "That's great. So should I call you Penelope from now on?"

"Penelope is your name but why do they call you P.J.?"

"My middle name is Jasmine but Penelope Jasmine is a very long name so we shortened it to P.J. Some of my college friends shortened Penelope to Penny and that's what they call me. What would you like to be called?"

"Penny is nice. You can call me Penelope or Penny." She ducked her head.

Parker pulled her into a one-armed hug. "How about Penny now and Penelope when you get older?"

"Okay." Maria clung to her and Parker kissed the top of her head, so grateful to have these children, this family in her life. She liked having a namesake.

Since Parker was getting tired and since she couldn't help put the girls to bed, they left after dinner.

"Wow, Detective Parker, you have a way with the girls."

Parker laughed at Corelli's playful comment. "With the little ones at least. I'm honored Maria wants to share my name."

"And the big ones?" Corelli asked as she merged onto the Belt Parkway toward New York City. "You have Deb Maynard and Michele Benson hot on your trail but what happened with Ndep? I heard she resigned from the ME's office."

"When we had lunch, she told me that for the last three months she'd been thinking about returning permanently to Nigeria to marry the man her parents picked for her. And, by the way, that's what she's doing."

"Wow. I know you'd been thinking it was over but did you have any idea?"

"I felt her pull away but I didn't know it was because she was considering such a radical change. It's hard to understand but I've had a small taste of what it feels like to live in two different worlds so I'm sympathetic. I'm sorry to lose her. I'd hoped we could be friends."

"I'm sorry it didn't work out." Corelli was silent, concentrating on driving. "Brett is at her apartment packing things for the move. It's still early. Are you interested in dropping in for a visit?"

"Definitely."

"Penny, Penny Parker."

Parker swiveled, looking around the lobby of Brett's building for whoever was calling her name. Had talking about her college friends calling her Penny triggered something? Was she hallucinating that vision from the past striding toward her? Nicole Summerfield, beautiful as ever, materialized magically. Parker was in her first year at Harvard Law and Nicole was a Harvard senior when they'd dated. It seemed like ages ago and yet it felt like yesterday. Nicole grinned and opened her arms. Somehow, despite the cast, she managed to wrap Parker in a warm and familiar hug. She kissed Parker's cheek. "I am so happy to see you."

"It's wonderful to see you, Nicole. I didn't know you were in New York."

"I am. And I've been reading about you in the newspapers and seeing you on TV for weeks. I've been intending to get in touch but things have been hectic. Do you live here in Battery Park City?"

"Not yet, but I'm thinking about moving into this building. What about you?"

"I live here with my wife." She put her arm around the waist of the attractive woman who had moved to her side. "Dr. Nora Tannen, meet the infamous Detective P.J. Parker, known to her old friends as Penny."

"And this is my partner, Detective Chiara Corelli." Parker extended her left hand to include Corelli who was watching the exchange with intense interest. "But it's not fair that you know all about me. What have you been doing since…Harvard?"

"It's all right, Penny. Nora knows we were an item my senior year. I went to medical school as planned so it's Dr. Summerfield. I'm a neonatal specialist at New York Presbyterian Hospital. I'd love to catch up but we're already late for an appointment. Let's get together soon." She pulled out a business card and wrote a telephone number on it. "That's my personal cell, call me. We're having a party in two weeks. I'd love for you to come, both of you.

I'm warning you, Penny, if I don't hear from you in a week, I'll show up at the police station and embarrass you."

Parker warmed to the affection in Nicole's voice. "I bet you would. Don't worry, I'll call."

Corelli grinned as the two doctors walked quickly toward the swinging doors. "Well, Penny, Nicole is really attractive and she seems nice. I'd love to hear the story of what happened to that relationship."

"Life is what happened. She went off to med school and I was in law school and neither leaves much time for a social life. But she's a great person and a lot of fun. She lived in a suite with five other seniors, one of them some kind of young genius. They studied hard but they were always laughing and joking. I'd love to reconnect with her." *And it would be great to have lesbian friends in the building.*

As the elevator rose to the thirty-third floor, Parker side-eyed Corelli, remembering how tense they both had been the first time they came to Brett's apartment, fearing a serial killer was holding her hostage. Corelli was not only more relaxed this time but seemed to radiate happiness. Brett welcomed them both with hugs and some kisses for Corelli. "Hey, I'm glad you stopped by. Watch yourself, P.J., I have stuff piled all over the place."

Parker was committed to this move but she wanted to see the apartment as a visitor before she claimed it as her own. "Mind if I look around?"

"Feel free to wander, but as I said, watch your step. I don't know how I accumulated so much stuff."

She went straight to the windows in the living room. As she remembered, the view was spectacular. At night the lights of New Jersey across the Hudson River twinkled and in the day the sun sparkled on the water. The modern kitchen had the same view as the living room and the master bedroom. The dining room and the other two bedrooms, faced east, so no water views. There were two bathrooms, one in the master bedroom and the other shared by the other two bedrooms. The smallest bedroom was set up as a home office. The apartment had everything she wanted, especially light.

Brett and Corelli were in the living room chatting. Parker joined them. "I want to accept your very generous offer to let me live here until you decide to sell. And if the offer still stands, I'd like you to leave all the furniture."

Brett jumped up and embraced Parker, as best she could with her sitting down. "Fabulous. I'm hoping to be out by next weekend. When do you want to move in?"

"I'll move my things when my lease is up in a couple of weeks but I'm planning to stay with Jessie and Annie until my cast comes off. If you clear out the closets in the master bedroom and leave room in the bookcases for my books and my records you can take your time getting everything out."

"You have vinyl?" Corelli shook her head. "Lately I learn something new about you every single day, Parker."

"Hey, I need to keep you on your toes. And I do have a large collection of vinyl."

Brett beamed. "You've taken a load off my mind. I really didn't want to leave the apartment empty. I know you'll be happy here."

"Yes, Parker, I wish you happiness in your new home." Corelli grinned. "And maybe your new neighbor, the lovely Nicole, has some single friends you can add to your list of admirers."

Brett touched Corelli's cheek. "What are you talking about, Chiara?"

Corelli stood. "Parker's eyes are drooping. Let's drive her home and I'll tell you all about it on the way."

CHAPTER FORTY-TWO

"Parker, I need to talk to you." Maynard sounded pissed. "Privately, please."

"All right. Get my jacket and let's take a walk around the block." "Sounds serious," Corelli whispered.

"It sure does." Parker slipped her arm into the jacket Maynard held for her. Maynard draped the other side over her shoulder and closed the top button, then slipped into her own coat as they left the station. It would be April in another week and the milder weather was welcome, especially since her cast made wearing her heavy coat impossible. "What's up, Deb?"

Maynard stopped and faced Parker. "Are you trying to get rid of me?"

"What?"

"I had a drink with Agent Day last night and she offered me a job with the JTTF. She made it sound like you think I should take it. So I assume you're trying to get rid of me."

Parker laughed. "No, I'm not. Day is hot to bring you over to her team. It sounds like a great career opportunity so I told her I wouldn't object if she offered it to you." She started walking. "It's not my job to make career decisions for you, Deb. You've done a fabulous job on this project, you're a natural leader and if I was in Day's position, I would want you to head up my computer unit too. But it really is up to you. I suggest you think about what you want. Would the work and the environment make you happy? Does the job fit with your long-term goals? Your decision should have nothing to do with me."

"But do you still want to work with me? I know I've been a pain in the past but I'm trying. And to be honest I'm hoping you'll agree to date me again."

"Since we talked, I've had no problem working with you. And as I said, you contributed a great deal to the success of the case. But this is your future we're talking about. We've had an intense three weeks but you know most of our cases don't require the level of computer expertise this one did. The JTTF job will not only be more challenging but it will provide exposure that could lead to big things for you. Whether we date or not shouldn't be a factor. But taking the job doesn't mean we can't date. We'll still be in the same city. I encourage you to think hard about this, get as much information as you can from Day, talk to some of the people who would report to you and maybe talk to Corelli to get an objective opinion. Whatever you choose will be fine with me."

Maynard touched her arm. "Thanks. I think that's good advice."

Parker had just settled at the conference table again when Dietz dropped a folder on the table in front of her. "Ballistics on the four handguns found in the raids. Day used her muscle to have them jumped to the head of the list."

Corelli moved to Parker's good side so they could read the reports at the same time. It didn't take long. They looked at each other. "Let's bring him in. I want to understand why someone so close to the family would murder them one by one over the years."

Reading reports was almost as bad as writing them so when Darla called just before lunchtime they agreed to meet her and Bear at Buonasola.

This time they could share a lot more about the cases but leave it to Darla to zero in on the only thing they couldn't talk about yet. "So, who murdered Harrington Davenport? And are the rumors true that multiple Davenport family members have been murdered in the last twenty or more years?"

Parker laughed. "Still working on that, so no comment."

Darla smiled. "I'd like to do a feature on you, P.J., about your work on your first homicide as the lead detective, your being attacked and getting right back to work. And of course, how you brought down a white nationalist plot to destroy our government, solved three—maybe more—murders, arrested a man who is a child rapist, a pornographer and a drug dealer. The bad cops are always in the headlines. I believe it's important that the public hears about the good cops to balance the scales."

Parker flushed. "I—"

"That's a great idea, Darla," Corelli said. "I'm sure the department will approve the request. Don't let Parker's false modesty get in your way." Corelli poked Parker. "You need a taste of what being in the limelight feels like."

"Okay," Darla said. "I'll follow up and get permission. I hear there's news on the personal front. Is it true that you're moving to Battery Park City?"

Parker frowned.

Corelli held her hands in front of her. "It wasn't me and I doubt Brett would have revealed your business."

"Then who?" Parker glared at Darla.

"Well, let's see...I may have called you on Annie and Jessie's landline the other night. You weren't home so Annie and I had a chat. She's really excited for you."

"I'm going to give you the benefit of the doubt and assume you didn't call to grill her about me." Parker gazed at Darla. "It's true."

"But Gloria isn't moving with you?"

"Nope."

"But I thought you were tight."

"We were."

"And now?"

"We're not."

"Is that why she resigned from the ME's office and isn't answering her phone?"

"That's not for me to say. And that's the last question about Gloria that I'll answer."

"So tell us about your new apartment. And do you need help packing and moving?"

When they got back to the station, they headed to interview room three to interrogate the murder suspect. Two uniforms escorted Meriwether Davis past them. He muttered "bitches" as the guards pushed him into the room. They ignored him. After the detectives from the Grand Larceny Division finished interviewing him about his financial crimes, the JTTF would address the terrorist charges. Davis would be in prison a long time.

Corelli and Parker entered room three and sat. Abel Clemson glanced up but seemed to look through them.

"Detective Corelli, please read Abel his rights." He listened as she read the words and signed when asked, but otherwise he didn't react.

"Please explain, Abel." Parker kept her voice low, hoping it would soothe him.

"Explain what?" He sounded surprised.

"Why you killed them?" She left it at that and waited.

"Them?"

"Harry, and Philippa's other children and grandchildren?"

"Does she know?"

Parker knew how to play this game. "Know what?"

"T-t-that I shot Harry? And the others?"

He sounded like a boy confessing to stealing cookies. "I thought you and Harry were best buddies?"

He looked up with a smile on his face. "We were. He was like my baby brother. I would do anything for him."

Parker exchanged a look with Corelli. This was weird. "So why shoot him?"

He chewed the cuticle on his thumb. It seemed like this was a deep question. "Harry never believed Philippa's white nationalist bull so from the time he was eight or nine, they fought. She hated him because he didn't like anything she believed in and she mostly treated me like the son I was, like I should have rightly been. But when he was going to run for the Senate, it was Harry this and Harry that. And it was as if she didn't like me anymore."

Parker was puzzled. "You killed him because you thought she favored him over you?"

He nodded.

"And what about her other children and grandchildren?"

"Them?" Abel's face hardened, his hands clenched. "When they were her favorites, she didn't pay no attention to me. I had to kill them so she would remember who really loved her."

Shit. The man was insane. "Did you know that just a couple of nights before you shot Harry, he and Philippa had a falling out and he decided to report her to the FBI?"

He stared at her as if trying to process the information. "Do you mean she stopped liking Harry? And even if I didn't kill him, she would have loved me again?"

"Yes."

Parker needed to get this right. "When Philippa favored a family member, you thought she didn't love you. Is that true?"

"Yes, ma'am."

"And you shot seven members of Philippa's family in the last twenty years because they were her favorite child or grandchild at that time?"

"Yes. So she could see I was loyal and loving, and no matter what, I was the one who would always be there for her."

He'd seemed simple in their earlier interactions but clearly he was crazy. Parker wondered whether he knew right from wrong. "Do you have any regrets about killing them?"

He stared over her shoulder so long she thought he'd become catatonic. "Yes, ma'am. If Harry wasn't her favorite anymore, maybe I shouldn't of shot him." He picked at his cuticle. "You think maybe if Harry wasn't her favorite anymore she won't be mad that I killed him?" He looked up and appeared to be waiting for an answer.

Parker didn't look at Corelli, afraid she'd be rolling her eyes. "Abel, I'm going to send someone in to take your statement. Tell them what you told me, all right?"

"Sure. I always tell the truth."

Though she realized he was in his own world, Corelli couldn't help herself. "But you lied to us about killing Harry."

Abel shook his head. "No, ma'am. You never asked me if I shot him."

Corelli couldn't remember whether they'd asked directly but it didn't matter now. "Abel Clemson, you are under arrest for the murder of Harrison Davenport, Phoebe Davenport Worth, Albert Davenport, Elliot Davenport, Willa Davenport, Harrington Davenport II and Fiona Medford."

CHAPTER FORTY-THREE

It had been a month since they'd wrapped the case up in a big red bow. They'd solved nine murders and the attempted murder of a police officer, plus foiled a domestic terrorism plot. Not bad for her first experience as the lead detective. Of course, as she teased Corelli from time to time, it was just a simple murder.

Tonight P.J. would sleep in her new apartment for the first time. Two days ago the cast had been sawed off and they'd had the great arm unveiling. Sure that the skinny, hairy thing would break, she'd closed her eyes when her physical therapist said she was going to straighten it. But she had and now it worked like a normal arm. It was weak though, and she had to be careful until she strengthened it in therapy. But without that awkward cast and its foam cushion, P.J. felt free and loose. Back to normal. Better than normal, actually.

She'd had a lot of help moving and unpacking. Annie and Brett put all her clothing away, Chiara, her sister Simone and their nephew Nicky set up her home office, installing her computer, organizing her paper files and supplies and hanging the framed copies of the many articles that appeared about her after they closed the case, a gift from Darla and Bear. They also unpacked her records.

But she'd left the boxes of her books, photographs, and mementos stacked in the living room so she could unpack them herself when she had two hands.

She piled a few of her favorite records onto the spindle of her phonograph and now with the sun streaming in and Miles Davis's *Kind of Blue* as background, she moved through the apartment enjoying the fact that it was all hers. At least for the next year. She returned to the living room and dragged the box with framed photos to the shiny black Steinway grand piano in front of the window. The place of honor was reserved for the studio portrait of P.J. and her mother. She was on Tasha's lap, wearing a frilly pink dress with tiny white socks and shoes. They both faced the camera but Tasha, in a pink dress, was looking down at her, her expression soft and filled with love. Tasha had intended to send the picture to Randall Young, Parker's biological father and she'd inscribed it, "To Randall, with love from Tasha and your Precious Jewel." P.J.'s alcoholic grandmother's intervention prevented the photo being sent and deprived her of her biological parents.

She stared at the photo. Jessie had shortened Precious Jewel, the name on her birth certificate, to P.J. and at her uncle's urging she'd changed her name legally to Penelope Jasmine. She arranged the pictures she'd selected from the many Annie and Jessie had taken of her over the years. They went from the very first pictures they took, the before and after of her first bath and haircut to her promotion to detective. She added a picture of her with Gianna and her family, another with Brett and Chiara, and her and Chiara with Amari DeAndre, the popular singer, now friend.

She stepped back and viewed her handiwork. In less than a year her life had changed radically. She had new friends, a new apartment, a solid reputation as a homicide detective and her romantic options seemed to be expanding exponentially. The record switched to The Pointer Sisters singing "Jump." Her body reacted to the beat. Without thinking about it her arms went up and her body dipped and swayed with the music. She sang along as she twirled around the floor but after two months of idleness she was breathless and she could only manage some of the words. "Jump...feel my kisses...my love...my touch...Jump."

Catching a glimpse of herself dancing to this song in the mirror over the sofa brought up images of Nicole, of the dancing, of a younger time when the world seemed full of possibilities, even love. Now as she pranced around her living room, eyes on the view, her thoughts on the future, everything seemed possible again, even love. She would find her person. She was sure.

The song switched. Her phone rang. She sank into a chair next to the window. "Parker."

"Hi, it's Deb. I hope you don't mind that I'm calling you at home. I heard you're taking a week off."

"Oh, hi. What's up?"

"I wanted you to know that I still haven't decided about the new job but I've been negotiating with Day and so far they're giving me everything I want so it's looking more and more likely." Maynard hesitated. "And I wanted you to know that whether I accept it or not, I want us to date again and see whether we can be together."

Parker smiled. She was sure Maynard would accept the promotion. It would be a great career move. She assumed the real reason for Maynard's call was for reassurance about the possibility of them dating again. "That's wonderful, Deb. I'm not ruling dating out but a lot has changed for me and I'm planning to take time for myself, by myself. I hope you'll respect that."

"Yes, of course, but you know me, I do not go quietly into the night." She laughed. "I had to make another try."

Parker laughed. "I do know you. Keep me posted about the job. See you next week."

Parker stared out the window. She still didn't understand what had shifted, whether she had changed or whether the universe was playing its games, but lately women were sniffing around her like she was a bitch in heat or her pheromone generator was overworking. Michele Benson had called last week to inquire whether Parker had totally cleared her of any involvement in any part of the case. When Parker said she had, Benson invited her out to dinner. It was weird. Even with her strange cast and cushion, four women had come on to her at Nicole's party. She gave two of them her number. Maybe it was all the publicity that made her sound like a superhero. Or maybe, as Brett suggested, something in her had opened and she was responding to attention she might have not seen or ignored in the past. Whatever. It was a good problem.

So far, she'd put everyone off, saying she wasn't ready to date right now, that she was adjusting to her new apartment and focusing on physical therapy and getting back into shape. And though she hadn't said it out loud, she was still adjusting to her newfound notoriety and her increased status in the department.

The sun streamed in, warming her. She was happy and at peace in way she'd never been before. Life was good.

Bella Books, Inc.

Women. Books. Even Better Together.

P.O. Box 10543
Tallahassee, FL 32302

Phone: 800-729-4992
www.bellabooks.com

CPSIA information can be obtained
at www.ICGtesting.com
Printed in the USA
JSHW021437230122
22188JS00001B/2

9 781642 473384